Copyright © 2021 Seeley James

All rights reserved. No part of this book may be reproduced or transmitted in any form or by any means, electronic or mechanical, including photocopying, recording, or by any information storage and retrieval system, without written permission from the author, except for the inclusion of brief quotations in a review. If you violate these terms, I'll send Mercury after you. So, watch it.

DEATH AND REDEMPTION: A Jacob Stearne Thriller is a work of fiction. All persons, places, things, businesses, characters and incidents are the product of the author's imagination or are used fictitiously. Any resemblance to real people, living, dead or somewhere in between; gods and goddesses or other divine beings; or events, locales, or places, is purely coincidental. If you think otherwise, you don't know the author very well—he's simply not that smart.

If you would like to use material from the book in any way, shape, or form, you must first obtain written permission. Send inquiries to: seeley@seeleyjames.com.

Published by
Machined Media
12402 N 68th St
Scottsdale, AZ 85254

DEATH AND REDEMPTION: A Jacob Stearne Thriller
First Edition, released June 22nd, 2021
Print ISBN: 978-1-7373223-1-3
ePub ISBN: 978-1-7373223-0-6
Distribution Print ISBN: 978-1-7373223-2-0
Sabel Security #11 version 2.36

Formatting: BB eBooks
Cover Design: Jeroen ten Berge

SEE THE SEELEY JAMES COLLECTION

SEELEYJAMES.COM/BOOKS

DEATH AND REDEMPTION

A JACOB STEARNE THRILLER

SABEL SECURITY #11

SEELEY JAMES

For my grandson
Shaw

CHAPTER 1

THE LAST THING PROFESSOR RAFAEL Tum expected to see was a woman in a thin silk dress with her wrists chained to the floor. He blinked in the daylight that bent around his back, illuminating a cascade of golden hair. She glared over her shoulder at him. Shuffling forward, his shackled feet gained only a few inches with each step.

"Are you hungry?" he asked quietly. He held the tin plate in front of him like an offering to a goddess. "Are you hurt?"

Anton slammed a fist into Rafael's lower back. He staggered a step and almost dropped the plate.

First in Belarusian, then in English, the young mobster said, "No talking."

The woman looked away. But in that brief instant, Rafael thought he recognized her. A famous American. Not internationally famous, not a politician, but a celebrity of some kind. There was something in her ice-blue eyes that called to him. She longed for a champion to save her.

His aging ankles crackled when he squatted to set the food in front of her. He examined the side of her face. A blindfold covered her forehead, lifted by a guard for dinner. A lowered gag wrapped her neck. Dirty fingers with manicured nails. Bare feet. Rafael sensed her flinching under his gaze. Not wanting to make her shame worse, he pushed the food closer and rose.

Facing Anton, he shouted, "You're an animal! You're all animals."

A fist landed in his stomach. Not as hard as he'd been hit by the junta's goons in the old days, but a solid gut punch, nonetheless. Anton was just a teenager, Rafael realized on second look. About the same age as his students back at the university. Could the boy be as dangerous as he tried to look?

Yes. Rafael knew that all too well. How many of his revolutionaries had killed by that age?

Rafael set aside any notion of overpowering the boy. While he had some tricks left, he was too old to overcome the youth's vigor. He would think of another way to free the woman.

Anton pointed outside and shoved him toward the door.

Rafael lurched forward, shuffling toward the abandoned apartment building across the alley where the gangsters had held him overnight. They tracked across a gravel parking area, then through waist-high weeds to the entrance on the far side. Pushed by Anton's pistol, he trudged upstairs, one tread at a time, his shackles barely allowing each foot to gain the next step.

Back in the large room with the bare wood floor, three of Anton's fellow gangsters milled about, waiting for orders. Rafael headed toward the dark hole that had been his prison for the last twenty-four hours.

Before he could shuffle inside, a new voice called out to him. "Aye, Professor, a wee word, if you don't mind."

A well-dressed man with black hair gelled straight back over his collar sat on a wooden chair at the far end of the room. Behind him stood another well-dressed man with his back to the room and a phone to his ear.

Rafael approached the out-of-place pair. They didn't fit in with the Belarussian mobsters who'd kidnapped him.

The Scot said, "My mates here tell me you've not coughed up where you hide your gold, old man."

"I've no gold to hide."

"That's not what I told them." He grinned and tugged at the lapels of his sport coat.

The man behind the Scot clicked off his phone and turned to face Rafael. The old man's heart froze. He'd expected the well-dressed men to be gangster bosses—not his old nemesis.

The man's name spilled out of his mouth before he could stop it. "Joe Griffith."

Griffith twitched a smile while pocketing his phone. He said, "It's been a while."

"Not long enough."

Griffith turned to the Scot and barked, "Everybody out."

The Scot relayed the message. Anton translated it to the other mobsters in Belarusian. They trudged out on command. The Scot turned back to Griffith with a satisfied and eager face. Griffith stared back without a word.

It took the Scot a few seconds to figure it out. He wasn't needed. When it dawned on him, he tucked in his hubris and left.

Griffith crossed his arms and strutted closer to Rafael. He said, "Is that how you thank me? Come, my old friend, let us be reasonable and talk like adults. Remember, I am the one who expunged the war crimes from your days playing Che Guevara."

Rafael stood still and kept his gaze on Griffith.

"As you no doubt surmised," Griffith said, "we want your little secret society to turn over the Chaac Equation."

Rafael shuddered when Griffith pronounced the Equation, named for the Mayan god of lightning, as *shock* instead of the correct way, *chalk.* He said, "I no longer belong to any society."

"You left the Keepers? I don't believe you. You are the Keepers." He paced a circle around Rafael. "Keepers. Ridiculous name, really. You should talk to a marketing consultant."

Griffith moved to the dirty window and peered through the grime. Rafael watched him. They were both silent while a neighborhood dog barked at some unseen threat. After a minute, the dog lost interest.

"Well?" Griffith prompted. "Not going to deny you have it?"

Rafael stood still.

"They won't hurt you, you know, these local gangsters." Griffith wheeled around. "Neither will Seamus. You'd die before you revealed anything about it, so I ordered them to lay off."

Rafael didn't believe him, not that it mattered. Griffith never let people walk away from an encounter. Long ago Rafael resigned himself to die for his noble cause. Now was as good a time as any. His thoughts returned to the chained woman and the dim glimmer of hope in her eyes. The best he could hope for would be freeing the unfortunate young lady before any encounter took place. A small objective in a long and tumultuous life, but he'd learned it was always good to have a goal to focus on before the beatings began.

Griffith paced another circle around him. Rafael didn't bother to follow but instead fixed his stare on the window.

"Ever regret walking away from the family fortune?" Griffith poked his shoulder. "You'd be the telecom king of Guatemala right now instead of your drunken brother."

Griffith stroked his chin and studied Rafael. He walked the length of the room. When he reached the end, he said, "Instead of torturing you and making all that mess, I have my people searching for something you value more than the Chaac Equation. We always look for the greatest point of vulnerability. Saves time. That brother of yours didn't even make the list."

Griffith held up a handwritten piece of paper just beyond Rafael's reach.

Struggling not to squint, Rafael took a mental snapshot of it to contemplate later. His eyesight had declined with his age, but he made out the names of several of the people Griffith threatened.

"I thought your gray-haired mother might fit the bill, but it turns out she died last month." Griffith slapped the paper back into his pocket. "And you didn't even bother to attend the funeral. Bad boy, Rafael. You taught me better than that, did you not?"

Rafael kept his gaze on the window, where a fly traversed the glass.

"Let the woman go," Rafael said.

Griffith's eyebrows raised in surprise. "Which woman?"

"The one in the storage shed."

"If you don't know her name, I know better than to think you'd tell me anything useful in exchange for her freedom. Come now, Rafael. There must be someone on this list you care about more than the Chaac Equation."

Griffith pulled the paper out and flashed it in front of Rafael's face once more, trying to evoke a response. The professor refused to play the game. But he processed what he could see. Twelve names, three of whom were people he would indeed die to protect. Should he stop this madness and agree to talk? No. Griffith would kill them all anyway.

An unexpected name rose from the list. Jacob Stearne. The man who saved three finance ministers at the G20 Summit. The man who stopped a terrorist attack on a cathedral full of worshippers in Paris. A man who saved the life of Rafael's niece. A true hero in a world falling far short of them. A man who survived impossible odds with great regularity. Rafael would not feel guilty for betraying Stearne should it come to that. He could feign interest in Jacob and embark on a false narrative to keep Joe Griffith going in the wrong direction. By the time his ruse was uncovered, he would be rescued or killed. Either way, his secrets would be preserved.

But there was no point giving up Stearne to Griffith. They knew each other too well. He would see Rafael's move and counter it right away, just as he had with the woman. The other man, though; the arrogant Scot. What did Griffith say his name was, Seamus? He might fall for it.

Then what about the woman? Should he try harder to save her? No. There was too much at stake. As much as it broke his heart, he couldn't give Griffith anything. She may suffer, but in the end, it would be for the greater good.

"Well?" Griffith leaned in close. "I want the Chaac Equation. Do you want to save someone the trouble of being tortured before your eyes?"

"Ultimately," Rafael said, "everyone has an appointment with fate."

CHAPTER 2

I WAS THINKING ABOUT HOW you get these big expectations in life. You visualize a future with whole scenes built up around holidays and birthdays and vacations and children and growing old with someone. You figure you'll both be there when you have that big Mardi Gras blowout everybody comes to, including the cops. Or you figure one of you'll cook and the other will clean and it'll never be discussed, it'll just get done. You take for granted that every Sunday the two of you will cuddle on the couch and read books. Maybe you can picture how one of you will push the other in a wheelchair after twenty thousand days of good times and bad.

And then one day—without any warning from the gods—she's gone.

No more holding hands. No more picking restaurants for dinner. No more arguing about the right way to bake a potato. No more dancing in the kitchen. It's over.

Life is a sucker punch. One day you're on top of the world with everything in front of you.

Slowly, I became aware that I was sitting in Pia Sabel's office on the top floor of Sabel Towers in Bethesda, Maryland, where Tania was rambling on about our boss. She sat on the sofa across from me, being chipper on purpose. Annoying. I felt like telling her to shut up so I could sink back into my funk. But Tania wouldn't, so I saved my breath. We had served together in some wars everyone knows about and others we're not allowed to discuss until 2045. We knew each other too well.

"You get that, right?" Tania canted her head as if there were something wrong with me. A bushel of her wild hair swung across her shoulders. "She's wound up tighter than an actress doing her first nude scene. Hey, Jacob, you in there? You hearing me?"

"Yeah." I blinked. "Actress. Screen test."

"That ain't what—" Tania went on about what was wrong with the boss. She wanted me to visualize a more satisfying and engaging life for Ms. Sabel.

Why bother? It would all end in the lightning flash of a bomb anyway.

I couldn't see anyone's future. All I could see was the past. A line of black cars, her parents staring daggers at me, a closed casket, a dark rainy day, a chunk of marble with her name on it, people standing around muttering words I couldn't hear. Ms. Sabel stood next to me from beginning to end. Never spoke, just kept her arm looped through my elbow, her shoulder pressed to mine. I appreciated that.

Six weeks ago. It felt like an hour. The wounds still bleed.

Without warning, Ms. Sabel charged into her office like a freight train plowing snow. I came back to the present.

Tania was still talking. I tuned in to hear her say, "—is why she needs to get laid worse than any white girl in DC. Stefan's a platonic relationship that'll never work. When he looks at her, all he sees is the night he had to blow his dad's brains out to save her life. And when she looks at him ... what? Why you staring over my shoulder? Shit. She's standing right behind me, isn't she?"

The ladies got into it, and I stayed out.

When women get snippy with each other, the smart men hide. There's lots of places I could go that didn't involve women. Not that there's anything wrong with them, it's just ... they remind me of Jenny.

The Mercury medallion Jenny had given me waited in my pocket for a chain. When we got engaged, I gave her a ring and she gave me a coin with an image of Mercury on one side and the planet symbol on the other. We were going to pick out a chain so I could wear it around my neck. We never got that far. I kept it in my pocket where I could rub it between my fingers at times like this.

I sank back into thinking about meeting Jenny in the hereafter. Ancient Roman views on *Romana Mors,* Roman death, or what we call suicide, came to mind. Virtuous suicide was an honorable path in certain circumstances. Cato the Younger committed suicide rather than face the tyrant Julius Caesar's subjugation of the Republic. Ethics over enrichment. While the Epicureans and the Stoics, philosophical rivals, agreed about Cato, they also made it clear that killing oneself for love or passion was not a noble end. Ancient Romans valued their *dignitas*, the accumulation of respect, charisma, and prestige in life. A wasted life, a pointless suicide, would destroy all of one's amassed *dignitas*.

And that's where I was stuck. Death in battle to preserve the nation held the greatest *dignitas*: *mortis honore*, death with honor. Or, as the officers at the back of the column used to tell the men at the front, *Dulce et decorum est pro patria mori*. How sweet and decorous it is to die for one's country.

That kind of sentiment carried me through my career as an Army Ranger, where they gave me medals and commendations. But I survived the wars. I left the military and joined Sabel Security. I met and fell in love with a wonderful woman. She died a death that would've had Cicero and Horace agreeing on something for first time since Cato. Even Zeno and Epicurus would've consented that she died with more *dignitas* than anyone in recent memory.

Jenny had moved on to the next world. I remained trapped in this one.

I needed to catch the next boat off this plane of existence. My only hesitation: It had to be the right boat, going in the right direction in case Dante was onto something about all those circles of Hell. But I had no wars to fight. I had no civilians to protect from the world's monsters. And Ms. Sabel wasn't letting me go look for any, either.

Before I could interrupt the ladies to discuss the operational topics of the day, Ms. Sabel got a call about the murder of an old friend.

She stumbled around her desk while she talked to a detective in Manchester, England. Devastated, Ms. Sabel staggered through her conversation with the detective. Then she needed air.

Ms. Sabel had been there for me when I needed help, so I escorted her to the coffee shop across the street.

We talked about why some deaths hit us harder than others. Why we'd both killed people in dire need of being killed without an ounce of remorse. Yet there were others who were innocent and should live a long and healthy life. People who lived in the safe zone. Ms. Sabel's friend was one of those. Someone in her safe zone.

Jenny should've been in mine.

She got her coffee and we sat in silence while we caught up with the messages on our phones. A handsome guy came in, distracting her momentarily. I was glad to see it. Tania wasn't wrong: the boss deserved a good fling, if not something more.

That's when I got the alert. Perimeter alarms were going off at the Sabel Security Operations Center. Only one group I could think of had the resources and motivation to attempt a break-in at our secure facility. If the legends were accurate, it was an ancient order of rich guys who supported each other with money, soldiers, anything it takes to keep the peasants toiling in the fields and the politicians under their thumbs. They had their own version of a special ops battalion called the Knights of Mithras. Knights who had traded in lances and shields for automatic weapons and body armor. They were every bit as tough as Navy SEALs and almost as tough as Army Rangers. Taking them on in a pitched battle might let me catch up with Jenny in the afterlife. Honorably. With *dignitas*. I considered asking Ms. Sabel to let me track them down to the ends of the Earth and extinguish them once and for all.

But she'd say no.

She wanted me to live here and now with the same pain and grief she lived with. Because she didn't want to be alone. She thought she was saving me from hell. Instead, she was holding me in it.

I know how to defeat those who want to save me: go looking for trouble.

CHAPTER 3

SINCE I'D BEEN PROMOTED TO a VP of something, the attack on the Ops Center fell under my umbrella. I had to oversee it—or manage it or whatever VPs do. Then I could build an ironclad case for going after whoever tried to break into our warehouse. Surely an encounter like that would turn violent.

I took my leave and headed out.

The post-rush hour morning traffic was maddening as I drove to the Ops Center with a man in my passenger seat. Not just any man. This guy wore a formal toga, the kind Roman senators wore two thousand years ago: white with red trim in an understated geometric pattern. He had a helmet with two ridiculous wings on the sides. And matching wings on his sandals. He was eating grapes. For many years, I thought he was Mercury, winged messenger of the Roman gods. But now, I just think of him as my imaginary friend.

Why imaginary? Because I'm not ready to believe my psychiatrist's diagnosis—that he's a manifestation of PTSD-induced schizophrenia, a byproduct of my eight combat tours—because that would mean I'm insane.

I'm not insane.

I'm disappointed.

An endless stream of traffic clogged my forward progress. Horns honked like dogs barking: it starts with one then everyone else jumps in. Driving in the Washington metro area would send the Dalai Lama into obscene tirades. Finally, there was an opening. I steered around a knot of cars to the lead and drove on.

I trusted Mercury to look out for me; that's why I'm disappointed. For years he saved my life in the hopes I could bring him back to the forefront of popular spiritual consciousness. He and his pals in the Roman Pantheon have been living off divine food stamps for fifteen hundred years and they're desperate for attention. To raise my profile— and thus his chances of revival—he turned me into the new American god of war. So much so that I've been festooned with Bronze Stars and Purple Hearts by the grateful colonels and generals whose lives I saved. Mercury claims he made all that happen. I used to believe him.

Not anymore.

If there is a god, why would he let Jenny die?

Mercury munched a grape. *You still moping around about that shit, homie? You gotta let it go. We got big things in your future and Ima place a bet on you pulling it off. I could win big on this one.*

I said, *I don't care. Leave me alone.*

Mercury said, *Leave you alone? What, and let you crash into that dump truck what's about to run the red light?*

No dump trucks in sight. I slammed on my brakes anyway. The anti-lock system shuddered me to a standstill.

He may be a figment of my imagination, but he's a figment with an unnatural ability to predict the future.

Cars behind me screeched and slid at odd angles. Four cars back, someone wasn't looking and hit the car in front of them. The car directly behind me couldn't stop safely so he swerved around me with a honk and a raised finger.

A dump truck flew out of the narrow cross street and t-boned him. The two vehicles slid across the intersection and crashed into three others on the far side. Glass and plastic and upholstery and metal bits flew in every direction. Bystanders screamed.

I glanced at the metal carnage. Plenty of other people could help. My lane was clear.

You're welcome, Mercury said. Biting off another bunch of grapes, he continued talking with his mouth full. *See what happens when you listen to a god? You get to live another day. Time you admitted it, boy, you believe in me—or you never woulda stopped.*

I drove on. *Shoulda been me.*

Mercury turned in is seat to face me. *What's all this 'shoulda been me' stuff? You already done ruled out suicide cuz that's for whiny bitches.*

I said, *I want to join Jenny in the next world.*

Mercury said, *What 'next world' izzat, homes? You're talking to the god who guides you to the river now, so go easy on the do-it-yourself theology.*

I said, *Hades, Orcus, Tartarus, whatever the Romans called it. Where does she go from there?*

Mercury said, *Uh-uh, no way. I ain't falling for that one, bro. You know damn well the Ethics Committee of the Gods would have me up on charges for telling you anything about the afterlife. That's a no-go zone.*

I said, *Why? What's the big secret? Why isn't there a single religion anywhere that has a verifiable afterlife scenario?*

If we proved to you the afterlife was wonderful, y'all would give up on Earth and move on, Mercury said. *Then there wouldn't be any mortals left to toy with. Where's the fun in that? May as well go back to the dinosaurs, all dumb as a box of rocks. That was boring. Which is why we tossed a meteorite on 'em. Unanimous decision by all the gods. See now, what you're trying to do is pull an Orpheus kinda-deal. That shit's above my pay grade.*

He filled his mouth with more grapes.

I tried to remember the myth of Orpheus but there are way too many Roman stories to keep track of. That's when the phone rang with Ms. Sabel's special ringtone. She had a few mundane questions for me. Just as we were ending our conversation, a text came through on my dashboard.

"Uh, Ms. Sabel," I said, "before you go. I just got a text message. It reads, 'We have Professor Rafael Tum. Contact us to make ransom arrangements.'"

Since we weren't particularly close to the old man, neither of us knew what to think of that. Ms. Sabel clicked off.

I stared at the text again. I considered a few responses but needed more information. Simple things like: who is "we?" How am I supposed to believe they have the professor? And why should I care? Rafael Tum was no friend of mine. He'd withheld a lot of critical information last time I ran into him. But he did the right thing a couple times too. I decided to blow off the text unless they were going to supply some basic information. But the back of my brain twitched with one idea: the only people who cared enough to kidnap the professor would be the Knights of Mithras. The same people I hoped were breaking into the Ops Center. If I tried to free the guy, I might find that *mortis honore,* death with honor, I was after.

I slowed at the next green light and looked both ways for dump trucks. Nothing this time.

To Mercury, I said, *The gods take pity on mortals all the time and hook them up with their true loves. I wanna do that. How do I appeal to the gods? What were you saying about Orpheus?*

Mercury said, *Dude. Please. Read the books I give you. Orpheus and Eurydice?*

I said, *Don't recall anything about them.*

Mercury looked disappointed. *Virgil, one of the greatest poets in history! Cannot believe they don't teach his stuff in schools. No wonder y'all are so messed up. Anyway. Orpheus was a rapper with a lyre, and was madly in love with his brand-new bride, Eurydice. Then she goes and gets bitten by a viper and dies. Poor Orpheus went around singing from deep in his soul about how he longed for her. He strolled his ass right on down into Hades.* Mercury wiggled jazz hands and added tremolo to his voice for effect. *He sauntered through the flickering shadows where the phantoms of the dead—shades, they were called— rose from the depths of Erebus to hear him sing. Women and children, warriors and kings, all whispering wisps of the departed, came to listen.*

Mercury ate some more grapes and pointed at a passing car. *Y'all oughta get one of those. What izzat?*

I said, *A Jaguar, out of my price range. What happened to Orpheus when all the spirits heard him singing?*

Oh yeah. Mercury smiled. *You sure you want to hear 'bout this, bro?*

I rolled my hand impatiently.

Mercury said, *So Orpheus pleaded and Ariadne caved. See now, Ariadne be Pluto's wife, so she's the real power down there in the underworld. She allowed Orpheus to take Eurydice back to the land of the living—as long as he didn't look back to make sure she was following him.*

I said, *Why would she be following him? Wouldn't she be walking with him?*

Mercury said, *C'mon now, y'know how we like to test you fools. He had to walk out alone and trust that Ariadne would release his woman to come up the path behind him. But mortals be what mortals is—sleazebags. Right when he got to daylight, he started thinking things. Nobody knows for sure what things he was thinking. Maybe he figured Ariadne lied. Maybe he couldn't take it any longer. Maybe he thought the gods wouldn't notice if he cheated. Whatever, he turned around to look at her.*

Mercury ate more grapes. A lot of grapes. He chewed. And chewed. I wanted to slap him.

I said, *AND ... ?*

And what?

And what happened when he turned around?

Whaddya think happens when a god tells you to do something and you don't? Eurydice cried out to him as she turned into dark smoke and vanished into nothingness forever. So, there's the lesson for you.

I pulled into the parking lot at Sabel Security Operations Center. It sits at the end of a half-mile unmarked driveway, surrounded by a neatly mowed, thousand-foot-wide perimeter. I turned the engine off and faced my forgotten god.

I said, *What lesson? I asked how I can join Jenny in the next life, and this is what you tell me? That Orpheus made a deal to get his wife back if he trusted the gods—but he made one little mistake and she's gone for good? It doesn't mean anything! Hopeless. No wonder the Jews survived the Christian takeover—and you didn't.*

Hey! Don't get snarky with me, muthafucka. Mercury scowled. *That's the first lesson of Orpheus: You think you'll do anything to get where Jenny's at, but you don't.*

I said, *What do you mean first lesson? What's the second?*

Mercury said, *You ain't ready for that. If you was, you'd know what the story means.*

I said, *C'mon, just tell me. I'll do what you ask.*

Mercury said, *Oh no. All y'all mortals ask the gods to do you a solid, then you cheat—and when you get caught, you complain. Y'all suck.*

I said, *You suck.*

You suck worse.

CHAPTER 4

SEAMUS MCLEOD RODE THROUGH THE streets of Brest, Belarus in silence, taking his cue from his boss, Joe Griffith. Griffith's anger rippled outward from the front seat like heat waves in the desert. Not that Seamus took it personally. He might get yelled at, but there were other factors Mr. Griffith would take into consideration.

The driver dropped them at the Hermitage Hotel's grand entrance. If one could call it that. While it was the finest in Brest, it would hardly qualify as a cheap motel elsewhere. The two men kept their silence as they rode to Mr. Griffith's fifth floor suite. As soon as Seamus closed the door behind them, Griffith unloaded.

"Why the hell did you let them saddle you with those stupid thugs?" Griffith's baritone rumbled the furniture.

"They didn't say a thing about it until we were in too deep." Seamus tried hard to keep his Scottish brogue from surfacing. It had a bad habit of bubbling up under stress.

"The Chief of the Brest Police wanted to keep his people at a distance from you." Joe lowered his voice a notch. "I get that. But why not let your people guard the captive?"

"Insurance. The cops keep our Knights at a distance. Then, if something goes down, they get a warning. Yet they can say they were never involved."

"You should've put your foot down."

"I bloody well did!" Seamus tried to lower his anger. "They arrested us for kidnapping. This arrangement was our only way out. Don't worry about it. I have them under control. All we have to do is make the exchange before they can mobilize."

"You'd better." Griffith crossed to the window and stared out. "Pour us some whiskey. Tell me your next steps."

Seamus found a bar cart in the sitting area and poured god-knows-what from a glass decanter into two glasses. He carried them to Griffith and handed him one.

"To getting the Chaac Equation." Griffith held his glass aloft.

"Aye." Seamus clinked and took a sip. It burned like diesel fuel.

Griffith swallowed the harsh stuff, stared at his glass, handed it back to Seamus, and pulled out his phone. Without preamble, he told his assistant, "Diane, get me a room in the nearest real city and arrange transportation. I'm not spending another hour in this godforsaken hellhole."

He clicked off and stared at Seamus long enough to make it uncomfortable. Griffith asked, "What did you want Betty Bardon for?" When Seamus looked confused, he added, "The woman captive."

"Aye, right. My own insurance. That old professor fancies himself a bit of a hero. If the Brest police muck up the works and slow me down, the old man will stop to free her. That gives me a chance to catch up."

"Smart move." Griffith gave him a nod. "Did you get anything out of old Rafael since I left?"

"You wouldn't let us question him properly."

"Are you questioning your orders?" Griffith's face contorted with rage.

"No, sir." Seamus almost saluted as if he were back in the SAS.

Griffith relaxed. "It's imperative that we come out of this with the Chaac Equation. You must be pragmatic in your methods to make sure I get what's mine. The people you're dealing with won't respond if he's harmed in any way. They don't want damaged goods."

"He had no cyanide capsule, no communications links. Who wants him?"

Griffith smirked. "Are you questioning the plan, Mr. McLeod?"

"No, sir. It's just that …" Seamus huffed. "He doesn't appear to have any value at all. We sent the message to all of them as soon as you said—not a single response. It's not been long, but I would think someone would've replied right away. Have we got the right man?"

Griffith eyed him in a way that made him understand he'd asked one question too many. "Not a single response, eh?" Griffith said and eased his stern expression. "I can juice some of your prospects. Sometimes it takes an extra touch. Have any favorites?"

Seamus bristled at how everything Griffith said pinned the whole thing on him: *your* prospects; *your* questioning; people *you're* dealing with. As if he were being set up for blame should everything go sour. And still he knew nothing of the master plan. He didn't need to question orders, but a hint about the expected outcome could help him understand where they were headed. "I'm not familiar with the relationships between the old man and those who got ransom demands. I've no idea who would want the old bugger."

Griffith nodded slowly with a condescending sneer. "All right, I'll let you in on a bit more. You see, Rafael Tum would die before telling you anything about the Equation. You could torture him for weeks and get nothing. God knows the Guatemalan government tried that back in the '90s. What we need is Professor Tum's greatest point of vulnerability. Someone who doesn't share the Keepers' maniacal devotion to their ridiculous order. That person will make him talk."

Seamus appreciated being shown a little trust. He considered the conversations he had with Tum and what they might have revealed. But the stone-faced old man had given him nothing. "His niece. She's family and that's always—"

"Cherry Crocker and her uncle had a falling out a couple months ago." Griffith grabbed his suitcase from the closet and began repacking it with clothes from the drawers. "She went the distance to help him clear up his past only to uncover his appalling atrocities. If she responds in any way, even to send her regrets, I'd be shocked."

Seamus watched the boss pull a suit from the closet and fold it carefully into the bag. Wracking his brain for any clue, and hoping he could get a morsel of advice, he found nothing but a growing silence.

Griffith retrieved his shaving kit from the bathroom and tucked it neatly into a small space. "Did he flinch at any name you gave him? Any twitch? Did he scratch his face or look away?"

"Aye. When I mentioned Jacob Stearne, he scratched his jaw."

Seamus squinted.

Griffith froze, a pair of socks in his hand. He smiled wistfully before tossing the socks into the bag. He said, "Stearne may well be the answer. They're not close; torturing Stearne won't do anything. But we could use Stearne in a different way. Rafael would trust the young man, and that would be a mistake that could play into our hands."

"Do you mean Jacob Stearne has the Equation?"

"No, but he's resourceful and can get it. And he has no maniacal devotions to Rafael Tum or the Keepers."

"Is he the one you want, then?"

"The real question is, do you?" Griffith asked as he zipped the suitcase closed. "Jacob Stearne destroyed your predecessor. Shot him nineteen times. A bit excessive if you ask me."

"Oh aye? Nineteen? Where'd he shoot? First in the shinbones, then the femurs?"

Griffith frowned. "Now that you mention it, I believe that's what the coroner said, yes."

"He's a professional. You don't die instantly from a single gunshot wound unless it goes straight through your brain stem. Even if you take one in the heart, your brain keeps functioning for a bit. He was torturing the man. Nineteen rounds is not excessive, that's pure hatred. He was motivated."

"Indeed." Griffith set his bag on its wheels on the floor. He turned for the door, leaving the bag for Seamus to roll.

Seamus frowned at the slight but took the handle and followed his boss.

"Stearne held your predecessor responsible for the death of a woman. Silly thing for a man to get worked up about when there are so many around, yet he did." Griffith sniffed as they waited for the elevator. "Suppose he holds me accountable in some way as well."

"He'd be the one old Rafael would trust the most, then?"

Griffith gave him an appreciative glance. "You would think so."

"We've some intel on Jacob Stearne. They haven't let him out in the field for weeks. Some concerns about his mental health, one might imagine, sir."

"Interesting. That means Pia Sabel is keeping him close so he stays out of trouble. That would be driving him mad by now. Impatience leads to mistakes. And he hasn't responded yet?"

"No, sir."

"He may very well be the one you need, then. Think you can handle him?"

"Americans go on about their Navy SEALs and Army Rangers, making movies and all that. I've fought alongside them in battle. They scream in pain same as you and me. Don't worry, sir, I'll get it done."

The elevator pinged and the doors thunked open.

Griffith nodded in deep thought. "All right then, I have an idea that might bring him charging into the fray. But be on your toes and don't say you haven't been warned."

CHAPTER 5

I SAT IN MY CAR, staring at the neatly mowed perimeter around the Ops Center. During his all-too-short reign on Earth, Alan Sabel built it to keep his sensitive technology, armaments, special weapons, and everything else out of the wrong hands. The walls are six feet thick, solid concrete with a system to cut off all unauthorized communications. The roof is a latticework of steel beams and cement. Only people named Sabel know how many basements lurk below ground, and there's only one person named Sabel still living.

I found a parking place near the main entrance and stopped. Before I shut the engine off, another notice bounced across my dashboard. A video waited for me on my phone. I grabbed it, locked the car, and leaned back against the door.

I played the video.

Joe Griffith, the man ultimately responsible for Jenny's death, grinned at me in a light blue sport coat and open-collared shirt. He said, "Jacob, we sent you the text. You didn't respond. We're disappointed. But we're guessing you need proof. Watch the next video and get back to us."

I wanted to rip out his hair and gouge out his eyes. But he knew that, expected it, and played into it. I rubbed Jenny's medallion in my pocket to calm my thinking and focus. Instead, it reminded me of how Griffith had deprived me of my fiancé.

A second video came in. I clicked on it. There was no sound. It was a dark room, a chained man huddled in a corner. His body language said it all: he was defeated, tired, sick, beaten. A light came on. A hand came from behind the camera, grabbed a fistful of gray hair, and pulled into view the face of Professor Rafael Tum.

As sickening as it was to see any human in chains, Joe Griffith had played his hand poorly. He should've put out more of a teaser. Something less personal. By putting his face on my screen, he was trying to provoke me. That much was obvious. Reacting quickly would be dumb. The best reaction on my part was no reaction—for now.

And yet the situation presented an ideal opportunity to meet Jenny in the next world by exiting this one in a blaze of glory. *Mortis honore.* Taking out Joe Griffith would be doing humanity a favor while giving me a shot at revenge. *Dignitas.* A win-win for everyone. Well. Except for Griffith.

But Ms. Sabel would need convincing before she let me go on a mission like that.

In the present, I had a job to do, so I pushed my darkness away and put on my corporate-VP persona like a tortoise shell.

Isaiah Reddick, shift supervisor for the Ops Center's perimeter security, stood ramrod straight next to a golf cart at the front door. The lean man looked like a sentry at the Tomb of the Unknown Soldier. He had twists with fade, a trendy style among young black men in DC that was a career-sideliner in the military. As I approached, he looked apprehensive for a moment, then slapped a Sabel cap on his head. That one small motion made me feel bad for him.

"There's nothing on the video, sir." Isaiah said. "Everything happened underground. We dug down and found their tunnel. It's on the other side of the building."

"Two things," I said and shook his hand. "First, drop the 'sir.' You're not military anymore. Name's Jacob. Second, be the man you want to be. Let the other guy worry about your hairstyle. You can lose the hat if you're wearing it to please me. I don't give a damn what someone looks like long as he shoots when he's supposed to and not when he isn't."

After a double take followed by a slow smile, he tossed the hat into the cart and shook his twists free. He checked me out with a once-over and stopped at the holes in my jacket. He asked, "Are those bullet holes?"

I didn't answer. Any combat veteran would check the back to see if they'd gone through. He did. And he saw there were no exit holes. I'd carried them inside me back to the infirmary. They didn't let me go out to play for two weeks after that.

When Isaiah realized we weren't going to discuss it, he gestured to our electric chariot. We got in and took off across the expanse of grass surrounding the building.

"When the alarms went off," Isaiah said, "no one knew what it was for. The warning flashed, 'Subterranean Area Six'. We had to dig out the manuals to figure out what it meant and where area six was. We lost valuable time. Were you aware of the alarm, sir?"

"Never heard of it, but it doesn't surprise me. Alan Sabel wanted the place to be impenetrable."

"Was he a subscriber to Stearne's Law?" Isaiah smiled with perfect teeth. "'Paranoia is the result of acute situational awareness'?"

I smiled and nodded. Isaiah was making points in the brown-nosing department. My proverb was the result of a thousand betrayals on the battlefield. It had saved more than a few lives. Even if he was just saying it for my benefit, it might save his life.

We finally rounded the last corner. Way out by the perimeter fence, a thousand feet from the building, several men stood near a big trench. A backhoe waited behind them. We got up close and hopped out. Steel plates reinforced the trench's soft loam walls. A ladder stood at one end. The workmen told us it was ready for inspection.

I led and Isaiah followed. The ladder took us down twenty feet to a landing and a second ladder. Another fifteen feet and we stared into the maw of a seven-foot, perfectly round tunnel. Smooth, wet sides and a muddy floor. Workmen strung lights on steel support beams. They'd made it a hundred yards before they ran out of line.

We stepped into the hole and smelled the wet earth all around us. It wasn't coated or shored up. I'm no engineer, but I had the feeling it could collapse at any moment and bury us all. While it didn't feel like that moment was in the next hour or two, it didn't seem much farther out than that.

"We sent a drone out," Isaiah said. "We found the other end of the tunnel. We're working on who owns the land. Your thoughts, sir?"

"I *thought* I told you to call me Jacob."

"Sorry, sir—Jacob. Habit. It's only been three months."

"Marines?"

"How did you know?"

I sniffed the air and crinkled my nose as if something stank. He laughed at the interservice rivalry.

"I think we should go see for ourselves," I started out at a cautious run. If the Knights of Mithras dug this, they would be waiting in ambush for us.

After my crack about Marine-stink, Isaiah took it as a competitive run. He pulled into the lead as if we had nothing to worry about. I noted his lack of concern seemed casual for a combat veteran.

When we saw daylight, we slowed. The tunnel had been bored into the side of a rise. The Ops Center sat on top of that rise. The soil at the entrance had been tilled by several large vehicles. Treads and tires had churned the area. Whoever had dug the hole had beaten a hasty retreat. We followed mud tracks running down an otherwise dry dirt road into the distance.

"Flatbeds, tractors, cranes, and a boring machine," I said. "What's that tell you, Isaiah?"

"Expensive. Someone spent some money on this operation."

"Which means they fully expected this operation to work. There had to be a payoff. What were they after?"

Before seeing the tunnel, I'd assumed it was the work of the Knights of Mithras. Since we didn't die when we arrived at the far end, I began to doubt that. Who else would commit time and effort on that scale?

"We have tons of pricey gear in there." Isaiah looked around. "This would make a great staging area to drag out Sabel Visors, Sabel Armor, Sabel Monoculars—"

"You can drop the Sabel part," I said and clapped him on the shoulder. "When you're talking to someone who has the same signature on their paycheck, you can bet you both have all the company gear, right down to the Sabel Toothpaste."

We shared a chuckle.

Isaiah gave me a tentative glance. One of those off-topic questions that must've been eating at him since he heard I was coming. He had a question burning inside him and it was now or never. I squared up to face him, giving him full opportunity.

"Sir, I mean, Jacob," he said, "I appreciate how the company has put their faith in me as a shift supervisor. But I'd rather be in the field. Could you advise me how to make that lateral transition?"

I felt Isaiah's pain. Back in the military, battlefield experience promoted a man a lot faster than securing a warehouse. The same was true at Sabel Security. His desire mirrored my own. Pushing reports and doing evaluations all day reminded me of watching the corn grow all summer in Iowa. But he had it backwards. He wanted *me* to get *him* back in the field? I wanted *him* to get *me* back in the field.

"I seem to be homebound myself these days," I said. "But I'll see what's going on. What kind of Marine were you?"

"Recon."

He only needed one word to convey his expertise. Recon Marines, formally Force Reconnaissance, or FORECON, were on par with Navy SEALs, almost as good as Army Rangers. But there were two kinds: green and black. The former being the ones everyone reads about in the papers. The latter were the kind whose exploits were unsealed twenty-five years after the fact. If then.

I stared him in the eye for a long second. His head moved from side to side about one millimeter. A movement telling me not to ask if he were green or black. He didn't want me to ask because the Black Recons couldn't answer. And not answering could get awkward. Which meant he was Black Recon.

I clamped a hand on his shoulder. "I'm sure we need someone to do laundry. I'll check around."

He relaxed and gave me that quick smile with those perfect teeth.

I said, "You were saying they were after our expensive secret weapons. You might be right. Still, that's a lot of money to put up for a speculative operation like that. All our gear has embedded serial numbers. You can't file them off and sell it on the black market."

Isaiah scratched his head and looked around. Surrounded by trees, the area the bad guys chose was isolated from inquisitive eyes. They operated in secrecy. He looked back at me. "Begging your pardon, sir. I mean, Jacob. I read your report about what went down in Germany a couple months back. The Knights of Mithras are a multinational operation with deep pockets. I don't see any evidence to conclude they were involved here, but could it be them?"

"You're right, not enough evidence," I said. "Let's think this through. For some reason they stopped boring three hundred yards short of their destination, then dragged a seven-foot diameter boring machine back six hundred yards. How long would that take?"

"No idea, sir—I mean, Jacob." He pulled his phone and started thumbing away.

"Seven feet is eighty-four inches." I tapped my chin while I thought. "That's the diameter of storm drains and urban sewer systems, right? Means whoever did this used a fairly common boring machine. For boring machines that is. Plenty of expertise around for construction. Plenty of equipment available. Could've been a contractor who specializes in storm drains got conned into building this. Could've been one of Ms. Sabel's competitors or enemies. I'm guessing boring machines crawl forward inch by inch. But how fast do they go backwards?"

"Says here—" Isaiah held his phone up "—there's one in New Jersey can travel at five miles an hour and bore at ten yards an hour, call for price and availability."

I did the math in my head. "To get it out of the tunnel, that's about five minutes to get 2,000 feet backwards. Add in ten minutes to switch gears or whatever they do. Once they reached the opening, they would've needed a crane to put the machine on a flatbed."

"That would take half an hour," Isaiah said. "Plus load up any other hardware? Generators, lights, cords, cables, porta potties—an hour, maybe two?"

"How long did it take you to figure out what the warning meant?"

"Half an hour." His face twisted up as he recalled the morning's events. "Area six turned out to be a big one, so we dragged out our ground-penetrating radar. It took another half hour to locate the hole. And another hour to get to it because the sides of the trench kept caving in. So, two hours. Damn, we just missed them."

Looking around at the tunnel, I noticed the bored walls were smooth and dry. It hadn't rained in over a week. While the ground at the entrance was churned into mud, most of the moisture involved had come from the boring machine they dragged out of the tunnel. I walked back in the dark hole and touched the sides.

I waved to Isaiah, and we ran back toward the Ops Center. I stopped at the Sabel property line. The dirt on the Sabel side of the line was soaking wet, barely able to hold the circular shape. Damn. Alan Sabel had used gray water, filtered from the facility drains, to keep the soil permanently soft and mushy around the property line. He anticipated a tunneling effort? The man had been a paranoid genius.

"They kept boring," I said while sticking my finger in the damp dirt, "even after they got into the soft soil that would collapse a tunnel over time. But they didn't go far."

"They stopped at the first sensor," Isaiah said.

"OK, here's the deal, Isaiah." I stared until I could focus on his retina. "I'm going to call it the work of the Knights of Mithras. I have my reasons." The primary reason being that I wanted to pick a fight with the meanest bear around. I had an inkling who the real culprits were, but it was best to leave that for later. "You back me up on that, I'll see about getting you a ride-along gig in the field while you're on administrative leave."

"What?" His face went wide. "Why would I be on admin leave? This isn't my—"

"They knew they'd been discovered," I said. "They backed out, loaded up, and bugged out. How did that happen?"

Isaiah stared at me, slowly turning a sickly green in the dim light. He knew how it had happened just as well as I did. And he knew what would happen next. And that part made him scared and angry. Scared because he knew his whole crew would be placed on leave while an internal investigation uncovered which one of them had alerted the tunnel borers that a "subterranean alarm" had gone off inside. Angry because he'd planned on rising fast at Sabel and this wouldn't look good on his record.

Isaiah's posture buckled a little under the crushing weight of leadership. His sad gaze met mine as he began to understand that Stearne's Law is no joke.

CHAPTER 6

I DROVE BACK TO SABEL Tower in downtown Bethesda thinking about one thing: squishing Griffith's head in a vise until it popped like a melon. Not that I'm the vindictive type, but the man was pure evil. He might have a different view of things. Maybe he thought he was keeping the world safe for international commerce that benefitted a few of his well-born buddies. I foiled his last attempt at world domination. That mission had cost Jenny her life. And that meant he had to die.

Who actually dug the tunnel was immaterial. I could blame it on the Knights of Mithras and Ms. Sabel couldn't deny me going after them and their leader, Joe Griffith.

Mercury said, *Great plan, homie. But she's gonna shoot you down like a dawg.*

I said, *Drop the act, will you? No one talks like that. I know you're trying to channel inner-city street or Compton or something, but you're not pulling it off.*

Did I mention Mercury is of African origin? Turns out, the Bible is spot-on when it says, "God made man in his image." Modern humans became sentient in the Rift Valley of Eastern Africa, and guess what skin tones are found in that part of the world? Artists of every culture make god in *their* own image because it sells better. Note that Jesus was a Mediterranean Jew, not fresh off the longship from Oslo.

Mercury has this theory that he needs to sound like a rapper to reach the influential generation of today. If he could talk like Snoop Dogg, maybe, but he sounds like an off-key singer in an *a cappella* group.

Mercury said, *What am I supposed to do, homie? You never bothered to learn Latin, the language of the gods. So whaddaya want from me?*

Preferest an Elizabethan affectation, wouldst thou? Speak thusly shall I? Were I to apply my words trippingly on the tongue and then yea in the very torrent, tempest, and whirlwind of passion, wouldst thou comprehend my meaning? Hesitating not a whit? He laughed and shoved my shoulder. *Fuck, homes, you should see yo face right now. So, fare thee not the ways of Shakespeare?*

I said, *Your version of street ... works. Just listen to more Kendrick and Drake. Now, back up. What did you mean about Ms. Sabel turning me down? Someone attacked our Ops Center and kidnapped a frenemy of hers—and I'm going to tell her it was the Knights of Mithras.*

Mercury said, *You gots to come up with a better pitch to get her onboard. Start thinking up something extra excellent, cuz I got plans for you out there.*

My long-abandoned deity had a point. Ms. Sabel instinctively knew I was trying to find a martyr-mission for my purposes. Somehow, I would have to trick her into letting me go. Throwing the Knights out there should work. Right?

Then I started thinking about why Griffith had sent me the message about the old professor. If you kidnap someone, shouldn't you send the ransom demand to someone who cares? What was he up to? He was trying to antagonize me. Draw me out. For what? If he wanted to kill me, he could send twenty Knights to my house, overwhelm my defenses, and get the job done. Five minutes and they'd be gone before the neighbors could dial 911.

So, why would a guy like Griffith make Rafael Tum's kidnapping my personal problem?

Somehow, I had to use that angle to help Ms. Sabel understand my need to slice Griffith into pancetta-thick pieces to be left in the woods for feral animals. That wouldn't be too cruel, would it?

Mercury said, *You don't know a damn thing about selling management, do you, dawg?*

I said, *Nobody says 'dawg' anymore.*

Mercury said, *That's a shame, it's a good word. Anyway. This is a big-huge-freaking deal, bruh. You gots to sell her on it. Be convincing. You got this. You got any spinach in your teeth?*

I glanced in the mirror. Clean. I said, *What's so important? Usually, you don't care what I do.*

Usually, you're getting into trouble all by your own self. From pissing off the manager of the Casino Monte Carlo to the maître d' at Mickey D's, you got a knack for getting people to shoot at you. I keep you alive. And that'd be hero stuff. Legendary stuff. But nowadays, just look at you. You been a desk-monkey for weeks on end. I got plans for you, my brother. Big plans. Might even be a movie deal in it for me. Holy Jupiter, will ya look at that?

He was pointing at my reserved parking space underneath Sabel Tower as I nudged in. Under my stenciled name, someone had added graffiti, "The Hero of" and underneath were six places—China, Monaco, Mumbai, Rabat, Skagen, Paris—all crossed out. At the bottom of the list, "G20." A short history of the cities, countries, and international conferences I'd saved from devastation.

Mercury said, *Ain't that sweet, homes? Even if they left out Tokyo, somebody cares enough to keep a list of your adventures going. That be the hero stuff I be talking about right there.*

I said, *Had to be Miguel. He's trying to cheer me up. Fuck him.*

Mercury said, *Dude, snap out of it, will ya? Nobody likes a Debbie Downer. This is gonna be great. Deliver your yet-to-be-dreamed-up reasons to Pia-Caesar-Sabel and she's gonna let you go whup ass on Griffith and the Knights of Mithras.*

Mercury believes billionaires are like the Caesars of Ancient Rome, one step closer to the deities than the rest of us because of their financial ability to build temples in his honor. A self-serving philosophy, but what are you going to do?

Mercury said, *You know you gots to take the blood with you, right homie?*

I said, *Who? You mean, Isaiah? Why?*

Mercury said, *Holy Apollo, homie! When a god tells you do this, do that, you just do it. What woulda happen to ol' Noah if'n he said he was gonna think about it for a spell? Just do it. Besides, here comes the son of Changing Woman. He'll help ya out, no questions asked.*

Miguel Rodriguez pulled into his parking space next to me and dragged his six-four, 230-pound linebacker's frame out of his Mini Cooper. My best friend glanced at the graffiti, then back at me with his irresistible Native American grin. I needed to cut him off before he said something that might cheer me up.

"Know a guy named Isaiah Reddick?" I asked.

"Shift supe over at the Ops Center?"

"Yeah. He was asking me about field work. You got anything on your calendar?"

He nodded. "Taking a squad to London with our CEO tonight. I could take on an apprentice for a tour. Why?"

"Nice guy. Deserves a shot. He's going to be sidelined while his crew is investigated. May as well get some work out of him."

"Investigated? And you want me to take him on? Nice."

"He's a good guy. Marine. But. Not one of *those* Marines."

We walked into the building together and I explained what happened. Promising to give the guy a shot, Miguel peeled off at the twelfth floor. I rode the elevator to the top and marched straight to Ms. Sabel's office.

I was about to knock on the open door but didn't see the point. She had a convention going on. Getting a word with a billionaire is like getting a celebrity autograph at a fan convention. People swarmed around Ms. Sabel. Finally, the crowds parted, and it was my turn.

I explained about the tunnel, how much the operation cost, and where it was headed. I explained how we had a mole in our team at the Ops Center. None of which seemed to bother her. So, I pulled out the video from Joe Griffith and the one with Rafael. She looked unmoved. Which was out of character for her.

Ms. Sabel squinted at me.

My pitch wasn't working. So I went over it with more details and wound up my pitch by saying, "I want to go after them. We take them down, free Rafael Tum, and tick off a good deed for the week."

"We could do that," she said. "But the FBI should handle this. That's what we pay taxes for. You called them, right?"

I almost pointed out that *I pay taxes* and billionaires don't, but that wouldn't help my case. Besides, we all voted for that craziness for some inexplicable reason. Problem for another day.

Mercury leaned an elbow on her shoulder. *Uh, y'know what homie? She don't look like she's gonna let you save Professor Tum. You gotta do something about that.*

I said, *She's distracted, she lost a friend in England. Usually, she'd be all over this.*

Mercury said, *Screw it, dude. You're gonna have to go it alone.*

I said, *What? You're the one who always wants me to convert her to the Roman Pantheon. I can't just run out on her.*

Mercury said, *We don't have time for this whiny bullshit. It's time you took a stand for doing the right thing. Time for you to go rogue.*

I said, *Go rogue?* He was up to something. Gods always are. Then it came to me. *Wait a second. Did you bet on this thing between me and Griffith?*

Mercury said, *Holy Minerva! Is that what you think of me? You think the only reason I help you is so I can win a few aurie off Mars and Juno?* He paused and gave me his best dumbfounded look. *Well. Yeah. OK. I mighta played the odds a bit. But this time, I bet on you to live through the ordeal. And let me tell you, that be risky AF with the mood you're in.*

I said, *How much?*

Mercury said, *What does that matter? Just talk to the woman. We need to get moving. There's a clock on this bet.*

I said, *How much?*

Mercury looked left and right and then he said, *I lost my wife to Mars in the last round, OK? I just need to get her back or she'll never let me hear the end of it. I ain't letting him keep her one extra day. They had a thing going back in the Jurassic cuz, let's face it, times was slow, and— hey, never you mind about that shit. Get your head in the game here. You gotta get moving.*

Ms. Sabel was searching my eyes. "Right? Jacob?"

"Yeah. FBI. I called them. They're tracing the message."

"Good, because we're going to England." She stepped around me and headed for the accountants waiting by her desk. Over her shoulder, she said, "Wheels up in an hour."

CHAPTER 7

ON THE FLIGHT TO ENGLAND, I acted like a disaffected teen being dropped off at the prom by his mom. Which was unprofessional of me. So, I tried to snap out of it. But then we were met at the airport by her long-lost friend, Dame Millie. The woman and her husband were right out of a Monty Python skit about the English upper class. They weren't Ms. Sabel's kind of people. Which struck me as odd. Just as odd as her refusal to let me go after Joe Griffith and the Knights of Mithras. Then things got worse.

On our way to the police station, where Ms. Sabel planned to help the investigation into her friend's murder, a mob of anti-rich protestors recognized her and attacked her. My attempt to act like a bodyguard was restrained by ten men who took out their marital and career disappointments on me. Luckily, Ms. Sabel held her own and came away with only a black eye. The people who attacked her got the worst of it.

While she tried to convince the detectives to let an American civilian help them because she's rich—which kinda played into the protestors' theme—I got a call from FBI Director Daniel Shikowitz. Since he was an old friend of Ms. Sabel's father, I almost handed her the phone. But Shikowitz knew her number. He was calling me for a reason. I showed her the Caller ID and stepped out of her meeting with the Manchester Police.

A second later, the Director said, "Jacob, good to find you. Hope you're doing well after that terrible business at the G20. We're still heartbroken about that. I've not much time so I'm going to cut to the quick here. Hold on. I'm trying to patch in Secretary Townsend. Ah. There we go. Neville, are you there?"

"I'm here, Daniel." An unfamiliar voice came on. "Thank you."

"Neville, I've found Jacob Stearne for you. Go ahead. Tell him what you told me."

"I'm sorry," I interrupted, "who is on the line?"

"Neville Townsend, Secretary of State," the new voice said. "But let's not worry about titles. I'm calling to impress upon you the importance of your mission. We need Rafael Tum back here at once. It's been nearly twenty-four hours and we've not heard a thing. Your mission to retrieve him is of the utmost—"

"Hold up." I didn't know the proper etiquette for interrupting a Secretary of State, so I just put it out there. "What mission is this?"

"To bring Rafael Tum back," the Secretary said. "Daniel told me you were negotiating with the kidnappers."

"I wasn't negotiating anything, sir." I felt a seed of hope rising in my soul. The promise of a dangerous mission dangled on a phone call just beyond my reach. My free hand rubbed Jenny's medallion for luck. At the same time, I saw a cloud of doubt. Two powerful men had the wrong impression about how much sway I held over Ms. Sabel. And by calling me instead of her, they were proving another point: they were afraid of her. "Ms. Sabel told me to let the FBI handle it. Don't you guys do kidnapping, Director?"

"In the US, yes," Shikowitz said. "They're holding him in Belarus. A little outside our jurisdiction. Jacob, we need you on this case. You have to mount a mission to rescue him right away."

In the gray hallway of an ancient building in a city far from home, I felt people pushing me around for their own purposes. The army had been different. There I had been a pawn of presidents and cabinet officers eight thousand miles from home, but at least I was surrounded by a few thousand other pawns with whom I shared a certain *esprit de pawn*. I also had a chain of command in which I invested a certain level of confidence, cynical as it might be. It's quite another thing being directly manipulated for reasons that are way outside normal channels.

"Permission to ask a direct question, sir?" I asked.

"Go ahead," Townsend said.

"What the fuck?"

I let that one sit there for a moment while the two of them realized I'd just cut through ten layers of management with three words. Shikowitz coughed and Townsend stammered. They were both waiting for the other to take the hard question.

"I can understand you may have concerns, Jacob." Secretary Neville's voice went soft and low, as if he were putting a baby down for a nap. "We certainly owe you a few answers. What do you want to know specifically?"

"Why does the Secretary of State give a damn about what happens to a British-educated Guatemalan national who once led a failed revolution and now teaches English Lit and Mayan history in his native country?"

There was a long pause while Director Shikowitz drew in a breath. It was clear to me the head of the FBI had no idea Rafael wasn't even a US citizen.

"Well, he's a friend." Neville took his time, like a kindergartner thinking up a good one. "His sister is a big supporter of the administration. She married into the Crockers of Nob Hill. Heard of them?"

"Yesss," I steamed. "Her daughter, Cherry Crocker, nearly got me killed a couple months ago."

"I see." He grumbled and drew in a breath to give himself courage. "Well, there's a lot to this operation. There's a certain amount of need-to-know going on here. You were a decorated soldier once. I'll appeal to your sense of duty and willingness to follow the requests of your superiors."

"Yeah, nice one. Let's define 'soldier and superior' here, Neville. We—"

"You should address me as Mister Secretary."

"Not happening, Neville. I asked you a question and you answered with a question, which is a huge red flag for me. You're a big shot living a stone's throw from the Pentagon. They have special ops guys who can do what you need done. I know. I used to be one of those guys. But you didn't ask them. And that brings up a big question in my mind. See, I'm not a soldier anymore. Right now, I'm a civilian being asked by you—Neville—to go out and die for something other than my country. So, this need-to-know crap comes down to one thing: I need to know."

There was a long silence. I could hear both men breathing. Then Neville stirred. "Daniel, if it's not too much to ask—"

"I'll drop off the line, Neville. Touch base with me when you're done. Jacob, I'll call you back later."

He clicked off. Neville stayed quiet for a while.

"You see," he said, "this is a big deal. Bigger than you or me. There's a lot—"

"Cutting you off there, Neville. You're circling the same load you dropped earlier. Let me tell you where I am. We did some research on the people who kidnapped your friend, the Knights of Mithras. They're a cagey bunch but we uncovered cells of these guys, 500 to 1,000 strong. They have cells in ten countries. And those were the ones we found. There could be twice that many. All of them get the same kind of training I had as a Ranger. They're every bit as good as me at killing people. And you want me to pop over to—where was it, Belarus?—and risk my life for an aging professor who lied to me to get me to rescue Ms. Cherry Crocker of Nob Hill, then withheld critical information that nearly wiped out my next mission. Stop trying to *manage the narrative*. No more dodging questions. What I'm asking here is: What do you want? And, like I asked at the beginning, why do you care about Rafael Tum?"

"Very well then," he said. "How much do you know about the Knights of Mithras through history?"

"Three ... two ..."

"Yes, yes, you've made your point. OK." He paused a beat. "This goes nowhere. Not even to Pia. Especially not to Pia. Understood?" He waited for a second before realizing he had no cards to play. "The Knights have been taken over by Joe Griffith. He's gotten hold of something the Russians were working on codenamed the Chaac Project. It's such a big secret, I'm not read in on it. So don't ask. What I do know is the Russians failed because they were missing a critical piece of information known as the Chaac Equation. We believe Griffith is after the Equation. If he gets it, he could dominate the world. We know he has a big meeting for investors planned in two weeks in Belgrade, Serbia.

He—"

"Whoa, investors? The Knights of Mithras are a bunch of rich guys. Why would they need investors?"

"The Knights are rich with titles, not unlimited cash. The Project is so vast it could bankrupt most nations. There are only ten countries wealthy enough to fund the research and development costs—estimated to reach $100 billion—and they would insist on ownership. Griffith needs several investors to spread the risk, raise the funds, and provide the expertise for the R & D phase. His people have ransomed Brother Rafael to several different individuals. We don't know why they included more than one; we assume they're working to leverage Rafael to get the Equation before the meeting in Belgrade. We must have him back before anyone else gets there. Because this is going down in Belarus, the USA will not be part of this operation. The DoD and the NSA said you were the man for the job. Were they right?"

"Yes, they were." It was my dream mission. Save the world, rescue some random professor, and get my revenge on Griffith. I had a hard time keeping the excitement out of my voice.

"Here's the deal," I said. "There are a couple twists you're not going to like but you're going to swallow hard and do as I say. First, you're going to have Shikowitz call Ms. Sabel and talk her into letting me accept this mission. Don't give her that crap about duty and country; she has a lot less tolerance for BS than I do. You're going to have Shikowitz tell her that you're a Keeper. She knows about you guys and the Knights; it'll save a lot of time. We need her resources, and she never turns down Shikowitz. Second, a Sabel Agent is going to drop a special phone off at your office. When I have Rafael secured, I'm going to call that phone. Before I release 'Brother' Rafael, you're going to tell me how long you've been one of the Keepers and what the fuck they do. Goodbye."

"What makes you think I'm a member of the Keepers?"

"Pretend you're not and I'm out." I clicked off and leaned against the wall.

Processing what he said and what he didn't, I made note of the fact he didn't argue about getting a Sabel phone. They're off the national grid, highly encrypted, satellite based, not yet hacked by our own intelligence agencies much less foreigners, so our communications would be unreported by anyone anywhere. And he was fine with that. Which meant, he needed a layer of secrecy the State Department couldn't offer him.

Sup, homes, Mercury said appearing next to me. I nearly jumped out of my skin. When I caught my breath, he said, *The gods work in mysterious ways, huh, bro?*

I said, *Don't sneak up on me like—*

Dude, the least you could do is say 'thank you.'

I said, *Oh c'mon. You did not get the Secretary of State involved. He said he spoke to the DoD and other people.*

Mercury said, *The evidence of a divine hand is all around you, yet you choose to say the sky is blue because of refraction. Well, who in the Orcus refracted it? Huh?*

I said, *Just give me a minute. I need to process this.*

Mercury said, *Well then process this here then, my dear mortal: Chaac is a good friend of mine. The lil' dude can party like P. Diddy, y'know what I'm saying? Wait right here, I'll go get him. Oh, hey, Neville keeps saying it like 'shock' because the whole Chaac Project is about electricity and Chaac, pronounced tja-alk, is the Mayan god of thunder and lightning. Electricity, shock, get it?*

I said, *Yeah. Not funny.*

Mercury dismissed my attitude with a wave. *Anyway, I can't wait to get you two together, we're gonna have so much—*

I said, *No, no, no. I don't need any more gods in my head.*

Mercury's face fell as if I'd insulted him—the same expression he always gets when I'm not ready to party with the gods. He melted into the background, shaking his head sadly.

My phone rang. Shikowitz. After brief and nervous-on-his-end salutations, he asked if he could speak to Ms. Sabel.

I pulled her out of the meeting with the local constabulary. She met me in the hall holding an icepack to her cheek. Facing me, she argued with Shikowitz for a minute. Then she muted the phone and looked at me. She said, "The Secretary of State is a member of the Keepers?"

I explained how she's the only person I know who's not a member of a secret society. She went back to her call.

Throughout the call, she kept her eyes hard on mine, knowing this was my end-run around her plan to keep me out of harm's way. But her friend Shikowitz was persuasive. Eventually, she said, "He's ready. He can take my jet to London, pick up his crew, and be ready to cross the border before dawn."

I hugged her, kissed her on the cheek, and floated out of the building.

CHAPTER 8

EXCITEMENT COURSED THROUGH MY VEINS like a drug when I picked up my squad, Miguel and Isaiah, in London where they were working security for our CEO. Isaiah thanked me across the Channel and over half of Belgium before I convinced him to shut up. I didn't need thanks. I needed time to relish the clash to come. Heading back into battle against evil fed my addiction to danger. I was higher than a kite.

Adding to the excitement was my bluff. The ransom was something called the Chaac Equation, which I'd promised to bring with me. Showing up empty-handed should piss them off even more. Hell, I didn't even know what it looked like. Was it a thumb drive or a black box? Was it the size of a postage stamp or a building?

The three of us flew to Warsaw, landing at 0200. We chartered a skydiving plane that took us to the edge of Poland's airspace by 0400. An easy jump took us over the river into a town called Brest. The Poles, Lithuanians, Germans, and Russians traded the city like a playing card over the centuries. None of them bothered to invest much in infrastructure. After the Soviets face-planted in '91, Belarus went its own way. Now they had a Hilton Hampton Inn. Things were looking up.

We stashed our parachutes and other equipment in a park on the edge of town. On the flight over, we'd worked out a detailed plan. Miguel and Isaiah took up their observation post and launched a Sabel drone to keep an eye on me.

I walked alone through city streets as dawn broke across a clear sky.

I made my way to the railroad park specified by the kidnappers in their instructions. It wasn't much of a park. Leftover rail cars and steam engines waited for locals. I made a wide circle first, and a smaller circle the second time. No one stood on the streets or looked out of windows. The kidnappers had specified an engine in their instructions, so I leaned against a nearby tree and waited.

Two tough guys swung around the freight cars fifty yards out. They separated from each other as they approached. The leader, smaller and swinging his arms in a way that he thought made him look strong, but actually made him look like an orangutan, kept his gaze locked on mine. He wanted me to notice the pistol tucked into his belt. He wore a long-sleeve plaid shirt buttoned to the neck with an odd turtleneck t-shirt underneath. The other guy was the muscle. No need for swagger. He worked the one-size-too-small trick to make him look bigger. His trilaterals bulged through his shirt sleeves, as did his biceps, his pectorals, and so on. Muscleman swept around my flank, checking the area for any associates I might have brought along.

"You are Jacob Stearne, *tak*?" Plaid-shirt said with a thick accent.

He skipped over the password protocol. Amateur.

"Too early for ice cream?" I asked.

His expression changed as he realized his mistake. He mentally backpedaled and pretended not to know my name. "You are looking for ice cream truck?"

"A little late for that now." I smiled nice and friendly. "What's your name?"

"Anton." He almost stuck out a hand to shake but pulled back. "You are well? OK? Good trip? Do you need anything? Water? Ice cream? I get. No problem."

"I'm good, thanks, Anton. What's your friend's name?" I nosed over my shoulder where the other kid made a show of doing a security sweep.

"He is Ivan."

I felt for them both. They were young, lacking scars and tattoos. Gangster wannabees who had already lost control of the game.

I wore a small earbud buried in my ear canal to keep comms live should they take my phone. You couldn't see it unless you went looking deep. I heard both Miguel and Isaiah groan in my ear. There's nothing worse than working with amateur criminals. They tend to spook easy and start shooting at the slightest twitch. Then the only way out is to kill them all. Local governments frown on mass murder. Especially by Americans. We had hoped to avoid that complication.

"You've done well, Anton." I smiled and clamped his shoulder. "Same for Ivan. Call him over here. Time to report in, tell your bosses I'm clean, unaccompanied, and have no tricks to pull. I'd like to get this over before we get old."

He stared at me blankly. Obviously, his first ransom exchange. The charade hardly ranked in my experience.

"Ivan," he called out, followed by something in Belarusian. An East Slavic language that sounds like—but isn't—Russian.

His associate trotted over to us. I held my arms straight out from my shoulders and waited. Ivan took the hint and patted me down while Anton made the call to his superiors.

We didn't have to wait long before a minivan pulled up in the parking lot and stopped. The boss gangsters. A small, wiry guy got out and fast-walked toward us. Nervous energy rippled through the air ahead of him. Older with a scarred ear, he kept his black curly hair piled on top. Prison tattoos peeked from the neck of his sweatshirt. Anton and Ivan deferred to the two new guys. That confirmed the new guys outranked Anton and Ivan. Which is how these things usually went: first contact was with the expendable kids, the next was mid-level for the delicate job of transportation, followed by negotiations with the head guy who I'd meet later.

As he approached, he tucked a black cloth bag under his arm. He said, "Jacob come for Rafael, yes?"

The driver got out and came around the front of the van. About my size, bald with what appeared to be a matching tattoo at his neck, he had the face of a prize fighter and the muscles to go with it. He came within ten feet and stopped and stared.

"Yes," I said. I nodded over my shoulder at the boys. "Get these guys out of here. They scare the hell out of me."

Wiry-guy took a moment to translate my English. As he figured it out, I caught a glint of appreciation from Anton. I may as well have given him a five-star review on TripAdvisor for Future Mob Bosses of Belarus. Wiry-guy gave them a job-well-done glance.

Anton and Ivan backed away. Within a few seconds, they were gone.

"Chaac Equation," the prize fighter said.

I raised my hands in surrender and turned to him. I said, "Do you speak English?"

He said, "*Nie.*" Which sounded like *nyet* but not quite. I took it for the Belarusian negative.

My options were clear: beat the crap out of these guys and threaten them until they took me to Rafael or do it their way. They looked tough enough to make extracting the location from them next to impossible. As dangerous as it was, I opted to go their route. After all, it was the most likely to produce my desired outcome: to work my way up the ladder to Griffith.

I said, "Nothing happens until I see Rafael Tum in person to make sure he's alive."

The prize fighter grabbed my wrists, wrenched them behind my back, and zip-tied them. He was strong. Wiry-guy reached up and threw the bag over my head. The big guy reached in my pocket and yanked my phone. They pushed me to the van and shoved me in the back.

"We're tracking you," Isaiah reassured me through the earbud.

The van drove over potholes at a good clip for what felt like an hour, driving in random directions to throw off any tail. I wasn't worried. Sabel drones are electric, nearly silent, and painted to blend in with the sky.

Periodically, Isaiah would give me updates on how far behind me they were. It ranged between five and fifteen minutes.

We finally came to a stop. The side door slid open, and the fighter's meaty hands dragged me to my feet. He led me into a musty-smelling building and pushed me up three flights of stairs. Someone ahead of us creaked a door open. I smelled plaster dust and heard plastic sheeting rustle. A room under renovation.

Isaiah gave me an update. "They circled back. We'll be there in ten minutes."

Without warning, the hood came off.

The light blinded me for a second. I winced and looked around. We stood on planks of worn, unfinished wood. Green and purplish swirls of wallpaper peeled back in places. The room was missing a good chunk of interior wall. Someone had expanded the living space with a sledgehammer. Construction plastic hung like a curtain over the hole. The space beyond was dark.

Wiry-guy took up a position to my left that formed a triangle with the boxer on my right. It was smart. If I attacked one of them, the other would slam me to the ground. Tough guys in the movies beat up two bad guys at the same time, but that's only because the director choreographed it for him. In real life, these guys were too far apart and, while they were amateurs, they weren't stupid. Wiry-guy sensed me making calculations and pulled back his jacket to reveal a pistol tucked into his belt.

At the other end of the small room sat a dark, brooding man in a rickety chair. He held a large pistol in one hand. He was well dressed with black hair gelled straight back. In my head, I labeled him "Slick." An assault rifle leaned against the wall behind him. Slick rose and looked me over. I maintained eye contact. Average build, average height, average looks, he moved like a professional warrior with purpose and awareness. He stomped his boot heels on the wood a little harder than required to emphasize his authority over me. Giving me a full examination, he tracked around behind me.

CHAPTER 9

SLICK CAME AROUND IN FRONT of me, then turned his back on me and walked away. In a slight Scottish brogue, he said, "You disappoint, Mr. Stearne."

"Well, that makes two of us. I was told you were handsome."

He snapped a look over his shoulder at me before deciding to let it pass. "You negotiate in bad faith. You were to bring the Chaac Equation."

"I did," I lied straight to his face. "When I know Professor Tum's alive, we'll make the swap."

"We?" He regarded me carefully and stepped closer. "You brought associates with you. You were told specifically, nae."

At some point, he'd had the Scot beaten out of him. Maybe he'd spent some time in America. I said, "I don't trust criminals. If I brought anything, you'd kill the professor and me. You know it. I know it. So don't play this like your amateur sidekicks over here."

"You've got bound hands and you're making demands?"

"Where's Griffith? Shouldn't he be here?" I asked. This whole operation was a waste of time if Joe wasn't coming.

A hint of surprise that I knew the name crossed his face. He said, "I'm in charge."

Isaiah's voice slid in my ear again. "Five minutes out. Streets are blocked off for some reason."

I had a feeling Slick's patience would run out in less than five. There were three of them. Two armed and one with dangerous fists. Bad odds, but not impossible. As long as I didn't get into a fight with the prize fighter, I could handle the other two. I turned my back to Slick and lifted my bound wrists.

"Tell me then, what was your plan?" he asked, ignoring my request for free hands.

"You show me the professor. When I verify he's alive and well, I tell my man to bring the Equation so close you can taste it. Then we work out how the exchange goes down. Everybody walks away alive."

"And how were you planning to tell your man?"

He didn't argue about my use of a singular noun for my associate. That told me he hadn't spotted my guys.

"Smoke signals," I said.

Miguel, my best friend and a member of the Diné Nation, spoke into my earbud. "Not funny." In a sarcastic voice, he added, "Ke-mo sah-bee."

Slick walked another circle around me. As he passed the prize fighter, he held out his hand. The big guy slapped my phone in it. He held it to my face to unlock it. Sabel phones don't work that way. They need double verification. There's a fingerprint reader hidden on the side.

He looked confused and waited for me to explain the phone.

I shrugged and turned my back to him once again. I lifted my bound wrists a second time.

He sighed, shifted his pistol to his left hand, pocketed my phone, whipped out a nasty looking stainless-steel stiletto, clicked it open, and freed my hands with a flick.

When I first started working for Ms. Sabel, she showed me how she could beat men in the boxing ring using speed over strength. We practiced her reflex exercises every day. Combined with all the fighting techniques the US Army taught me, I am stronger, faster, and smarter than just about anyone I come up against.

Slick was no different from the others who thought they could keep me contained: they placed too much confidence in the mere possession of a firearm.

The instant my wrists were free, I grabbed his right hand, yanked him over my hip, twisted him around in a circle that ended with him on his knees, in a headlock, his own stiletto pushing against his jugular. My left hand grabbed his left wrist, brought it up, and aimed his pistol at Wiry-guy.

For a second, everyone froze as they processed what just happened to the balance of power.

When the adrenaline spike reaches the brain of an untrained civilian, thousands of fight-or-flight responses pop into their heads at once. Their brains overload and cross signals. It takes hundreds of hours of training to get those signals under control. Which is why combat veterans tend to be calm in emergencies. Wiry-guy wasn't a veteran—he was a gangster. No training. He pulled the pistol out of his belt a second before all the untrained synapses in his brain short-circuited. The barrel had just cleared his belt when his trigger finger spasmed. He shot himself in the gut. He fell to the floor, his pistol spinning across the room. He writhed.

The boxer stared at his friend, then at Slick and me. I'd already brought Slick's pistol around to him. The boxer was looking down the barrel.

Mercury chose this moment to stride through the tense situation as if he were at a garden party. He said, *Homes, you ain't supposed to get yourself killed here. Seamus here—that would be Slick's real name— ain't worth it. You need to get Griffith before you check out.*

I don't trust gods when they give out advice. *Why do you care when I check out?*

Mercury said, *I done told you, bruh. I got a lot riding on this.*

I said, *Oh, right, you lost your wife to Mars in a bet, and you want her back—same as I want Jenny back. How about we make a deal? I help you get Larunda back and you—*

Oh no you don't. Mercury started backing up, holding his palms up as if he were pushing me away. *You ain't tricking me into making a deal with a mortal. That's for Juno or Ariadne, Neptune maybe, but not in my portfolio. No. I didn't hear you trying to make no deal. Anyone asks, I wasn't here.* He backed to the wall and almost disappeared into it. Then he stopped. *Dude, don't get killed here. You got bigger things going down. Defuse. Defuse. Ya with me?*

How come we always have to accept the will of the gods, but they never want to make an even trade? Is it me, or are we getting the short end of the stick here?

"I don't want to hurt anyone," I said to Slick. "Tell him to empty his pockets and drop to the floor."

Slick was shaking. Not like an amateur, but with the rage of a commander who'd lost his battle. He said something in Belarusian. The boxer dropped to his knees, then spread his hands on the floor.

I relieved Slick of his pistol and knife, took my phone, pushed him down next to the big guy, and zip-tied their hands. Slick had a ring of small keys that I palmed. I grabbed Wiry-guy's pistol. I emptied the chamber and magazine and stuffed it back in his hand. When the authorities got there, I wanted them to know who shot who. Then I remembered the car keys and snatched those out of Wiry-guy's pocket.

A quick check of Wiry-guy's wound didn't give me much hope for him, though. He would bleed out if he didn't get help soon.

Not my problem. He chose his path.

In my earbud, Isaiah gave me a status update. "We're stopped in traffic, another five minutes, maybe more. But—bad news—the drone picked up two squads of armed men converging on your building from all directions."

The front door was no longer an option.

At the far end of the dark room, a lean, older man with a weathered face and gray hair sat on the floor, his hands chained to a radiator. Rafael Tum. I knew from experience his look was deceptive. He'd been a guerrilla leader back in his day and understood how to survive. He nodded a silent thanks, then raised his chains to reveal a keyed lock.

Slick's ring of small keys had the right one. A flash later, I had Professor Tum freed.

He patted my shoulder with an assessing look. We'd had a difficult history. He wasn't sure if I were there to rescue him—or kill him.

"Window?" I asked. "We have company closing in from all sides."

We ran to the other room as we heard tromping on the ground floor stairs. He spotted the rifle and pointed at it. A silent request for permission to take it. I nodded. He slung it and climbed out the window.

Tum and I thought alike. People rarely look up when searching for adversaries. Even soldiers. The old man scrambled to the roof. I followed. It was made of sheets of corrugated steel. Cheap and easy to build, but slick and unforgiving. We scrambled, slipping as much as climbing, until we reached the stack of three brick chimneys near the middle. We squeezed in together between two of them. It was all the cover we could get. We stopped moving.

Below us, voices shouted to each other. We could tell they were freeing Slick and the boxer.

Rafael Tum turned to me with the look of a seasoned revolutionary who had been through many impossible jail breaks. He whispered, "You did not kill those men?"

"I thought it best to defuse the situation."

CHAPTER 10

RAFAEL TUM AND I REMAINED stuck between two chimneys for too long. I needed a bathroom break, but armed men searched every apartment, bush, and pothole below us. All I wanted was a way off the roof, to sneak past the armed killers looking for me, and find my way back to the park on the river so we could get across to Poland.

While my bored gaze wandered the skies, I spotted a drone five or six blocks away. If I could see the drone, it couldn't be Isaiah's. Which meant the Knights had eyes in the sky. They would be onto us shortly. But the drone appeared to be stationary. A little too far away to pinpoint us. Why became apparent a moment later.

Isaiah spoke in my ear. "Bad news, dude. Turns out, the traffic we're stuck in was caused by six personnel carriers blocking off the 'hood. They unloaded about fifty cops, full armor and automatic weapons. Some of them are looking at us funny. We don't look Belarusian."

A Native American and an African American would stand out amongst the all-white locals. The largest minority in Belarus were the Poles. A fact I might've considered more carefully before conscripting them for this mission.

Isaiah continued, "The Knights have a drone. We're going to take it out, but it looks like they're watching the cops. Hang on—I see the Knights in your building are scrambling to get out."

I updated Rafael on this development.

"To operate in Brest," the old man said, "Seamus had to make deals with the gangsters and the police. Naturally, he lied to both parties. They think you have a diamond that he valued at roughly €20 million. They believe he's trying to cut them out of the deal."

Great.

"They've cleared out of your block," Isaiah said. "One guy is going back in. A civilian with black hair, slicked back. The rest are scrambling. There's a platoon of cops in full battle rattle doing a house-to-house. You've got five minutes. Oh. Wait. Cops are looking at us. They're coming for us. We're surrounded. Nowhere to go. Sorry, bro. I'm turning drone control over to you. Until we get clear: out."

Damn.

It took a minute for me to realize what his second-to-last sentence meant. I scrambled to find the drone app on my phone. If you leave a drone uncontrolled too long, it becomes a target for twelve-year-old boys with slingshots. Once I had the app running, I turned the ship around to get my bearings. I found the Knights' drone. Maneuvering mine directly above theirs, I dropped the drone-killer: a foot-long steel wire with weights on each end. It fell across two of the enemy drone's rotors. The thing fell like a rock. And its operators would have no idea what happened.

Which wouldn't be anytime soon from the look of the Belarusians' ground game. I found Miguel and Isaiah standing in front of an armored personnel carrier with their hands up. So. No support crew coming to my rescue.

I turned the drone around and scanned the streets. From their formation and tactics, it appeared the Belarusians were after the Knights, not me. Which made sense. Slick had made promises that they wanted him to keep. But that distraction wouldn't last long. As soon as the Belarusians learned I was in town, they'd be after me for their ransom: a diamond that didn't exist.

That meant we had little time to get out of Brest. We had to fly while the Knights and police were still preoccupied with each other.

We made our way back down the roof toward the window we'd fled through earlier. The surface was so slick and steep, we had to spreadeagle for safety. There was a one-foot overhang that we'd done pull-ups to get up and over. To get back in, we'd have to position ourselves directly above the window without being able to see it. If we were off and missed it, we'd drop three stories. That was going to hurt.

And Rafael's bones weren't young anymore.

Mercury floated down on his absurd wings and lay on the corrugated steel next to me. He propped his head up and smiled. *How's it hanging, bro?*

I whispered, *Where's the window? Am I close?*

Mercury said, *No way, homie. I'm not helping you. You were mean and nasty—all up in my business, acting like we were equals who could work out a deal.*

I looked up quickly. *Why not? Back in the day, you were supposed to take Larunda to Hades, but you fell in love with her and fathered two children. You stashed her in a cottage where Jupiter would never find her. You cheated death on her behalf. That's what I want to do with Jenny. Why can't I do something like you did?*

Mercury said, *You're just a mortal. You guys don't have any real capacity for love and family, bruh. Nothing like us.*

I said, *We don't have capacity for love? Isn't that the justification slave owners used when they sold off families to different bidders? Leave me alone. I'm done with you.*

Mercury said, *Oh really? You don't want me to tell you the window is two feet to your left then? Fine. Have it your way.*

"At what are you staring?" Rafael, still above me on the roof, was looking over his shoulder at me. "I thought we were in a hurry."

"Yeah, uh, just trying to align with the chimneys. If I recall correctly, we should be over this way a bit."

I made the adjustment, got to the edge, dangled my feet over, lowered myself, and found the window. Right where Mercury said it would be. For just a second, I wondered if there really is a god.

I dropped into the apartment and stepped cautiously forward, looking for danger. Wiry-guy lay on the floor. As I expected, he'd bled out. His pals never saw the need to call an ambulance.

Then I saw what I was expecting. A pair of shoes peeking out from behind the construction plastic. Slick hid in the room where he'd held Rafael. I considered shooting him through the drywall. The advantage would be in saving a step. The disadvantage would be losing intel about Joe Griffith.

"Step out of the dark, Slick," I said. "Or I shoot you through the wall. Oh, and don't forget to hold your pistol by the barrel."

Behind me, I heard Rafael's foot scrape the windowsill and miss.

In front of me, Slick stepped out holding his pistol as instructed.

Rafael made another scrape on the window. I realized his problem. I'd barely made it in and I'm six foot one. He's half a foot shorter. He was going to need help, or he'd land on his back three floors down.

Slick grinned. He saw the problem too.

"Slide that pistol too me," I said. "Nice and easy."

Slick shook his head. His grin grew more confident.

Holding the iron sights on his center mass, I backed to the window and reached outside. I felt Rafael's knee. Not a good hold. I felt around higher until I found his pocket. It gave him enough confidence to let go of the roof. He dropped.

But he didn't quite land inside. His butt hit the windowsill. His torso started falling backward. His momentum started tugging me as well. Already off-balance because I had reached outside, far behind my center of gravity, I had the ominous feeling I could get yanked out along with Rafael and crack my head open on the cement below.

Slick calculated his risks. If he charged me, I'd let go of Rafael and kill him. If he ran, I'd save Rafael and let him live. Slick took off running down the hall.

Which told me he was a smart adversary. He almost won this round. Too bad the cops found out he was double-crossing them, or he'd have gotten away with it.

I dropped my pistol, spun around, slammed a foot to the wall, grabbed Rafael's belt with my free hand, and pulled hard.

Rafael flew into the room, sliding across the floor, only stopping when his feet hit Wiry-guy's corpse.

"Thank you," he said through gritted teeth.

He rolled up to seated and checked himself for injuries.

I grabbed my pistol and ran after Slick. He was taking steps two and three at a time, heading for the ground floor and the only exit. If I were him, I'd wait there for another shot at capturing me.

I used the drone and brought it in close. He stood outside with his back flat against the wall, waiting for me to open the door.

The drone also showed me an advance squad of police coming our way. The street leading to our building was blocked by the van they brought me in. The soldiers would come around it on both sides. Which meant we weren't leaving by the street.

Rafael looked over my shoulder at the drone feed. He saw what I saw.

Then the battery light came on. The drone had ten minutes left. This was supposed to be a quick operation. My guys didn't have time to recharge it while they sat in traffic. I parked it on the roof where Rafael and I had spent such a great morning.

Rafael was ahead of me. He ran down two flights of stairs and stopped at a window on the second-floor landing. He started elbowing his way through the glass. Slick heard the noise and turned in the doorway to see what we were doing. He swung around the jamb, leading with his pistol.

If I shot him, the noise would bring the cops straight to us. I pressed the unlock button on the car keys to draw the cops' attention to Slick. He heard the chirp. I locked and unlocked it a couple times to make sure the Belarusians didn't miss the point.

I tossed the car keys to Slick. Professional courtesy: Here's your only chance for escape.

He scowled at me. He pocketed his weapon, scooped up the keys, and made a break for it. Of course, he wouldn't get far. He just didn't know it yet.

Rafael was out the window, dropping to the ground. I followed.

No matter how easy they make it look in the movies, landing from eighteen feet up hurts your feet. Even when you roll. I limped off the sting, heading toward a footpath that ran between buildings in the opposite direction of the soldiers. Rafael grabbed my arm.

"We can't go yet." He shoved his hand in my pocket and pulled out the ring of small keys. He took off around the corner of the building.

From the opposite direction, I could hear the unmistakable sound of officials yelling at Slick to drop his weapon and get on the ground. Police orders sound the same in any language. Twenty yards and an old apartment building separated us. At best, sixty seconds.

I had no choice. I followed Rafael. Maybe he knew a better way out.

Rafael led me to a long row of storage rooms crouched between two buildings. Each had wooden doors, weathered and faded. Every door had strong locks. Rafael went straight to one and found the key, threw away the lock, and yanked the door open. He stepped inside.

I trotted over. "Dude, we don't have time for whatever—"

Behind him, a golden-haired woman cowered in the corner on a dirty concrete floor. A thin and dirty silk dress clung to her body. Chained to a rusted chunk of steel, she sensed our presence and quivered under a blindfold with a gag in her mouth.

CHAPTER 11

"IT'S ME," RAFAEL SAID AS he approached the huddled figure slowly. "Close your eyes."

He held out a hand and waited for me. Still surprised, I stared at his hand a second before figuring out he wanted a knife. How he knew I'd gotten a knife past the gangsters and Slick, I wasn't sure. I pulled the small tactical knife hidden in my belt buckle and handed it to him. He sliced off her blindfold and gag, handed me back the knife, then pulled away her blindfold.

The woman blinked in the dim light. She looked at Rafael. "Thank—" She noticed me and froze.

Something about her flooded my mind with a memory of Jenny. My fiancé had been tied to a chair with a bomb strapped to her chest and left in the middle of seventeen schoolchildren. There was a striking similarity to the strain of terror on both Jenny's face then and this woman's face now. My heart shattered. I couldn't breathe for a moment. I felt the weight of Jenny's medallion in my pocket.

"It's all right," Rafael cooed. "He's here to rescue us."

He searched through Slick's keys to unlock her chains.

"Wait a second," I said, coming back to the present. "That's …" I snapped my fingers trying to remember her name. "The movie star. From that movie about the girl."

"That movie?" Rafael mocked me while he unlocked her chains. "About the girl? Such eloquence."

"Um. Yeah. Betty Bardon."

She rolled her eyes and looked away.

Rafael pulled Betty's chains free. She rubbed her wrists, then checked me out again. Her bright blue eyes pierced through me, half-fearing for her life and half-wanting to kill me. Or was it humiliation and rage?

Stearne's Law crowded into my thinking. *Paranoia is the result of acute situational awareness.* I'd learned not to trust Rafael the last time I hung with him. I wasn't sure how he was wrapped up in the current situation. If Betty Bardon was a trap, it was a good one. He knew I'd never leave a woman behind. I asked, "What's she doing here? Is she with the Keepers? The Knights? My exfil plan is to free one hostage and—"

"Then change it," Rafael snapped. "It's two now. And no, she has nothing to do with this and has never heard of Keepers or Mithras."

Betty rose with that mix of humiliation and rage still glowing in her eyes. Her hands were dirty. Her fingernails clotted with blood. Two filthy plates and a metal cup lay in the corner. She tried to hide her bare and dirty feet.

"Then what's she doing here?" I asked.

"Not all men are honorable, Jacob." Rafael put a hand on my shoulder.

A sick feeling came over me. Now I understood why Rafael had asked me about killing Slick and his men. I'm not a big believer in the wholesale slaughter of strangers, but now that I knew what they did to Betty Bardon, I regretted sparing their useless lives.

Police voices grew closer. They were seconds away.

Betty Bardon looked at me as if I'd slaughtered children. Her rage grew by the second. She was ready to claw my eyes out.

"He's with me," Rafael repeated in his reassuring voice. "It's OK. He's a good man. Betty, do you hear me?"

She snapped her glare to him. He kept up a rhythmic nodding. Slowly she began to calm herself. She took an anguished breath, burst into tears, and threw her arms around him.

"They sent me in with food and water yesterday," he said over his shoulder. "And again this morning."

Outside, men's voices grew louder. One issuing commands. Others replying in the Belarussian version of "clear." They were one building away.

DEATH AND REDEMPTION

I checked out the blood under her fingernails. Something I'd seen more than once in war zones. When people start killing each other, men have a bad habit of resorting to their inner animal. Women often respond in kind. Ms. Bardon made Slick and his boys pay for their animalistic transgressions. Although I didn't recall seeing any claw marks on their faces or necks, the first places usually marked. From what I recalled of her career, she played sexy temptresses in movies. In real life, she was a fighter. I could work with that.

"Yeah. Well," I said and stuck my head out the door. Our alley was still empty. "We have to run."

My eyes swept the bare floor. "Do you have shoes?"

She remained locked on Rafael. He said, "They brought her here as you see her."

A quick glance at her back showed no underwear lines through the tight dress. "We'll get her some clothes somehow. Right now, we need to leave. Ma'am, can you run?"

She let go of Rafael and backed up. Fear and rage built up again.

I knew the worst thing you could do to a victim was get in her space. But there was one thing even worse: letting her abusers take her back. I leaned over, shoved my shoulder into her gut, hoisted her up, and ran.

Rafael didn't argue. He kept up with me.

Ms. Bardon argued. "Put me down, damn it."

She clawed my back and pounded her fists on my kidneys. I kept going. I could explain later. Rafael tried as we ran. He kept telling her this is what we had to do. I doubt she heard him.

Old ladies stuck their heads out of windows and stepped to their doorways to watch as we made our way out of the apartment buildings and into a neighborhood of shabby homes with ragged fences. Apparently, the sight of a man with a struggling woman over his shoulder didn't ring any alarms in Belarus. Dogs barked and kids stared from their backyards. We ducked into an area filled with gray concrete apartment buildings. We ran between two of the largest buildings and out to a larger road.

When I thought we were clear, I set Ms. Bardon on her feet. She backed up ten feet, glaring at me, her fists and jaw clenched. She was about to shout obscenities at me. Rafael stepped between us and tried talking to her again. Over her shoulder, I saw a cab.

Two blocks behind the cab, I saw an armored personnel carrier stop and unload ten soldiers. They headed down a side street. We were good for a few minutes. I hailed the cab.

He pulled to the curb. I opened the door and tried to usher Betty in.

"If you think I'm going anywhere with you, you're nuts!" Her screech echoed through the apartment buildings.

"Please," I said, "we will get you to a store and get some clothes."

"It'll be OK," Rafael added.

"Those soldiers are looking for us." I pointed up the street.

She tried to keep one eye on me while the other followed my finger. When she saw them, she waved and let out a piercing whistle. "Over here! Over here! These men—"

Rafael clamped a hand on her mouth. "These are not American police. These are just as bad as the others. Jacob is our best hope. Please, get in the cab."

She gave him a look that would've shriveled a lesser man.

To the general public, we had every appearance of a daylight kidnapping. The cabbie had witnessed enough. He hit the gas and let the door close by his forward momentum.

"He's here to help us," Rafael pleaded. "He's going to get us back to the West."

That appeared to get through to her. She gave me another close inspection. "Who are you?"

"Jacob Stearne, ma'am. Sabel Security."

"Never heard of you," she sneered. "What are you doing here?"

"I came to rescue Professor Tum."

"Who's that?" She scrunched her nose.

I thumbed at Rafael.

He held out a hand. "Pleased to make a proper introduction, Ms. Bardon. Call me Rafael."

"You're a professor?" She shook his hand hesitantly. Then she turned to me. "How do we get out of this godforsaken place? Where the hell are we anyway?"

"Brest, Belarus. Where were you abducted?"

Her eyes darted left and right. "Kobryn."

That was the next city east of Brest. Rafael and I leaned in toward her with curious frowns. Kobryn and Hollywood were not in the same social quadrant.

She said, "My mother was Belarussian. I was born Yulia Nyakhaychyk. When I went into acting, I wanted to honor the Golden Age of Hollywood. So I combined Bette Davis and Bridget Bardot and came up with Betty Bardon."

I didn't know what to say. I looked at Rafael for help. He didn't have any answers either.

"My grandmother lives in Kobryn," Betty explained. Anger clouded her face. "She sold me out. That bitch! That fucking bitch! Told me some guys wanted my autograph. Everybody sells you out when you're famous. Everybody. You can't trust producers, or directors, or..." She planted both hands on my chest and shoved me out of her way. "I'm just a piece of property to you fucking people."

She stormed down the broken sidewalk. She stepped on something sharp and shouted, "Fuck!"

Rafael and I trotted up to her. I said, "Let's find a store and get you some shoes."

She gave me that look of fear and rage again. Then she let her guard drop just a notch. She said, "Are those police really in on it with that Scottish guy?"

"They were planning to share your ransom," Rafael said. "But the Scot double-crossed them."

"Then we have to hide." She picked her way across a gravel parking area at the back of a building. "You'll have to get me some clothes. Sweats. And shoes, size 39 Euro, and sunglasses."

I nodded and took off around the block. I checked on the cops searching buildings. I had a few minutes. I found a convenience store three blocks away and picked up what I could. They didn't have bras, undies, or socks. Just sweatpants, a hoodie, shoes, and big sunglasses.

Mercury stood behind the cash register. *Homie! Did you notice how much Betty Bardon looks like Jenny Jenkins only with bigger—*

I said, *Where's the clerk?*

Mercury said, *—and rounder—*

I said, *She's nothing like Jenny.*

Which was a lie. When we saw that movie about the girl, I told Jenny that she was better looking than Betty Bardon.

Mercury said, *Little trivia for you, bro: Betty's grandma was a dyed-in-the-wool Soviet. A true believer, party member. But Betty's mom couldn't hack it. She left for the West when she was seventeen and never spoke to her mother again. Betty had probs with her mom and thought Grandma might bridge the gap. That's why Betty went looking for her roots.*

I said, *Yeah. Fascinating. Where is the clerk?*

Mercury said, *Why you in such a big hurry, brutha? We're just having a chat here.*

Gods don't chat. You can learn that much from a quick skim of the Bible. Did God ever say, "Hey, Moses, how's it hanging? You catch the Packers game last night?" No. You know why? Because when gods speak, they're always up to something. They want you to crack down on people with a batch of Commandments or give all your money to the poor and proselytize for the rest of your life. Maybe clean up your act and love your neighbor. Not that anyone's ever done that. But nowhere, in any culture, in any pantheon, do they just stop and chat.

He wanted me to shed my victims so I could get on with winning his bet for him.

I leaned over the counter. An old lady in a uniform lay on the floor clutching her chest. Whatever Mercury was doing to the poor clerk would stop when I left, so I didn't worry about her. I tore the tags off the merchandise, laid them on the counter, and dropped a hundred euro note on them. I gave Mercury a dirty look and left.

As I marched away, Mercury called out, *You gotta admit, she looks a lot like Jenny. Except she has bigger—*

I put my hands over my ears and started shouting in my head, *La-la-la! La-la-la! La-la-la!*

It took a few minutes, but I found Betty and Rafael hiding behind dumpsters near where I'd left them.

Rafael and I turned our backs while Betty donned her clothes. She fluffed her hair and asked, "What's your plan to get us out of here?"

I tugged her wrist and said, "Let's go."

We had to swing wide of the search area by jogging a mile out of our way, then cut back to get to the river. Betty wasn't a fast runner like Ms. Sabel, but she was no stranger to exercise. She kept a good pace with seven-minute miles. Revolutionaries spend a lot of time running through the jungles avoiding the government, so I didn't worry about old Rafael.

As we ran, with an overtone of suspicion in her voice, Betty asked, "You do have a plan, don't you? Mr. Rescuer?"

"There's a park at the Mukhavets River. I've stashed a two-seater electric airplane. You two will take it four miles south, then turn east, cross the Bug River and you're in Poland. My people will meet you there, get you home."

"A what?" she asked, her voice rising in volume and pitch.

"Electric airplane. Ultralight. Takes off in fifty feet, flies at about five hundred feet, runs around 100 mph, flies for about fifteen minutes. Easy to operate."

"I don't know how to fly a plane," she said. She turned to Rafael. "Do you?"

He shook his head.

"You have to fly us one at a time then," she said.

"Not enough juice for two trips. Besides, I've only flown the thing once for training. It's not that hard. Although, landing is kinda … Look, it's the only way out of here. One of you will figure it out."

A hornet buzzed my ear and a piece of brick twenty feet in front of me turned into a puff of powder. Bullets sound like hornets when they pass by. The crack of a rifle reached us a split second after the supersonic bullet missed.

CHAPTER 12

RAFAEL UNDERSTOOD WHAT THE CRACK of the gun meant, but Betty turned around to look for the source of the noise. Rafael and I dragged our companion into the nearest alley. We ran down it and around a corner. We flattened against a brick wall.

Betty shouldered up next to me for protection. Rafael checked the alley's other end.

I pulled out my Sabel Monocular. It's a tube the size of your hand that works as an invisible periscope. A built-in laser heats the air an adjustable distance from you, creating a mirage-like mirror in the air. When I look through the monocular telescope, I can see around corners. This time, I saw my ex-friend Slick running down the sidewalk toward us. He had a rifle in one hand and a radio in the other.

There was no time to figure out who he was talking to. It didn't matter. He must have wormed his way out of custody. I had to assume his crew of eight others, who searched the building for us before the cops got there, were also free. Which led me to conclude the locals had patched things up with the Knights of Mithras and were hunting us as well.

I checked the drone app and raised it up. It came toward us, using GPS. The battery light came on again. I needed just a few seconds. It found us and hovered above our alley. The soldiers were two blocks away and closing. Slick had four men with him and was closing from the opposite direction. We had one direction to go, which would take us across a wide boulevard between the two factions.

The drone blinked off. I heard it crash to the ground near Slick.

My thoughts turned to Jenny. Something about this mission felt doomed, just like that icy mountain in Germany where she met her fate. Which led me down a dark tunnel of endless regret. I'd saved Jenny and the children the first time. I failed her the next.

I pulled the medallion out and looked at it as if it could help.

Betty watched me with a suspicious side-glance. "What is that, a good luck coin?"

I shrugged and slipped it back in my pocket. With no time for tragic memories, I pushed off the wall and huddled with my charges.

Pulling up my mapping app on my phone, I showed them the route to the park. In case something happened to me, I showed them where we stashed the plane. I explained everything I know about flying it: make sure you have fifty feet, push the energy lever forward slowly, pull back on the stick softly, use the pedals to bank, find an empty road to land on and set it down gently. They listened with grim expressions. Then I explained our slim chances for survival. Which they accepted.

"Now or never," I said.

We ran down the alley and crossed the boulevard, sprinting as fast as we could go. The soldiers saw us right away. Slick saw us a split second later. We had enough of a head start to give us a slim chance of getting away.

We jogged right and left at every alley until we were lost. When I checked the map, we were still a mile from the park. The soldiers were north of us and Slick to the east. We were in a business district, nice and clean and fairly new. There was a long boulevard that led to the park in a straight line. We couldn't go that way or they'd shoot us like air-gun targets at the fair. The rest of the neighborhood was a grid pattern. Nice straight streets with clean sight lines. A rifleman's dream.

Rafael pointed at a delivery van. The driver stepped out with an armful of boxes and walked inside a shop.

Three blocks behind us, Slick and two of his minions rounded the bend. They looked in the wrong direction. That bought us three seconds.

Rafael pushed Betty toward the van.

I pulled up the rifle and aimed at Slick. A mom with two kids walked out of a shop and into the line of fire. I slung the rifle and chased after my companions.

Rafael took the wheel. Betty jumped in the passenger side. A bullet ripped through my skin between my arm and ribs. The searing pain felt like a flame. The truck was rolling when I jumped in the sliding side door. Bullets ripped through the sheet metal.

Betty screamed and covered her head.

Rafael rounded a corner, then another. No way Slick could catch us.

But then bullets pinged through the windshield from soldiers in front of us.

There is nothing in automotive bodywork that will stop a bullet other than the engine block. All three of us tried to crouch behind it. Rafael steered with one hand on the wheel and one eye above the dashboard. Five seconds later, another burst of gunfire ripped through the sliding door. We'd just passed more bad guys. Now they were behind us.

I sat up and got my bearings. We were driving up the street we'd just left. I looked at Rafael. He sensed my question about why we would go back the way we'd came when that would bring us straight back to Slick. He pointed at a gas station three blocks up. The road had a slight bend in it. I understood his plan.

I climbed into the back of the van and rummaged around for something heavy. I grabbed a toolbox and clambered back up front. I opened the door and pushed Betty out. She screamed. Rafael opened his door and stepped halfway out. He kept one foot on the gas while I dropped the heavy box on it. Then he jumped. I rolled out after Betty.

Hitting the ground rolling, I got up, ran to Betty and scooped her up.

Our van hit the gas station with the screeching of shredding metal as it plowed directly into the pumps. Screams followed as everyone nearby ran from what would happen next. The fireball wasn't instantaneous. The spewing pumps and the leaking tank from the van had to pool around something hot enough to ignite it all. But an explosion was inevitable. Everyone knew it.

I ducked into a store with Betty in tow. She didn't argue. We backed against the wall and watched the people running from the station. Slick rounded the bend with his gang. As soon as they ran by our window, I stepped out, dragging Betty with me. We started running away from Slick and the gas station, heading for the park. Rafael joined us.

That's when the explosion hit.

The shock wave knocked everyone on the street to the ground. While the fireball drew their attention, we got up and ran.

Six minutes later, we reached the waterfront. A stone seawall held back the land ten feet above the river. A brick and cement boat dock stepped down from the park to water level. There were no boats. We ran to the edge of the dock. The sides of it wrapped around the seawall, giving us a temporary hiding place. We stopped to catch our breath.

The noise of diesel personnel carriers approached the park entrance.

The ultralight was on the other side of the long narrow green, half a mile that may as well have been the other side of the world.

Rafael pointed across the Mukhavets River. "Is that Poland?"

"No. That's a tributary to the Bug River. We'd have to swim a mile into the heart of Brest to reach Poland."

Betty shrieked, "Blood!" She pointed at my wound.

I said, "Keep it down. Worry about it later. We need to find a way out of here."

She pulled her sweatshirt off, leaving herself exposed, ripped a sleeve from it, then slammed her armless top back on. She ripped the sleeve in half and wrapped the material around my arm and tied it.

Then she pointed upriver about sixty yards. A storm drain was half-exposed, its arch rising four feet above the river.

We heard the pounding of boots closing in on our position.

She dove in and started swimming. Rafael dove in after her.

No one asked me if I'd like to infect my wounds by diving into a murky, swampy river. Then I heard the whump-whump of a chopper heading our way. We couldn't hide from that on a boat dock. I dove in and followed them.

CHAPTER 13

SWIMMING WITH A COUPLE OF shattered ribs and a wounded arm is not easy. I made the storm drain and swam into darkness until I felt hands grabbing me. Betty and Rafael dragged me to my feet on a steep slope of cement. I could see nothing. I could feel their hands and I could tell we were in an ancient brick drainage system. It stood about five feet at the center with an arched ceiling. Being a storm drain, not a sewer, we were blessed with the smell of mud and decaying leaves and nothing worse.

I pulled my phone out, turned on the light, and looked around. The slope was gentle and straight. That meant if soldiers looked in here, they'd find us quickly. Rafael understood my thinking and started hiking up the hill. I followed.

"Where are you going?" Betty asked.

"To find a junction or a corner." I pointed back to the river where a hint of daylight glowed between the arch and the water level. "And I need to get a signal."

"We were so close," she said in a dejected tone. She fell in behind us.

We made our way up the hill a quarter mile until we found a workman's access point. Steel rungs ran up to street level from a small landing attached to the side of the culvert. Finger-wide shafts of light came through two holes in the manhole cover where they connected the removal tool.

We huddled together for warmth in the cramped space.

Rafael climbed the ladder to the top and listened. We both recognized the sound of the personnel carriers as they rumbled overhead. He shook his head and climbed back down.

"Let me see that wound," she said.

She took my light and unwound the covering. As soon as she saw the damage, she clamped a hand over her own mouth to stifle her scream.

Rafael nudged her gently aside. Out of necessity, rebels were their own doctors. He knew his way around an injury. He pushed my shirt into my rib-wound to clot the blood. We didn't have anything resembling clean to wrap around it completely. He re-tied the sleeve a lot tighter and finished it with a better, tighter knot. I grunted my pain away. He gave me a nod.

We knew the scenario: get antibiotics and pain killers or swirl around the gangrene drain.

"Why did they kidnap you?" I asked Rafael.

He looked at me before swiveling his gaze toward Betty and back, letting me know he couldn't tell me everything in front of a civilian. Since he was the one who insisted we bring a civilian, Stearne's Law tingled the back of my neck. Then he said, "They're looking for information. They tried to get Cherry to come to my rescue. They believed they could torture her to force my hand. Alas, she has become disillusioned by the deeds of my past. You came instead."

There was little light, making it difficult to read his face, but the part about Cherry hating him sounded true. After her staunch defense of him in front of the International Criminal Court, she learned the charges against him were true. In a rage, he had wiped out an entire village during the Guatemalan Civil War. That Cherry was disillusioned was putting it mildly. As a soldier, I knew Rafael's atrocities had weighed on him for years. There's no way to atone for sins of that magnitude. I imagined that guilt fired his altruistic involvement in the Keepers.

I checked my phone. No satellite signals this deep underground. I considered turning on the 5G service. Velcom, the local phone company, would turn over my location to the authorities without a warrant. I kept it off.

The app showed my ear-canal bud had died. I used the special tool to pull it out and shoved it in my pocket. It's built for a morning, not a whole day.

"Tonight?" Rafael asked. Meaning we wait until dark, then we wait until darker, then we make a break for the ultralight.

"If they're anything like the Russians, the Belarussians will go home at 5 PM. The Knights will stick around, though."

"Diversion?"

"Yep."

"What are you guys talking about?" Betty asked. "What diversion?"

I let Rafael explain it while I took a shot at climbing the rungs. I needed to update headquarters to make sure they had an exfil plan for me. Every movement of my left arm sent searing pain straight to my head. I used it to hold my balance while I repositioned my feet and right arm. When I got high enough, I stopped to let the Sabel satellite find my phone. Below me, Rafael explained our end game.

"The Knights will watch the park," Rafael said. "Jacob will create a diversion up the street somewhere. If they go for it, two of us get in the ultralight and head for Poland."

"What happens to him?" she asked.

"His company will get him out."

"What if they catch him?"

Rafael shook his head.

"They'll kill him," she said. "Right? Oh my god. He can't do that. We can't let him do that."

I couldn't see my companions below me in the dark, but I found a signal up at the top. I called HQ's emergency command. The backstop. They answered right away and switched me to special operations, where someone named Emma answered quietly and calmly.

I reported, "Miguel and Isaiah were taken by authorities—"

"We know, sir." Emma had a calm voice. "They got a call in before they were taken. Embassy personnel are working on getting them released. The good news: the operation you're up against is regional, not national. What's your status?"

She was putting a good spin on it. Regional in a highly militarized country like Belarus was like taking on the National Guard in New Jersey. Not as bad as the US Army, but still a damn powerful force.

"I've freed two hostages and we're hiding in a storm drain."

"What's *your* status?" she asked again. She was no novice to macho operators in the field.

"Bullet wound in the bicep and a couple cracked ribs. We need to get the hostages out. Prime objective."

"You're not supposed to have two hostages. Just one."

"I have two. Rafael Tum and Betty Bardon, the actress."

Just like me, Emma took a moment to process the dynamic. She said, "You have a two-seater."

"I'll create a diversion while they get away."

"It's not that easy."

"Make it that easy."

"Poland backed out of the deal." Her voice softened. "You can't go there."

I ran options through my head. When we sketched out the mission, we'd ruled out Ukraine because it was too far for the ultralight. Forty miles, if I recalled correctly. Not enough battery for the payload.

Emma's voice went a notch softer. "Ms. Sabel left specific instructions: you are coming home alive no matter what. You are to leave the hostages and take the ultralight. It has enough range to carry two hundred pounds to the border. Ukraine is onboard."

"Not happening."

"We checked the options; the team has discussed it. The operation is scrubbed. It's exfil and regroup."

"Find another way," I said. "I'm not leaving them behind."

I hung up and made my way back down the ladder.

From the silence that greeted me, they'd heard the conversation.

"There's an echo," Rafael said and pointed up. "It works like a megaphone."

"Thanks," Betty said. "But she's right. We can stay down here. Why the hell not? Call my agent. I'm his meal ticket. He'll find a way to get me out. It's about time he did something for his fifteen percent."

I didn't answer.

Betty shivered as she squeezed river water out of her one-armed sweatshirt. She said, "No one in Hollywood would leave a sex object in a foreign country. That's all I am to them. Objectified to the point of being no more important than an orange. But an orange who can make them rich if I show enough boob."

Rafael and I stayed quiet.

"Fuck. Who am I kidding?" She got up and tried to pace in the tight confines of the storm drain. She plopped down across the culvert from us. "My sexy-bitch days are numbered, I can't land a serious role, and I'm too young to play someone's mom."

She huffed and sat quietly.

We still didn't know what to say.

"Most of my life," she said, "I've been on my own. People started taking advantage of me when I was fourteen. Making me do this or that. Humiliating, horrible things." She shuddered. Her voice cracked. "It gets lonely fending for yourself all the time. You know? You fake a smile and pretend it's all good. But you're alone. Isolated in a cold, mean world. What I'm trying to say is … I'm not used to saying thank-you. And … well, what you did there, telling them you're not leaving us behind, that was a first for me. No one's ever stood up—" She choked and took a moment to collect herself. "So. It's a hard thing for me to say. But. Thank you."

My first thought was to say, forget it, or it was nothing, but that wasn't what she wanted to hear. I thought for a moment, then said, "You're worth it."

After a while, she got up and squeezed her shivering shoulders between us again. "Like I said, being on your own your whole life is a lonely way to live. You know what that's like, don't you, Jacob?"

"What do you mean?" I asked.

"Being treated like baggage." She snorted. "I read how Pia Sabel dumped you a few months ago. Boy toy no more. Left you in Greece or Albania or someplace."

"Thought you never heard of me."

CHAPTER 14

FROM THE SOUNDS FILTERING DOWN from the street, the Belarusians were going house to house. They even came up the storm drain from the river, missing us with their flashlights by inches. At some point toward afternoon, we marched up the hill toward the center of town with our throats parched and our stomachs growling.

During the long day and evening of pacing, we had time to talk. Betty did most of it. She told us the inside story on Hollywood. Turns out it's one big cult of eating disorders based on ever shifting pseudo-science made up by high school dropouts twisting the odd concept gleaned from a random doctor. She explained all the groveling one has to do for work. Her first role was third bikini on the beach. Not a speaking role. She went back to college for a master's in science but acting money called her back. From there, things went well but never Oscar-well. Lately the calls had stopped coming in.

While she talked, I went over things in my head. The Knights weren't the ones who dug the tunnel to the Ops Center, so who had the resources to mount an operation of that scale? The government came to mind, but they had great relationships with Sabel Industries and Ms. Sabel was a big supporter of President Williams. Then there was the matter of the blood under Betty's fingernails. Since none of the guys I saw were visibly clawed, whose blood was it?

Somewhere near 2200 hours, Betty realized Rafael and I hadn't said a word since we skipped lunch. Her voice turned to me, "What's your story? Why didn't you follow your company orders?"

I let a long silence stretch between us.

"He has demons," Rafael explained.

I shot him a nasty look he couldn't see in the absolute black of the tunnel.

He continued, "He seeks redemption."

The old man was an experienced soldier; he knew my soul without knowing much about me. I both appreciated and resented it. But he had clarified what drove me better than my used god: deliverance from the ghosts of my past. For a moment, I could see Jenny reading on the sofa with her legs lying across mine. I could see Jenny making a face when the gorilla at the zoo pooped in his hand and ate it. I felt Jenny holding my face in her hands as she told me I was the best cook she'd ever eaten—then laughing at her unintended double entendre. I could see Jenny running through a cave with a bomb, hoping to throw it over a cliff before it went off. I turned her medallion over and over between my fingers.

"Well," Betty sounded moderately pacified, "if you get us out of here, I'm not going to sleep with you. Just so we're clear."

"Good." My answer came too quickly because she sniffed her disappointment.

As planned, we waited until dark, and then waited until darker. When the noises at street level died down enough for us to emerge through a manhole, I climbed the ladder and pressed my back against two hundred pounds of steel. I waited and listened and felt. No nearby voices, no tremors from heavy vehicles.

Risky as it was, I pushed up. My wounded arm sent shockwaves of pain through my body. Keeping it under control, I gently moved it high enough to clear the lip on one side. Rafael jammed up next to me and pushed. Together, we moved it halfway to the side. I peeked out.

Business district. Dark. Quiet. The street was empty for a couple blocks either way. I crawled out and pulled Rafael, then Betty. Together we pushed the cover back in place with a street-echoing clank. We had the 9 mil I'd taken off Slick. The rifle would make us stand out in a crowd, so we left it behind.

Surveying the area, I spotted a KFC occupying the corner of a high-rise office building two blocks north.

In the opposite direction, an armored vehicle idled, its headlights lighting up the street away from us. Next to it, silhouettes of soldiers milled about aimlessly. I'd been on maneuvers like that. They were waiting for orders so the search could resume. The brass was trying to figure out if they should sweep the city again or expand the search beyond. Since it was a city search, not a national thing, going wide would create jurisdictional problems and require lots of creative explaining. Regardless of their final decision, they were putting a lot more effort into this than I expected.

At least it would give us enough time to grab fried chicken and steal a car.

The KFC staff looked disappointed to see us. They were in the midst of cleaning up for closing time. I waved a hundred euro note under their noses. Suddenly, they were glad we stopped by. When Betty translated for me, they eagerly turned the fryer back on and loaded it up. But that gave us a good fifteen minutes to wait for our order to go. I looked over their uniforms and asked if they kept extras in the back. They had a woman's outfit that would fit Betty and a top for Rafael. Nothing in my size. It cost me another €100.

Betty went to the bathroom to change. Rafael put his on where we stood. Any camouflage was better than none.

That's when Mercury appeared. *Hey homie, must've been hard getting turned down by a hot actress before you had to beg her for sex.*

I said, *I'm not interested.*

Mercury said, *Whacha mean? You gotta thing for actresses. Remember that auburn-haired beauty, what was her name?*

I said, *Sylvia.*

Right. That's the one. Whatever happened to her, anyway?

I said, *Still serving time for art fraud.*

Mercury grinned and spread his arms wide. *That's what I love about you, bro, such fine taste in women. For the record, my sweet Larunda ain't never been convicted of art fraud. Hey, here's a tip for you: this one is not an international art thief. Here's another tip: if a woman—outta the blue—says she don't wanna sleep with you, what she really means ...*

I said, *It doesn't matter what she means.*

Mercury started to dissolve slowly. *One place the two of you agree on is not wanting the Knights to find you. So keep frosty, cuz you're gonna get real close now.*

"Rafael," I said. "Go to the men's room."

We exchanged glances. With a look, I told him it was serious. He didn't question me, just marched straight in. His Mayan ancestry stood out in an all-white country.

I moved to the rack of utensils and condiments. It's amazing how fast-food places all look the same from Bakersfield to Brest. A car pulled up outside and two men got out. As I pulled sporks, napkins, and various other options, two familiar voices came in. They were jovial, teasing each other. They moved to the counter behind me and ordered in Belarusian.

Pulling the Glock from under my jacket, I stepped behind Anton and raised the muzzle to his skull. At that moment, Betty Bardon came around the wall separating the bathrooms from the dining area. Anton and Ivan turned to see her. Then three things happened in rapid succession. First, Betty squeaked in surprise. Second, both young men recognized her. Third, Ivan noticed me and my pistol.

I couldn't threaten both at once, so I gambled that Ivan valued Anton's life because he was the brains of the pair. My gamble paid off. Ivan raised his hands in surrender.

"Put your hands down," I ordered. With two picture windows facing the street, the last thing I needed was an obvious stickup. "Betty, grab their wallets, keys, phones, anything in their pockets."

Betty fumbled everything into a pile on the counter. One pistol, two wallets, two phones, one hunting knife, two switchblades, and forty-eight Belarusian rubles. I had Betty tell the chefs to add all the trimmings and any extra chicken lying around—our order to go had just doubled.

A squad of Brest Police marched by the windows. They wore full riot gear and carried automatic rifles. Times like these separated winners and losers in the game of life. Betty broke out in a sweat and trembled.

I said, "You're an actress and you're in a KFC uniform. Play the overworked fry cook ready to go home."

She trudged to the door as if she'd worked twelve hours straight and put the closed sign out just as the cops reached for the handle. In light but tired banter, she explained they were sold out and closed.

Anton, Ivan, and I never took our eyes off each other. For all their youth and inexperience, they were cornered untamed animals and therefore unpredictable and dangerous. I pressed the 9 mil into Anton's abdomen, the barrel inside his ribcage, aimed up at his heart. Young enough to make brave decisions yet old enough to know they'd be the first to die in a shootout, their nervous energy poisoned the air between us.

CHAPTER 15

IN PLEADING, TEASING VOICES, THE cops begged Betty for dinner. Betty politely refused. The men claimed sour grapes with laughs and a dismissive waving of arms. They left.

The real employees set two large bags on the counter. After a nod, a pimply young man scooped the goods from my mobster-friends' pockets and dumped them in a third bag. Betty retrieved Rafael.

The old man was shocked to see Anton and Ivan. He bristled with rage and whispered to me. "We should kill them."

His vehemence was understandable, but his tactics were terrible. I put a calming hand on his shoulder.

"Dude, gunshots? Dead bodies lying around?" I stared at him until he understood the futility of his idea.

"We don't need them," he hissed. "We can swim the river."

"They had personnel carriers and helicopters. Do you think they forgot to put boats on the river?"

Realizing I was right, he nodded. A minute later we were on the road.

Ivan drove, I rode shotgun, and Rafael kept Anton from making any sudden moves by holding the young man's revolver to his ribs. Betty sat behind me. We traveled on farm roads and back roads and through private property until we were out of the area the Brest Police had cordoned off. Then we hit the M10, what passes for a highway in Belarus.

We headed toward Pinsk, not to be confused with Minsk, 150 miles north. The road headed in the opposite direction from Poland and ran parallel to the Ukrainian border, offset by forty miles. It was the only direction where there weren't battalions of Belarusians looking for us.

Along the way, I texted back and forth with Emma. As my main contact for operations, she decided to stay with me until I got home safely. Which was nice of her. She kept me updated on several new developments. Others on her team tracked police and military radio traffic to see if we'd been spotted. So far, the officials in Brest appeared to have given up. I doubted the mobsters or the Knights were as easily thrown off the scent.

As the ride wore on into the dark, Betty put on a show. That's what actresses do. It took a few miles, and a lot of banter, but she wore the boys down. Eventually, she had them singing a Belarusian pop song. They accepted their fate and the mood improved as we drove into the night.

Then the fun died down and quiet set in.

"Ever wonder why a science geek would go into acting?" Betty asked anyone listening.

I almost said no but decided it wouldn't stop her.

"I've always had this driving desire to be the center of attention," she said. "I never knew my father. I never felt that patriarchal love flowing to me and that created a need. A need to be adored by masses. It's a real kick when you get it."

I saw no reason to respond. Neither did the other guys.

"You have that need too, don't you, Jacob?" she asked.

"No."

"It's a different kind of stage for you, but it's the same thing. Come on, admit it. Public attention is a real high, am I right?"

"No."

She persisted. "When you save lives you become everybody's hero. You get your picture in the paper. They give you medals. For you, it's like winning an Oscar. Like when that French president gave you that medal last spring and then a few weeks ago when that German lady, Angela—"

"I didn't do it for the attention." I snapped a little louder than necessary. I softened. "I did what anyone would've done."

I couldn't see her sitting directly behind me, but I sensed her slump in her seat. A quick glance at my companions found some surprised faces.

My value rose in Anton's estimation. In their language, he translated my exploits to his compatriot. Ivan looked me over from the driver's seat.

We were quiet for a few miles. A car had been following us at a distance ever since we left Kobryn. At 0400 in farm country, it was reasonable that someone might be going the same direction. But Stearne's Law didn't allow me to let it go unnoticed. I checked their phones to make sure they were off. They were.

Would Ivan's car have a tracking device? Young stallions in a mob with bosses more paranoid than me? Conceivable. I kicked myself for not thinking of it earlier.

I pulled my phone and punched the company app for checking such things. Sure enough: there was a tracker in the back.

After rounding a broad curve, Ivan followed my instructions to turn off the headlights, downshift to slow the car, and coast into a gas station just off the M10. With no brake-light flare to alert our pursuers, it would take them a few miles to realize my ruse.

Rolling into the mini mart in blackout mode, I watched the only car on the main road pass by at full speed. I let Anton pump gas while Rafael kept a pistol trained on him. I dug around in the trunk until I found an old Soviet tracking unit the size of a pack of cigarettes.

I fit it neatly between the windshield wipers of a delivery truck idling in front of the store. From the look of mud hanging from its undercarriage, the truck's next delivery was down a random farm road.

Everyone dropped back into their assigned seats. Ivan took off fast.

It was a long drive. An hour later, we crossed into Ukraine on the smallest road I could find on the map. Arriving long before the border station opened, we followed a well-worn path of tire tracks skirting the building through the mud. That put us only four hours outside of Kyiv.

It was late morning when we climbed out and stretched in front of the Hyatt Regency Kyiv. I thanked the boys for the ride. Betty gave them hugs. While the movie star occupied their attention, I fished their phones out of the bag, turned them on, and slipped them under the seats. Then they drove away.

"They'll get around the corner, call their bosses, and turn us in," Rafael said.

"I'm counting on it." I hailed a cab. "They're criminals and that's what criminals do. Which is why I made reservations at the Fairmont Kyiv across town."

The cabbie took us around St. Michael's Golden-Domed Monastery so we could marvel at the onion tops that looked freshly polished. According to our driver, the place was built in the 12th century. Parts of it were demolished by the Soviets during their war on religion.

We checked in at the Fairmont. Emma had cleared the way for our lack of identification. The Presidential Suite awaited us.

When our butler opened the door, a doctor, Miguel, Isaiah, and a local Sabel Agent named Nadia greeted us.

Nadia had new clothes for us. The doctor had bandages and antibiotics for me. Nadia escorted Betty to her room while Isaiah marched Rafael to his. Between them, Rafael understood the drill, but Betty had no clue about why she needed her own Sabel Agent.

When the door closed, Miguel nodded towards Betty's room and said, "She looks a lot like Jenny."

"Don't go there."

Miguel and I caught up on each other's escapades while I showered and changed. He liked my choice of Isaiah for the mission. The man never spoke while under Brest Police scrutiny and never complained afterward.

Miguel finished his report on his ordeal with a question. "Why did you put so much faith in a new guy?"

"Got out of the Marines three months ago, rose to shift supervisor, and was looking for something bigger."

"But his team had a mole. Someone alerted the tunnel monkeys we were on to them. How do you know it wasn't him?"

"I don't."

It was clear he wanted to ask if Mercury had approved of Isaiah, but he didn't. While he and Ms. Sabel were my trusted confidants regarding my divine connection, he knew I didn't like to talk about it.

Rafael came back, dressed smartly in black slacks and a blazer. He took a chair in the living room and waited for his fate. In the unspoken dialect of operatives, Isaiah gave me a nod that let me know Rafael had asked no questions, requested nothing, and behaved as a suspect should.

Nadia dragged Betty in by her bicep. Despite being dressed in bright and attractive pantsuit, she had fire in her eyes. "What kind of rescue is this? I mean, don't get me wrong here, I appreciate the Dolce & Gabbana outfit, and I appreciate you taking a bullet for me, and ... all the other stuff you did. But why can't I make a call?"

I said, "Tell her, Rafael."

The professor cleared his throat. "You have given him reason to doubt the sincerity of your captivity."

"What the fuck does that mean?" Her voice rattled the fine china tea set on the coffee table.

Met with silence, she dropped into a chair across from him.

"He will explain in his time," Rafael said.

I put my phone on speaker and waited for the other end to pick up. When a curious voice answered, I said, "Slick, good to hear your friends in the Brest Police let you live. Jacob Stearne here. We need to meet."

Betty's eyes went wide, her mouth dropped open. Rafael gestured with a finger to his lips to keep her quiet.

His voice came through with a little static. "The name's Seamus. Why would I meet with you?"

"Consider it professional courtesy," I said. "I have something you want. You didn't say 'please' when we last met. In fact, you were quite rude. Since your boss will likely have you drawn and quartered if you come home empty-handed, I propose we sit down like gentlemen and discuss an exchange."

His answer sounded like it slithered out of a snake's throat. "Where are you?"

"Hyatt Regency Kyiv. Announce yourself and they'll show you to my rooms. Tonight at seven."

I clicked off.

Betty nearly hyperventilated with shock. When she calmed herself, she said, "What the hell are you doing? We barely got away from that guy alive. You want to meet him?"

I tracked between the furniture to stand in front of her.

"I've never been raped," I said. "But I've helped victims in recovery.

I've seen some victims consumed by fear and others by rage. Everyone reacts differently. There's one thing I've never seen—a woman who gets in a car and sings songs with men who were her tormentors."

CHAPTER 16

JOE GRIFFITH SURVEYED THE VIENNESE skyline from the rooftop penthouse's sun deck. Preparations were going fine except for the overdue phone call that would seal his triumphant mood for the board meeting. He checked his watch and cursed. Then he relaxed. It was too nice a day for worrying. Feeling the perfect breeze caress his face, he pointed to a greenish-blue dome across the skyline. He called out, "Konrad, is that the opera house?"

"This is the Karlskirche, Herr Griffith. Eighteenth century Catholic church." Konrad jogged over to him and pointed to another building in the near distance. "Staatsoper is just there."

"Catholic?" Griffith took in Konrad's black jeans and disco-esque shirt. "I thought you were all Lutherans."

Konrad stiffened. "The Hapsburg dynasty was the last of the Holy Roman Empire. Ja, this is Austria's history."

Anything labeled "Hapsburg" was a part of history Griffith had always found murky, shifting, and unfathomable. He grunted. "Of course. I was thinking of Germany for a moment."

"The ladies arrive now, Herr Griffith." Konrad waved at the roof deck. "Would you like to inspect them here or inside?"

Griffith squinted into the clear blue sky and smiled. "Out here would be splendid. They're all government registered and have had recent medical checkups?"

"Of course, mein herr. And all results are in. Those who do not pass are not here."

Griffith dismissed the man with a nod. He looked up the opera house on his phone and noted what was playing. Given his cultured guest list for the evening, he would do well to have some idea of the obscure and, in his opinion, ridiculous art form. It turned out to be an unpronounceable title by Monteverde. He did catch one word: *Poppaea*. If he recalled correctly, she was the scheming mistress of Emperor Nero who convinced him not only to divorce his wife, but also to have the ex-wife executed. Not satisfied with mere execution, Poppaea had her rival decapitated and the head delivered to her. Griffith admired such determined individuals.

Konrad let out a short whistle while leading a parade of women clad in string bikinis along an opposite wall. He lined them up in the sun and stood by, beaming with pride.

Griffith counted them, eighteen in all. They were between five feet and five-six, none too tall. That was good. A shortage of blondes, but that was acceptable. At least there weren't any green or blue dye jobs. Three had that slight-Asian look often found in the countries ending in *stan*: Kazakhstan, Kyrgyzstan, Uzbekistan, and so on. "Konrad, I told you no slant-eyes."

"They are just in from Moldova, I swear."

"Well, either they traveled there from China, or their parents did. You have reserves to replace these?"

"Only with tattoos, Herr Griffith."

"That won't do." He hated being forced to choose between two evils: tattoos and Asians. "Even so, you've only eighteen. I have twelve board members. What do you expect them to do, share? We need twenty-four."

Konrad looked exasperated. He chewed his lip, looking for an answer.

Griffith's phone rang. The awaited call from Seamus McLeod. He turned his back on Konrad and answered. "Success, Seamus? We've chilled champagne just waiting for your report."

"Aye," Seamus hesitated and blew out a breath. "About that. The gang we were forced to use failed to properly pat him down. Soon as he arrived, he pulled a knife, took the top man's pistol and gut-shot him. Since the Chief Constable of Brest wouldn't let my men near, I had to subdue him alone. Unfortunately, that Belarusian stood between me and—"

"You son of a bitch!" Griffith hurled his phone over the balcony and watched it disappear into the street six stories below.

Seamus had underestimated Stearne despite being warned. And he'd let the Brest police chief make demands that undermined his mission. Not only did they not have the Chaac Equation, they had no Professor Tum for a bargaining chip, and no Jacob Stearne. He steamed until he caught his breath.

Still looking over the city, he held out his palm and said, "Konrad, your phone. Now."

He heard the man's footsteps on the wooden deck and felt the phone firmly slapped into his hand. Konrad's phone was shiny, clean, and newer than his. He noted this, then dialed Seamus.

"What steps are you taking to rectify your failure?" he asked.

"Stearne requested a meeting."

"You didn't agree to it, did you? It'll be on ground he controls. A trap."

"Nae, of course I wouldn't fall for that ruse."

"What is your plan then?"

"That'd be the reason for my call, sir. I'm asking for your wisdom on the matter since you know Stearne and that bitch who pays his bills."

Griffith chafed at the Scot's petulance. He said, "Now you listen closely. Before you go throwing around references to Jacob Stearne taking down the Knights of Mithras in his last engagement—before I was named Protector—I'll remind you it was not I in charge of that mission. It was your predecessor. He failed in spectacular fashion, and he paid the ultimate price. Be sure you don't do the same."

"Wasn't planning on it," Seamus said. "All that notwithstanding, you've a better handle on the man and his methods than I. It would benefit us both should you share a wee bit of your wisdom in the matter."

"You chose Jacob Stearne for the ransom drop and I made plans for him based on your confidence. The Board of Directors holds their monthly meeting here this evening at seven. They are expecting a progress report on the Chaac Equation. What do I tell them? That you have failed? I must have this before Belgrade!"

Griffith seethed with anger while Seamus stammered. Losing his patience, he said, "Don't force me to solve this problem myself, find him. Bring him to me. I know how to make him do what I want. I need only a few moments with him—in person."

Griffith clicked off. He tapped the phone in his hand while sensing Konrad waiting nervously behind him. He had one more call to make. He dialed northern Finland. His contact answered on the first ring. "Joona, is your team ready?"

"Yes, sir."

"The Highlander Garrison has disappointed me once. He gets one more chance."

"We are ready, sir."

Joona Forss needed few words. Griffith liked that. They were ready and waiting. Griffith liked that even more. And by saying nothing about his Highlander peers, Joona spoke volumes. Griffith considered making the change sooner rather than later. Unfortunately, Finland was too far away from Ukraine for an immediate response. He'd have to give Seamus one more chance. He clicked off.

He turned his attention to Konrad. "You will need a new phone."

Konrad's jaw dropped.

Griffith pointed at the women who blew him kisses as his attention passed over them. "This is all you have who fit the description?" When Konrad nodded, he continued, "Then subcontract with a reputable brothel. Clean girls. Nothing that can be traced by a suspicious wife."

CHAPTER 17

SINCE BETTY WASN'T YET IN a mood to explain herself, I had Nadia take her back to her room and give her the silent treatment. On her way out, Betty looked to be having second thoughts about holding out on me. In my estimation, Betty was the kind of person who would rather have her feet sliced with razors than go half an hour without talking to another human being. Her willingness to tell me the truth would multiply in that much time, so I sent her off to stew.

Rafael, on the other hand, would shrug off either punishment. He remained in his seat. I perched on the arm of a chair opposite him. A bowl of fruit topped with a huge bunch of purple grapes sat on the coffee table between us. Miguel and Isaiah left to make preparations for the evening. All was ready for the call to my new bestie, Secretary of State Neville Townsend.

Just to be a jerk, I chose video mode. There are few joys in life that compare to waking the Secretary of State before dawn on a video call.

Townsend blinked into the camera and ran a hand over the plume of hair sticking up like gray straw. He made Bernie Sanders look well-coifed. Still staring at the screen, he ran the same hand over his swollen eyes and took a deep and weary breath. Pulling back silky sheets and velvet covers, he rose and looked over his shoulder then looked back at me. He moved to a different room, one that betrayed hints of a home office. He plopped into a chair and said, "Jacob, why are you calling at this hour?"

"I'm making good on my promise," I said. "Thought you'd like to say hello to your Brother Keeper, Rafael Tum."

I flipped the camera mode so he could see my hostage. Rafael raised a hand half an inch. Neville nodded with less movement. I figured Keepers aren't big on using their words. But then, they both knew this was a situation where the less said, the better.

Flipping the camera back to me, I said, "When we last spoke, you told me, and I quote, 'We need Rafael Tum back here at once.' To facilitate that, I have Sabel Two arriving tomorrow morning. It's a ten-hour flight, so he's almost there. All you have to do is answer that question I asked you."

Neville squinted one eye and chewed on my statement for a moment before the light went on in his eyes. "Ah yes, you mean your incomparably eloquent question: *what the fuck*?"

I waited.

"Yes, well." He blinked and rubbed sleep out of his eye. "This all revolves around some project the Russians abandoned. Griffith got hold of it and seems to think the Chaac Equation will solve his problems. He believes we have it. That's all I know, Jacob."

"Rafael is fit like no other man his age," I said. "You know, yesterday, we ran several miles and he never complained, never got winded, never slowed up. Still, if you don't answer, he's going to be pissed about walking five thousand miles back home."

Rafael's interest in the conversation was no greater than if he were watching paint dry.

Neville bit the inside of his cheek and worked his jaw. "There are no more details to share, Jacob. We're a compartmentalized organization and I've told you everything I know."

"Hardly."

I couldn't let this end with the simple return of Rafael Tum to a warm, safe bed and call it a good deed done. I needed a mission that would get me a chance for revenge against the most dangerous man in the world—Joe Griffith—and it was slipping through my fingers.

"What do you think I know that I'm not sharing?" Neville asked.

"Nice dodge, but you forget the obvious evidence in front of us. Why would you care what happens to Brother Rafael if Griffith's after a project even the Russians couldn't get up and running?"

"It might surprise you to learn, young man, that we in the Keepers value the lives of our brothers. I'm genuinely concerned about Rafael's wellbeing and—"

"Bullshit. Using only eight words, I once convinced a Knight of Mithras to take his cyanide capsule. If your archenemies are that dedicated to the cause, the Keepers could be no less committed. You would leave him to die if the stakes were high. Yet you wanted him back. You think he learned something during his short stay at the Hotel Mithras."

Neville pursed his lips and frowned.

Rafael spoke up. "Tell him, Neville."

"I can't," Neville shot back with heat. "He's not a Keeper."

Rafael raised his head to me. "Jacob, do you want to be a Keeper?"

"Sure, why not?"

"Oh, for Christ's sake, Rafael." Neville's face blistered red. "You can't induct members like that. He didn't even ask what's involved."

"OK," I said. "Do you guys have a dental plan? If not, that's a deal-breaker right—"

"This is not a joke!" Neville came out of his chair. His Bernie-hair rose to accentuate his anger.

"We need him, Neville," Rafael said. "We got lazy and now we have a price to pay. Over the last two decades, we lulled ourselves into complacency. The youngest Keeper is over fifty while the Knights have recruited and trained relentlessly. They've kept track of us and yet we had no idea they put the Scottish Highlander Knights in charge. We need youth and vigor, a sharpness of mind. You've read his military record and I've seen him in action. We need Jacob. We can work through the formalities of induction later."

Neville thought about this for too long.

I said, "What he really means is, you guys need someone willing to die for your cause."

Mercury plopped down in a chair next to Rafael. *Didya miss me, homie?*

I said, *No.*

Ima let that slide, yo. Mercury plucked the grapes off the coffee table. *Yeah, so I was tied up at the Convention of the Underappreciated Gods.*

They wanted me for the keynote address. Y'know how it is. Famous and all that.

Or underappreciated, I said. *What do you want?*

Who, me? Mercury pointed at himself. Then he hoisted the bunch of grapes and stuffed too many in his mouth. One fell to the floor. *I want my temple to be the biggest in Rome, throwing shade all over that funny-looking little dome the Pope's got. Oh, you mean, what can I do for you? Well. This might be a good time to think about the Chaac Project that Griffith has and the Chaac Equation that Rafael has, and why not put them together? Why izzat such a big deal that all y'all mortals be leaving dead bodies all over the place?*

I thought about it for a minute. He was right, it was important. I said, *Neither of them is telling me anything, so asking that outright is a losing proposition. But taking Rafael up on his offer to induct me into his cabal is the way into this. If Rafael trusts me, I can steal the Chaac Equation, offer it to Griffith, and then kill him for his role in Jenny's death.*

Mercury smiled. *Now you're talking. By the way, I gotta remind you that back when you was playing tour guide in Brest's storm drains, ol' Rafael here told Betty you had demons and sought redemption.*

I said, *So?*

My gaze fell to Professor Tum, who watched me the way a raptor watches a lizard. Neville thought long and hard about my worthiness to join his merry band of whackos.

Whaddya mean, 'so'? Mercury said. *Dude, the man ain't seen you since Germany. How's he know your mood? How's he know your feels?*

My idle god had a point. Rafael had me dialed in. He knew I wanted to die for a glorious cause against an unbeatable foe. That's why he wanted me to join the Keepers. He didn't mind if I died for his cause. But how did he know that's where I was in life? I said, *He doesn't just feel my pain; he's been there in his life journey. Personal experience? He lost someone. Maybe more than once?*

Suddenly, I felt a connection to the old man.

Mercury touched his nose. *Finally, you get it. He's whatcha call complex and layered. Say, you mind if I take these grapes with me? They want me back at the convention for a wrap party and I'm starving.*

And with that, my god and my grapes were gone.

Rafael stared at me with concern creasing his brow. He was in the middle of saying something I'd missed. I rewound the video in my head and caught up with his conversation. He had said, "He is correct, Neville. We need someone willing to join us in our cause, make it his cause; live it and breathe it. Thus it follows that he would need to know what we know. We should hold nothing back."

Neville's lips moved but his tongue refused to form words. Then he stopped thinking about *managing the narrative* and took a deep breath. "On your recommendation, I concur we should make him a temporary Keeper until such time allows for the formal process can be completed."

"Agreed," Rafael said.

Neville said, "Here's where we are, Jacob. I'm serious when I say we don't know a good deal about the Chaac Project. There are indicators that it would shift the balance of power in the world. For the last two generations, the Keepers and the Knights achieved a standoff, a working understanding. Not unlike the US and Russia with little skirmishes here and there, but no outright wars.

"Something changed earlier this year. The Knights began fighting to the death. Their bold move at the G20 conference shocked us. They've not done anything like that since they started the First World War. After you tripped them up, they changed leadership. Joe Griffith runs things now and he has big plans. As I said, he acquired the mothballed Chaac Project and came after us. We don't know what he wants or why."

"He wants the Chaac Equation." I raised a finger in the camera window to stop him.

"Yes." Rafael's interruption was authoritative. "Somehow it helps complete his Chaac Project. In his upcoming investor meetings, he must prove it works. Financing R & D is high-risk for investors. They'll need tangible evidence that he has more than smoke and mirrors. We need to know what he has."

My gaze bounced between Rafael and Neville a couple times before I got it. "You want me to figure out what his project is and why he needs the Equation to complete it. You want me to get close to him."

Rafael nodded. Neville said nothing.

While it was more than they told me last time, it was far less than everything.

My brain formed the decision in my head. I could say forget it and move on, or I could take a long shot at killing Joe Griffith. The downside to taking on the Knights was the likelihood of dying before getting close to hurting any of them. Had it not been for the Brest Police, the Knights would've killed Rafael and me on the rooftop.

Before I made up my mind, I found myself rising to my feet and heard myself say, "I'm your man."

They began to thank me, in their typical understated way.

Something squished under my shoe while they talked. When I lifted my boot, I found a crushed grape. The bunch on the bowl of fruit was gone. Or did I imagine it to begin with?

"Before you get too happy," I said, "there are things we're going to need."

"Fire away," Neville said. "I'll get you anything."

"For starters, you'll need to have Shikowitz call Ms. Sabel again. She thinks I'm going to run off and get myself killed, so he'll need to move her past that problem. Then, just so we understand each other here, and there are no misunderstandings: I get to kill Griffith in the end, right?"

Neville looked shocked.

Rafael said, "Naturally. But only after we know about the project and the goal. The Knights could easily replace him, and we don't want to hit replay on this drama."

Neville clicked off the video feed while his partner was in midsentence. Understandable. As a government official, he couldn't sanction a hit on a US citizen, so he chose not to hear the words.

"One last question for you, professor," I said. "You're the only living person I've met who managed to beat death more often than I. How is it Seamus McLeod got the better of you?"

CHAPTER 18

NADIA DIDN'T DRAG BETTY IN this time. The actress charged in with fire in her eyes. I held up a hand to stop her in her tracks, then pointed at a chair as I took a call from Emma, head of my operations team. Betty gave me the stink-eye while she ignored the chairs and paced the living room. Nadia stood at ease by the door.

Emma said, "We just uncovered news, sir. Betty Bardon's last two movies were financed by Joe Griffith. She stayed at his place in Chicago last winter."

My brows rose. I turned away from Betty's scowl. "Were those major investments?"

"Critics panned them both as sexploitation films, but they still cost several million each. The last one was a total bomb, and the one before might have broken even. We can't be sure of the numbers. Our financial team says the movie industry uses accounting techniques that are considered felony fraud anywhere else."

"Good work."

"Next topic," she said. "The internal investigators want to talk to Isaiah about the tunnel at the Ops Center."

"It can wait. He's with me and we're busy."

"OK. Also, Ms. Sabel approved you for an unlimited operation, sir." Emma's voice held a good deal of admiration, as if she hadn't known I was blessed by both gods and billionaires. "She also doubled my staff to support you."

"That's terrific news, Emma. You sound like you've been up as long as I have. On our end, we're going out to dinner, then we're going to drink too much, then we're going to sleep. We'll be flying out twelve hours from now, so you and your team can go home, feed the dog, get some rest. After that, sleep may be hard to get."

"Thank you, sir."

"Oh, and Emma, please drop the 'sir' part." I clicked off. If everyone was going to call me sir, I wasn't sure the VP thing would fit my style.

My gaze found Betty Bardon staring at me with the eyes of an underappreciated actress.

"I don't need her following me around," Betty said as she nosed over her shoulder at Nadia. "Thanks to you, I have no money, no ID, clothes, so I'm not going anywhere."

"It's not where you might go that concerns me. It's who you might call."

A blush of anger ran up her neck. "What's that supposed to mean?"

"You had dried blood under your fingernails. None of Slick's thugs had visible scratches. Either it was faked, or you clawed someone other than the five men I saw. Which is it?"

Her face reddened. Her mouth opened to protest my assumption. Then she slammed it shut after realizing her best option was silence. Finally, she said, "Stage blood."

I dropped an octave, slowed my cadence, and asked, "What does he have on you?"

Betty faced me, curious. "Who?"

"Slick, the Scot who tied you up in Brest. Great acting, by the way. I believed it right up until you got in the car with Anton and Ivan. So, how did Slick get you to play the part?"

She took a moment to think. After viewing the room and furniture, her deflated gaze came back to me. "Not Seamus. It was Griffith. He threatened my *babulia*, my grandmother."

"Is she safe now?"

"I don't know."

"Then she didn't sell you out?"

"No." Betty collapsed into the chair, her arms dangling from the sides, and stared at the fruit bowl.

"Tell me about you and Joe Griffith."

"There's no me and that bastard," she said with ice.

"He financed your last two films. The first one didn't make any money, yet he bankrolled a second. Why?"

"He didn't finance anything. He laundered a few million and skimmed the profits." She eyed me suspiciously. "What's your interest in him?"

"He has sins to atone for."

I watched her mull that over. She didn't have any questions about which or what kind of sins. Her pensive silence implied she knew of his crimes firsthand.

"Why did you stay at his place in Chicago?" I asked.

Betty's knees squeezed together while her arms crossed tightly over her chest. She stared hard at the piano. Eventually she said, "Obviously, you have ears and eyes everywhere. Do your spies tell you what kind of man he is?"

"He's the kind of man who fits his guest rooms with locks on the outside." When her gaze snapped to me, I explained, "I went there to free a kidnapped woman a couple months back."

She looked surprised and relaxed her grip on herself just a little. "People think Hollywood cleaned up its act," she began slowly and gathered steam. "Far from it. Weinsteins are a dime a dozen in Tinsel Town and Griffith's the worst of them all. He doesn't just threaten your career—he holds your family's lives in his hands. I didn't land the lead in back-to-back bombs because I wanted or auditioned for them." She shuddered, then raged, "He owns me."

"He forced you to act like a hostage. Why?"

"In case someone rescued the old man. They knew Rafael wouldn't leave the Damsel-in-Distress behind. I was supposed to slow them down. Make noise, stall, get word to them about where we went. I didn't do any of that because you showed up. You were the last person in the world I expected to see."

I asked, "How did you come to know so much about me?"

Her gaze rolled across the carpet a couple times before coming back to me. She rose and looked me in the eye. "There was a time when I had a fantasy. I thought I could hire a mercenary or seduce a hero who would rescue me from Griffith. I researched people and organizations. But it was hopeless. I couldn't afford the companies and the heroes were accidents of time and place. Not real men driven by real principles. Then one day I found a video of you getting a medal. I felt your spirit in my bones. You hurt the same way I hurt. You have that pain deep in your soul—knowing you're adrift in an emotionally desolate world. Not many people know what that feels like, do they?"

"I don't know what you're talking about."

"Yeah, you do," she said, nodding. "Like I told you, I've been manipulated, humiliated, victimized for the enrichment of others. They want me to forget what they made me do. They want me to move on. They didn't give me roles because it would do me any good. Just like they didn't give you medals because it did you any good. They do it because it profits them. That's how I get roles. That's how you get medals. They want you to smile and wave like nothing you did bothers you. The things I did bother me. And I see that same conflict in your face—the things you did bother you."

There was no denying it. I was barely eighteen, lost in the rubble of Nasiriyah, separated from my unit, under fire—and running for my life. A horde of enemy soldiers chased me into a bombed-out amphitheater where a platoon of Marines had been pinned down by a company of hostiles, outnumbered five-to-one, and running out of ammo. That's when Mercury first appeared to me. He convinced me to take over a .50 BMG and guided my aim until I'd taken out twenty-nine armed combatants. The rest fled. The Marines hailed me like a hero. They paraded me around on their shoulders. But what stayed with me was the dead. Sons, brothers, fathers, all with their heads shattered, their blood and brains spilled by my hand. There's nothing heroic about killing people. And she was right. They gave me medals, a full page in *Stars and Stripes*, interviews on *AFN*.

Not for my benefit. For theirs.

"I learned to hide it," she said. "I practiced in the mirror. Faking my smiles, faking my speeches, 'What an honor it is…' and 'I want to thank…' all that stuff. I tried to forget the bad parts. Then I watched the President of France hang that ribbon around your neck. You had that smile. The same one I'd practiced in the mirror. Fake. You were covering up the dead."

She had me there. When I close my eyes, all I ever see are the faces of the dead. And for the last six weeks, all I see is Jenny, running with the bomb, trying to save my life.

I looked out the window and took a long, slow breath. She might have my problems nailed, but they were my problems, not hers. Right now, she was my problem.

"Thanks for the psychoanalysis," I said. "My focus is sending the people I rescue back home so they can practice whatever they want in front of their mirrors. So, tell me the truth: have you reported back to them about where we went?"

With pained, sad eyes, she shook her head. "Didn't you hear what I said?"

"That is exactly what you said. How do I trust you?"

"Because I need your help." She put on her best defiant face. "I'm going to kill Griffith."

"No, you're not." I handed her purse to her and turned her toward the door. "I am."

CHAPTER 19

ACROSS TOWN, MIGUEL RODRIGUEZ ADJUSTED his tie in the full-length mirror in the Presidential Suite at the Hyatt Kyiv and gave his blue business suit a tug. Had he gained weight since the last time the company took his dimensions? Must be the extra iron he started pumping a few months back. One more check and he decided to take out his ponytail. His shiny black locks spread across his shoulders. A look both disarming and threatening at the same time. Perfect.

Isaiah watched him from the doorway. "Never figured you for the kind to spend big on expensive suits."

Miguel smiled and opened the jacket to reveal the designer label. It read: Sabel Fashions. "There's one waiting for you back at the Fairmont. They keep our sizes on file."

"Do we wear suits that often?"

"In case they need a body bag."

Isaiah laughed nervously. "Mind if I ask you a question? You and Jacob have worked—"

"You're going to pussyfoot around the question everyone asks, so let me spare you the time: 'Am I his sidekick?' Yes and no. My first deployment went south day one. Ugly firefight. A hundred hostiles swarmed over the ridge. Some guy walks through the crossfire like he had an invisibility cloak. He saves my platoon with no more effort than turning off a light switch. From then on, when violence is about to break out, I become his shadow. Hand him fresh magazines, guard his flank, scare the shit out of some guy with my size, whatever needs to be done." Miguel held up his arms. "I know what you're thinking—standing in a white man's shadow means all the blame for his shit falls on us, the people of color. But no, the cops always talk to him—and they take his word for it. So far, I'm alive and kicking when I could've died or been jailed a thousand times. The gods love him. I figure, if you can make a bigger difference in the world by helping someone else than you can on your own, that's what you do."

"Then what's the 'no' part?"

"When the shooting stops. I'm my own man. We're friends. We're equals. All leveled up. Jacob thinks of me as the big brother he wished he had."

"He must trust you a lot to handle this meeting."

Miguel frowned. "You need to be in the lobby."

"Yessir."

"Save the 'sir' for Jacob. It annoys him."

Isaiah smiled and headed to the door. Miguel watched him go and realized why Jacob pulled the man for this mission. No one in Griffith's camp had ever heard of Isaiah Reddick. If they asked any spies, he was an unknown quantity.

It took nearly an hour, but Isaiah reported in on the comm link. "Worked exactly like you said. The cops have detained all but Seamus McLeod and two others. Question for you: why let Seamus bring two guys?"

"He'd scrub the mission rather than go alone. It would be too obvious."

"Right. You're pretty smart. For Army." He clicked off.

Miguel pulled up his phone and watched the video feed from the camera he'd put in the hall. Before long, the elevator doors opened, two Knights exited with guns drawn. After they cleared the first two corners, Seamus stepped out and followed. Their confidence rose with an empty corridor in front of them. They marched in a triangle to the suite.

Miguel stepped into the bedroom, switching his phone to the camera in the living area. The advance men entered first. One went left, the other came straight to him. Too easy. On bare feet, he moved silently behind the wall near the bedroom door. As the Knight stepped cautiously into the room, Miguel's arm flew out and stabbed the man in the neck with a handheld Sabel Dart. He caught the Knight before the body hit the floor and laid him down gently.

His next victim was a level more complicated. The man finished his sweep in the other bedroom directly opposite and turned to see Miguel crossing the space. The Knight had time to swing his pistol up and grunt the first syllable of a warning before the Sabel Dart hit his arm. Miguel did a quick check of the camera outside the door. Slick waited, looking impatient. He hadn't heard the warning. Perfect.

Miguel opened the door with a big smile and waved Seamus McLeod inside.

Slick looked Miguel over, then glanced around inside the suite before taking two cautious steps. He looked up at the big man and asked, "Who the hell are you?"

"Ever watch westerns?"

"Aye."

"I'm the sneaky Indian." Miguel gave him a big, disarming grin. "Many of us prefer 'Native' or 'First Peoples.' But that's like calling you a European instead of Scottish. So, if you want to show you care, take the time to know a man's tribe. I'm Diné, known to colonial sympathizers as Navajo."

"Oh aye?" Slick nodded slowly, then walked into the living room and stood in the middle. From there, he saw a pair of feet in both directions. He minimized his reaction and tugged his leather jacket. "Where's Jacob?"

"They're not dead." Miguel pointed at the Knights. "I used a Sabel Dart. They inject a non-lethal dose of venom from the inland Taipan snake mixed with a heavy dose of sleeping medication. The venom creates instant flaccid paralysis that lasts about five minutes. By then the sleep medication has kicked in. They'll be fine in about four hours. Which won't be a problem if you answer my questions in the next five minutes."

Slick puffed out his chest and looked up at Miguel. "And what's going to happen in five minutes, eh?"

"The Kyiv police show up and arrest you for that kilo of cocaine in the fruit bowl."

The Scot leaned over the coffee table and rolled his eyes. "You rented the room."

"In your name," Miguel grinned. "Using a facsimile of your passport and credit card."

"I'll tell the chief of police it was yours."

"He knows." Miguel shrugged. "He gave it to me." When Slick looked surprised, Miguel continued, "See, my dad is an aerospace engineer who makes good coin. He raised us in El Segundo, California. Damn nice town. And he—"

"I don't want to hear your fucking life story—"

Miguel's huge hand grabbed Slick by his jacket, shirt, and undershirt and lifted him off his feet. "Don't be rude, Seamus. I'm telling you a story here. You're eating into your five minutes."

Slick's eyes widened and rolled left and right, trying to figure out how Miguel could lift him one-handed.

"As I was saying—every summer," Miguel said, "Dad sent me to visit my grandparents on the Rez. Oh, Rez is what you guys call the Navajo Nation. Anyway, I saw a lot of colonial-perpetrated alcoholism there. I promised myself I'd never drink, never do drugs." He set Slick down. "Every now and then, I find myself outside a bar or a brothel where some white guy drank too much firewater and someone's taking advantage of him. I help the dude out, cuz I'm nice like that. And most of them appreciate it. So this one time, I'm in Odessa and this drunk guy is getting jumped by some pimps. I wade in and save the guy's life. He's not the forgetful type." Miguel squinted at Slick. "Am I boring you? Cuz your eyes just rolled."

"No, no, no. Just trying to keep track of my remaining minutes."

"Four, more or less," Miguel said. "Yeah, so, anyway, turns out the dude is in charge of Kyiv's vice squad. You know what that is? You got those in Scotland? Oh, good. We're on the same page here. So, I'm in town and ask the dude if he can do me a solid and slam this Scottish prick in jail overnight."

The light went on in Slick's brain. His head rolled back. "You. You're the reason six of my men were detained outside the building."

"See? I told Jacob you weren't as stupid as you looked."

"Just overnight? Not, uh …"

"Depends on whether I believe your answers."

Without warning, Miguel bear-hugged the smaller man, then spun him around, held him tight with one arm, fished his finger into Slick's mouth, and extracted a false tooth containing a cyanide capsule. He let Slick go. The Scot gagged and coughed. Miguel held the capsule between them. He said, "I like you, Slick. You're not bad for a white man. Manageable. I'd hate to see you take the easy way out."

Slick squeezed his eyelids down tight for three seconds. Then he opened them and said, "What do you want?"

"Where can I find Joe Griffith?"

"Who wants to know—you or Jacob?"

"I'm asking the questions. You've got two and a half minutes left."

Slick cast a desirous glance at the cyanide capsule. "I refuse."

Isaiah's voice came through Miguel's earbud. "Miguel, your friends arrived. Whole SWAT team and everything."

"Here's the thing," Miguel said. "You knew this was a trap. You knew coming here was dangerous. Yet you did. Why? Because you're desperate. You had no other leads. I'm offering you a chance to turn the tables on Jacob Stearne. He's going to go wherever he thinks Griffith will be, and you can lay a trap for him. A chance to get even."

"Aye, you're cocky as they come, aren't ya? Think you'll outwit me somehow?"

"You know it's a trap, I know it's a trap, he'll know it's a trap—may the best man win."

Slick had to think about that. Miguel watched him. The Scot curled a finger over his lips and stared at the floor. He paced a small circle, keeping his face away from Miguel. Which concerned the big man. He wanted to see the Knight's face, read his cues, get a sense of how big a lie he was going to tell.

Isaiah reported in. "They're on your floor. Fifteen seconds."

Slick looked up with a prepared and unreadable face. "Griffith's due at the Casino des Grottes Royales in three days. Don't ask me more. I'm not in charge of his personal security to prevent just this sort of problem."

Someone knocked on the door.

Miguel wished he had five more minutes to grill the Knight. He shrugged. "You're out of time anyway."

He landed the Sabel Dart in Slick's shoulder and let him drop to the floor. Opening the door, he ushered the cops in and tracked out past them. He paused to slap the Kyiv vice squad captain's shoulder and said, "Thank you, I appreciate your help. Say, would it be too much to ask if you kept them for four days?"

"Hard, my friend. Three days is the law."

"Don't bend the rules." Miguel held up his hands with a grin as if planting a kilo of impounded cocaine wasn't a rule already bent. "That should be fine."

He walked away and dialed Jacob. His friend answered as he pressed the elevator button.

"Are you OK?" Jacob asked.

"The man came through for us, like I said he would. Full SWAT and all that. Slick decided to stay in Kyiv for three more days."

"What did he tell you?"

"Casino des Grottes Royales, three days from now."

"Where's that?"

"How would I know? You're the one plays around in tuxedos and shit. I'm just your sidekick—Ke-mo sah-bee."

"Oh, c'mon," Jacob said. "I thought it was funny. You know I didn't mean it in a derogatory way. You weren't offended. Were you?"

Miguel clicked off and smiled to himself. Always good to keep the white men on their toes.

CHAPTER 20

I CLICKED OFF MIGUEL'S CALL still wondering if he was offended. I need to be more respectful. The big guy and his friends in high places have bailed me out a hundred times over.

I went back to adjusting my tie in the full-length mirror in the Presidential Suite of the Fairmont Kyiv. It fit well, although I didn't see why Emma felt the need to put me in a tuxedo. I'd prefer something casual, like a sport coat and slacks. But when you're five thousand miles from home and someone has a tux tailored and delivered, you don't quibble.

I transferred my pocket stuff to my tux: wallet, phone, pistol, extra magazine, suppressor, and Jenny's medallion. I held it a moment while I remembered our last time in Ukraine. I'd just blown up an arms dealer's yacht on the Black Sea and Jenny saved me by showing up in a personal submarine at just the right time. Great times. But those days were over. A sigh escaped me.

Miguel came in wearing a sharp blue suit. Isaiah followed in a light gray. Rafael was the only other guy in a tux. I checked my phone. Ms. Sabel had yet to return my call, but I wasn't sure which continent she was on at the moment. With her schedule, she could be anywhere.

Nadia texted. The women were running late and would meet us in the dining room. I told the men. We groaned and eye-rolled in unison. Then we headed downstairs.

White linen, gilded decor, and flowers dazzled my eyes. My tuxedo was one of many in the room. Emma knew her stuff. The restaurant's silver place settings had more utensils than the state dinners Ms. Sabel drags me to at the White House.

It occurred to me that I'd never taken Jenny anywhere fancy enough for a tux. Partly because she had self-esteem issues stemming from her homicide conviction. I should've ignored her doubts and taken her anyway. A missed opportunity. I always thought we'd have years together. I never thought our time would end so suddenly. There's no time like the present to enjoy the one you love.

We finished off a platter of oysters on the half-shell and a round of vodka and chatted about our favorite topic: weapons.

A commotion at the entrance caught the attention of everyone in the room. Shimmering sequins that transitioned from silver at the shoulder to gold at the floor made Nadia glow like an apparition. The soldier she had been two hours earlier bore no resemblance to the next-Ukrainian-supermodel who floated toward us. Heads at other tables turned. The four of us rose to our feet and nearly fell to our knees.

Betty Bardon followed in a dress of liquid black velvet with the skirt slit to the hip. Beaded designs drew one's eye to her flash of leg. Her blonde hair swirled gracefully around her neck in a way that ensured her bare shoulder remained bare.

A Frenchman at a nearby table exhaled, *"Mon Dieu."*

Before I could find words, Betty smiled for the first time since I'd met her. She had dimples. And her eyes sparkled. She said, "Wow, you certainly fill out a tux in style. Is that your ass or did it come with the suit?"

Without my god of eloquence handy, I managed to say, "Uh …"

In her element, the world of pretend, Betty charmed with a mischievous flutter of eyelashes. And dimples. A real mirth flickered in her expression as if she were in on a big joke with the punchline about to come out. Stearne's Law crept into my head. Had she been freed from her burdens through confession? Did that mean she'd told me the truth? Or was this an actress doing a great job of obscuring her motives by distracting me?

Leading with her bare leg, she stood toe to toe with me. She ran her fingertips along my satin lapel and suppressed an impish grin. I tried to breathe. As she waited, she let her smile spread. The dimples deepened.

Finally, I said, "You look stunning."

"Thank you, Mr. Stearne."

Miguel pulled out the chair he'd been sitting in next to mine and motioned for Betty to take it. She gave him a gracious thank-you nod. While she swept her gown to the side and sat, exposing as much leg as possible in the process, Miguel gave me a knowing nod.

Ms. Sabel chose that moment to return my call. On video, no less. She was dressed up as much as Betty, only—being a billionaire—she had a few pounds of diamonds draped around her neck.

Before I could answer, Betty leaned across my shoulder to stare at Ms. Sabel and her glitter. She looked up at me with a jealous scowl.

Rising before pressing accept, I stepped away from the table. I said, "Griffith will be at a place called Casino des Grottes Royales in three days. I can't find anything about it. Either our source lied or—"

"Shit," she said. "You won't find it. It's in Monaco. The first casino in Monte Carlo, called *Les Spelugues* or The Caves, failed in 1857. *Des Grottes* also means caves. They used a different word to escape bad luck. It's not open to the public because it's exclusive to the Russian oligarchs and mobsters who live there. Mikhail Yeschenko owns it. He'll never let you in."

It occurred to me that she knew a lot about it considering she wasn't a gambler. I said, "What do you mean? Yeschenko loves me. I'll give him a call. I'm sure he'll open the doors."

"This is the guy who is pissed at me—which means he's pissed at you—for having the US Treasury trace the $28 million you owed him. They uncovered his methods of working around the sanctions."

I was about to remind her she was the one who stole the $28 million from him in the first place. And that Yeschenko blamed me based on bad information. And that she never bothered to correct the international mobster's invalid assumptions. But then I remembered rich people—even nice ones—don't like being reminded of things like that. I let it pass.

She eyed me in the video. "Is that a tuxedo? Hold the camera back farther, I want to see the look. Say, that's nice. Where did that come from?"

"I don't know. Emma had it tailored and sent to my room."

"We finally found a desk manager who can make you look good. Thank god! I'll make—"

"Excuse me?"

"—sure she's assigned to you permanently. Back to Yeschenko. I don't want you going to Monaco."

"All I need to do is deliver the man he hates more than you and me put together."

She thought for a moment before she understood my plan. "Yuri Belenov?" She started shaking her head.

"Don't worry," I smiled. "I've got this."

Ms. Sabel clicked off with her eyes full of sadness, as if she'd never see me again.

Betty squeezed my thigh as soon as I sat down. "Is she my competition?"

"You have no competition." The words came out of my mouth before I thought about the message they would send. Her dimples deepened and her eyes sparkled again. I added, "Ms. Sabel's like a sister to me."

"Every man who's said that turned out to be lying."

Suddenly feeling defensive, I asked, "What do you know about her?"

Betty glanced away, slightly embarrassed for a moment. When I didn't let up on my stare, she faced me and said, "Well, I know she had a tragic childhood, orphaned at four. Her natural father was a promising scientist. If I have it right, her mother was strangled right in front of her during a home invasion. She was adopted by Alan Sabel, became an international soccer star, and inherited Sabel Industries."

She left out Ms. Sabel stabbed her mother's killer with a vegetable knife, hitting his femoral artery and letting him bleed out. Nor did Betty mention that Ms. Sabel tracked down the man who arranged the home invasion two decades later and pumped nine bullets into him. But she was close enough. I let her off with a smile.

After dinner, Nadia recommended a nearby club. We walked over. I flashed my American Express Centurion card. It's black and made of titanium. Doormen and managers the world over recognize it instantly as being invitation-only with no spending limits. At all. The manager came out and escorted us past the line and gave us a tour.

Hands waved over the dance floor like wheat on the prairie. House dancers writhed on pedestals scattered around the room. Dry ice machines dropped wisps of cooling fog from the ceiling. Colored spotlights swept across bodies squirming like a clew of worms.

Galactic was opening for Snarky Puppy—my two favorite bands. Heaven on Earth.

Because of my Centurion Card, the manager sat us at an exclusive VIP table and brought an overpriced champagne. We toasted to freedom. Even Rafael relaxed and drank a little. Then Betty ordered shots of vodka.

After that, things got murky.

AT SIX THE NEXT MORNING, the sun had risen but I couldn't see it. Whether that was due to my hangover or the fog, I wasn't sure. A chilly wet mist greeted us when my crew climbed out of our Ubers. Two bright white Gulfstreams waited with airstairs deployed and beckoning, the Sabel Industries logo in deep blue splashed along their respective fuselages.

Betty slapped an arm across my chest and said, "Hey, why are there two?"

"You're going to Hollywood, right?" I asked with my head pulsing as a monkey banged my brain between two cymbals.

She reached into my open jacket and tugged my Henley's buttons. "You wanted to see where I live, didn't you?"

"Nadia will give me a full report once she's sure you're safe." I pushed her hands away.

"Nadia?" Regretting the sharpness in her voice, she brought it down to a whine. "Where are you going without me?"

"Don't ask. You don't want to know." I turned and followed Isaiah around the first jet's nose heading for the second.

Miguel, who doesn't drink and was therefore functional, ushered the ladies and Rafael up the airstair to Sabel Three, then trotted to catch up with us as we climbed aboard Sabel Two.

After feeling the weight-shift at wheels-up, Isaiah asked, "Did you want to clue me in on Brazil? Like, what's there?"

I couldn't think because of that monkey and his damn cymbals.

Mercifully, and with a touch of side-eye, Miguel answered for me. "Deep in a fortress, guarded by fifty Spetsnaz veterans, is one of the most dangerous and murderous cybercriminals in the world. We're going to sneak in and kidnap him."

"OK. Do we have a map of the grounds I could study?"

Feeling the need to be useful, I said, "Nah."

"Do we have a plan?"

"Nah."

CHAPTER 21

A FEW MILES OUTSIDE SALVADOR, Brazil, the air stuck to us like hot molasses while the sun baked a hole right through our skin. Miguel and I sipped our coffees on the beach while we listened to Isaiah's chatter through our earbuds. His impression of a Jamaican accent was hysterical. It was also an ingenious way to cover his lack of Portuguese. The Russian killer he spoke to handed over the Ferrari's keys without a question.

"All pard of de service, mon," Isaiah told the guard. "Have her back in no time."

He kept the man distracted by chatting about the Brazilian beauties lying on the mansion's beach. The Russian agreed they were nice to look at but would offer little more. Guarding a world-renowned hacker kept the man suspicious of strangers. But he never tried to stop Isaiah from loading the boss's Ferrari SF90 onto the flatbed. A bit of misdirection expertly done by our new guy.

A short while later, we saw Isaiah drive by in his official Ferrari dealership truck. That was my cue to send up a drone. As beach mansions go, Belenov's was not bad. Certainly, a grade above the neighboring estates. Not that the neighbors could tell given the distances between the houses. The nice touch was the brick walkway from the main house to the sprawling palapa on the beach. Lowers the sand maintenance for the staff. The two bathing beauties Isaiah mentioned tanned topless on lounge chairs in the sand.

Mercury said, *See the problem with that, bro?*

I said, *I don't have a problem with nude beaches.*

Dude. Mercury slapped his forehead, knocking his helmet off his head. *You know Romans ain't got no probs with nudity, given the baths and such. So think about what the problem might be.*

He picked up his helmet and blew sand off its little wings.

I zoomed in on the women—for purely logistical reasons. I said, *It's not a problem.*

Miguel, looking over my shoulder, also for purely logistical reasons, saw what I saw. He launched the second drone and sent it over the long drive that led from the beach villa to the only paved road in the area.

Then what we were waiting for happened. The man guarding the women on the beach put a hand to his ear. No doubt getting a frantic message from his compatriot in the driveway. A moment later, he ran up the walkway to the main house at full gallop.

I said, *See that? It's working exactly as planned.*

Mercury frowned. *You got a plan you didn't get cleared through me?*

I said, *You were busy with the Unfortunate Gods Conference.*

Underappreciated. He slapped the back of my head. *And that ended yesterday?*

I said, *Where have you been, then?*

I negotiated a conjugal visit with my wife. He sighed. *Don't ask how that went.*

I noticed my derelict god had bite marks on his bloody ear. Recalling he'd lost his wife in a bet, I imagined how well his booty call went. And I thought mortals had problems. The gods are always running around impregnating virgins, cheating on their wives and husbands, sharing lovers, and blaming us for the world's mess.

Miguel showed me his drone feed on his phone. A Land Rover slid to the front door. The guard from the beach cleared the entrance and jumped in the passenger seat. They took off down the driveway. In the comm link, Miguel said, "Isaiah, they're leaving the property now."

"I've made the first turn," Isaiah reported. "But I'm a mile from the next one. Can you slow them up?"

No way. Mercury leaned over Miguel's shoulder to see the phone, then looked at me. *Did you guys do that on purpose?*

I scanned the walkway up to the house and around the pool deck outside. No other guards visible. Sending the drone in a circle around the property, I tried to get a look under the myriad coconut trees. No guards hiding anywhere I could see.

Zooming in on the mansions' acres of glass, I turned on the thermal imaging. One occupant, upstairs, left of the pool deck. The room featured floor-to-ceiling windows facing the beach. I tagged Miguel and started walking across the sand.

The big guy followed me while monitoring his drone feed. He clicked a few buttons and hooted, "Direct hit! Massive bird shit on the windshield. They're stopping to wipe. Just bought you a couple minutes, Isaiah. Use them wisely."

Sabel drones have an array of interesting options. Simulated bird shit was news to me.

A few minutes later, we passed the bathing beauties with a nod and marched up the walkway. From my drone's feed, it didn't appear our victim had seen us yet. Most likely had his head down in his six display screens. Such is the life of a hacker.

Mercury flew alongside with his wings beating like a bumblebee's. *How did you get the guards to follow your man with just enough delay?*

I said, *We had the dealer call the guards about a recall this morning. They were expecting a tow truck. But Isaiah dropped a few remarks about the women who were on the far end of the property. It took a few minutes for the guard to realize a tow truck driver wouldn't know who's on the beach. That's when it sunk in that he'd just let a man steal the boss's brand-new Ferrari.*

You cleaned out the guards on duty with a simple thing like that? Mercury dropped to his feet, stuck a fist for a bump and said, *Damn proud of you, boy.*

I said, *I can handle life without any gods, thank you.*

Oh, izzat so? Mercury's inflection held an ominous undercurrent. *Then how come you don't listen to me about Betty Bardon? Did you see her on the dance floor? She's got some moves, homie.*

A few spotty memories of her dancing like a cat on a hot tin roof came to mind. I said, *I don't care how hot she is.*

Mercury said, *You should care. You need her help. She's a genius. Know what her undergrad degree is? Quantum physics. Do you even know what that means?*

Of course. Everybody knows all about that stuff. I had the vaguest of ideas that it was a topic way over my head. *If she's so smart, why didn't you start with that instead of talking about her big—*

Just talking in a language you understand, dawg.

I said, *Wait, why did you tell me about her undergrad? Does she have a post-grad, um, thing ... whatever they're called?*

Mercury said, *Said you don't need no gods.*

With that, he was gone. Maybe pissing off a god wasn't my best move. Regardless, there's no way I drag a movie star into an operation where her implants could get popped. That, and I didn't trust her.

Our victim was not at his desk watching his multiscreen display. It was his bedroom. He was sound asleep. I stuck him with a Sabel Dart.

One of the bathing beauties stepped in the room, still topless. She said something in anger that sounded Portuguese.

I shrugged and crossed to her while Miguel slung our victim on his shoulder.

"*Borracho,*" I said before remembering that was Spanish. I racked my brain for Portuguese. Somewhere in there I knew the word for drunk in twenty languages. Next to *fuck you,* it's one of the handiest words in an international assassin's vocabulary. "*Bêbado.*"

She looked at me funny. Something was wrong. I wondered if our victim had gone clean since I saw him last.

Miguel headed out of the room. While the stunning woman shouted something to make him stop, I stabbed her with a Sabel Dart. I dragged her to the bed and pulled the covers up to her chin. One of us had to be modest.

Downstairs, Miguel made for the front door at a good clip. The second bathing beauty stood in the living room, a phone to her ear, jabbering in Portuguese with fire in her eyes. When I approached, she ran away. And she was quick. I didn't have time to pursue, so I ran through the house.

Miguel was out front, our victim unceremoniously dumped in the wheelbarrow, feet and arms dangling off the sides.

"We're going to get company," I said. "She sounded the alarms."

Checking his drone feed, Miguel said, "They passed your turnoff, Isaiah. You should be clear. But they just slammed on their brakes and are pulling a U-turn. We believe they're coming back here."

"I'm behind a barn," he reported. "Mind if I take this Ferrari off the truck and take it for a spin? Just in case they see me. I think I can get ahead of them better in this."

"Permission for a joy ride granted," Miguel said. "Meet us at the airport."

I picked up the wheelbarrow handles and started pushing our guest down the driveway.

Miguel pocketed his phone, shoved me aside, and took over. He grabbed the handles and started running.

We made it to the main road and down to the next mansion's driveway, where we'd stashed our rented Audi SUV. We shoveled our victim into the back and drove away. Miguel cranked it up and drove flat out.

Seconds later, two Land Rovers flew by heading for the mansion. One kept going. The other burned rubber to a stop, slid around, and gave chase.

Jumping into our SUV's back, I pushed our victim aside, grabbed an MP7 automatic rifle and opened the back end. As soon as the hatch rose high enough, I put half a magazine into their radiator. Radiators can't be bulletproofed. Steam poured out over the hood, washing the windshield. The wipers came on. Antifreeze streaked the glass in bold orange.

A man leaned out of the passenger window. I brushed him back. Even tough-as-nails Russians know it's best to stay behind the bulletproof glass. That gave me time to take out a tire, which is a tougher target than it looks. I hit it on the third try. Their truck swerved hard right, the blowout caving the front end to the pavement at speed. The driver overcorrected. The car flipped.

Just then, the feet of our victim began to slide past me as his body nearly fell out of the car. I grabbed his belt and pulled but had no traction. I felt both of us sliding out. My butt neared the final lip, which would be the end of my life given the speed we were going.

I yelled at Miguel, "BRAKES!"

Without questioning my order, he jammed us up. Belenov and I slid forward into the seat backs. The back door slammed closed. Miguel looked us over, assessed the absence of damage, and resumed his full pace run for the airport.

A few minutes later, we careened around the executive terminal on two wheels, rubber squealing and smoking. A beautiful Ferrari sat next to Sabel Two. Slathered across the paint from the wheel wells to the backend was a ton of flung mud. Isaiah must've taken the scenic route. A very scenic route.

He called out from the top of the airstair, "I'm starting to like field work with you guys."

We dragged our prize up the stairs and dropped him on the sofa in the back. I snapped a photo of him with a Sabel Industries coffee mug next to his head and sent it to Mikhail Yeschenko. I followed with a text that read, "I'll call you at 0600 Moscow time. That is, if you're still looking for Yuri Belenov."

CHAPTER 22

IN KYIV, THE NINETEENTH CENTURY jail's iron bars slammed like ships colliding right behind Seamus McLeod. His chains scraped the stone floors until the guard slammed the club into his stomach again. He didn't speak Ukrainian, so the guard used whacks with the stick. This one meant *stop*.

In the next room, his men waited. A thick yellow line divided the space. Six were on his side, while two others stood across the line. The two across the line had been processed out. They pulled personal effects from paper bags. Good. They were being released. It was the first thing he'd understood since they dragged him in and slammed him in solitary confinement. No food. No water. No phone call.

Someone shouted the name of one of his Knights. His man stepped toward a wall where someone unseen stood behind an 8x10 hole. That unseen person pushed a paper bag out the window. It fell to the floor before his Knight could catch it. He and his effects were kicked across the yellow line. The next name was called out.

And so it went, until all nine of them were outside standing in a sooty drizzle.

Seamus checked the street. His men did the same, each examining a different quadrant. No sign of that Indian. Or Native, whatever he wanted to be called. No sign of Stearne, either. Just dirty streets, industrial brick buildings, and colors that invoked genocidal thoughts.

His phone rang with a video call.

His men turned to him. Everyone knew who it was: Griffith.

Seamus turned to protect the others from being seen with him. They appreciated it with sympathetic looks.

"Thank you, sir," Seamus said. "We appreciate—"

"You have failed me for the last time," Griffith roared. "Do you hear me?"

"Aye, sir."

"You chose Jacob Stearne, did you not?"

"Aye, sir."

"I can allow for how he escaped you in Brest. You let yourself be hamstrung by the local cops. But letting him land you in jail is unacceptable."

Seamus glanced around at the eight faces focused exclusively on him. Griffith had shouted loud enough for everyone to hear. They knew their fate: stand still and wait to be assassinated.

"What the hell were you doing in Kyiv when I told you not to meet him there?" Griffith kept going.

"I met an intermediary who could lead me to him, sir."

"An intermediary? You didn't think it would be one of Stearne's tricks?"

"It was a drug dealer, sir. One who knows every inch of the city. He could lead us to where Stearne was hiding."

"Hiding? You think Stearne was hiding? Have you ever heard of Instagram? He partied downtown at the Dejavu. Posted pictures of Betty Bardon and him grinding on the dance floor."

"Aye, sir. That would be after our troubles, sir."

"And how did you get into those troubles?'

"The drug dealer, sir. We had no way of knowing the cops planned to bust him that night. He had a kilo of cocaine on him. We were swept up in the mess."

"And the drug dealer?"

"I've no way of knowing his fate, sir." Seamus took a deep breath and glanced at his Knights for support. They nodded encouragement. "They separated us all right away."

After thinking about it, Griffith nodded. "That sounds about right. They would do that to compare stories under questioning."

"We're ready to have a go at the bastard, sir."

"Ha! He's slipped through your fingers twice and you think you should get a third shot at it? What is this, baseball? I've already called the Finns. They're ready."

"If you don't mind me saying so, sir." Seamus paused a split second to see if Griffith would let him speak. "The Finns are a fine group, the deadliest of the Knights to be sure, but they're two hundred miles north of the Arctic Circle. They're five hundred miles from an airport. We can get to Stearne today."

"If only you knew where he is, is that right?"

"I won't pretend I tracked him while spending the last day and some in the slammer, but no one has pissed me off more than Jacob Stearne in my life. I give you my word on that. Same goes for my men."

"AYE!" the Knights shouted on cue.

Griffith's head snapped back at their ferocity. Then a sly smile grew on him. He looked like a man who'd just figured out which cards were left in the shoe at a Hold 'Em table. He said, "I hear motivation to succeed!"

"That's us, sir."

"How long will it take you to bring him in?"

It was a test question, Seamus knew that. He calculated the answer in his head. It had to be less time than it would take the Finns to reach civilization and become active. "Forty-eight hours, sir."

"Very good. You have until then. Any longer and you're nothing but mud under the boots of Joona and the Finns." Griffith clicked off.

Seamus pocketed his phone and looked at his men.

"What are you thinking, man?" a Knight asked. "How're we going to find him?"

At the same time, another Knight asked, "Why forty-eight hours, Seamus? You've got us all killed."

He held up his hand and lowered it between them. The discord died down.

He said, "Stearne will be in Monaco tomorrow."

CHAPTER 23

ISAIAH STOOD ON THE BALCONY of the Hotel de Paris Monte-Carlo watching the Lamborghinis and McLarens cruising Casino Square in the late afternoon sun. What I like most about expensive hotels is that they don't ask questions when you tell the bellman to bring your hostage to your suite with the luggage. Though he was rather rude about the tip until I added an extra €100.

"You could help once in a while," Miguel said after finishing the last knot securing Yuri Belenov to a folding chair.

"You're the BDSM expert," I said.

Isaiah ripped his eyes off the action in the square to check us out.

"He's kidding," Miguel said. "And quit watching the rich guys and the pretty women. You're supposed to be looking for Knights of Mithras."

"I was." Isaiah showed his palms in protest. "I didn't see any."

"Then what were all the whistles and 'whoo-ees' about?"

"C'mon, this is the first trip to Monte Carlo for this ni—" He cut himself off, uncertain of his audience. "Pretty amazing place. Like I said, I didn't see anyone who looks like they're watching us. Come see for yourself."

"New guys," Miguel looked at me and shook his head.

"We're known in this town," I said. "One of us sticks a head out on the balcony, bad things happen."

"But you're the Hero of Paris," Isaiah said.

"This ain't Paris," I said. "Whole different country. And that was only good for a week anyway."

Miguel joined Isaiah on the balcony but stayed back from the rail.

Mercury materialized in front of me and said, *How's this supposed to work, homes? I got a lot riding on this deal and you're not making sense. You're gonna trade your kidnap victim, Yuri Belenov, to mobster Yeschenko so he'll hook you up with Griffith?*

I said, *Right.*

Mercury said, *But Griffith's Knights are gonna ambush you and kill you first. I don't get my wife back if you die.*

I said, *Slick and his Scots won't kill me. They still want the Chaac Equation and they think I can get it.*

Mercury said, *You might be underestimating how pissed they are about making them look bad in Brest and Kyiv. They'll kill you then tell Griffith, 'Oops.'*

I said, *Then you'll have to make sure that doesn't happen. 'Bout time you started pulling your weight around here.*

Mercury turned bright red. *Pulling my ... dude! You DO NOT talk to gods like that, you hear me? You need to respect—*

My phone rang. The way overdue video callback from Mikhail Yeschenko.

I said, *Yo. Hold that thought. I have to take this.*

Mercury shot through the ceiling like a rocket.

I moved to the part of the suite where we held Yuri and took a folding chair next to his. Behind me, a large sheet of hastily erected cardboard made it impossible to tell my location by the background.

"I told you 0600 Moscow time." I scowled.

"Waiting for call from Jacob Stearne not my top priority." His accent was thicker than usual. American sanctions were keeping him inside Russia. Theoretically. "When do you deliver Yuri Belenov?"

"We need to talk about the conditions first."

"No conditions. You owe me Belenov." His voice rose with anger. "I let you live last week. This is deal. You understand, da?"

"Ms. Sabel paid you the $28 million in full. That's a done deal unless you want her to claw it back. If that's the way you want to go, let me know. I've got a top hacker right here. He can get the job done while we talk." I shared the screen with my gagged hostage, who glared first at me, then Yeschenko. "New day, new deal. You ready to hear my terms?"

"Sabel, *shlyukha*." The way he said the Russian word, I guessed it was a slur. "She send money through US Treasury. Held up in ridiculous sanctions. No good. Debt is still on you. You gave your word, Jacob Stearne. We had deal."

"You had a deal—"

"You break your word? Is this kind of man you are, Jacob?" After he asked his question, he put his phone on mute.

Most people feel safe pressing the mute button. But they forget that if Siri can hear you, someone like my operations team can hack into that. A Russian translator, part of Emma's team back at headquarters, listened to Mikhail's background conversation with his lieutenant and sent a transcript to Miguel.

"Who are you to talk about keeping your word?" I raised my voice. "You invited Ms. Sabel for tea on your private island then threatened to throw her off a cliff. We both lied. So what? Now I have Yuri. Work with me here."

In my peripheral vision, Isaiah's eyes blew wide open. Few people outside her inner circle knew the kind of hostile work environment she dealt with.

Miguel showed me the translation of Mikhail's sidebar. It said, *Why can't we trace his call? Work harder. Find him and save me the indignation of dealing with this kozyol. I want Belenov now!* The translator decided to skip *kozyol*, Russian for "goat," a prison insult for snitches. It wasn't the first time Mikhail had called me that.

"OK, new deal," Mikhail said when he unmuted. "Fine. You bring Yuri Belenov to me. I let you live one more day."

"Well, this call is going to hell fast. Forget it, then. I'll sell him to the Arabs. He stole ten times as much from them. I'll bet there's a sheik or a crown prince somewhere in Monaco. Wish I could say it was nice talking to you again, Mikhail."

I made a show of reaching my right hand high to bring it down in an arc toward the disconnect button.

"Wait, wait." Yeschenko steamed red from the neck up. "I listen for ten seconds. No more."

"You have a customer coming to the Les Grottes," I said,

mispronouncing it just to make him wince. "I need a few minutes alone with him. You can arrange that, can't you?"

"Who is customer?"

"Joe Griffith."

His eyes flared with recognition. He knew Griffith. He wasn't afraid of him. That meant he wasn't in league with him, which was a huge relief.

"You tangle with Joe Griffith?" He huffed. "You mess with me sometimes, but everybody know, Mikhail Yeschenko nice man. Very nice. I let you live, see? I let your boss the *shlyukha* live. I am merciful. Griffith is not merciful. He is big man with big resources. Maybe biggest man in world now. He send men every day to take you out. You win one day, maybe next day too. But one day soon, Joe Griffith win that battle, Jacob."

"Yeah. Heard that before. Can you arrange a meeting or not? Like I said, this town's lousy with Arab princes looking for Yuri Belenov."

"Selling out customers is bad business," Mikhail said. "Although. Meetings can be arranged. That is, provided known assassins not bring weapons."

It was a condition I could live with. I could easily kill Griffith with my bare hands. I said, "Same goes for his bodyguards, then."

"You want I should control whole world for you, Jacob Stearne? No bodyguards in casino. Never. That goes for big Indian too."

Earlier in the day, we studied the layout at Les Grottes and found five places an ambush could happen outside the casino. If I lived long enough to get past Slick and his Knights, meeting Griffith would make running the gauntlet worthwhile.

"'Indian' is so twentieth century. His name is Miguel, rhymes with Mikhail. Should be easy for you to remember."

"Whatever," he shrugged. "You want Griffith or nyet?"

"I'll be at your casino at 2000 hours."

"Deal," he said. "I come get Belenov now. Where you are staying?"

Miguel gave me a cutoff sign. I understood his desire to kill the call before we made a mistake and gave away our location, but I felt it was better to finalize the terms. Especially since he said he'd come get him now, meaning he was in Monaco, not Moscow. Since he never traveled without a few of his special guards, it was a big problem. He would be ruthless in his search and kill the three of us for delaying him.

"No way, Mikhail," I said. "You get Yuri after I meet Griffith."

The Russian billionaire nodded his head and stroked his chin as he thought. A light went on in his head. "OK, you win, Jacob Stearne. See you at casino, eight o'clock."

He clicked off.

"Damn," Miguel said. "He figured it out. Well, it was nice while it lasted."

"You got the meeting set. What's the problem?" Isaiah looked back and forth between us. "What'd I miss?"

"He knows me too well," I said. "He's going to out-bribe me at hotels in Monaco. It's not a big principality; it won't take him long. That means you're in charge of the hostage and you're now—officially—on the run."

"Hold up," Isaiah said. "You told me this Yeschenko guy travels with ten to fifteen guys as highly trained as we are and that he wants this Belenov dude bad. That's like making me be the guy who steals the salmon out of a Kodiak's claws."

"That's a fair assessment," Miguel said.

"Why me? Why not you?"

"You're the new guy."

Isaiah complained the whole time the bellman loaded our hostage into the rented delivery van. I told him to get a cheap motel in Marseille. After Isaiah finished complaining, Miguel said, "I thought you liked field work with us."

CHAPTER 24

RUSSIAN THUGS PATTED ME DOWN in the lobby of the Tour Odeon, Monaco's 49-story luxury skyscraper. They took every conceivable weapon from me including a pen and the secret tactical blade hidden in my belt buckle. They let me keep Jenny's medallion. One of the men tugged on the stiff support piece under my tux that surrounded my ribs. He asked, "What this?"

"For the back pain." I gave him a sheepish look and whispered, "I'm not young anymore and the lifestyle …"

He nodded his understanding of living with aches. My secret was safe with him. He and his friends finished the search. They never saw the comm link buried in my ear canal. At least I had a connection to Miguel. Without him, my only hope was a lost god.

My ears popped on the elevator ride to Mikhail Yeschenko's penthouse casino. More Russians and a second pat-down awaited me before they let me into the main room.

Looking through the crowd, the only language I heard was Russian. No surprise since the principality is a tax haven for kleptocrats. They like to rub shoulders with Europe's racing champions, tennis stars, movie stars, and art dealers.

There was a time when I wouldn't consider going into a den of thieves like this without Jenny. She was smart and grew up among the ridiculously wealthy. She could spot those who belonged and those who didn't from three gaming tables away. I missed her. I rubbed the medallion in my pocket. And that reminded me of why I wanted to meet Griffith: To watch him die.

I moved between poker tables and roulette wheels, searching for my prey with fingers just itching to get around his throat. With any luck, I'd remember to ask Neville's questions about the Chaac Project and Equation before turning his lights out, but one can never tell about these things. Heat of the moment and all that.

Griffith led the most dangerous group of rich people ever assembled in history. They were responsible for keeping the Dark Ages dark. They profited from wars both hot and cold. They hated an educated and healthy populace because it drove up labor costs. They resisted any and all taxes for any and all reasons. They insisted all government expenditures benefit them in some way. They demanded roads be built to their buildings, stadiums for their teams, enemies invented for their defense industries, and diseases ignored to maintain production. They are welfare queens—but their checks have nine zeros on the end. Over the last forty years, the world had given them everything they asked for. Griffith and his cabal were riding high.

None of that swayed me one way or another. As Plato warned us, people will vote for whoever tells them what they want to hear, not who is best for the job. That's not my problem. What I hated about Griffith was his involvement in a plan to kill the world's top finance ministers. My dearly beloved Jenny became entangled in thwarting that plot. She paid with her life.

So would he.

Mercury stepped in front of me, forcing me to a roulette table, *Dude, you hang here too? Ima win back my bride. What about you?*

I said, *I'm here to kill Griffith. Nothing more.*

Mercury said, *What'd I tell you about working with Betty Bardon, huh? You shoulda listened to me when you had the chance. If'n you had, you wouldn't be on this wild nymph chase you're on right now.*

I said, *Has any god ever said something concrete to prove his or her existence?*

Oh, izzat how it's gonna be? Mercury said. *Again you want proof. Like the Grand Canyon is something all y'all mortals could dig on a Sunday afternoon. And what is the human masterpiece you place against the beauty and grandeur we provide? Walmart. You always want more proof. Fine.* He nodded at the roulette wheel. *Black fifteen, straight bet.*

I said, *How will that help me kill Griffith?*

Have faith. He grinned and his little wings wiggled.

I need a new god. One who isn't so rude. But it was Ms. Sabel's money, so what did I care.

I threw down a big pile of yellow chips on black fifteen. The croupier looked at me funny and said something in Russian. Everyone else at the table stared at me like I was stupid. I shrugged. The wheel spun, the ball rolled, the crowd leaned over the table watching with eager eyes and bated breath.

Over their lowered backs, I scanned the room. The shadows of three men in the back corner were staring hard at me. They were obscured by the low light and the many people milling about the room. They didn't look like Yeschenko's men. Not that I knew all his boys, but Yeschenko's thugs have that born-in-a-steel-furnace look. The guys watching me were scrawnier, hungrier.

Yeschenko had said bodyguards weren't allowed in his casino. Slick and his men were more assassins, so technically he hadn't lied.

Behind me, people shouted and made a big fuss. It was all in Russian, so I didn't know what they were saying.

I found myself drawn to the three men in the corner. From their silhouettes, I pieced together a picture of them. Small-framed and wiry, they worked like predators, observing every breath I took and waiting for the right moment to descend on me like a pack of jackals.

A drunk slapped me on the back. With 150-proof breath, he shouted in my face, "Congratulations, American! You break bank at Les Grottes!"

Turning to the croupier, I watched him shrug and close the table to fetch more chips. All the faces around the wheel watched me with energetic glee. They were happy for me.

The men in back left their drinks and moved in my direction. One flanked left, another right, leaving Slick in the center heading straight toward me. We kept our eyes locked on each other in preparation for mortal combat.

The croupier stepped up next to me, a stack of chips in his hand. He followed my gaze, saw the tension building between the Knights and me, poured the chips in my pocket, and fled.

Slick and I were six feet apart and closing.

That's when three men who grew up in a Bessemer converter appeared. Two of them escorted the flanking Knights out of the room. The Russian blocking Seamus and me grabbed us both by the shirts and pulled us close enough to smell his cologne. He hissed, "No fighting, no swearing, no kissing. Talk like adults or I throw you both off roof."

He shoved us to the bar, then backed up an arm's length.

Slick and I looked each other over with pure hatred in our eyes. Then we turned our glare to our intercessor. He pulled a collapsible baton from his jacket and slapped the business end into his other palm. Some people were allowed to bring weapons into Les Grottes. Apparently.

Slick and I turned back.

With a nod at the Russian, I said to Slick, "Don't think your boyfriend is going to save your life. You lied to me. When—"

He finished my sentence. "This is over, I'm going to kill you for having me thrown in jail."

We growled at each other until the bartender set Stingers in front of us. He said, "Compliments of the lady."

Neither of us acknowledged him. We couldn't take our eyes off each other—and not in a nice way.

"Where is Griffith?" I asked through clenched teeth.

Slick didn't answer, he just sneered.

"If you don't tell me, I'll make you look bad in front of your boss again." I watched while he considered that option.

The Russian stepped forward. "Mr. Griffith send his regrets. He change schedule after Mr. Yeschenko warned you are out for blood."

He stepped back.

Slick watched the Russian with raised eyebrows. He quickly scanned the room for his boss.

I laughed. "You were going to put on a floor show and disembowel me in front of him."

Suddenly, I felt sorry for him on a professional level. He'd racked up losses without demonstrating value to his superiors. Not a good position to be in.

"Aye, something along those lines." Slick picked up his drink and took a sip. "What was your idea then?"

"Defenestration."

He nodded his approval of my proposed solution. A definitive option from 550 feet up.

I reached for my drink. Slick tilted his.

"There'll be hell to pay when I report," he said. "He's the most powerful unelected man in the world right now. You'd do well to talk to the man, Mr. Stearne."

I thought it was odd suggesting I talk to Griffith. I was under the impression he wanted me dead. I thought that over. I said, "Why would I do that?"

"I won't pretend I didn't come to kill ya, but the man wants a word with you. He thought you'd leave Brest and lead us straight to the Chaac Equation. You didn't do that. Now he wants to talk."

"I've nothing to discuss with him."

"Told him you'd say just that."

"Management never listens."

"Aye to that." Slick clinked his glass to mine.

We stood there, shoulder to shoulder, nursing our drinks for a long, somber moment. He sighed his disappointment and took a good-sized swallow. I felt his pain and did the same.

"A bit anticlimactic, isn't it?" I offered.

"Bloody Russians." Slick sighed.

Miguel's voice came over the comm link. "Doesn't sound like you need emergency extraction, but if you do, I'm on the roof, set up and ready. Your exit will be the third window from the entrance on the French side."

With a casual turn away from the bar, I surveyed the gigantic sheets of glass that made up the outside walls. They were two stories tall. I pinpointed the third from the elevator banks. The Tour Odeon sat on the municipality's border and cast long shadows over the neighboring French town. But in the dark, it was hard to tell which side of the building faced the Mediterranean. I watched for a moment until I spotted bobbing lights on yachts. The opposite side would be France.

"You missed your chance, mate." Seamus took a long swig from his drink. "And I missed mine. I'm sure we'll meet again. Until then, take every breath like it was your last."

"Yeah, yeah, whatever. Watch your back, I'll be out there—and all that."

Slick looked over my shoulder, saw something, then grinned at me. He finished his drink, slammed the glass on the bar, patted my shoulder, and left.

Our Russian referee appeared satisfied we were professionals who'd called it a draw. He decided no further babysitting was needed and also left.

Miguel said, "Ambush set up outside the entrance. Eight Knights. You'll need the dramatic exit after all."

The bartender leaned across the wood. "Sir, it's good manners to thank the lady who bought your drinks."

"Oh, right," I said. "Who was it?"

He pointed toward the end of the bar. My gaze traveled past twenty well-dressed Russians to find my benefactor where the bartender pointed.

Betty Bardon.

Looking better than any of her movie roles, she gave me an electric smile, baring her dimples like a shark. She added a flirtatious little finger wave. If I thought the slit dress she rocked in Kyiv was hot, the plunging-neckline minidress she wore sucked the air out of the room.

Mikhail Yeschenko stepped into my line of sight. "Now you owe me Yuri Belenov."

The Russian oligarch looked like a marble statue. Hair plastered to his head like a thin sheet of silver, his suit molded to his body with laser precision, his gaze was like solid rock.

"You warned off Griffith," I said. "No deal. Besides, the Emirates are willing to pay cash."

A thug moved in on the left, another on the right. Yeschenko said, "We have deal, Jacob. You said Griffith would be here, not me. You owe me Yuri Belenov."

One of his thugs extended his collapsible baton and readied a blow.

"Yeah, OK," I said. "I never liked the Emiratis anyway."

"There you are," Betty slid a hand around Yeschenko and grabbed my wrist. "You promised me some of your magic on the roulette wheel."

When she tugged, Yeschenko looked her over and immediately recognized her. He squinted at me with a curiosity that said, *how did a clown like you land a woman like her?* He looked around the room. Movie stars have a way of getting all eyes on them and Betty was better than most. The entire room watched our conversation. Yeschenko calculated this was no time for a scene.

Before he stepped out of her way, he said, "One spin, then you come with me."

I pointed at the wheel nearest Miguel's window. "Three spins and I'll tell you where you can find him."

"Why I should trust you?"

"He'll be standing on a street corner in Marseille. When I arrive home safely, I'll text you which street corner."

"We take you downstairs to soundproof room. You tell me street corner."

"My man is driving around waiting for my call. I won't know which street corner until I make the call. But I give you my word that I'll text you the address."

It was all he'd get, and he knew it. Yeschenko nodded, then stepped aside.

Betty squeezed my arm and pressed her cheek to my shoulder as we crossed the room. She whispered, "You could say thank-you, but there's a better option."

She squeezed me.

I said, "Oh?"

"You could help me kill Joe Griffith."

"Why should I help you?"

"Because you know where Joe *isn't*—he isn't here. But I know where he *is*." She smiled up at me with that damn gleam and those dimples. As if killing a man meant nothing more than going to brunch.

Yeschenko followed on my heels, his bodyguards on either side. We crossed to the table. I looked at Betty and squeezed her hand. I whispered, "Follow my lead and don't scream."

I announced to the room, "This table is rigged! Rigged I tell you."

I kicked the table over and ducked behind it, dragging Betty with me. Mikhail and his bodyguard stared down at us in that confused instant before they realized something bad was about to happen. Before they could react, the third window from the entrance exploded, sending shards of hurricane-proof glass across the room. Some caught my host in the face. Screams and shouts echoed through the room. A smoke bomb flew in, adding to the confusion.

Grabbing Betty by the wrist, I ran toward the smoke while others ran away. We stopped in front of a hole thirty feet tall and twenty wide and stared at a five hundred foot drop outside.

"Do you do your own stunts?" I shouted over the shrieks.

"Hell, no!"

"You do now."

A thick rope flew into the open window. I grabbed the stainless-steel buckle and gave a shake that sent a wave back up to Miguel on the roof. I attached the buckle to the harness under my tux that the guards thought was a back support.

Betty stared at me with eyes as big as a tarsier's.

"Hold onto me like your life depends on it—" I wrapped both arms around her and jumped out the window into the dark "—because it does!"

CHAPTER 25

JOE GRIFFITH FOUND THE ARCHITECTURE of the executive terminal in Copenhagen calming. It was a pre-war terminal designed to ease concerns of early aviation travelers. The undulating tile ceiling mimicked the waves of the sea. As he waited for a minor repair on his jet, his problems mounted in his mind. A complication of stress.

He'd had an iron-clad deal to trap Stearne before that double-crossing Russian Yeschenko flipped on him. No weapons allowed, the ungrateful bastard had said. What the devil had Stearne promised him that leveled the playing field in matter of hours?

Griffith's stomach roiled with hate. He'd send someone to mop up the Russian. He didn't care what everyone said about Yeschenko having small armies at his command; Joe Griffith had large armies at his. The Knights would find a way. But that was a score to be settled after Belgrade. Right now, he needed the Chaac Equation.

Flaked paint in the corner told him the airport's budget lacked proper funding. That reminded him of his own childhood, also lacking in funding. Lacking in everything.

He had started life as a schoolteacher who couldn't afford to buy a house. His first stroke of genius was recognizing something about men. They were all exactly who Mother Nature made them. Many stifled their desires, or kept them secret, but all men had desires. Women did too, but Griffith's early realization included the fact that, as a man, he could not as easily grasp and manipulate a woman's desire. Therefore, he decided to focus on men. In particular, the wealthy men who placed their children in the exclusive private school where he taught psychology. Instead of selling them on some brilliant business opportunity, he watched their eyes. Men's eyes spoke volumes about their desires. He made a note of what each of these industrialists desired.

Next, he found the women those men desired. Aspirational women who lacked the funds to achieve their dreams. Athletes, actresses, dancers, whoever might fit a rich man's need. He explained the terms to the young ladies. They understood what was expected. What it took to get a wealthy man to support her. The matches he made at his parties were the stuff of legends. A skill that launched his career as a venture capitalist. Most men are easy to satisfy: a little attention, a bit of adoration, and a whole lot of sex will do the trick. Such introductions opened doors for young Joe Griffith. He helped the wealthy men fulfill their desires, and they helped him.

But one of the doors he opened blew open all the others. It was a school function when he saw fashion billionaire Roy Benedict's eyes follow a high school girl across the room. He knew what he had to deliver to earn Roy's trust. And Joe delivered. How many over the years, twenty? Fifty? He'd lost count long ago. It didn't matter. What mattered were the loans. At every exclusive party he arranged for Roy and some underage girl to meet, he hit up Roy for loans. Big ones. By the time Roy died, Joe had several hundred million dollars in undocumented loans he never had to pay back. Loans the heirs never knew about.

That's what drove Joe Griffith's success. That was his strength. Knowing what needed to be done and having no reservations about doing it.

That's how he got into the Knights of Mithras in the first place. The Duke of Kingston didn't consider himself depraved. He merely had standards. No one spoiled by other men. No one under thirteen. No one over sixteen, either. After five exclusive parties meeting the Duke's standards, Joe was promoted to run the whole operation. That's where serving the rich gets you. And because of the Duke's support, Joe had survived what nearly became a lynching at the board meeting in Vienna. The Duke's backing, and the entrance of twenty-four beautiful women, calmed things down nicely. Of course, the exclusive room set aside for the Duke and his two special guests—unseen by anyone else—sealed the deal.

That was one problem settled. For now.

Building on those strengths, how should he deal with the long game? They needed what Rafael Tum had—the Chaac Equation. If properly motivated, Jacob Stearne could be leveraged to retrieve it. Everyone liked Jacob. He had unnatural luck and was revered by the masses. Rafael would trust the young man. And that would be the end of the Keepers.

What alternatives did he have to Stearne? None. Neville Townsend didn't have enough imagination to have needs like other men. The insufferable bastard desired only his wife. It was settled, then: Stearne was his only option. And they'd already engaged. Stearne didn't let it go after escaping Belarus. He showed up in Monaco. No doubt he'd keep coming.

That raised a question in Griffith's mind: why did Stearne keep coming? Did Stearne care about the professor? Did Stearne blame him for the death of that girl in Germany? Or was Jacob Stearne just another sucker for that stupid thing people called "duty"?"

Where was Stearne's weakness? What leverage could he use to turn Stearne into an asset? He would need a trap.

He could come up with one while out on the hunting trip. Five days of isolation in Greenland's wilderness would leave him plenty of time to think.

Then, like the snap of an icicle, he knew the trap that would bring the great, invincible Jacob Stearne to heel. It was right there the whole time.

He pulled out his phone and dialed. When the other man picked up, he said, "Joona. It's time to deal with the failed Scots. Have you ever been to Greenland?"

CHAPTER 26

BETTY BARDON SCREAMED LOUDER AND with more feeling than in any of her movies as we fell five hundred feet off the skyscraper. She shattered my eardrums before we passed the twentieth floor. Terminal velocity for a drop like that is about 120 mph, so she had good reason to worry. Still, the way she managed to do it all in one breath was astonishing.

Just above the tenth floor, the tensioners began to kick in, slowing our descent.

Pulling her up and leaning back, I landed us on our feet and hit the quick release. My painful bullet wound from Belarus howled like a wolf.

Miguel ran ahead across the small, wooded park that served as the building's green space. He leapt to the top of a retaining wall and leaned back, extending a hand to help me. It was the first time he saw Betty; the rest of our escapade having been in the dark.

He said, "Where did she come from?"

"Nice to see you again." She grabbed his hand.

He pulled her up, then pulled me. He said, "My plan is for one passenger."

"Well, there's two," I said.

He clicked the button on his key fob. The lights blipped on a glow-in-the-dark, lime-green Lamborghini Huracan Spyder.

The three of us stared at it as shouts and flashlights filled the park below us.

"There weren't any Range Rovers?" I asked.

Miguel shrugged.

"We can fit," Betty said optimistically. Obviously, she'd never been in a Lambo before. Then she added, "We have to."

Miguel folded his bear-sized body into the otter-sized driver's seat. Betty and I stood on the passenger side, staring at the tight confines.

"I'll sit in your lap." She giggled. "Just promise me you won't say, 'We'll see what comes up.'"

A second after my butt hit the leather, she was on top of me, cramming her legs between mine and into the footwell. Miguel hit the accelerator without waiting for buckled belts, banging us into the racing seats. Momentum slammed the door shut.

Monaco doesn't have streets. It has walkways barely big enough for two people to pass sideways. Lamborghini doesn't make narrow cars. The passenger-side mirror whacked the first parked car and twirled into the darkness. A good deal of paint stayed with the do-not-enter sign we blew past.

Miguel wisely chose not to take the direct route through the town of Monte Carlo, instead aiming for the switchbacks up the hill behind the city.

I could barely breathe with Betty squeezed on top of me, but I managed to ask, "Why a Lamborghini?"

"The valet gave it to me."

"The valet just *gave* you this car?" Betty asked.

"In a manner of speaking."

"What manner?"

"I was holding him two feet off the ground when I asked him for the keys."

At the first turn, I was able to see the freight train of cars snaking up the hill behind us. Led by black SUVs, the favored but unwieldy choice of bodyguards the world over, a series of other cars trailed by inches. Some had flashing lights as if they were police cars. The distinct whiz of a bullet passed by as we made the next switchback.

Some crazy locals decided to put their garbage cans out for collection. They clattered over the hood, scattering their filthy contents in every direction. A large dressing-drenched lettuce leaf stuck to the windscreen directly in Miguel's view. Not missing a beat, Betty reached over the top, plucked it off, and chucked it over her shoulder. It fluttered away in the wind. Pulling herself back into my lap, she wiped her greasy hand on my pants.

"Thanks," I said.

"Well. You didn't offer me your handkerchief."

I couldn't. It was flattened in my breast pocket under her back.

At the next turn, flashing blue lights came at us. A police truck careened down the intersecting lane, trying to head us off. Miguel downshifted, put his foot down, and accelerated straight toward them. A game of chicken on a mountainside. Betty screamed just as loud as she had during the free fall.

The police chickened out first and swerved into a driveway. We flew by them.

"What were you thinking?" Betty shrieked.

The big guy shrugged. "If they hit us, we would go under them. Their tires would have launched off the nose of this car like a rocket."

"No, they wouldn't," she said. "This car is all carbon fiber. It's made with torsional stiffness in one direction only, front to back. When their weight reached the center, this car would've imploded, collapsing both vehicles into a lump the size of a toaster."

Miguel stole a glance at her as he upshifted. I tried to get a look at her to see if she were serious, but I couldn't see past her shoulder.

After a few seconds driving on a relatively level road, Miguel said, "I think I missed our turn. Check the map."

I squirmed before determining what I already knew. "I can't reach my phone."

Betty shoved a hand in my pocket, pulled it out, and said, "Where are we going?"

"Aéroport Nice Côte d'Azur," Miguel said in perfect French. Showoff.

Betty played with the screen a moment. "You're right. That was our turn."

"Alternatives?"

"None."

He slammed on the brakes, clicked off the anti-skid and traction controls, slammed the accelerator, and shifted gears until the back tires squealed with burning rubber. He spun it around in the body length, then roared back the way we came.

The police truck had just backed out of the driveway when they saw us coming. They pulled back in to let us pass.

We exited the side road straight into the hairpin turn inches ahead of the lead vehicle chasing us. Now hot on our trail, a gunman leaned out to take potshots at us. The winding road didn't give him much chance and he wisely held his fire. But there were straightaways on the map Betty held out for Miguel to see. He nodded and kicked up the speed another notch.

I managed to tug my Sabel monocular out of my suit and got a look behind us.

"Who are they?" Miguel asked.

"First car, Slick and the Scots. Second car looks like Yeschenko. Third car … I don't know. I think it's that guy who owns that soccer team."

"Abromowitz?" Betty asked. She opened the glove box, fished around for the registration, read it, and slammed it shut. "Holy shit. You stole Abromowitz's car! He'll have us killed. We're going to die."

"Never say die," Miguel yelled. "Get the drone."

He pointed at the footwell while the tires screamed a high-pitched wail around the next corner.

Betty fumbled around between my calves before saying, "I can't reach it. I'm going to stand up. You get it."

Then, insane as it might seem, she stood up, just like she said she would. I wrapped my hand around her thighs to keep her from falling out as the next corner threatened to eject her like a watermelon seed at a spitting contest. She gave our pursuers a salute with both middle fingers.

When she dropped back into my lap, she moved to one side, allowing me to access my phone. I pulled up the drone app. Miguel handed her the flying machine. She held it aloft.

Bullets pinged off our back end.

"Don't worry about those," she said. "Torsional stiffness works in our favor against bullets."

She sounded reasonable although I had no idea if she was right. I turned the drone on. She launched it. Stabilizing it, I managed to bring it under control.

"Birdshit the lead car," Miguel shouted over the wind noise.

"Where?" I asked. "There's no control for bird shit."

"Right there." He was too busy spinning the steering wheel to point.

"Yeah," Betty said. "Right there where is says '*Fimum iacere*.'"

I looked at my phone. There were ten buttons. Nine in plain English and one that read, *Fimum iacere*. She leaned over and pressed it for me. The display showed a half gallon of goo splatter across Slick's windshield. His car slewed left, then right, then crashed into the retaining wall, spinning the oversized SUV across the roadway before it flopped on its side, blocking the road.

"Direct hit!" I announced.

Miguel slowed to a sane pace.

Betty twisted to look at me, her face full of disappointment. "You didn't study Latin? *Fimum iacere*: to throw shit."

"No, I speak Arabic and Pashto. It was useful in the wars."

Her disappointment didn't fade.

We drove the rest of the way in relative peace.

I called Isaiah and told him to leave Yuri on a street corner, bound but not gagged. I texted Yeschenko the address. Then I called the police in Cannes, which Yeschenko would be passing through on his way back to Monaco. I gave them Yeschenko's plate number and let them know he was kidnapping a Brazilian man, and that he wasn't supposed to be in France due to the international sanctions. I hadn't lied to the Russian; I gave him Yuri Belenov. But I couldn't let him keep the guy.

CHAPTER 27

WE LAY FLAT ON OUR bellies, peering over a ridge twenty miles outside a village called Kangerlussauq. Which is just north of the Arctic Circle on the western edge of the Greenland ice sheet. A hundred miles down the fjord to the west was either the Labrador Sea or Baffin Bay—the maps didn't distinguish where one began and the other ended. Two hundred more miles west lay a frozen and uninhabited piece of Canada. We were in a rocky, barren terrain covered in moss, lichen, and, where dirt accumulated, quick-growing short grasses and calf-high bushes. No trees. The forecast called for subfreezing temperatures overnight and a good chance of sleet.

The four of us shared two high-powered binoculars, keeping an eye on the hunting party half a mile down the slope from us.

Miguel handed me the massive binoculars and slid back down the muddy rise to where Isaiah waited. I nestled the mini-tripod in the dirt beneath my chin, lined up the viewing range, and dialed in the focus. I counted seven people: Griffith, two other European-looking guys, and four local Inuits. The latter I figured for hunting guides. Judging by the tents, cooking setup, rifles, and other equipment, they were expecting a large group to join them.

Three months ago, Griffith had invited Betty on an exclusive, expensive, and incredibly hard-to-set-up hunting expedition for musk ox. She found both hunting and Griffith disgusting and declined his invitation. After Monaco, she'd promised to tell me where to find him—but only if she rode along. Which I refused until Miguel overruled me because, without her, we had nowhere to go.

"That's him," Betty said too loudly.

I clamped a hand over her mouth, shoved her head down, and gave her my best shut-the-fuck-up glare. Sound travels ten times farther in the silent, featureless terrain. A whisper can travel hundreds of yards. You can hear a gunshot for miles. We'd discussed this before landing.

She nodded. I let go. She exhaled and mouthed, *sorry*.

She elbowed her way back to her mini-tripod and binoculars.

After a few minutes, I tugged her parka and nosed back at Miguel and Isaiah. We slithered down the low slope until we could stand up without being seen by our prey.

We hiked back to the glacier and through a narrow, blue-tinted ice channel. We emerged on the far side of a glacier finger as smooth as polished marble. The afternoon sun had warmed a significant stream that flowed from where ice met land. Our base camp was set up in a ravine just above the high-water mark.

I checked in with Emma and our support team. With clear skies, unearthly quiet, and miles of visibility, the small drones that worked for me in the city would last five seconds over Greenland. I'd requested a Sabel Weapons Systems drone. One of the big ones with missiles and machine guns normally reserved for the exclusive use of the military. Sometimes, there were test drones and others lying about. My request had been rebuffed by Sabel Weapons executives until Emma asked Ms. Sabel to approve it. Suddenly, they were moving quickly. Which was nice. Unfortunately, the available test drones were based in California, over three thousand miles away. With prep, refueling, and whatever else, two would arrive by morning.

Isaiah checked the sky for other people's drones. Miguel checked radio frequencies for monitoring devices. Both came back clean.

Joe Griffith did not subscribe to Stearne's Law. He had no early-warning system to let him know if assassins were in the neighborhood.

Isaiah squatted in front of a tent and lit up a propane burner to warm our dinner.

Betty said, "Why don't you break out that big sniper rifle and shoot the son of a bitch right now? Give it to me. I'll do it."

Miguel scoffed. "I said you could come along. I didn't say you could give us away by missing our target."

"I wouldn't miss," she hissed. "Believe me."

"It hasn't been dialed in for temperature, range, air density, and all that," I said. "It could be off by ten feet at that distance. You could kill one of the Inuit guides instead."

"Why did you bring it, then?"

"Because I expected to be out here with professionals who would know we needed to hike several miles away, calibrate it properly, double check it, and then follow him until he's a good distance from anyone else."

Isaiah stirred the stew. Miguel brought an oven out of his tent, squatted next to Isaiah, and began to preheat it.

"All right," she said, "let's do that."

Her voice had risen with her frustration. I put a finger to my lips. "There are no trees or bushes to stop sound waves from traveling—"

"I know," she stage-whispered. "Sorry. Just do whatever you have to and shoot him."

In a voice three notches quieter, I said, "I have to talk to him first."

"About what?" She put her hands on her hips and stuck out her jaw. "What kind of man lets a sick bastard like Joe Griffith walk around a free man? You killed those terrorists in France, you killed those terrorists in Germany. What's the holdup?"

"Look, I'm not your personal assassin who kills people on your orders. A couple times, I prevented imminent deaths because I could. This is different."

She crossed her arms and turned away. "Not for me it isn't."

Miguel and Isaiah pretended not to listen in. One stirred stew, the other baked biscuits.

"Why is that?" I asked Betty.

"I told you." She turned her back on me.

"No, you didn't," I said. "You told me a story. A good one with lots of sympathetic overtones ripped from the headlines. When are you going to tell me the whole story, Betty?"

"What's that supposed to mean?" She glared over her shoulder, her golden hair gleaming in the remaining sunlight.

"You said he threatened your *babulia.* Or did you forget? Most people would've wanted to make sure grandma was safe before they flew 2,500 miles into the Arctic."

She trembled, pulled her hood up, and turned away again.

I waited.

After two full minutes, she said, "No. He didn't threaten my *babulia*. I was visiting her when he threatened me. I turned myself into him before he found where I was staying. I didn't want him taking another family member hostage."

She shook her head as if arguing with herself about how much more she wanted to reveal. She faced me.

"Freshman year in high school," she said, "Joe Griffith told me I could make a big splash in the world. All I had to do was humor this English guy. Royalty, he said. A duke. I ..." She sniffled back some tears before composing herself. "Well, a couple years later, he was pressuring me to recruit my classmates. I couldn't live with it anymore. I told my dad. He went to Joe Griffith's house in Chicago—and never came back."

She cracked and sobbed. I let her work through it. After a minute, she pulled out of the dive and wiped her eyes.

"I sent the cops," she said. "I sent private investigators. Nothing."

"He has a crematorium on premise," I said.

"How do you—?" She snapped a curious glance my way. "Oh, that's right. You told me you went there to rescue someone. Too bad you didn't rescue my mother."

My brows rose.

"She bought his whole story," Betty said as tears rolled down her cheeks. "Didn't care that the man murdered her husband—because he's rich. She figures rich people can do whatever they want. She told me I was a prude. Said I should do as he says. It's all fine. She claimed a couple hundred years ago, she would've married me off to a prince by fourteen. He had her brainwashed. She's been helping him ever since."

"That's why you said you see yourself adrift in a lonely world."

She turned away again. "That's why I'm going to kill him."

I considered her story. I wanted to believe it. It rang true. But she was an actress and part of me remained cynical. That part felt bad for doubting her, but plenty of good people tell lies. And then there's

Stearne's Law: *Paranoia is the result of acute situational awareness.* Everyone really is trying to kill you.

"Now." She faced me with a huff. "What's your excuse? Why are you a hero to strangers at the top of a mountain in Germany but won't be my hero?"

"Risks."

She wrapped her arms around herself.

"I'll go into his camp tonight, extract him, set him in a chair, and ask him some questions about Rafael Tum. After he answers, I'm going to shoot him in the head."

"I'll do that part."

"No," I said. "You're not going on that mission."

"I can handle it. I interviewed mercenaries, I read up on heroes. None of them compare to you. You can do this for me. You have to do this for me. Put him in a chair and let me pull the trigger."

"Not happening."

"Why not?" she asked.

"You couldn't deal with the aftermath."

She stared at me, a list of unspoken questions crossing her face.

After a long, tense silence, Miguel said, "Hey, you two White Privilegers—the brown people made your supper."

With unspoken guilt, we sat and ate in relative silence.

Then it was time to recheck Griffith's camp. As far north of the Equator as we were, the sun never gets high in the sky. There were only four hours of darkness in early May. Even though we had a couple hours of daylight remaining, our shadows were long, the crevice through the ice was darker, and the breeze was colder. Clouds darkened the eastern sky.

We elbowed back up to the ridge. Miguel and I surveyed the area first.

Everything had changed. Several new vehicles had arrived carrying a lot of people. Seven six-wheeled ATVs and two regular ATVs shimmered the air with heat waves.

Griffith, wearing gloves and a parka worthy of the South Pole, stood with his men forming a circle around something. The Inuit guides were gone. Maybe setting up the next camp site farther into the wilderness. Griffith spoke to a tall, thin man with a shock of white hair. The newly arrived men wore body armor and carried automatic rifles.

Miguel switched off with Betty. She snugged the eyepieces to her face and watched.

I was about to hand mine over to Isaiah when something strange happened. The newly arrived men moved to one side, revealing nine other men kneeling in a row.

Betty whispered a question to me. I didn't hear it.

I said to her, "Give the binocs back to Miguel. Do it now."

She didn't move.

Joe Griffith pulled out a large SIG Sauer with an extended magazine. He stepped up to the first man in the row and put two bullets into the man's skull. His head jerked an instant before his body slumped. Two and a half seconds later, the reports reached us. Betty gasped. Stepping sideways, Griffith fired two more bullets into the next man.

Seamus McLeod knelt at the end of the line, stoically awaiting his fate.

I repeated, "Give the glass to Miguel. Now."

Betty didn't move.

Griffith made his way to the next man and repeated the execution.

After the fourth killing, Betty backed up at high speed and scrambled down the slope. When she got to the bottom, she stood up, leaned over, and puked her guts out.

I didn't need to watch the remaining executions. Griffith was finishing off the Scots for their failures.

I handed off my binocs to Isaiah and crawled back down until I reached Betty.

She gulped and heaved, swaying in place, eyes on a distant cloud.

I put an arm around her waist, holding her up. Her body vibrated with fear, anger, and revulsion. Another load came up and splashed at her feet. She dry heaved and gulped more air. Then she turned and buried her face in my parka. I wrapped her up and held her.

CHAPTER 28

HOURS LATER, WE SET OUT on our mission to capture Griffith. Betty would've been in a better mood if I'd hacked her leg off with a machete. She was not an operative, had never handled a weapon with live ammo, never trained with night vision, and still hadn't recovered from losing her stew. Miguel backed me up this time. So did Isaiah. We had no choice. She could not come with us.

We left her in an ice cave two hundred yards from camp at 0200. She had a direct line to Emma in case anything went wrong.

Fighting a strong, cold wind coming off the ice sheet, we made our way back to our ridge. Night vision only illuminates a hundred yards or so. With heat being rare on the open tundra, our low-resolution thermal imaging binoculars worked like a dream. It allowed us to make informed guesses based on lumps of heat signatures. The canvas hunting tents were like glass to our visors. The only thing we couldn't see through was insulating material, like ice chests. We scanned with thermal binoculars in different directions then regrouped below the ridge to discuss our findings.

The scene had changed again. Only five men remained in camp. Two were prone in a single tent, two more patrolled a wide area, another stood in the center tent. The lone figure appeared to be standing at a table while examining things on top. Since it was a hunting trip, it could be topographical maps.

"Not good," Miguel said. "We're missing more than half the party and all of the dead bodies."

"Burial detail?" I offered with little conviction.

"Permafrost," Isaiah said. "They'd need dynamite to dig more than six inches."

"They had to do something with nine bodies. Drag them off to the fjord, set them out for scavengers, maybe?"

Miguel said, "Maybe isn't good enough to bet your life on."

"The center guy has to be Joe Griffith," I said. "We agree on that, right?"

My companions nodded.

The wind picked up another notch, blowing toward Canada. The chill that came with it forced me to zip up my parka and tighten the hood.

Isaiah looked east. "Katabatic wind. We could be in for an ice storm."

"Where did a Marine learn a big word like that?" I asked.

"Ski trips with Dad. We went backcountry camping and skiing in the Canadian Rockies every year. Katabatic wind is when heavy air forms over the glaciers and falls downhill. This one feels wet. Like a big storm coming."

"Skiing's an expensive sport," I said.

Miguel shook his head and looked at me with utter disappointment.

"My dad's a surgeon." Isaiah patted my shoulder as if I were a school kid who'd just scored against his own team. "We don't all grow up in the ghetto."

If there had been any, I'd have crawled under a rock. Trying to save face, I asked, "So why the Marines?"

"I had no interest in med school," he said. "Dad suggested I serve my country after Dartmouth, and I liked that idea. I was planning to go to law school after my commission, but I discovered I liked releasing my pent-up rage in combat. Trouble was, I didn't care for the military so much. When I heard Jonelle Jackson was Sabel's CEO, I figured you guys would offer a good career path."

I was about to ask about his pent-up rage was about when names like Trayvon Martin, George Floyd, Ahmaud Arbery, and hundreds more flew through my mind. A company like Sabel Industries, run by a black woman, might not be perfect, but it offered him a better chance at fairness than many law firms.

"OK, so between the three of us, I'm the only one who didn't go to private school."

"And you're in charge," said Miguel, son of an aerospace executive, "because you're white."

"Then you can be in charge," I said.

"No." He grinned. "I like it better when you take the blame."

"Whatever. I'll go after Griffith; you guys create a diversion."

"That's such a bad idea," Miguel said. "You're not in charge anymore."

We looked to Isaiah for ideas. After all, he went to Dartmouth.

He glanced at us and shook his head, knowing he was on the spot. "We have to answer the obvious question before we march in there. Where are the other five? And then the more subtle questions about where the Inuits went. And of course, where are the bodies?"

Which was exactly what I was going to say. Probably.

We went in three different directions, comm links on but reserved for special reports to keep things quiet. Miguel jogged upstream, glacier side. Isaiah went downhill, fjord side. I went straight ahead to slip between the patrols and check out the campsite.

Our thermal combat suits were bulletproof and dissipated body heat through small exhausts. We'd barely register on thermal imaging systems. I moved down the ridge, wide open with nothing to hide behind and praying Sabel's engineers got the suit right.

When I came within range, I switched to my Sabel Visor, a combination of light amplification and high-resolution thermal. The patrols were on opposite ends of the camp heading outward.

I checked the tire tracks. The six-wheel ATVs Griffith had rented had different treads from the four-wheeled ones the Inuits used. There were two sets of four-wheeled ATV tire tracks heading back to town. Did Griffith send them home so they wouldn't witness Seamus's execution? If that was the case, what happened to hunting for musk ox?

There were three of Griffith's ATVs in camp. Four were missing.

Rounding the cooking area, I kept low to the picnic tables, examining the heat signatures in the tents. The men had moved positions, as if turning in their sleep. The lone figure in the central tent continued to pace. This close in, the heat signature was better defined. He appeared to hold a phone to his ear. Definitely Griffith. Who else would be making calls this deep in the night?

Isaiah's voice came over the comm link. "Caribou herd two miles south of their camp. The guides's tire tracks indicate they went to town. Nothing else in sight. Heading back."

Miguel reported next. "Three miles north and I've found three ATVs. No men, no bodies. Footprints lead to an ice field a quarter mile east. There's no warmth left in the footprints; they don't show on thermal. If they did that on purpose, it was a clever move. I can't track them until daylight. But no drag marks anywhere. That means we're still missing nine bodies."

Mercury said, *Whazzat tell ya, homie?*

I nearly jumped to Mars. *Don't sneak up on me like that.*

Mercury patted my back like he was burping a baby. *If you apply that paranoia rule of yours, they're out there on the ice for a reason. If it's not burying the Scots, what is it?*

I said, *Can you just tell me the answer?*

Mercury looked like he smelled rotting meat. *C'mon now, no cheating. If I tell you the secrets of the universe, you'd go blabbing it to everyone. Some people would believe you and sing your praises. They'd start worshipping you and calling non-believers heretics. Next thing you know, they're burning people at the stake, invading foreign lands, stealing all the world's treasures—and telling everybody I told 'em it was cool. Nah. Been there, done that.*

Regardless of his non-answer, his question burned in my mind. That's when I saw the meat lockers. Just beyond the normal camp kitchen with scent-sealed, bear-proof coolers sat four refrigerator-sized meat lockers. Meant for big game meat like musk ox, they could easily hold two or three Scots each. I'd solved the Scottish question.

Mercury said, *You solved it? Excuse me? What am I, a potted plant? Bro, props here. Huh? A hug? A dap? Anything? No? OK fine, then tell me this. I told you Betty Bardon was smart. I told you to work with her. When did I tell you to bring her to the Arctic Circle?*

I said, *No choice. She wouldn't tell us where he was unless we brought her.*

Mercury said, *Well you're the white man in charge, which means you shoulda lied to her. Get the location, then send her home on that fancy sled Pia-Caesar-Sabel lends you. What were you thinking?*

I said, *I was thinking you were right about her being smart.*

Mercury said, *And now she's a liability. A huge liability. A really, really huge—*

I get it, OK? She's safe for now. We've got that handled. I don't need your help.

Oh izzat so? Mercury faded into the night.

I never know what he's talking about. All I know is that I'm a constant disappointment to my god.

I went back to thinking about the problem at hand: Where did the five men on three ATVs go? Night hunting? Miguel was three miles away. The men were farther out. At that distance, the five were no threat. There were two on guard duty, and two asleep, leaving Joe Griffith alone.

One more sweep of the perimeter told me the patrols were both heading back to camp. They were making an arc of a hundred yards. Both men had eyes in my direction. If I returned to rendezvous with Miguel and Isaiah, there was a solid chance they would see me crossing the open tundra. The moonlight was weak, but the area was featureless, and I didn't look like a caribou. My best chance for escape—and the riskiest—would be to take Griffith hostage.

Whispering into the comm link, I told my squad, "I'm going after Griffith."

"No!" Miguel and Isaiah replied in unison.

"We don't know where five men and one ATV are," Miguel said. "It's suicide."

"No choice," I said. "Patrols are heading straight for me."

Holding my rifle at the ready, I marched into Griffith's tent.

He stood in the center greeting me with open arms. "Welcome, Jacob. Good to see you finally decided to come in from the cold."

CHAPTER 29

MIGUEL RODRIGUEZ STOOD AT THE top of a ten-foot-high finger of glacier when his heart stopped beating. Griffith's calm welcome of Jacob—live streamed through their comm link—threw all their conceptions about the mission out the window. A claw of guilt reached inside his gut and crushed everything into a compressed lump. They'd made a huge miscalculation.

It was the biggest miscalculation Miguel had made since telling his dad, in a fit of teen rage, that he didn't want to study astronomy anymore and instead joined the army. Once enlisted, he'd found the same rage-release in battle as Isaiah and embraced it. After seeing Jacob Stearne in action, he found his calling: saving the world. Even if it meant being a white man's sidekick. But now, all those life decisions were in peril.

Jacob had walked into a trap.

"Isaiah," he whispered into the comm link as he checked the landscape around him for the missing five Knights.

"I heard. What was he thinking? Is he trying to get himself killed? He should've waited for us."

"Wouldn't have mattered," Miguel said. "This is no hunting trip. This was an ambush from the get-go."

"I thought you said this guy doesn't get shot."

"He hasn't." Miguel looked around for the quickest way off the ice. "Yet. We need to get him out of there. Are you still two miles south?"

"Yes, and you're three north." Isaiah sighed. "Do they have a drone we didn't see? How did they time this so well?"

"No drone." Miguel found the edge of the ice and jumped to the ground. "This is old-school hunting. They knew we would come for

Griffith. They were expecting us."

"We relied on modern technology and they went by what, sense of smell?"

"That and known behaviors. Everyone knows Jacob and I were Rangers."

The Katabatic wind picked up speed, whipping Miguel's thermal suit. If it flapped his, it would flap the Knights' as well. He listened. All he heard was a storm in the distance.

Isaiah stayed quiet a beat until he understood Miguel. "They knew you guys were trained for zero-dark-thirty operations. They planned on us attacking by night—the way Rangers always do."

"Exactly." Miguel started out at a full run. "I'm heading there now. If we move in a pincer from our separate directions, we can take down …"

"I'm on my way," Isaiah said, his breathing picking up.

Miguel stopped and looked at the loose dirt in front of him. He said, "Damn. Hold up."

"What is it?"

"There were three ATVs, but only two sets of real footprints."

"What does that mean?" The sound of Isaiah's footfalls stopped. "How can you tell?"

"They walked backwards in places to make it look like four or five people. They only did it on the soft dirt where I'd see it but not examine it closely. Now that I'm on my way back, it shows up like a neon sign. The tracks look like the letter N if you visualize them from a bird's eye."

"Why would they do that?" Isaiah asked.

"Had to be a good reason. Let's think this through. They made it look like five were gone, two were sleeping, and two were on patrol. In reality, there were only two gone, leaving three unaccounted for."

"I see what you're saying," Isaiah said. "If we charge into Griffith's tent, three of them are going to pop out of somewhere. That's what happened to Jacob. They hid behind insulating material so they wouldn't show up on thermal imaging. They're one step ahead of us."

"We put our heads together, we can out-think them. Why did the two go across the ice?"

They both stood still nearly five miles apart, listening to the wind and

Jacob's conversation with Griffith coming through the comm link.

"Jacob doesn't seem to be in immediate danger," Isaiah said. "They're talking."

"If Griffith didn't shoot him right off, he's not going to. And that raises a big question: Why not?"

"Does he have some other way to leverage Jacob?" Isaiah asked.

As soon as the question left his mouth, they both knew the answer. In unison, they said, "Betty."

"I don't know him like you," Isaiah said, "but I'm guessing he lost his woman on a mission like this. He won't let that happen again."

"You're closer to her ice cave," Miguel said. "Go get her before the Knights who crossed the ice get there. I'll try to free Jacob."

"On my way." Isaiah's footfalls resumed, bolting across the tundra.

Lightning flashed across the eastern sky. The sound of hail on ice came to him. In the bitter cold night, an ice storm barreled their way.

Miguel ran to the ATVs. They had motorcycle handlebars, a single seat in the middle, and a large cargo area that dominated the back. Two Knights couldn't ride three, so one had been brought up after a long walk back. Leaving them under a time crunch. That's when mistakes are made. He checked all three. Sure enough, one of the ATVs had keys in it. He checked the compartments and found what he needed: a small bungee cord.

Miguel had long admired how Barboncito, Crazy Horse, and Sitting Bull waged battle: Fearless, heading straight in like a game of chicken. The first one to blink died. He fired up the ATV, letting the noise roll across the frozen grass and rock. Let them know the Native was on his way to the rescue. Coming straight at them.

Riding it at a good clip, he made sure to drive it no faster than he could run. He let the headlight play across the ground. Nothing presented itself as a target over the first mile. In the second, the tracks ran through a low canyon with sides ground smooth by glaciers. Stearne's Law crept into his mind. Shadows on the ridge above him looked like monsters. Dips in the ground looked like tank traps. At his steady speed, he kept his rifle ready in his left hand and his legs coiled, ready to jump off at any moment.

He could hear Jacob and Griffith shouting in his earbud, but the conversation was obscured by the engine beneath him.

As the canyon widened, Miguel wound the bungee cord around the throttle and made it tight. Stretching out the other end, he felt for a place to hook it and found a couple options. He rode tall in the saddle, his eyes scouring the ground ahead for Knights of Mithras.

CHAPTER 30

I STOOD VERY STILL, NOT wanting to spook the three Knights holding rifle muzzles to my head. One behind, one on the left, the other on the right. They were incredibly efficient. I'd entered the tent leading with my rifle to push through the double-layered entry used in cold climes. Before I could acquire my target, they'd stepped out of insulated blinds and wrenched the muzzle from my grip. Joe Griffith remained alive for now. He stood directly in front of me and talked like a meth addict, ninety miles an hour. I wasn't listening. I was trying to hear what Miguel and Isaiah had figured out. With Griffith yammering on, and Miguel and Isaiah piecing things together, I found it hard to focus on any single voice.

I figured out Isaiah went to save Betty, which was good. They shouldn't waste time helping me. I was quite content to die here. What I worked over in my head was how to take Griffith with me.

The noise of the ATV through the comm link told me what Miguel was doing. He was coming to save me, and there was nothing I could do to stop him. The roar of the motor cancelled out further communications.

I started listening to Griffith while thoughts of him using underage women like Betty Bardon to line his pockets ran through my head.

I said, "You're talking too fast, Griffith. This is all new to me. Take me through your story again."

He sighed, pulled out a chair, and sat, legs crossed. With a finger, he instructed his well-trained Finns.

One of the Knights pushed a chair to the back of my knee and pulled my shoulder back. I had no choice but to sit. They readjusted their barrels, keeping them in contact with my head. I'd made a lot of daring and miraculous escapes in my day, but these guys weren't giving me an inch to operate.

"Listen carefully, Jacob." Griffith said in professorial tone. "The industrial revolution began with coal. In the beginning, the coal barons ruled the world. Then the Rockefellers displaced them with oil. In time, the Arabs replaced the Rockefellers. Today, thanks to climate change, humanity stands at a crossroads. Every nation in the world is seeing the effects already. Iceland has invested in deep-water ports for when climate change makes the Northwest Passage a reality. They think that will happen in the next ten years. Chinese cities are so choked with coal soot, they've committed to going all-electric by 2030. Everyone knows clean energy is the future.

"The generation of it is easy: solar, wind, nuclear, tidal, geo-thermal—take your pick. But the future will not belong to those who produce energy. It's too cheap and easy now. No, the future kings, the next Rockefeller, will be the man who holds the patent on storing it."

"You mean, the lithium-ion battery?" I asked. "Several people and companies were involved in developing that. It's in all the electric cars made today and—"

"Yes, yes, yes." He threw up his hands as if tired of hearing the Li-ion argument. "Lithium-ion rules storage today. It's a forty-year-old technology, Jacob. It's explosive, it has a limited number of recharges, it weighs a ton, and it's made from rare earth materials. It's not the future. Think, man. There has to be something better out there that has the potential to change the world."

"And you found it?" Skepticism dripped from my question.

"Not yet. No one has. But many are looking. That's where you come in." Griffith leaned back with a smug look.

I pursed my lips and frowned. "You think I know how to build a better battery?"

"Every invention requires an army of people to build its temple. Each person carries a brick to be put in place. I have a master plan for my temple of energy storage. And you, my good man, have the potential to lay the cornerstone."

"Potential?"

He leaned forward, put his elbows on his knees, and clasped his hands. "Your mother is a drummer of some regard. I find that fascinating. How a farm wife in the middle of nowhere-Iowa is remembered fondly from Montreal to New Orleans is remarkable. And your sister gave up touring to plant corn. How does that happen?"

That he knew about my parents was not shocking. Mom and Dad have been immortalized on Wikipedia. My sister Joyce wailed on her trumpet but hated the idea of being a jazz musician. The constant weekend road trips were bad enough when we were young teens, but what she hated most was being billed as a novelty rather than an accomplished artist. Not many women blow the horn. By the time she went to college, she would only play in the living room with the family. That he knew about Joyce meant one thing: Griffith had done a lot of homework. Which was meant to intimidate me. And it was working. Were it not for the rifles pressed to my scalp, I would've strangled the man.

I shrugged in response.

"You've had quite a ride as a hero, Jacob. The local papers from Iowa City to Dubuque describe the time your family homestead was shot to pieces in a small war between you and five criminals—and only you survived. Astonishing. No doubt you could do it again. Especially if you were defending your family against the likes of hired Creoles from New Orleans or Seamus McLeod and his unfortunate Scottish brigade."

A couple years back, some Creole gangsters made the mistake of taking a contract to kill me. At the time, I was staying with my folks when the Creoles decided to earn their commission. After exchanging several hundred rounds, I was alive and the Creoles weren't. In a small town like Donnellson, Iowa, a shootout like that got around. But the story never made it to the big cities like St. Louis or Chicago. How did Griffith know?

"There were only four Creoles," I said. "It wasn't that big a deal."

"So modest." He smiled like a snake. He pointed at the men who hadn't wavered their aim a millimeter since popping out of their hiding places. "Nonetheless, you've noticed my Finns already outwitted you. And I only brought a squad. There's a whole battalion of them in

Lapland dying to lay waste to your pastoral family farm. I can do that tomorrow, or next week, next month, next year—you know you can't maintain a secure perimeter forever."

I glanced up at my adversaries. His mention of northern Finland explained why they were in single layers instead of bundled for the cold like the rest of us. They weren't even wearing gloves. No body fat, intense eyes, muscles that didn't bulge from lifting weights but rippled from hours of hard work. These were a far cry from any other Knight I'd seen. They were hardened killers. They'd been training for a long time.

"I foiled your tunnel into the Sabel Ops Center. I'll find—"

"What the devil are you talking about?"

"You dug a tunnel from half a mile away trying to get into our company warehouse."

Griffith looked disgusted. "You think I need to steal body armor and those ridiculous little darts you love to poke people with? Please. As you can see, we don't need your fancy technology to beat you. We do it with our wits. You're impressed, admit it."

He sounded sincere about the Ops Center. Confirmation of what I'd already guessed: that it wasn't the Knights. But if it wasn't them, who was it?

"OK," I said. "I'm impressed, Joe. What is this potential I have?"

"What I want from you is simple. Rafael Tum has something that belongs to me. He trusts you. I want you to get close to him. Find what is mine and bring it to me."

I've always admired how rich people believe that if they want something you have, they first convince themselves that you stole it. In this case, I'd known the professor for a couple months but doubted he kept anything belonging to someone else. I'd never seen him in possession of anything more than his own clothes.

"Whoa," I said. "You've got a lot of unpacking to do there, Griffith. What does he have? Why do you think he trusts me after he lied to me on several occasions? And, the big question, what's in it for me?"

"In reverse order, there's a fortune in it for you. But you won't believe me, so we'll come back to that when you have leverage and reason to trust me. In his defense, Rafael never lied to you. He omitted a few things at my request. At the time, I held his war crimes pardon over his head. The pardon's gone through now, so he has no reason to hide things from you in the future."

When he finished answering two of my three questions, he waited for me to bite. I remained insistent on the third question. "And what does he have that you want me to steal?"

"Not steal, Jacob. Let me make that perfectly clear. It's mine. It is called the Chaac Equation. It cannot be described. When he trusts you, he will show it to you. He cannot help himself in that regard. When that happens, you will recognize it and you will return it to me."

"The thing I was supposed to bring for ransom?"

"I knew you didn't have it." An evil grin spread across his face. "If you'd had it, you would've left Rafael to die."

A lightbulb went off in my head. "That's why Seamus said you wanted to talk to me. You wanted to make a deal. Why not just ask me?"

"Seriously?" He laughed. "You hate me. I need someone relentless who will do whatever it takes. It didn't have to be you. But you were the one who answered the call. And kept answering it. Like tonight."

He had me there. My blind hatred of him led me straight into his trap. And now I was in it. "How does this Chaac Equation make you king of the future?"

"It is the key to a new form of electrical storage. It's unlike any battery we have today. It stores a thousand times more energy. Whoever holds the patent will be the new Rockefeller."

"The king of energy storage."

"Indeed." He smiled broadly. "And you will be one of my princes."

The bargain was my mother's life to betray Rafael Tum, a likable man with a sordid history and no loyalty to me. Not a difficult decision. As much as it sickened me to let the man responsible for Jenny's death live, I could go along with it for now. I wanted to kill him right then, but the Finns wouldn't let me get to my feet alive. I would hunt him down later.

"How long will it take him to trust me enough to show me this thing?" I asked.

In the distance, I could hear an ATV approaching.

"He already trusts you. You saved him."

"So the kidnapping was a setup?"

Griffith shrugged. "Call it what you will. It worked out for both of us. He trusts you now. Seek him out, buy him a drink. He will take you into his confidence. He must. He has no one else."

I saw no reason to tell him Rafael already wanted me to join his tribe.

"OK," I said. "I'll do it."

The ATV roared ever nearer. Miguel, channeling Crazy Horse, was charging into the camp, head-on and fearless. There has never been a braver man.

One of the Finns looked up, alerted to the sound. The other two held their weapons tight to my head, trusting their brother to check on the threat. Perfect teamwork. Formidable enemies.

"Not so fast," Griffith said. "You're a smart man who—by now—has figured out three ways to screw me in this deal. So naturally, you'll need some skin in this game."

Griffith rose and pulled a pistol from his parka, squeezed his gloved finger inside the trigger guard, and aimed it at me.

Outside, Miguel opened fire with his automatic rifle.

CHAPTER 31

GRIFFITH WAS NOT A BATTLE-HARDENED veteran like his Finns. He freaked at the sound of Miguel's bullets ripping through his tent. He dropped to the floor, pale and shaking. His Finns did not. One bullet bounced off a Knight's body armor and landed in my lap. Another took a round to the shoulder and shrugged it off.

One of the Knights glanced at the entrance and exit patterns, lined up where they were coming from, adjusted for the speed of the ATV, and fired blind through the side of the tent. Not perfect, but a better and quicker deterrent than running outside and starting over. I was impressed.

The ATV's engine accelerated suddenly, sounding like it was coming straight for the tent. Knowing Miguel, he'd fired, rigged the throttle wide open, and jumped off. Most people would follow the ATV, allowing him to come up behind them.

A flash of lightning lit up the tent and silhouetted the Knight out front.

The Finns didn't work like most people. One stayed with me, pushing my head with his rifle to let me know he was there. One went out the front door while the third leapt over Griffith and rolled to the back of the tent.

To warn Miguel, I said, "Your man just rolled out an escape hatch in the back. That's clever, Griffith."

Through the comm link, Miguel said, "Thanks. I'm tracking him."

The ATV zoomed past the tent, the Doppler effect telling me it was going in a straight line flat-out. Five seconds later, we heard a thump, like a tire hitting a rock. The sound changed to that of a small airborne vehicle with a wide-open throttle, then it crashed to the ground. The engine cut off in a clatter of broken metal and plastic.

In the comm link, Isaiah said, "They have Betty. From what I saw in the ice cave, she put up a fight. I see ATV tracks on the far side of our campsite. They have more wheels than we realized. They're a few minutes ahead of me."

As he spoke, the sound of two ATVs reached us. They were inbound and coming fast.

My host regained a little composure and got to his hands and knees. Looking at me, he became angry that I witnessed his moment of cowardice. With a glare, he staggered to his feet and aimed his pistol. Then his ears registered the approaching ATVs. He smiled, comforted by the return of his Knights. He resumed his large-and-in-charge persona and lowered the pistol.

Outside, Miguel and one of the Finns exchanged fire for a moment in syncopation with a round of lightning.

The ATVs slid to a stop outside and shut down.

Suddenly, everything was silent but the wind.

Two men came in holding Betty between them. They shoved her, bound and gagged, to Griffith's feet. Her face landed on his shoes. With wild, wide-open eyes, she screamed in her gag and struggled to her knees.

Griffith grabbed her arm and helped her up. "Betty, I'm disappointed in your decision to join forces with Jacob."

Her distinct but muffled "fuck you" made him smile.

"Her decision to join us?" I asked with cynicism. "You knew we were coming. Who else could've told you besides her?"

He was about to respond when the sound of something bad came to our ears. The Finns and I recognized it at the same time. Betty and Griffith had never heard a stampede before. Isaiah's herd of caribou were heading straight toward us from the south.

The Finns exchanged glances, telepathically discussing tactics to deal with the problem and assigning roles. Two men ran out, the one guarding me explained the situation to Griffith. "Caribou stampede. We need to go right now."

Outside, the Finns fired in the air to ward off the panic-stricken animals. Even if they were successful, the approaching storm could spook the herd right back in our direction.

"Sorry guys," Isaiah's voice came over the comm link. "I set charges around the herd before I left the area. I thought they might come in handy. I realize it's incredibly dangerous, but I couldn't think of any other way to counterbalance their numbers."

"You done good," Miguel answered him. "The gods always look out for Jacob."

Griffith raged at me. "You think she did this? You think I would rely on a woman for intelligence? My network is extensive! I have eyes and ears all over the world! No, she merely played a part. She was supposed to slow you down so we could catch you in Brest. She failed. She has no more value to me than she does to Hollywood."

"Sir?" The Finn raised his voice. "We must go. Now. Right now."

Griffith steamed, his face red, the veins in his eyes popping out. "I'll show you what she's worth to me."

He pushed her an arm's length away and shot her in the chest. Dead center. Point blank.

Betty's eyes blew open in shock. She staggered back a step and fell to the ground on her butt.

He turned to me and shot me in the chest. "Now go do as you're told. Get me what I want. You have a week."

I fell out of the chair, writhing in pain. My state-of-the-art liquid-metal body armor saved my life, but the impact equaled taking a baseball bat in the chest. Betty groaned a few feet away.

A second after he stormed out, the man who'd held a rifle to my head bolted after him. Outside, the ATVs raced away.

Miguel rolled in the escape hatch at the back. He cleared the room, saw Betty, then checked out front. When he was certain Griffith and the Finns were gone, he went straight to Betty.

I struggled up on one elbow. The stampede was close. Way too close.

Mercury stood over me, his arms crossed and a scowl that would shrink a believer. *Mm-mm-mm. What am I looking at here?*

I said, *Not now.*

Mercury said, *Oh yes, now. D'you ever read them Bible stories about the wrath of god? Same goes for the wrath of the Roman gods. Especially seeing as how my wife is being held as collateral and you said, 'I don't need no help.'*

I said, *Please. I'm in pain here. Besides, I never use the double negative. I might've said—*

Don't matter what you said exactly. Mercury strutted around the room with the wings on his little sandals flapping. *What matters is you need my help all a sudden or you gonna be reindeer feed.*

I said, *Caribou.*

Are you messing with me? You gonna be correcting me at a time like this? Do you need my help, or do you want to take your chances with four thousand hooves?

I need your help, I said. *Please.*

Mercury said, *Are you gonna listen to me next time I tell you something?*

I said, *Probably. I'll try. You make it hard sometimes.*

I make it hard? Mercury's scowled deepened.

Thundering hooves came straight at us. They charged at full speed. The lead animals tracked around the back. Some animals were caught up in the guy lines of nearby tents. Their pained wails echoed through the camp. The herd kept coming, trampling a few of their own in the process.

Miguel kept working on Betty. She cried out in pain when her gag came off. She stifled it when the exertion caused her even more pain.

Mercury said, *Aight then, Ima let you have a freebie this time. I placed a big bet on you, and I need my wife back. Which means you gotta stay alive—and quit DOING STUPID SHIT, homie.*

With that, he disappeared.

Hundreds of hooves pounded the ground around us, shaking the tent poles and rattling the fixtures. The tables and chairs danced from the seismic rumble.

After several terrorizing minutes, it began to die down. Stragglers came after, still in numbers, still charging fast, but with less energy. The aging members of the herd.

Betty screamed in pain. Miguel apologized.

Isaiah's voice came over the comm link. "Hang on, I'm almost there.

Oh my god. All the tents are destroyed. Oh god, I'm so sorry."

"We're fine," Miguel said.

"Where are you?" Isaiah asked.

"Griffith's tent," I said and let out a groan as I got to my feet.

"Can't be," Isaiah said. "This place looks like a bomb ... wait. There's one tent untouched. Is that where you guys are?"

He ran in the front door, throwing back the flap and stopping immediately. He stared at me with moon-sized eyes popping out of his head. He took in Miguel and Betty.

I stood, gripping the table to steady my stance while my chest screamed in pain. "Stampede was a great idea."

"Broken manubrium," Miguel said to me, referring to the top bone of Betty's sternum where the ribcage comes together in front. The military trains combat soldiers to deal with traumatic injuries. He pointed at her chest. "Armor on these winter suits has a weak spot right there. We need an air evac."

CHAPTER 32

JOE GRIFFITH FELT THE C-130 transport aircraft sliding across the glacier before lifting into the air. Joona Forss and his brigade knew how to mount an operation against the vaunted Sabel Security team, that much was certain. All their gear was stowed aboard the craft. Their tracks swept clean as the ice storm poured glaze ice across the landscape. They were never there.

Joona brought him a mug of coffee and handed it to him.

Griffith took it and smiled at the Knight. "Well done, Joona. Give my compliments to the men."

Joona nodded without any further expression and walked down the cavernous cargo hold.

Pulling his laptop, Griffith prepared his report in his mind before beginning to type. This should bring him back into the board's good graces. Things were on track. Triumph was in sight. After typing a paragraph, he deleted his overly optimistic opening and started again. He'd given Jacob Stearne a week, to which the man too readily agreed, as predicted. Stearne planned to betray them, a duplicity they would use against him.

Griffith estimated Stearne would need two weeks to complete his quest. Stearne would spend the first week looking for a way out. In the second, with pressure mounting and things like photographs of his sleeping family members texted to him, he would act quickly. Even so-called-heroes had weak spots. They tended to care too much about others.

Griffith re-read his report, made a few adjustments, and pressed "send."

His thoughts ran back to his own family. Stearne would miss his people. Joe Griffith hadn't shed his fast enough. After years of beating his three children, his alcoholic father succumbed to cirrhosis. There wasn't much of a funeral. Three teenagers struggling to pay the medical bills had no interest in paying an undertaker even more. On cue, their absent mother showed up, asking about inheritance. When his older brother took over the liquor cabinet to fill his father's shoes, Joe started booking his fifteen-year-old sister at strip clubs. At least she brought in enough for his tuition before she elevated herself to "independent sex worker" and struck out on her own. He wouldn't have guessed either one of his siblings ever read the *Journal,* but the minute his profile as a successful fund manager hit the front page, they both showed up with empty palms outstretched. Fuck them.

If he and Jacob Stearne reversed roles, and Jacob threatened Griffith's family, he would've laughed in the man's face.

Stearne hadn't laughed. Not at all. He'd calculated the skill of the men who'd subdued him and paid attention. His casual shrug was betrayed by his loss of color. The man cared about his sister, Joyce. Far from a sex-worker, Joyce Stearne was engaged to the local sheriff, Louis Kirby, and ran the largest organic farm in the Midwest. A remarkable businesswoman, if the Cedar Rapids *Gazette* was any judge of such picayune things. And the parents? Taking a back seat to their charging daughter, on the verge of retirement. Waiting to shower their love on grandchildren as they had on Joyce and Jacob. Sickening.

The Duke of Kingston sent a reply to Griffith's report. Before he opened it, he checked the time. London was three hours behind him, so it's one in the morning there. It seemed the young Duke was a night owl. The reply was short and terse. "That Sabel woman will do anything to protect Stearne's family. What precautions have you taken?"

Griffith double-checked his encryption, not wanting any details spilling out over the internet. They'd only recently confirmed their new system was safe from the prying eyes of Sabel Technologies, the NSA, and the rest. He replied that Joona's men were already operating a trucking company outside of Iowa City with regular routes to Fort Madison. The trip took them past Stearne Farms four times a day, with the first before dawn and the last at dusk. A parallel team had been set up going the opposite direction. One of the outfits took a more public stance, intending to distract Jacob or anyone the Sabel woman sent for protection. He sent it.

The Duke replied almost immediately. "What about Betty Bardon? Is she pulling her weight?"

Betty had done some things asked of her and then gone rogue. Should he tell the Duke that? Unnecessary. She would soon come back into the fold. She had before. As much as she loathed Griffith, who else could help her get what she wanted? And she wanted it bad.

Things were on track, leaving no need to include the board on every detail. They would only use it against him later. Yet the Duke required a response. Could Betty still be properly motivated?

Griffith thought carefully before typing his reply. "Betty Bardon is an unknown quantity. Does she still care about her mother? It's anyone's guess. The two women had a tumultuous relationship before Betty cut it off."

The Duke replied, "You job is not to guess. Your job is to make things happen."

Griffith stared at that one for a moment. Then the system erased the message as part of the security system. It rankled him, but he couldn't let that show. He carefully explained that he had leveraged the actress to the breaking point. Any additional threats may overwhelm her and make her immune to them altogether.

The Duke replied, "Then send the girl one of her mother's fingers. That should make her pay attention."

CHAPTER 33

"HOW THE HELL DID YOU survive the stampede?" Isaiah's gaze traveled to Miguel. "Is this what you were talking about? Become the man's shadow because the gods favor him?"

Miguel rose. "You need to get her flat so she can breathe."

"You're doing just fine right—"

"You're the new guy."

Isaiah managed to calm Betty with a silky voice and reassurances that she would survive. From past experience with a broken sternum, I knew it felt a lot closer to dying than Isaiah realized. Every breath, no matter how small, brings incredible pain. But the new guy had her breathing with her diaphragm in no time. It made a huge difference.

Betty summoned me with her hand. When I knelt next to her, she whispered, "You saved me. You're my—"

"Don't talk," I said. "The extra breathing hurts. And no, I didn't save you. I let you come with us. Big mistake."

"You're going to get him?"

"Yes. But that's a battle for another day. Stay quiet, rest."

Isaiah spoke to her in soothing tones. He should've followed his father into medicine—he had a great bedside manner.

Emma took the opportunity to chime in on the comm link. She said, "I've made calls to emergency facilities in Greenland. Help is on the way. When the man threatened your family, I dispatched a team from the Chicago office to Stearne Farms. They should be onsite in two hours."

"Make it an *invisible wall operation*," I said. My family would kill me if I brought a deadly threat to their doorstep a second time. The invisible wall kept our people out of sight without alerting anyone local to the danger.

"That requires more people," Emma said. "I'll work it out."

She clicked off.

Miguel and I went to survey the damage outside. As we stepped through the double entryway, Miguel pointed to the brand name on the insulating flap: Sabel Security. A quick glance around and I understood why the contents of the campsite hadn't attracted my full attention. It was familiar, and therefore normal background. All of it Sabel gear.

We stepped through to the bitter cold.

Sleet was still coming down. A layer of ice covered everything in sight. The camp had been leveled, including the oversized ice chests. Strewn across an acre around us lay the trampled bodies of nine Scots.

Miguel led us to his crashed ATV. Squatting to open one of the storage compartments, he pulled out a destroyed first aid kit with a Sabel Security logo on it. Disgusted, he tossed it back, stood, and studied the terrain. "It was a setup from the beginning, Jacob. I heard you ask him, and I heard his reply. But he might be covering for Betty. So tell me, do you think she told him we were coming?"

Crouching next to the ATV, I gauged the weight at a thousand pounds.

"Sabel Security doesn't have a Greenland office," I said.

He knew what I meant. The equipment had been stolen elsewhere and brought in. And that meant planning and logistics had been done days in advance. If Betty had divulged information about us, it had only confirmed what Griffith already knew: that I'd come after him anywhere he went.

Miguel walked south, following the trail of the Inuit ATVs. He stopped twenty yards away and called back to me. "I saw these same tracks coming in from the side of the canyon north of here. The Inuits weren't guides. They were locals who stopped to say hello."

Unlike city people, those who live in the middle of nowhere always stop and talk to strangers. In the wilds, people need each other. If something went wrong for either party, if someone broke a leg, or someone never came back, there would be someone who would sound the alarm. That's how people were back in the small towns of the

American Midwest—neighborly. They were even more so out here where everyday life depended on people helping each other.

He tromped back to where I stood.

"Griffith set this scenario in motion when Betty was with us in Monaco," I said.

"You can't rule out the possibility her job was to lead us to the slaughterhouse."

"No. I can't." I picked up a broken piece of ATV, looked at it, and tossed it back. "But she didn't fake puking her guts out when he executed the Scots."

"True that," he said. "And he shot her. If she was his mole before, she won't be anymore."

"Maybe," I said.

"Hey. Going into Griffith's tent was a dumb move on your part."

I didn't answer. Maybe I'd been too quick to dismiss Mercury. Maybe I'd been too focused on *mortis honore*. Either way, I'd endangered the team. They deserved better.

Emma called with an update. Paramedics had been summoned but would have to come from Nuuk, an hour by air from Kangerlussauq and another hour's drive away from our location. The ice storm had grounded all air evac in our area. They planned to stabilize Betty and wait for the weather to clear because the bumpy overland trail was no place to haul a broken sternum.

I asked Emma, "Please check for any Sabel Security offices that have been robbed lately. I'm thinking one of our facilities is missing several ATVs, Arctic camping gear, all kinds of things."

"The Hudson Bay office was cleaned out three days ago." Emma hesitated a moment. "There's one other thing you should know. The team picked up some chatter on Greenland's police radios. They believe you executed the Scots. Griffith set you up for it. I've alerted the company lawyers, but they'll be working out of Denmark."

She left us on that note.

"We're going to need help getting out of this one," I said.

Miguel studied me. "How did you leave things with your buddy, Neville Townsend?"

"I wasn't nice."

He nodded and picked up a piece of camp stove. "You know the State Department has a consulate in Nuuk."

"No." I did a double take. "How do you know?"

"It's right next to the Inuit Cultural Center. First peoples stick together." He grinned. "Common enemy."

"OK, I've got a couple hours before I have to beg Neville for help. Let's see if we can find anything to back up our story."

We walked silently through ground churned by caribou hooves. We found what might've been Seamus' body. It was so badly disfigured, it was hard to tell. When we reached the end of the camp, we stopped. Nothing had presented itself as useful in our legal defense.

We looked back across the devastation at the light glowing from inside the lone tent.

"We haven't gotten our asses kicked like that since Nuristan Province," the big guy said. He started back to Betty and Isaiah. "Was it worth it?"

"We learned we're up against some dedicated Finns." I checked out a bear-proof storage locker, its Sabel logo the only part still intact. "Where did they learn their tactics?"

"According to their recruitment brochure, the Knights have been around for thousands of years." Miguel glanced at the clouds as the sleet let up. "They must keep in practice through mercenary operations. Most likely, they've fought with and against Rangers. They know our methods. They knew our electronic perimeter is a hundred yards and they stayed well outside that range."

His assessment felt spot-on to me. The Finns were used to barren tundra and knew they could see two hundred yards without alerting us to their presence. They also knew we wouldn't use drones. I said, "And they know we'll adjust, which means so will they."

"We'll have to set the terms next time." He pushed what looked like a log. Turned out to be a body. "Not the Arctic."

He went ahead, leaving me to make my decision. Was it better to talk our way out of this with the local authorities or call Neville Townsend and eat crow? For the sake of the team, I would have to work up an appetite for fowl.

I called Neville on the special phone I'd given him. As before, he answered with bleary eyes and electric hair. A voice behind him said something about rude people calling at three in the morning. He squinted at the screen.

"Hey, Neville," I said in a cheerful voice. "How you doing? Say, I could use some help."

I explained the situation to him. He groaned and promised to send a note to the consulate. Then he rolled over and dropped the phone on his nightstand. He had an interesting ceiling.

Back in the tent, the guys were comforting Betty.

"Consulate will bail us out later in the day," I said. "The company will send lawyers. But. We may be stuck here for several days."

"Why?" Isaiah asked.

"Because Griffith set us up to take the fall for killing the Scots."

"We can just show them the video."

"What video?" I asked.

"When you went to help Betty," Isaiah said, "I put my phone to the binoculars and recorded Griffith executing those guys."

CHAPTER 34

THE INQUISITION TOOK A FULL day. When I finally got stateside, I went looking for answers. A little after three in the morning, I jumped out of a perfectly good airplane over Rosslyn, Virginia, and floated across the river to Georgetown to land on Neville Townsend's roof. The upper stories are where alarm companies take shortcuts and use outdated hardware because no one is expected to break in up top. I attached jumper wires to the alarm sensor on the dormer window.

While I should have thanked the Secretary of State for sending in the consulate staff to rescue us from murder charges, it was Isaiah's brilliance that sealed our release. I didn't feel charitable toward Neville, Rafael, or the Keepers. I wasn't even clear what the Keepers were, what they kept, or what they wanted. As much as I welcomed the opportunity to kill Griffith, there was a lot more to the Chaac Project than I was told. And the Keepers had answers they weren't sharing.

I slid the window open and squeezed into a narrow space inside. An attic clogged with steamer trunks and bookcases with little room for maneuvering greeted me. A quick check of the unlabeled chests revealed nothing but old clothes and family mementos. Nothing that looked like something the Keepers would keep.

But then, I had no idea what I was looking for. Something with an embossed title that read, *Master Plan for World Domination*? A pocket-sized nuclear weapon? A picture of the Queen of England holding a severed head by the hair?

Griffith promised I would know it when I saw it, but he was talking about Professor Rafael Tum. No one knows where Rafael lives. Not even our tech people could trace his movements after our driver dropped him at a diner in Adams Morgan, the artist's neighborhood a mile away. That left Neville's crib as my only option.

I threaded my way to the door and eased the knob a millimeter, trying to avoid squeaks. Neville's house had an attached guest house where the State Department's Bureau of Diplomatic Security kept a man overnight. The personal security detail was staffed with new recruits eager to work their way up the ladder to an embassy posting overseas. In my experience, that was how trigger-happy young men ended up making regrettable decisions. I didn't want to become a regret. I twisted the knob. It let out a cry for lubricant.

With a map of his house in my head, gleaned from his last renovation permits, I made my way down to the bedroom level. Typical of historic homes, several additions had been cobbled together by each successive generation. They hadn't necessarily been level with each other, requiring oddly placed landings and short staircases here and there. I stood below such a stair leading to a hallway lined with overstuffed bookshelves.

The hall led to the master bedroom, where a snoring duel was in progress. No winner yet declared. If I remembered correctly, Neville's home office lay beyond the duelists.

As I crept up the stairs, using the edges to minimize noise, the top one groaned like a stepped-on dog. One of the snorers forfeited with a snort. Neville's voice clattered into the dark. "Someone there? Hello?"

Looking for a hiding place, I stepped into a doorway on one side of the hall and checked the space. It was a TV room where a pair of La-Z-Boys faced a flat screen. I turned to face the hall, stood still, and watched through the open door.

Neville's feet thumped to the floor and padded toward me. Dressed in black, I was nearly invisible. As he neared me, I checked the bookcase opposite. Lots of old books, mostly history and biographies. A few knickknacks and pictures. A model of a DC-3, the WWII-era workhorse of an airplane, gathered dust between Plato's *Republic* and McCullough's *1776*. The old man stopped and looked right at me. He looked over his shoulder to his bedroom. "Anyone there?"

The Secretary shuffled forward and tottered down the steps I'd just come up. He turned the corner heading down.

I moved on silent feet to the bedroom and tried to cross it.

Mrs. Neville rolled over in the sheets and grunted. "Evmm phinf OK?"

"Shhhh…"

She smacked her lips and snored softly.

I resumed my tiptoe across the room, my skin electric with tension. Neville's office doorknob turned quietly in my hand. But the hinges screeched before reaching a nine-inch opening. Sliding through, I entered a lair smelling of ancient books and wood. A sound behind me caught my attention.

The lady of the house was awake, searching the dark room. "Neville?"

Did you miss it, homie? Mercury said.

Jumping out of my skin, I said, *Jesus Christ!*

C'mon now, we've been over this a million times. I'm Mercury, winged messenger of the Roman pantheon. Bro, if I be Jesus, you'd be in a mess of troubles right now. He'd be yanking you around by your ear. Besides, you know me.

Not in the dark.

Izzat some kind of reference to my skin color? Are you making a joke, my bruth-ah? He stretched out the last word.

No. I took a deep breath. *So, what's up?*

Mercury gave me some serious side-eye before he said, *Just wanted to make sure you saw the picture behind the DC-3. No need to get all anxious.*

I'll look on my way out. My mind raced back to why a model airplane caught my eye. I had nothing.

Mercury said, *Dude, you need to check it out.*

I said, *Save me the trip back across the creaky floors and just tell me.*

Mercury said, *I do that and I'm disqualified from the bet, and you know what that means.*

I said, *You lose your wife.*

Oh yeah, her too. So do some digging around by your own self. But what are you looking for?

I said, *Griffith wants the Chaac Equation. Rafael and Neville want me to find out how badly he needs it.*

Mercury said, *Why would they want to know that? Why wouldn't they send you in to destroy what he has?*

I thought about that for a moment. *Because these days, his research could be stored in a hundred places. We'd never get it all. And that means they want an assessment of how close he is to solving this battery thing. Because ... because why would that matter? I don't know.*

Mercury said, *Both Neville and Rafael mentioned Griffith had a conference coming up to find partners for R & D. Why does Griffith need partners?*

I said, *Because the Russians burned so much money, they gave up. He needs a lot of money. And that means he's inviting all kinds of criminals and hostile countries. The Keepers want to know how big a threat he poses. If he gets funded by China and they figure out this super-battery, that could upset the USA's standing as the global superpower.*

Mercury said, *Not bad thinking for a mortal who claims he don't need no divine intervention. Say, where do you suppose ol' Neville went?*

I said, *To get his security guard?*

Mercury said, *Maybe he went for milk and cookies.*

I looked around the office using my Sabel Visor and the ambient light from the windows. Awards, photos with presidents and prime ministers, diplomas, and other stuff hung on the walls. More bookshelves filled with books. A government-issued secure laptop, obvious for its extra thickness, lay on the desk. A crystal globe paperweight held down a thin stack of papers. Nothing screamed *secret stuff* to my gaze.

I slithered back through the bedroom. The Sabel phone I'd given Neville lay on his nightstand. No other phones nearby. I was honored.

A door closed one level below me. I froze an arm's length from Mrs. Townsend. She wasn't snoring.

Muffled voices and groaning floorboards crossed the living room below.

"Neville?" Her voice trembled. She rose on an elbow desperate to make out my shadowy form.

"Shhhh ..."

"Who the hell are you?" Each word rose on the alarm scale. She was two seconds from screaming.

I jabbed her with a Sabel Dart. She slumped back into the pillows. I pulled the covers up and tucked her in before making it to the hallway. Two pairs of feet tromped toward me from below. I barely had time to back into the TV room and press my back to the wall next to the light switch, the open door to my right.

Neville led the way. Someone else stopped at the landing and opened a door. His footsteps led away from me momentarily. He was clearing the room, using standard procedures. Neville stood still, waiting within my reach.

Then the guard's footfalls came toward us, getting the same bark out of the top step I'd gotten. The one that woke Neville. I sensed the minute electrical charge given off by humans in close proximity. He was on the other side of the wall from me. Cautious, maybe sensing my charge, he pushed his flashlight into the room followed by his head.

The Sabel Dart landed neatly in his neck. I caught his weight and laid him out in the hall at Neville's feet.

The Secretary stared at me like a horror movie character at first sight of the chainsaw, speechless with his mouth wide open.

I pointed at my victim on the floor. "He's just taking a bit of a nap for the next few hours. He's fine."

"Wha…"

"Let's not report this incident. It'll be a blot on the poor guy's record, and he'll never get a promotion. It wasn't his fault they trained him badly." I pulled off my balaclava.

"Wha…" He began to recognize me.

"Just chill, Neville. You'll get your voice back in a second. There's something I wanted to ask you." Moving aside the DC-3, I pulled the framed photo out from the back. I blew off a layer of dust and showed it to him. "Tell me about this."

His gaze dropped to the photo, then back to me, then back to the photo. After round three, I glanced at it. Four men and a young woman smiled for the camera in front of a log cabin in the pines. On the left, a much younger Neville Townsend. On the right, a much younger Rafael Tum sporting a beard. Next to Rafael, a boyish looking Joe Griffith, not yet thirty. In the middle, a much younger Alan Sabel. And next to Alan, a tall, athletic—not to mention unhappy to be hanging with Dad and his pals—teenaged Pia Sabel.

I repressed *what the fuck?* before the words bubbled out of my mouth.

"Just a friendly camping … Fishing. Right. Uh, fishing trip." Neville's face drained. He took the photo from me and placed it back on the shelf and moved the DC-3 in front of it.

"Hold up." I handed him the model airplane, pulled my camera, and snapped a picture of the picture. "Alan Sabel was one of you guys? A Keeper?"

Neville glanced down the hall toward his bedroom, nervous as a whore in church.

"I gave your wife a dose of the same thing I gave him." I pointed at the young man on the floor. "Answer the question."

He said, "Let's go downstairs anyway."

I gestured at the stairs. He led the way.

We went to the white-marble-and-stainless-steel kitchen, where he poured two glasses of milk and produced a plate of ginger snaps. We sat at the breakfast bar on high stools. He dipped a snap in his milk and munched.

I waited for my answer.

"What did you learn from Griffith?" he asked.

"Not how this works, Neville." I eyed the cookies. I love ginger snaps. "What I know or don't know stays with me until I get some answers."

He dipped another cookie and chomped.

Of course, I couldn't resist cookies and milk forever. No one can. I took one, dipped it, and ate. Homemade. You can tell right off. Crisp, not too sweet, and fresh ginger. "Mmm, your wife's a great cook."

"Dan, actually." He pointed upstairs. "The best cook in the service."

I made a mental note to trade recipes with him. If he wasn't too pissed about getting darted. After inhaling my second cookie, I said, "And the answer is?"

"Alan Sabel turned us down. Didn't have time to commit, he said. I couldn't blame him. That daughter of his was traveling all over the world playing soccer, you know. He was a single dad, with a thriving business, and he never missed her games."

"Is she one of you guys?"

"The first rule about the Keepers ..." He smiled without finishing the famous line adapted from a movie. I finished it in my head: ... *is never talk about the Keepers.*

"And why is Griffith in this?"

"He was Rafael's apprentice. Obviously, he has since turned to the dark side." Neville chortled and glanced at me with mischievous eyes. "Since you're going to show her that picture, be sure to ask Pia what happened about an hour after it was taken. Don't look at me like that—she never told me."

CHAPTER 35

MS. SABEL LOOKED AT MY phone again and huffed in anger. She said, "Where did you get this?"

"Of all people," I sighed, "I thought you would answer the question straight up instead of deflecting."

Our gazes met. She wasn't used to me challenging her. It wasn't often. Her jaw flexed with tension. My jaw flexed with tension. She leaned back against the massive slab of oak that is the desk in her home office. She'd just returned home from solving a murder in England. Traces of bruises incurred on her trip still showed. An insomniac who put in a two-hour workout before breakfast, she had already dressed in a business suit, her ponytail still wet from the shower. She had meetings and I was holding her up. I didn't care.

She turned and paced. I gave her the space.

"I was fourteen." On the far side of the cavernous room, she crossed her arms and turned her gray-green eyes my way. "He wasn't the first adult to hit on me. Crazed fans, stupid coaches, hotel employees. Someone posted a countdown website for when I would turn eighteen and become 'fair game.' Don't look surprised. I'm not alone in handling that crap, Jacob. Most women have to deal with it. Anyway, Griffith came on a little too strong for my taste. My left hook broke his orbital socket, and the follow up haymaker destroyed his nose."

It wasn't hard to picture. I'm six-one and her eyes are level with mine. I've sparred with her and seen a ferocious woman unleashed, fueled by a lifetime of fury at her fate.

She stared at me, letting me fill in the blanks about what Griffith had done to deserve a vicious beatdown. I already knew Betty's story. Betty was older than Ms. Sabel, but nowhere near as tall or strong. Betty had been at the man's mercy like a sparrow under a cat's paw. How many young women submitted to his assaults? After Betty, I'm sure he felt emboldened and tried the same thing with Ms. Sabel. But, due to her wealth and privilege, Ms. Sabel has always gotten away with taking the initiative against people she doesn't like. She'd taken up boxing around that tender age. Thin-shouldered Griffith probably never worked out, much less studied a martial art. Unprepared for a powerful young woman, he had never seen it coming.

"From the story Betty told me," I said, "you went too easy on him."

"That's not how Dad saw it."

"Did you tell him the details?"

"No." She turned away. "He was proud of everything I ever did, but that day, he never asked what happened, he just lit into me. I'd never seen him so angry before. After his reaction, I felt like the whole thing was my fault."

As much as I wanted to give her a hug, I knew it was the wrong time. I waited.

After a few foot taps and looks out the window, she strode back. "I know it wasn't my fault. I've dealt with it. Now tell me about Betty."

She was deflecting my original question, which pissed me off, but that would have to wait. Her problems outranked mine.

"About Betty," I said, and related the story.

She listened intently. When I finished, she said, "Where is she?"

"Guest wing, the Blue Room. She's OK but won't be going for a run in the next couple days."

"Broken ... what was it?"

I pointed to the center of my chest.

She nodded. "I'll go talk to her."

"Before you go: I asked you a question."

She took a deep breath, recrossed her arms, and looked at a piece of carpet between us. "I had no idea what Dad was doing with those men. I was too young and uninvolved in the business. I never told you about Rafael because, frankly, I didn't recognize him. It was a one-night trip, years ago."

"Are you involved in the Keepers?"

"No." Her usually steel gaze never rose to mine.

"What's the Chaac Project?"

"I've no idea." She stammered a few times, then she said, "That's not entirely true. I have an idea. One that's far out on the fringe. I'd like you to find out. You're a more dispassionate analyst than I."

None of her answers matched my wildest expectations. Too much missing information.

She tilted her head. "Are you OK? You still look angry."

"Not anger," I said. "I'm confused. I've always trusted you. Right now, you admit you're not telling me everything. I get it, you'll tell me later. I don't like that. My problem is: I don't know who the good guys are."

She stood still.

"Betty told me a series of lies," I said. "Neville and Rafael have told me so little, I have nothing to trust. And now you—keeping something from me. I feel like a castaway. Abandoned by everyone for reasons I don't understand. The only person I'm sure is evil is Griffith. And the worst part is—he's the only one who's told me the truth. You know what? You're right, I am still angry."

She squeezed my arm and looked at me with sympathy. "You don't know who to trust because you don't trust yourself. You ran into Griffith's ambush knowing it was a bad idea. I know why. Jenny died on your watch, and it pains you. And then the Keepers gave you a mission that let you dig deeper into those wounds. Now you're seeing plots against you everywhere you turn. How far will you go before you pull out of this dive, Jacob?" Her voice cracked. "I can't trust a man on the verge of doing something dysregulated."

Dysregulated. A word used by psychologists because it sounds nicer than self-destructive. Her words hit me like a sledgehammer to the foot. My heart pounded in my chest; my brain froze then boiled over. Before I went ballistic, telling her how wrong she was and how I was fine, I saw the tears welling in her eyes.

Ms. Sabel wrapped her arms around me and squeezed tight. She said, "You need to see Dr. Harrison."

The psychiatrist had been treating her for a decade. They had a close relationship.

"I know what you're thinking," she said. "I know you talked to him a couple years ago and you didn't care for it. But this is serious, Jacob. And it's not me who doesn't trust you. It's you."

CHAPTER 36

DR. HARRISON STOOD IN THE doorway with a welcoming arm graciously gesturing me inside. Round spectacles reflecting the windows behind me obscured his eyes. His gray goatee was trimmed shorter than I remembered, as if he had turned hipster. All he needed was a two-inch ponytail. After hesitating, I stepped into his inner sanctum and sat at the end of a loveseat. He took a wingback opposite, steepled his fingers above his beach ball belly, and began with the standard pleasantries.

Mercury stood behind him. *Is this guy going to let it go, homie?*

I said, *Let what go?*

Mercury said, *That you missed your last appointment—three years ago.*

I said, *He's bigger than that. Now leave me alone so I can concentrate.*

Mercury said, *Concentrate? On this loser? Dr. I-Went-to-Harvard-and-You-Didn't Harrison? He wrote a paper about you and me, y'know. Sent it in to* Psych Today. *Know what happened?*

I said, *Please. I'm trying to focus here.*

Mercury said, *They laughed at him. Set him up on a Zoom meeting with all the editors just to laugh in his face.*

I said, *That was mean.*

What'd you expect from a bunch of psychos? Mercury laughed with his mouth wide open. *True story, I swear.*

I said, *Quiet. I want to hear what he has to say.*

Mercury said, *Why listen to him? You've got me. I got your analysis right here, bruh. You're Orpheus pining for Eurydice, that's the start and finish to all your problems.*

"You don't want to be here," Dr. Harrison said. "And that's fine with me, Jacob. But Pia wants me to help you. You'll give me a few minutes for her, won't you?"

"That's why I'm here." I grinned like a madman trying to silence the voices in his head. "If she recommends your services, I'm all in."

"First, let's not open that box of worms with the Roman god, whatshisname, in it. We can let that come up organically if he plays a part." He adjusted his glasses and waited for me to test him. I let it go. He continued, "I want to know the real Jacob. Let's start at the beginning, shall we? Tell me about your childhood."

Mercury jumped back. *Did he call me 'whatshisname?' Did he say, 'if he plays a part?' Damn, boy. He thinks you're crazy. Y'know that? You're not crazy. He's crazy. And you know how crazy people are—they go talking smack about you behind your back. Make everybody think you're the one who's crazy and a threat to his community. Y'know what you gotta do about that. Shoot this muthafucka right now. Shoot him in the head. Show him who's crazy.*

I said, *Why are you worried about this guy? Wait, you think he's going to put me on meds again and make you go away.*

Mercury recoiled in shock. *No I ain't. Not at all. Cuz you wouldn't take them.* He stared at me, then leaned forward. *Would you?*

When I didn't respond quickly, Dr. Harrison tried another question. "How did your parents shape you into the finest warrior in the world?"

My brain started working over Dr. Harrison's question. What is it that shapes us? Is it something we do ourselves? Are we a product of our environment? Are we guided by the gods? Is everything inevitable, a fate we can't escape? Why am I me?

I said, "My parents are pacifists. Always have been. Hippies from the '60s. The last thing they wanted was a warrior."

I went on, uncertain if I was talking to the doctor or the winged messenger. Addressing them both, I told them my parents only care about two things: jazz and farming. As teenagers, my sister and I rebelled against touring as the "Stearne Family Quartet." But Joyce never rebelled against farming. She loved plants, seeds, rain, drainage, seasons. She was born with dirt under her fingernails. She learned to drive a tractor before she could ride a bike. Mom and Dad loved that about her. I couldn't make a chia pet sprout. I was forgotten, left behind. Joyce rose to the top of the 4-H Club and was elected president of the state chapter on the same day I set the state 10K record in track. Guess which award ceremony they attended?

Is that why I went to war? I wanted to do something they'd be proud of—or die trying. What I thought was duty, honor, service was actually self-destructive behavior?

"We call it dysregulated," Dr. Harrison said. He explained that trauma victims rely on self-destructive tendencies to blow off emotional energy they might otherwise talk through and deal with logically. Some dysregulated behaviors are minor, such as snacking on junk food, while others, like drug abuse, come with major complications. He had explanations of the stages I would come to recognize and handle without resorting to dangerous activities. The stages were precontemplation, contemplation, preparation, action, maintenance, and termination. Every time I felt compulsive, I would think through those six steps.

Mercury said, *A guy is aiming a rifle at your head and your compulsive reaction is to shoot him before he shoots you, but instead, you're gonna think through six steps? You're already dead, bro.*

I said, *That's not how it works. At least, I don't think it is.*

Mercury said, *How do I get a gig like this dude? The man's been helping Pia-Caesar-Sabel with her insomnia for ten years now. She still has insomnia. He still gets paid. I could fail at curing her insomnia for half what he charges. And I thought telling people to leave lambs and gold next to my statue was a racket. Holy Minerva!*

I said, *Harrison is helping me here. Think about it. My parents didn't pay attention to me, so I chased heroism to get it. They remained Christian pacifists, preferring to turn the cheek rather than violate a sacred commandment. When my medals didn't impress them, I got the attention I craved from Ms. Sabel.*

Mercury said, *See there? You're working things out now, homie. You're almost there. And that's cuz I'm helping you, not this witch doctor. Let's go on to the next step in thinking. Pia-Caesar-Sabel knows you want her approval. Why'd she send you to this quack?*

I said, *She said I don't trust myself.*

Mercury said, *And in reality, when mortals tell you something about you, they really mean ... what?*

I said, *She doesn't trust herself. Wait. About what? The Chaac Project? She didn't want to tell me what it is because she didn't trust her analysis.*

Mercury said, *And that's because ...*

I said, *She knows damn well what it is. And when rich people know what something is, they immediately convince themselves they own it and the person holding it now has stolen it from them. But there's something else she doesn't trust about it. Like what? Why doesn't she trust herself with it?*

Mercury said, *So if you want to kill Griffith—and make sure yours is* a mortis honore, *death with honor—first you need to ...*

After realizing Mercury was prompting me, I said, *Get my hands on the Chaac Project and figure out who the rightful owner is. No. Not the rightful owner—the best owner. The one who'll make sure the whole world benefits from it and not make one person the richest in history. No matter who that is, it sure as hell isn't Griffith.*

Mercury said, *Sounds like a mission worth living for, don't it, bruh?*

When I came back to the present, Dr. Harrison was wrapping up a lengthy monologue. But I'd lost the plot. He was saying, "... which represents the fear of the father's penis."

"Let's skip the penis-stuff, Doc. Thanks for your time, this has been enlightening. Now I know who to kill."

Mercury slapped his palm to his face and said, *Homie, telling your psychiatrist you 'know who to kill' might not be your best move. Look at his face.*

I said, *He'll get over it. Let's go.*

CHAPTER 37

EMMA CALLED WHILE I WOUND my way through the guest wing at Sabel Gardens. She said, "Here's an update on our Betty Bardon research. In her teen years, she landed a few bit parts and extra roles. Then she won a prestigious scholarship to UC Santa Barbara for Quantum Physics. Before you say, 'that's a beach school,' it's in the top ten for quantum research. She's no slouch. From there she got her masters at Caltech, then started on her PhD. She landed a research project abroad where she studied for over a year. Then, she dropped out and came home. That's when she starred in Griffith's movies."

I thanked her and clicked off. Why would Betty return from overseas to work for the man who abused her as a teen?

I found Betty propped on pillows in the Blue Room reading a dog-eared copy of *The Morpheus Decision*. Neither of us spoke when I gave the open door a hasty knock and walked in.

After a second holding my gaze like a bad kid watching the principal approach, she decided the best defense was a good offense. She said, "I know you're pissed about the ambush. I don't blame you. But I didn't have anything to do with it. I thought you would kill him—but you failed." She leaned to the nightstand, retrieved her phone, and tossed it to me. "Check the latest text about my mother."

It wasn't a text. It was a picture. A severed finger lay on green felt, blood dripping from the joint. My stomach turned. It wouldn't rank in the top one hundred of the worst things I've seen, but the cynicism of it spoke volumes about the sender.

"Griffith?" I asked.

Her face tightened up and a tear rolled from the corner. "She's my mother. I care. But I stopped feeling for her years ago. I haven't even spoken to her in two years. God, that sounds horrible and sickening, but it's true. She's his enabler, coconspirator. She tells underage girls to do what he wants. I hate her. This is appalling, even for Griffith, but if he did that, she brought it on herself."

Ms. Sabel's voice came from behind me. "Came from a burner phone over a European carrier. The phone hasn't been to North America since it was activated last night. Griffith hasn't been within a thousand miles of it. Our people are working on it, but we think someone cleaned the photo of metadata and forwarded it."

Having twisted to look at her, I turned back to Betty. "How do you communicate with Griffith?"

Her eyes fell to the covers.

I searched her phone for the most common secure texting app, *Signal*. She had it installed but the history had been wiped.

"Our people checked that too," Ms. Sabel said. She tracked around and sat on the foot of the bed. "All messages self-erase thirty seconds after being opened. There's nothing left."

"I know how that looks," Betty protested. "But I don't have anything to hide. He set the expiration—"

"My team's lives were at risk," I said. "I need to know what you're not telling me. I'm not challenging your story about the underage rape. But you had a decade to settle that score. So tell me, why go after him now?"

"Why didn't you use the sniper rifle?" she snapped at me.

"Too many risk factors."

"Same." She pulled the covers up. "Tarana Burke started the *Me Too* movement in 2006 and Alyssa Milano blew it open in 2017. Both paid a price for speaking up. Death threats from strangers, anger, resentment, and no new jobs. Ask anyone, man or woman, who's filed a rape or assault charge against someone. Even if you win, even if you're vindicated—it's a career-ender. No one wants to hire a troublemaker. On top of that, the cops can't file charges without evidence, so how do you get that? Gretchen Carlson had the expertise to record Roger Ailes' sexual comments at Fox News—and even then, Fox paid Ailes more in severance than all his victims combined. But what did I have? How does a fourteen-year-old record an adult? How does she say no?"

Ms. Sabel's stare burned a hole in the side of my head. I didn't need her help to know that line of questioning was off limits. It was time to change the subject.

"Was that stuff you said about the Lamborghini true?" I asked.

Betty squinted at me until she remembered Miguel playing chicken against the cops. "Just a quick calculation and basic physics. I'm not a hundred percent certain the SUV would've cratered the car's structural integrity. I'd rate it at an 80 percent probability. But I'm not a mechanical engineer."

In my peripheral vision, I could sense Ms. Sabel's rising curiosity about that story. I filled her in. "We borrowed a Lamborghini from Abromowitz and took a run at the cops. Betty warned us of the downside."

Ms. Sabel said, "You stole a car from Abromowitz? You'd be better off running away with his wife."

She turned to Betty. "You said you're not a mechanical engineer and stressed mechanical. Are you some other kind?"

"Electromagnetic engineering," Betty said. She checked our surprised looks. "I have a BS in quantum physics, electromagnetic engineering, and a masters in quantum electrodynamics. QED for short."

Ms. Sabel's shock was unmistakable. Suddenly pale and anxious, she left the room in a hurry.

"That's not public knowledge," Betty called after her. "I'd never work in Hollywood again if it got out. No one hires a smart actress." She turned to me. "Yes, I know, Hedy Lamarr invented radar for torpedoes, but she got away with it because there was a war on."

I waited for her to settle down. I asked, "With degrees like that, why become an actress?"

"Gal Gadot made $300,000 for Wonder Woman and ten million for the sequel. Guess how long it would take an electromagnetic engineer to make that?"

"What do you know about the Chaac Project?" I asked.

The actress in her came out. She snugged up the already snugged sheets and tried to look confused. "What is that?"

"I'll let that go for now," I said. "You studied my history long before you went to Belarus. You lied about being a hostage. You lied about your relationship with Griffith—"

"I didn't lie!"

"Dissembling is the same thing," I barked back. "If you ask for my help and don't tell me everything, you're lying."

"I want Griffith dead," she said angrily. Then she lowered her voice. "That's everything you need to know. You want the same thing. I thought we would be allies not … whatever this is."

"You and I don't have a 'this.' We aren't 'allies.' I have an agenda and ridding the world of Griffith is part of it. If you're so keen on the same thing, tell me where I can find him, and I'll handle the rest."

"I thought we could be friends," she said. "Yes, I left the door open hoping for something more. I thought you were done being alone. I thought you'd be ready to let someone get close. But you're wallowing in a past that's never coming back. Don't you want someone to care about? Aren't you ready to get on with your life? Don't you want to be a hero again?"

I tensed up. The answer to her questions was yes. Just—not yet.

"You know what your problem is?" she asked with heat. "You won't let a woman get close to you for fear of losing her. Well, I've got news for you, mister: When you do that, you've already lost."

She crossed her arms and pouted.

Ms. Sabel came back in the room holding a framed photo of her biological father, who had been murdered when she was four. She shoved the picture in front of Betty and said, "Do you know this man?"

Betty checked the picture carefully before turning a curious look at her. "Lloyd Aston?"

Ms. Sabel turned a serious gaze my way. "Could you give us a moment?"

"Sure, but—"

"I need the room," she said.

"I was just getting her to tell me where I can find Griffith."

"Belgrade, Serbia," Ms. Sabel said. "He's pitching R & D partners in two days. We're going."

"I need to be there," Betty said.

"No way," I said. "This is the end game. We're not risking it having a civilian—"

"She's coming with us," Ms. Sabel said. "Griffith thinks you're a couple. We can use that. Diversified distractions. Now give me the room."

The discussion was over. Apparently.

I backed out with a nod.

Mercury leaned against the wall in the corridor. *'Sup dawg? Did I tell you Betty Bardon is just like Jenny only with bigger—brains? Here's a test question for you: Why is Lloyd Aston's name on the lips of every grad student in the field of QED—not to mention a Hollywood actress?*

Instead of answering, I looked up Lloyd Aston on Wikipedia. Everything on the page was written by a science geek of the highest order. The only thing I could understand was his birth and death dates. One phrase jumped out at me even though I didn't know what it meant, "His groundbreaking research in quantum electrodynamics (QED) set the stage for everything we know today."

Looking up at my used god, I said, *How does that fit in with Griffith, the Knights, the Keepers, the Secretary of State, a mad Finnish mercenary, and a Mayan professor?*

Mercury said, *You left out Pia-Caesar-Sabel, who all-a-sudden took over your little quest for* mortis honore. *Whazzat all about, bruh?*

CHAPTER 38

BOARDING THE BRAND-NEW BOEING 777, recently christened as the new Sabel One, was a shock. Like a flying cathedral, it was wide, spacious, and well lit. And came with an executive chef. When I passed the kitchen, he was prepping dinner for a lot of people. Ms. Sabel bought the big jet as a flying office building because it was cheaper than building a second Sabel Tower and it impressed the hell out of business partners. A friend in marketing told me none of our customers would fire us for fear of being kicked off Sabel One trips to Shanghai or Sydney. There were three different client groups already on board when I got there, each with their own living room-like area.

Miguel, Betty, Isaiah, and I sat in one of the back rooms, waiting for Ms. Sabel to finish wining, dining, and impressing those clients. She had a plan for Belgrade she hadn't shared with us yet. Clients first.

After the paying customers were fed, the chef came aft to let us know he'd be serving us two at a time because the clients used up all the dishes. Someone was scrubbing like mad. Miguel and Isaiah opted to play Xbox games on the big screen in another room, leaving me with Betty. The smirk on their faces made it clear they thought they were doing me a favor.

We faced each other across a dining table for four. White linens, real silver, candles. The chef started us with wine and a citrus-and-avocado salad. Betty wore a tasteful business suit with a high collar. I guessed her chest was still red and swollen from the broken bone.

"Are you feeling up to this trip?" I asked.

"As long as we're not jumping off skyscrapers, I'll manage." She leaned back with her wine glass, taking in the aroma like an expert. And appraising me like a side of beef. "I won't be running through the storm drains either."

"Here's to putting those days behind us." I clinked my wine glass to hers.

"Here we are," she said, "just the two of us enjoying a romantic, candlelit dinner. It seems you were wrong about there not being an 'us.' Does that bother you?"

"There is no 'us,'" I said. "We're playing roles in Ms. Sabel's game. Each of us brings a different skill to her plan."

"Belgrade will be nothing more than a business meeting about R & D funding. It's Shark Tank on steroids. That's not a game."

"Not to you and me. But to billionaires, it's a game. 'Partnerships' is how they play poker."

"She doesn't need you for that. I can calculate those risks in my sleep."

"This game is different. The stakes are far higher than the biggest poker game ever played. There will be no winner, no loser. No single investor will bankroll the whole thing—too much risk. That means there will be partners. Not all those partners will be equal."

She finished her salad in silence. I savored the unexpected pistachio nuts hiding between the grapefruit and avocado slices. Then I noticed something unexpected: a hint of mustard in the dressing.

Swirling her wine before sipping, she savored the flavor, then asked, "What's the big deal about partners? I still don't see a game."

"Whatever Griffith is developing will require more than money. If you put in a million and I put in a million, your million is worth more than mine if it involves quantum physics. My million is worth more than yours if it involves a shooting war. In either case, for you and me to accept the terms of who gets 60 percent for the same amount of money requires a lot of trust and deep background. There will be folks from all walks of life: big money managers, private equity people, spies. Then there's the criminal element: Mikhail Yeschenko representing Eastern Europe's mobs; OPEC's consulting and mercenary firm called Remmo Nidal; and a man named Deng Zhipeng, who's either a brilliant businessman or a front for China's Red Army, or both. If Ms. Sabel gets in on the action, who will be her partners?"

Betty kept her gaze locked on me. "She needs you to read things about people that won't show up in dossiers. Clever. How do you answer those questions, Mr. Stearne?"

"Lots of research, a good deal of footwork, and I read people."

"What's your secret to reading people?"

"Unlike most assassins, I look them in the eye when I hold a pistol to their heads. I find them easy to read."

She looked a little sickened. "That makes all the difference, I'm sure."

The chef arrived with the main course, giving it that personal touch for special friends of Ms. Sabel. Filet mignon with morels in bone sauce for me, Vietnamese lemon grass shrimp for her. Family style sides for both. He refilled our wine glasses before leaving us.

She finished her first bite of the side of corn before asking, "How do you read me?"

I went for the steak while it was still hot. "You want something out of this adventure, and you've not been straight up about what it is."

Her eyes snapped up from her dish. "If you're so good at reading people, what else are you reading? What drives me?"

Playing games is not my favorite thing, but she was smart and wouldn't reveal her agenda easily. I let her wait while I sampled the johnny cakes, a fried cornmeal flatbread. I sipped my wine while she worried her fingers.

"To understand what drives you," I said, "first we have to look for your deficiencies. Those parts of you that you find—rightly or wrongly—lacking. Despite what you said about aging out of the good roles in movies, that's far from reality. You have enough beauty to last a lifetime. You're the sort of woman who could win Oscars at any age."

"Thank you." She batted her eyes.

"That's not a compliment—it's an observation of fact." I lopped off another slice of meat and chewed it slowly. The bone sauce amazed my palate with rich texture and delicate peppers.

"What else?" she asked.

"You're intelligent to a degree I'm not even smart enough to assess.

You've proven that. I asked Emma and the support team to research the structural integrity of a Lambo's hood. You were right. We would've died."

She covered her satisfied smirk by taking another sip of wine.

"And both those things are a problem at times. Especially in Lotusland. Your lethal combination of beauty and brains intimidates men and drives women into fits of jealousy. That's what limits your career, not your age. You said you love to be adored, so why would you come along on this trip just to be the girl on my arm? That's why you're looking for a new path. You'll never catch Gal Gadot in the salary department and quantum physics doesn't pay what you feel you deserve, so you're after something else."

Her eyes said it all. She couldn't lift them from the linen to look at me. I was close but still couldn't work out what she was after. It was right there on the edge of my thinking, just out of reach.

"There's a question," I said. Leaning forward to force her to look at me, I refilled our wine glasses. "Why? Why isn't either career good enough for you? The answers don't require a therapist. Horrific as your rape was, plenty of survivors go on to lead normal lives. You want more than normal. And that's a question for society as a whole: What do we collectively owe survivors in addition to our empathy? Does it justify a civil suit? Without a doubt. But as you pointed out, those aren't easy to win against a powerful man like Griffith. Where does that leave a woman like you?"

Her face flushed with anger. I was digging too deep.

Ms. Sabel arrived, instantly breaking the tension. I rose like a gentleman, but she pushed me back in my chair with a laugh. She said, "Don't let me interrupt. From the body language, you two were getting serious. Go on, I'm dying to hear it."

"I don't judge these things about you," I said to Betty. "I weigh them. How do I work with a woman who asks me to guess what she's after instead of being honest and laying it out there?"

I cut a piece of steak and enjoyed watching her squirm. I could beat her at poker, no problem. But I'd be a fool to play her in chess. I could see her making the calculations about where to go from here. How to get what she wanted from me without telling me what it was.

The chef brought Ms. Sabel a German chocolate cake for dessert. She smiled and thanked him. As soon as he left, she wolfed it down in seconds while Betty's jaw dropped. The world-class athlete who runs ten miles before sunrise every morning—as her warmup—can eat with impunity. Ms. Sabel put the plate down, rested her chin on her knuckles, and watched us like a spectator at a tennis match.

"All right," Betty said after regaining her composure. "My turn. How do I read a man like Jacob Stearne? What's missing from his Wikipedia page? You've done a great job of self-educating yourself. Not many are familiar with Hollywood's nickname 'Lotusland.' But you've read *The Odyssey* and understand the reference to the lotus eaters who forget everything they ever knew. Impressive. Then there's your fashion. You wear a tux or jeans with equal ease. You handle your silver like a born gentleman. That means Pia dragged you out of the muck of soldiering and taught you how to fit into her world. You don't like it, but you do it for her."

It was her turn to let me wriggle on the end of her assessment. She finished her shrimp and sipped her wine and kept her gaze hard on me. Ms. Sabel gave her an amused nod to continue.

"When I saw you in Brest," she said, "I thought it was my lucky day. My knight in shining armor had arrived. But those days are over, aren't they, Jacob? The hero I hoped for has fallen from Olympus."

While Betty spoke, Ms. Sabel grew tense. So did I.

"You always wanted to save the world," Betty said. "There was a time when you expected to live through it, like some invincible, immortal deity. And you did. But that was then. Losing your girlfriend changed all that. Now you're engaging in risky behavior. You're self-destructive. You don't care about life anymore. You want to save the world *and* die trying." She swirled her wine, took a sip, leaned back. "I've played the love interest in those movies. They're always badly written scripts. They would make better tragedies than heroic adventures. I've no interest in watching you play your part. If I still thought of you as a hero, I wouldn't hesitate to tell you what I'm after."

She tossed her napkin on the table, rose, and left before I could fully stand. I sat back down slowly.

Ms. Sabel watched me. I couldn't look at her. After a minute, she pulled Betty's wine glass over, filled it, and took a deep drink. With a nod at my empty plate, she asked, "How was the steak?"

"Like me. Grilled."

She smiled, emptied the bottle into my glass, and asked, "Does Mercury ever tell you to do self-destructive things?"

"Quite the opposite," I said. "Romans were a bloodthirsty bunch. If you offended them, they didn't sue you in court, they didn't tell you off in public. They destroyed your businesses, burned your crops, enslaved your children, and humiliated you before the world."

Now you're talking, homie. Let's burn some crops. Mercury sat on the arm of Ms. Sabel's chair and wrapped an arm around her. Not that she noticed. *You've got an agenda: Revenge killing of Griffith. Betty's got an agenda: Revenge killing of Griffith. Why not cut the girl some slack and hop in bed with her?*

I slowly turned my gaze to him. *Jumping into bed with someone is no way to solve problems. But she's told me she wanted to kill Griffith before. Why does it feel different now?*

He said, *Dude! You figured it out.*

I said, *Figured what out?*

Mercury scowled. *Dude, you just figured out Betty Bardon from top to bottom. Now you know what she wants, you can quit thinking about Jenny and start thinking about Betty and her big—*

Don't say it.

—brain. Mercury leaned back like I'd offended him. *Dude, you gotta give me credit for being a decent god.*

I said, *I will when I believe it.*

Then the lightbulb in my brain flashed. He was right. I finally understood Betty, and that made me one degree happier. Betty Bardon, B-movie actress, child victim, abused adult, planned to burn Griffith's crops, enslave his loved ones, and humiliate him in front of the world. She chose me to help her.

Maybe I would.

CHAPTER 39

THE HYATT BELGRADE'S GLASS-AND-STEEL STRUCTURE gleamed over a tired city in desperate need of a paint job. Traffic looked like Europe's used car lot. Considering it's one of the oldest continuously inhabited cities in the world, you'd think they could spruce it up a bit.

Miguel, Isaiah, and I went our separate ways to scope out the extent of security for the attendees. Each faction brought their own people, the quality of which would speak volumes about their intent to participate. Ms. Sabel brought in extras from the Rome office for her personal protection, leaving my squad free to surveil like jewel thieves.

Somewhere in the crowd, Joe Griffith carried the Chaac Project. He would give a sales pitch to the larger crowd. Those who trusted him enough to make a bid would get a deeper briefing, and a select group of those, who were ready to put in billions, would get to see and verify his material before writing a check. Since he hadn't yet gotten his hands on the Chaac Equation, his Chaac Project had to be in Belgrade for show and tell. I wanted a look at it before choosing who to support and who to betray.

Several of the big-time financiers also employed Sabel Security, so we saw some friends on duty. Nadia from Kyiv strode by watching over the Ukrainian delegation; I gave her a nod and a smile.

Serbian security forces roamed the streets in unusually high numbers. There were plenty of rivals strolling the lobby, each with their own security detail. Which meant there were a lot of tough guys striding around like sumo wrestlers stomping onto the mat.

I crossed the river and walked through the half-finished Belgrade Waterfront district where I found Rafael Tum enjoying a cup of coffee with a CIA agent. CIA spooks are easy to spot: shifty eyes and an underlying jumpiness from having a big target on their backs. That, and the haircut circa 1959. Our man in Belgrade was short and wiry, with dark eyes and a cap of black hair. I kept walking when the professor failed to acknowledge me despite making direct eye contact.

Back at the hotel, I joined Miguel and Isaiah for morning tea in the restaurant. We compared notes. Miguel had seen the Koreans, Germans, and General Motors people, as well as Remmo Nidal's contingent. Isaiah had spotted the French and Indian delegations, as well as Berkshire and Amazon. I told them about seeing Rafael. I'd also observed Deng Zhipeng, the Chinese internet billionaire, discussing something with a general from the Red Army. It wasn't clear if Deng's entourage was officially sanctioned by the government or if he'd gone rogue again. And no sign of the Finns. That worried us the most. When my guys finished their snacks, we headed for the suite.

Four men stepped in from different directions as we crossed a wide expanse of marble in the hotel lobby. Isaiah formed a triangle with Miguel and me, watching my 4 and 8, as if we'd been together for years. One of the men said, "Mr. Yeschenko would like to speak to you."

"Tell him if he hasn't found Griffith's security team, he's got bigger problems than me."

The man looked puzzled before tugging his lapel. "Come with me."

"Or what? You're going to shoot me in the lobby while fifteen Serbian soldiers watch?" While the man turned his head to count the soldiers milling about with automatic weapons, I grabbed his lapel mic and spoke directly into it. "Mikhail, don't send me errand boys. You want to talk, I'm in suite 1015. One floor above yours. Be there in five or lose out."

I pushed the man back, enjoying his shock that I knew which floor his boss was staying on. The three of us turned our backs on them and strode to the elevator.

Yeschenko waited outside my suite with a scowl on his face. A bodyguard stood next to him giving me the stink eye.

"C'mon in, Mikhail." I keyed the door and threw it open. "Like I said, we—the collective we—have a bigger problem than worrying about what you got out of Yuri Belenov. We need to join forces."

Yeschenko stepped in, his shiny suit glistening as he moved. He'd been on the verge of yelling at me, but my statement unbalanced him. He tilted a curious look my way and asked, "Join forces?"

I said, "We got our asses kicked by some Finns from Lapland a few days ago."

Shocked that I would admit a defeat, he leaned in, waiting for more.

"Remember Griffith's Scots?" I continued. "Sure you do. You sold me out to them at your casino. Set me up for an ambush. Ima let you skate on that one for now. Anyway, these Finns executed all nine of the Scots. Know anything about them?"

After a quick questioning glance at his man, they both shook their heads.

"They're Griffith's men," I said. "They're good. And they're nowhere to be seen."

Yeschenko found a chair and sat in it. "Nowhere? This is not good."

"That's why we need to stick together, even though we don't trust each other."

"We help you." He pointed at himself and his man. "This trip only. You still owe me Belenov."

"I gave you Belenov." I did my best acting job. "Wait a minute. Did you let him escape? And that's my fault somehow? Miguel, we're going to need better partners for this."

"You cheat me out of Belenov!"

"And you let Griffith's Scots set up an ambush for me in the lobby of your building. I knew you'd double-cross me because that's what you do, Mikhail. That's why I had the window escape planned. We're even, so get over it. We have a problem that rolled in from Finland."

Yeschenko squeezed the arm of his chair. "Griffith uses Serbians for security."

"For the forum, yes. Not for him. If you see him, you'll notice he doesn't have any Serbians nearby. And the worst part is, you'll never see his Finns."

"Da. This is bad." Mikhail rose and looked at his lieutenant. The man kept a stoic face. Mikhail turned back to me. "We notice this too.

Security precautions look right, not feel right. OK, we look. You look. We share information."

With a nod at his man, the two of them left.

"That was easy," Isaiah said. "Are they any good?"

"He tried to kill our boss once." Miguel let out a laugh. "Not a trustworthy bunch. At least we have a truce for the weekend, and that's what Jacob went after. One less group to worry about."

We sat down with laptops and began plotting who we'd seen stationed where on the outside. Next, we would surveil the inside. We reviewed what we knew: Yeschenko was temporarily neutralized. The greatest physical threat after that was Remmo Nidal. They were based out of Libya, where they had no pesky government interference. They had a surprisingly small contingent in Belgrade. After that, Deng Zhipeng and his Red Army general were an unknown quantity. And, scariest of all, no sign of the Finns.

Isaiah looked over his screen at us. "Why are we examining security details for these players? Why not steal their phones or hack their messages?"

Miguel said, "Messages can be faked, secured, encrypted. Feet on the street is a direct correlation to their commitment."

Isaiah squinted, uncertain about that answer.

"If they take Griffith seriously," I said, "they'll bring important people. And that means tons of security. If they think it's a scam, they'll have light security."

"Right," Isaiah said. "Then Yeschenko thinks this is serious. He brought a lot of muscle."

I smiled. "Not for him. He has a lot of enemies. This is traveling light."

We mapped out assignments for the hotel's interior. Miguel and Isaiah went to their suite to prepare for their assignments. Finally alone, I took the opportunity to change my outfit. The morning had been all about tight Euro-fashions. The afternoon would be American sweatpants. I dumped my pocket contents into a tray on the counter.

Among the detritus was Jenny's medallion. Staring at it for a moment, I decided to leave it behind. At some point, I would have to face a future without Jenny. It felt bad even thinking like that. Like ending an era with a betrayal. But it was the right thing to do. The pockets in sweats tended to dump their contents during a fight. I might lose it.

With a sad glance at the mirror, I checked my look. Casual observers wouldn't recognize me. Maybe.

The suite's door opened before I put on a shirt. I pulled my Glock, edged to the bathroom entry, and peered into the living room. Betty Bardon dropped shopping bags from Paris on a chair. I'd forgotten Ms. Sabel forced us to bunk in a two-bedroom suite for appearances. Betty snapped a look at me when I relaxed and holstered my weapon. Her color was gone, but not from seeing me with a 9 mil.

"You're here," she said as if it were a shock. No smile, no dimples, no sparkle. "I have a message for you."

I strode out of my room toward her.

She stared at my abs. "You could model for romance novels."

"That's the message?"

"Griffith wants to see you."

CHAPTER 40

MIGUEL RODRIGUEZ CHANGED INTO HIS afternoon fashion statement even though it would fool no one. What people remembered about him was his size, not his French neck scarf or his Italian loafers. Across their shared suite, Isaiah stepped out of his room. He looked like a different man with his twists hidden under a straw fedora and his sloppy NFL regalia swapped for Italian casual. Isaiah had talents beyond soldiering.

Isaiah had a funny look on his face. He pointed to his ear, indicating something Miguel should hear on the comm link.

Screwing his earbud in place Miguel heard Jacob mid-sentence: "… did you meet with Griffith?"

Betty answered, coming through from Jacob's mic. "His man pulled me off the elevator and dragged me to his room."

Jacob: "Which room?"

Betty: "Third floor, I didn't see the number. I was being shoved—"

Jacob: "I get it. Where does he want to meet me?"

Betty: "Klub 20/44. It's a—"

Jacob: "Splav, a houseboat on the verge of sinking that's been turned into a nightclub. It won't open for hours. Did he take you shopping?"

Betty: "No, Pia called Emma. These bags were at the front desk. Don't look at me like that. I swear, Jacob. Call her, ask her. I'm not conspiring against you with Griffith."

Miguel muted their comm link and motioned for Isaiah to gear up. Jacob had fired up his comm link to keep them aware of a rapidly evolving scenario. By the time the two of them met back in the living room with body armor and pistols, Jacob knocked on the door. He handed off a Russian-made Sumrak sniper rifle. Miguel took it. Without a word, he and his friend knew exactly what had to happen next. Jacob gave him a nod of trust and bounded down the hall for the elevators.

"Looks like you two have a plan," Isaiah said. "Are you a sniper?"

"Not my area of expertise," Miguel said. "How about you?"

"I did all right in training. But never put it to the test in combat." Isaiah looked up Klub 20/44 on the map. "That's more than half a mile."

"Your choice," Miguel said. "Cover Jacob's meeting, or break into Griffith's hotel room."

Isaiah looked him over and reached for the rifle. "I'll take the roof."

Still wary of the missing Finns, they went to the roof together to clear it. Miguel planted perimeter warning devices on the access points while Isaiah took advantage of the suppressor and ambient city noise to calibrate the rifle. They kept in contact with Jacob as he made his way through a weedy park to the river. Isaiah gave Jacob an appraisal on which parts of the Klub he could cover.

Satisfied of Isaiah's safety, Miguel trotted down the interior stairs to Griffith's suite.

A quick dose of spray-glue clouded the hallway camera before it could record him. An app on his phone ran through a wide spectrum of magnetic signals before finding the one that clacked the door open. Miguel slipped in and checked the room with his senses. No sound, no scent of people, nothing in sight, no visible cues. He was alone.

On his comm link, he heard Jacob give Griffith a cold greeting that was returned with an equal chill. They were starting up right where they'd left off.

Miguel checked the rooms, the closets, the spaces under the bed, even the cabinets in the bathroom. All empty. All suitcases stored in the central closet. Each with a single British Airways tag. The drawers in the master bedroom were neat. Six pairs of socks, six underwear, six undershirts, ten dress shirts, four casual shirts, five pairs of shoes, no athletic gear. Four suits, two dinner jackets, two sport coats, and one winter coat just in case the weather changed. No computers, no laptops, no phones. Only one USB charging cord on the nightstand. It was the missing items, things he didn't find, that rang Miguel's alarms.

Miguel fired up another app, one that looked for bugging devices. It checked the Bluetooth and Wi-Fi signal strengths. He found a transmission emanating from the reading lamp over the headboard. A surveillance camera, judging from the high data traffic. Audio and motion sensors wouldn't need anywhere near that much bandwidth. He didn't look at the device. Instead, he texted Emma and the support team. Texting reduced chatter on the comm link, allowing Jacob to concentrate.

Emma texted back: they could trace the data through the building's network, but it would take a few minutes.

He went back to work, appearing to continue his search. While he did, he began to think about his friend.

Jacob had confided in him about Betty's rant on the jet. There was more to combat veterans than being friends who watch football on the weekends. They were each other's confessor, therapist, support group, and, in Miguel's case, spiritual advisor. It was uncharacteristic of Jacob to have words cut him as deeply as Betty's had. He trusted Pia when she'd refused to tell him her game plan. But when an actress with an obvious crush on him did the same, he began to doubt himself. Self-doubt is dangerous territory for a covert operator.

In Miguel's estimation, Jacob hadn't strayed too close to the precipice. But doubts could mount up and become crippling. Was Jacob on the edge after Betty's tirade?

When Miguel had discovered his brother's body, Jacob was second into the room. From that shared tragedy, Jacob knew how Miguel felt about suicides. The last time they talked about it, Jacob appeared to understand how much everyone valued him. Miguel had said all the right things: I hear you; you're not alone; your feelings will change; I care about you.

Had it made a difference?

What else could he do to save Jacob? At some point, Jacob had to want help. So far, the man seemed to ignore the fact that Betty was right. He used to be a hero, not a fool with a death wish. But telling him that was counterproductive.

Jacob's conversation streaming through Miguel's earbud grew heated.

Griffith: "I gave you seven days. You've burned through four already. You're supposed to get Rafael to trust you, bring you into his confidence.

Yet you walked right by him this morning without so much as a nod."

Jacob: "CIA escort. I aborted the contact. So what?"

Griffith: "You've skated through life on luck alone, Jacob. That's no secret. You're an empty vessel. Living in the shadow of your former glory. I'm giving you a chance to dig out of your hole. I'm the one who listens to you. I'm the one who cares. I would never leave you out in the cold the way Pia has. If I know you, you're thinking she hasn't abandoned you. But be honest with yourself, Jacob. How many times has it been? How many times has she left you to figure things out for yourself? And where's that big Indian of yours? Not within half a mile of us right now. Ask yourself, who really cares about you? Who is offering you a big slice of future riches, and who is keeping secrets from you?"

Jacob: "You have a point."

Miguel noticed Griffith using the right scenario to coopt a man. His words were right out of the spymaster's playbook. Not to mention the therapist's handbook. Was Jacob vulnerable to manipulation? Six weeks ago, Miguel wouldn't have thought twice. Since then, Jacob had grown increasingly harder to read.

Griffith: "Right now, she has you believing she sent Sabel Security people out to protect your family. Do you believe that?"

Miguel's jaw clenched tight, waiting for Jacob's answer. His best friend said nothing.

Emma came on the line. She said, "Don't listen to him, Jacob. Tania Cooper led a team out there three days ago. They're incognito. Your family is safe."

A moment later, Emma texted Miguel separately. "Video feed is going to room 318. The hotel register shows it unoccupied."

Decision time. Is the video room a ruse? Or will he find the Finns there? Going in alone would be a mistake. While movie heroes do it every day, only an idiot would go in without backup in real life. He walked into the hall.

"Jacob," he said into the comm link, "bail on Griffith. As Emma pointed out, he's full of it. The room I just searched is a decoy. Too many socks, no laundry, and British Airways tags on the luggage. Isaiah, meet me at room 318."

They would have a two, maybe three-minute window to launch a surprise attack on Griffith's monitors. He had to hope Isaiah was on his way. Talking about it over the comm link would make it harder for Jacob to concentrate. And how long would it take to convince the new guy it was OK to stop covering Jacob? Counterintuitive command. The dialogue had indicated Griffith was going for a psychological angle, not a violent one. If it had been the latter, the move would've come ten minutes ago. Isaiah went to Dartmouth. He would know all that. Miguel hoped.

He didn't need to explain anything to Jacob. They knew each other well enough.

Coming from the roof took Isaiah an extra thirty seconds, but he came flying down the fire stairs two at a time. He propped the unwieldy sniper rifle in the corner and pulled his pistol. With a nod, he let Miguel know he was ready.

Miguel opened the app to unlock doors and snapped 318 open. They burst in together.

A small room, single bed, with a desk against the wall filled with monitors. Two men craned over their shoulders with stunned expressions. Pistols lay within easy reach. The tension rose but no one moved. Miguel took that as a good sign. He crossed the cramped space and jabbed each man with a Sabel Dart.

They tossed the sleeping beauties in the double bed together and bound their hands and feet.

Miguel went to the monitors. Using a thin cable, he connected his phone to one of the book-sized computers under the monitor. The data would go back upstream to the Sabel Ops Center, where they would hack it for everything they could find.

Emma sent a message seconds later. "Don't leave the room. These computers aren't on the internet, they're only connected to the local network. When you walk away, we lose our connection."

Miguel looked around the room. How long before the other Finns showed up looking for their brothers?

While he tried to work out the amount of time available, Isaiah pointed to one of the monitors.

The video was sideways, looking at a steaming bathroom. A woman's figure soaped her hair behind etched glass.

Betty Bardon.

Isaiah found a volume button and raised it. She was singing. No one who knew they were on camera would sing in the shower. Or let Finns watch her. Somehow, they'd planted a camera on her.

Time for a second bug sweep of everyone within reach of Pia Sabel.

Emma sent another text. "OK, we have them hooked up to the internet. You can go now."

Miguel started for the door, then noticed Isaiah had found a Sharpie and was writing big letters across Betty's monitor: *RUNKKARI*. He tugged Isaiah's sleeve and nosed at the door.

Out in the hall, Miguel asked, "What was that word?"

"It's Finnish for wanker, jerk-off."

"You speak Finnish?"

"No, but after Greenland, I looked up a few choice words. I was hoping they would come in handy."

Miguel gave him an appreciative side glance.

The elevator clanked open. Jacob looked up slightly surprised. They got on with no more than a nod, knowing the car could be bugged.

"I got the socks and laundry," Isaiah said, not caring if their adversaries heard this part. "But what was that about British Airways?"

"Turns out the Finns aren't invincible," Miguel said. "We caught them by surprise because they made a mistake when they set up Griffith's fake room: BA doesn't fly to Serbia."

CHAPTER 41

PIA SABEL WAITED BEHIND A tree for several minutes after Jacob left his meeting with Griffith. She made sure he went back to the hotel before calling her expert again. She bit her lip as she scanned the area for the missing subject matter specialist while the call went to voice mail. Pia had no idea what the Chaac Project looked like, she needed the damn expert. But time was up. She cursed and strode up the gangway to Klub 20/44. Stopping at the entrance, she did one last scan of the park, looking for her consultant, now fifteen minutes late. A no-show.

Proceeding inside, Pia tossed her purse on the table in front of Griffith and held her hands out as if nailed to a cross.

"No specialist to help you?" Griffith asked. "Are you qualified to verify things yourself?"

"I can manage," she said.

The man smiled like a viper as he ran a wand over the purse and checked the results. "I'm surprised. I thought you'd record our meeting."

"My memory is all I need." Subconsciously, she brushed her hand over the button-camera on her jacket's zipper pull. The tiny, self-contained camera passed all but the most advanced bug-sweeps.

"It's an honor to be so memorable." His voice dropped an octave to match his scowl. "I've never forgotten any of our encounters, either. From that nasty sucker-punch to humiliating me in front of the Canadian prime minister, they're all etched into my memory forever."

Pia smirked.

Griffith waived a hand at the empty seat across from him. "I'll let you keep that Glock you carry under your jacket. Now tell me why you asked for this meeting."

"I came to offer you a deal."

His eyebrows rose. "Do tell."

"The Chaac Project belongs to me. You know the history. By seeking R & D partners for something you don't own, you're committing fraud. I'm offering you a deal to turn it over so you can stay out of jail."

"Amusing," he said, his reptilian smile creeping back. "I bought it from the Russians. Abromowitz and Yeschenko put in bids that ultimately failed. I don't recall you even being invited, much less bidding. Face it, Pia, you missed your chance."

"I can prove ownership."

"Don't pull that bullshit with me." He crossed his arms. "If you had any evidence, we'd be in a courtroom armed with lawyers, not on the banks of the Danube." He stabbed the table with a finger. "You never sued the Russians for it. And they sold it to me. It's mine."

A man brought plates. He served them sarma, pickled cabbage leaves stuffed with meat and rice; burek, a baked phyllo pastry usually filled with meat but in this case, feta cheese; and cevapi, grilled meatloaf the size of egg rolls; and a pita with sour cream.

Pia watched the waiter until he left. "I thought this was a night club."

"It is." Griffith smiled. "I asked them to bring in local flavors specially for you."

Pulling a stapled stack of twenty pages from the chair next to him, he slid the document to Pia. "Here. Proof I have the Chaac Project."

He dug into his food.

Pia stared at the package for a moment, then leaned forward to ensure the button-camera had the right angle. She scanned the pages carefully, turning them slowly, looking for anything recognizable and making sure the camera had every chance to record a good image. When she reached the end, she slid it back to him.

He twitched a triumphant smile.

She picked at her plate as grease pooled beneath the burek.

"You'll never complete the project," she said. "The Russians couldn't after what, twenty years? What makes you think you can solve the problem?"

Griffith chuckled while he ate. He let her wait until he'd finished two of the sarmas. He wiped his fingers on his napkin and smacked his lips. "Do you even know what it is?"

"Not only that, but I know where it came from and why it's named 'Chaac,' after the Mayan god of lightning." She watched him struggle not to show his surprise. "You have no idea what's involved or why the Russians never got it off the ground."

"And you know all about satellites because you own Sabel Satellites?" he asked while licking his fingers. "You and I are owners. We have people who understand the details for us."

She ate a piece of the burek. Delicious despite being incredibly heavy. She tried the sarma next and found it less heavy, but still far from light. Griffith gobbled down his remaining slice of burek.

She said, "You don't understand the premise, and that means you have no idea how to find the right people for the project. Exactly the problem the Russians faced. You're doomed to fail. If Deng Zhipeng becomes your lead investor, how do you think he and his Red Army overlords will react?"

"I've no worries about Deng. It amuses me that you think my offering is a fraud. Belgrade would be quite a public venue if that were true. Why would I invite the superpowers if I didn't have the Equation in sight?"

That was a point she had pondered for days. Yet she couldn't believe he'd solved the Chaac puzzle. What genius could he have hired? All the known experts were employed elsewhere. None had gone on sabbatical or even extended vacations. Was he bluffing? Would he bluff on such a global scale?

She tried the cevapi. Perfectly spiced with onions.

Griffith tapped the table. "If there are problems, they are my problems. You're fishing for something here." He gave her a thoughtful appraisal. "You ditched your security team to meet with me. You don't want anyone inside Sabel Industries to know what you're up to." He pointed his fork at her. "You devious little bitch."

She fought a rising anger from boiling over, but in the end, he had hit it on the head. She didn't want anyone knowing about their meeting.

"I've told you it belongs to me," she said. "I offered you a chance to stay out of jail. Now, take it—"

"Or what? Dare you threaten me only days after your boys failed in Greenland?"

"I'll pay for the expenses you've incurred so far."

He laughed. "Pay for the lives forfeited when the Russians tried to retain copies of their research? Have you any idea the lengths my people went to ensuring there were no other Chaac files lying around? You have nothing. Your show of force failed. Your only option is to invest like Deng or Yeschenko, or anyone else."

She had no response. When she sought her CEO's advice, this is exactly the exchange Jonelle had predicted. Pia no longer intimidated Griffith, which meant he must have the Chaac Equation within reach. Had Jacob found it and withheld that because she wasn't telling him everything? Jacob might be mad at her, but he wouldn't do that.

Would he?

Seeing her squirm, Griffith leaned forward. "You want it badly. I can see that. And that means you believe you can make Chaac work. If you can, it could make you a lead investor. What do you bring to the table, Pia?"

She tried another slice of the addicting burek while she thought. "I suppose we could work together. Sabel Technologies has the best geniuses in the world. Our AI system is cracking encryption around the globe right now."

"Exactly what Deng Zhipeng said about the Chinese." Griffith waved her off. "And due to their excessive population, they have a higher probability of solving the problems. Quantity has a quality all of its own, as Stalin so aptly put it." She started to say something, but Griffith cut her off. "And don't trot out Betty Bardon. I'm aware you've become besties with the renowned-in-her-own-mind quantum theorist recently. Just remember, there's a reason she became an actress—when it's obvious she can't act."

Pia sat still.

Griffith gained confidence, sneering as he said, "You might do as a secondary to Deng. Perhaps you should talk to him before the bidding starts. Form an alliance. Or would that upset someone? Would you do anything that might anger Jacob Stearne?"

She wanted to break his orbital socket again. But she needed to stay in the game. She needed the Chaac Project. "Jacob is an employee, not a partner. He does as he's told."

CHAPTER 42

I LET MIGUEL TAKE THE lead on retrieving the video camera from Betty's clothes. She'd fallen for one of the oldest tricks in the clandestine playbook: a street vendor gave her a free necklace and put it around her neck. Buried in it, a wireless camera. Still dripping from the shower in hastily donned casual wear, she turned a sickly shade of green as the big guy extracted the device.

"I feel so fucking violated!" She stormed around her room, throwing her hands in the air. "That damn monster just plants a camera on me and peeps on my shower? Damn that creep! All men are fucking creeps!"

Miguel and Isaiah backed out quietly and left to finish their threat assessments inside the hotel. Being immune to creep-accusations, I tried to calm Betty.

There wasn't much I could do. Griffith had been victimizing her for fifteen years. I listened with sympathy, saying nothing. Sometimes patient listening helps. Not this time.

Instead of having a calming effect, she became increasingly agitated. Then she said, "I'm going to Klub 20/44."

"Bad idea."

The door slammed behind her. I didn't try to stop her. She had every right to confront Griffith. I doubted he was still there, so maybe the walk would calm her down. I still needed to finish my part of our threat assessment.

Mercury leaned against a chair. *Homie, tell me you gotta good reason for not killing Griffith at the Klub.*

I said, *I'm trying to figure out who should have Chaac. Not to mention where and what it is.*

Mercury said, *So you ain't in no big hurry to check out and join Jenny anymore? That's good, 'cuz I need a guy who's gonna get me my wife back.*

I said, *Uh. Just temporary. I figure I owe Ms. Sabel, you know, a little help figuring out … whatever she's trying to figure.*

Mercury said, *Oh, izzat right? Well then, if you're gonna stick around, you need to sharpen up and start thinking.*

I said, *What do you mean?*

Mercury said, *I mean, back when you was on top of your game, you'd be asking yourself questions like: those Finns had no way of knowing Betty would go for a shower mid-afternoon, so they wasn't creeping. Then why'd they put a camera on her?*

I said, *They wanted to see who she's talking to.*

Mercury said, *Even Orpheus knows who she's talking to, and he be dead three thousand years.*

I said, *They wanted to know what kind of security we gave her.*

Mercury said, *And that's because…*

I said, *Because I didn't look worried when Griffith threatened my family. I knew we have that covered. By not being anxious about them, he knew he needed a new threat. His Finns are planning to do something more immediate.*

Mercury said, *And what immediate plan could that be?*

I said, *They're planning on abducting Betty.*

I ran for the door and bolted down the hall. Her elevator doors closed before I could squeeze a finger in. I rushed to the stairwell across the way and bounded down the steps.

Mercury waited at the lobby door. *They grabbed her on the elevator once before, bro. Whazzat tell ya?*

I said, *They control the elevators.*

I ran down to the garage level and ripped the door open. There were three levels to underground parking. On the first, three people waited for the next ride up to the lobby. To kidnap her, they would use the bottom level. Fewer observers. I jumped to the next landing and flipped over the rail to the lowest level.

She'd been a victim long enough. It was time to put an end to Griffith using her like a toy. I couldn't let them take Betty. My heart raced with panic. I couldn't lose another innocent woman on my watch.

When I opened the stairwell door, I stood right behind a surprised man who craned around to look at me. I recognized him from Greenland: one of Griffith's Finns. He was waiting for the elevator doors to open across the way. I popped him with a Sabel Dart and pulled him back into the stairwell. He wore a dark blazer, which I stole. I straightened up and did my best to look Finnish.

Fifteen feet away elevator doors clunked open. Inside, two men had hands on an enraged and savage Betty. I raised my Glock with its sound suppressor. Shocked at the unexpected sight of me, they reacted quickly. The first Finn shoved Betty toward me, while the second took cover behind the steel of the elevator car. Both drew pistols.

Betty had never been in a real crossfire before. She screamed and covered her head but remained standing. If she dropped and rolled, I could've finished off the Finns in seconds.

The first Finn advanced, using Betty for cover while the second started shooting. With no other options, I tackled her, wrapped my arms around her waist, and drove her to the concrete. The first Finn scrambled backwards.

"Stay down," I said and started to roll off her.

Screaming, she spasmed, as people always do in deadly situations. Her knee slammed my right arm. My pistol skittered away. Two bullets buzzed my forehead. I jumped to my feet and ran straight at the first guy.

The second man, hiding in the elevator, couldn't get a shot without hitting us both.

Betty kept screaming.

The first guy was shocked by my aggressive charge and held his fire. He knew that even if he killed me, which was unlikely with a pistol, he was about to get knocked over by a large, fast-moving object. He rolled left.

Unable to change my momentum, I threw both my feet sideways, hitting him in the face, and landing on my side. Elevator-man came out to cover his friend. Bullets sparked off the concrete while I added a roll to my slide.

I stopped, jumped to my feet, and charged the concussed and wobbly first Finn while he tried to find his feet. I picked him up, using him as a shield, and tried to throw him into his buddy.

My victim regained his motor skills before I could get a good grip on him. Spinning around, he slammed his elbow into my chest and followed with a right cross. I twisted sideways, letting his fist glance off my collarbone, hooked his arm, used him for leverage, and kicked the second Finn. He was too far away to land a solid kick, but I managed to smack his forearm, which sent his pistol flying.

The first Finn used my position to grab my arms from behind and yank backwards. I felt like a chicken getting dressed for the oven.

Using my captor as leverage, I picked up my feet and pounded them into the second Finn's face. He went down hard, his feet twitching. The sign of a serious concussion.

Directly behind where the Finn had stood a second earlier, Betty stood with my pistol.

I stared directly into the black hole of my own suppressor.

Betty was in the act of pulling the trigger in the manner most amateurs use: eyes closed and head turning away, anticipating the blast. When her eyes were last open, she had been aiming at the Finn. She missed that he was down for the count.

I flung my body to the right. But the man holding my arms had seen the same thing I had. I was his shield; he wouldn't let me go.

Betty lost her nerve, relaxed her trigger finger, and looked back. She saw me. Shock filled her face.

My feet were falling to the ground after my failed attempt to go sideways. I picked them up again and kicked forward, throwing my weight toward Betty. The move caught my captor off balance and hurled us both to the ground. I landed with my feet stretched out in front of me and a fully grown adult on top of my shoulders. The impact nearly shredded my hamstrings. It also gave him an advantage.

He spun off my shoulders and landed on his feet. He turned to face me, pulled his pistol, and aimed for my head while I scrambled to my feet sideways.

Before he could pull the trigger, his face blew out in a shower of blood and brains. He collapsed like a dropped puppet.

Betty stood behind him, my smoking pistol in her hand.

The last Finn gained his feet, his eyes rolling in his head. Through the haze of concussion, the man knew it was do-or-die time for him. Desperate to aim at me, he swirled around trying to bring the muzzle in front of him.

Taking two steps, I smashed him in the face with a haymaker and laid him out cold. As a precaution, I jabbed him with a Sabel Dart. I took inventory: one out, one dead.

Silence.

Betty dropped the pistol and crumpled in on herself, sobbing. "I killed … I killed him."

I put a comforting hand on her shoulder. She turned and buried her face in my chest. She shivered. My arms instinctively wrapped her up and held her tight.

CHAPTER 43

BLOOD AND WATER RAN OFF my body and swirled around the drain before disappearing. It was nothing new to me. A shower I'd taken too many times. I let the water run clear for a few minutes before I shut it off and toweled dry. My thoughts ran across the suite to the other bathroom where Betty washed her first kill from her skin.

It had taken ten minutes to get her out of the garage. Another ten standing in the suite's foyer, holding her while she trembled and moaned.

Mercury checked my reflection. *Aw now, Dawg, that is the second time this week you've held Betty Bardon in your arms. Tell me that don't feel good.*

I said, *She's not Jenny. I'm just doing the right thing for a woman in a bad situation. After all, she saved my life. I'm helping her get through this.*

Mercury grinned. *That's what all y'all mortals say. Right up until her husband comes home.*

I said, *It's not like that.*

Mercury said, *At least you're not doing something self-destructive. Having Babelicious Betty Bardon in your arms makes a man want to live a little longer, don't it?*

I said, *That's a demeaning adjective. We don't do those anymore.*

Tying the towel tight around my waist, I began my cleanup routine.

Ms. Sabel appeared in the doorway and watched me shave. Or my abs flex, I wasn't sure.

She said, "Betty's fallen for you."

I caught her gaze in the mirror and asked, "What makes you say that?"

"Women can tell these things." She came in and leaned her butt against the counter. "She told you off on the jet. She wouldn't have done that if she didn't care."

I paused my razor in midair while I thought that one over. There could be some truth to her theory. Wouldn't it be nice to think so? And all this time I thought Betty was trying to seduce me to further her agenda.

I resumed shaving. Between swipes, I said, "How do you know she's not playing a part?"

"Instincts." She crossed her arms and stared into space. "Say, what happened to her this afternoon? She's a wreck."

"I want her to come to Griffith's big dinner tonight."

"Why?" Ms. Sabel watched me stretch my neck and scrape the blade across it.

"She saved my life." I finished and cleaned up the remaining rough spots.

"From the look of her, I'd say she killed someone in the process."

"She didn't tell you about it?" I rinsed off.

"She's blubbering about something going down in the parking garage." Ms. Sabel picked up a hand towel and dried my face, forcing me to look her in the eye. "She's not one of us, Jacob. Not used to fighting for her life. Right now, she's falling apart. She's not going to dinner."

"I can get her there looking like the homecoming queen."

"You want to prove something to Griffith, is that it?" She pursed her lips and tossed the towel. "Let me guess: he tried to have you killed and she foiled his plan. I'm not going to object, but—you can't do that to her. She's not in a sound frame of mind."

Betty joined us wearing a hotel robe, her eyes red and swollen, cheeks puffy. When she saw Ms. Sabel, her mouth formed a silent "oh."

"We're not a thing," Ms. Sabel said, pointing back and forth between us. "We're discussing business. He wants you at the party tonight."

"I … No. I couldn't. I … I just came in because it occurred to me that …" She stared at my reflection, her lips trembling. "I faked the scene in Brest. That was a terrible thing. He forced me to do it. I know, I shouldn't have. But this … I didn't want you thinking—"

"I read people." I waited until her eyes came up. "That wasn't staged.

He wanted you for leverage to force my hand."

Ms. Sabel's face snapped to me. "Griffith wasn't after you?"

"Tried to take Betty."

"And you fought back. Good for you." She patted Betty's arm, then looked at me. "What do you mean, he wants to force your hand?"

I hadn't told her everything yet. I gave her a right-back-at-you look and swept my razor and cream into my kit.

Betty started crying again. Ms. Sabel reached out and put an arm around her shoulder.

I picked up my boxers and wondered how long the ladies would linger.

Putting a knuckle under her chin, I lifted Betty's face until she met my gaze. I said, "You took the sleeve off your sweatshirt to make my bandage in Belarus. Today, you shot a man who was about to kill me. Thank you for saving my life. Twice."

Betty managed a nod, then looked at the floor.

"Now we need to save yours." I paused while both women turned their curious eyes my way. I put down the shorts, pulled out a toothbrush, and pointed it at Betty. "The last thing Griffith will expect is you waltzing through his cocktail party ready to take on the world."

I let her start shaking her head, no, before continuing. "I've seen you in action—you are a great actress. Under pressure, you convinced the Belarus cops you were a fast-food worker closing for the night. Masterwork. Now. Are you ready for your second act, Ms. Bardon?" I paused. "This scene is called 'The Victim Rises.'"

Her face came up slowly, questioning as she met my gaze. After a second, her eyes filled with understanding.

"Yes." She took a deep breath, swallowed a few tears, and fixed her jaw with resolve. She gave us both a determined look. "The man murdered my father, coopted my mother, abused me ... He's not getting away with any of it."

She lifted her chin and left to get ready.

With an approving nod to me, Ms. Sabel followed her out. If there was one thing a world champion like Ms. Sabel had down pat, it was the inspirational pre-game pep talk. She would put the finishing touches on Betty's psyche.

CHAPTER 44

GRIFFITH'S COCKTAIL PARTY WAS ONE step down from formal. A distinction lost on me, but the dinner jacket Emma had tailored for me came with regular trousers, not satin-striped tuxedo pants.

While Miguel and Isaiah pulled street duty, still looking for the remaining Finns, I escorted the ladies to the ballroom.

Betty trembled like a phone on vibrate-mode. The fear and guilt and terror of killing a man tore at her soul. Ms. Sabel gave me a glance that suggested we scrub my plan. Then the elevator doors began to open. Betty took a long, deep breath through her nose and transformed before our eyes. By the time the doors were all the way open, she was a different person. We entered the ballroom.

Ms. Sabel's height and athletic figure draws stares no matter where she goes or what she wears. On that evening, she drew plenty with the plunging neckline of her deep-red, embroidered gown. Betty Bardon's shoulderless dark blue drew an equal number. Both the ladies sparkled in Ms. Sabel's diamonds. A hush came over the hundred, virtually all-male, attendees. A bigger splash than Kyiv. Every man took them in as if comparing Titian's *Venus of Urbino* to Botticelli's *Birth of Venus*. Once fully appraised, the men's gazes drifted to me for a moment as if to say, *You lucky bastard*. Although more than a few were thinking, *I'm going kill you and take your women*.

Slowly but surely, the men worked up their nerve to talk to the beauties. The first was Deng Zhipeng. The Chinese billionaire had been trying to get in Ms. Sabel's pants for a couple years despite her standing nearly a foot taller. A prime minister whose name I should know went for Betty like a bee to a flower.

Mikhail Yeschenko slid in front of me and said, "Word on street is you kill three Finns in parking garage after lunch. I thought we share information."

"Street talk is always exaggerated," I patted his shoulder. "Only one down and it was minutes ago. I thought it best to tell you in person."

"And two more in hotel room."

"Yes, well, it was a rapidly evolving afternoon, Mikhail." I smiled. He didn't. "My friends are looking for the remaining Finns."

"All five dead," Mikhail said while examining me like a jeweler appraising a stone. "Confirmed with coroner."

I did a double take. By my count, Miguel used darts on two, I used darts on two, and Betty dispatched one. I said, "Not by my hand. It seems Griffith has taken to executing his failures."

"Not good way to keep men." Mikhail watched me closely. "While we look for Finns, someone steal my notebook from suite. This is your purpose?" He didn't wait for an answer. He gave me a look that said we were enemies again and turned to Ms. Bardon.

I listened in to Ms. Sabel's discussion with Deng. The Facebook-of-China founder wore four-inch platform shoes that barely brought his nose to her chin. But it wasn't a discussion. They were holding two parallel monologues. Hers about a partnership on the Chaac Project. His a peacock-strut about how she would love the view from his mansion overlooking Shanghai. Apparently, that was where any partnership discussions would take place. Such is the life of women in business.

Next to Deng stood the Red Army general I'd heard about. He was uninterested in the conversation. His gaze shifted about the room until he met mine. He did an evaluation of me for a moment, then continued searching the room with the eyes of a thief. He was into something he didn't want his bosses back in Beijing to know. I noted his demeanor for future reference.

Then an odd thing happened: Rafael walked up and started talking to him. There was no preamble, no shaking hands, no exchange of business cards. Was the general a member of the Keepers? Did that explain his edgy behavior?

Betty Bardon attracted a crowd as if she were a Southern belle with a large dowry here to choose a suitor. I kept my fingertips lightly on Betty's lower back. A prearranged signal. If she wanted out, she would bend back into my hand, and I would make excuses for her and exit. So far, she was leaning into her role with ease.

Ms. Sabel turned to my ear. "I've gotten word the Serbs want to talk to you about the garage incident. I'll be here another day or two. You are to take Sabel One stateside tonight."

I almost choked. Not that I worried about brushes with the authorities. I'd brushed authorities so many times I'd become friends with a good number of them. But ordering me home was highly unusual. I looked at her to see if she were joking. She'd already turned to someone else. No mirth on her face at all.

Joe Griffith pushed his way through the admirers, heading straight for Ms. Sabel. She was easy to spot in a crowd. When he came close enough and caught sight of Betty, he rocked back on his heels. My plan worked: he was stunned. His glare swept to me a second later.

Stepping toe-to-toe with me, he said, "You're looking awfully smug. But the night is as young and naïve as you, Mr. Stearne. I suppose news travels slowly in farm country."

It took all my willpower not to pull my pistol from its holster and put a hole in the man's head. There were no Finns in the room and the Serbian soldiers remained outside the ballroom. I could shoot him and make a break for the balcony on the far side. But I didn't want to get blood all over Ms. Sabel's dress.

Griffith turned to Ms. Sabel. The two of them talked like old friends.

My pocket rattled. The special ring tone for a call from Tania, Ms. Sabel's best friend and the lead for my family's security.

I told Betty I'd be close by and stepped away from the crowd to take the call.

The first thing I heard sounded like an explosion. "Tania, what's going on?"

"Jacob," she said with yelling in the background. "Don't worry. I've got it under control. Your family doesn't know what happened."

"What do you mean? What happened?"

"Jacob? Can you hear me?" Her voice turned away from the phone.

"Fuck you, motherfucker." Several pistol shots followed. "Jacob, apparently, there are more Finns than we thought. At least two teams. I gotta go. But don't worry about your family."

"What about my family?"

"They're fine. I've got them all going to Chicago for the Jazz Festival. Tell me something—this Louis Kirby guy, is he considered family? Do we take him or leave him to fend for himself?"

Personally, I didn't care if Louis Kirby lived or died, but he was my sister's fiancé and she'd kill me if anything happened to him. I said, "Yes, he's family."

My gaze turned to Griffith. This was what he meant by news from farm country.

Another explosion in the background obliterated Tania's next words. After another exchange of gunfire, she said, "I couldn't hear you."

"I said, yes, he's family." Suddenly, there was nothing but quiet in the background. "Tania? Are you OK?"

"Yeah," she said, sniffling. "These Finns take forever to die."

"Hey, one question. Did you volunteer to protect my family, or did Ms. Sabel ask you?"

"Do I look like a girl who's wanting to vacation in flat-as-a-pancake dullsville?" Tania hesitated. "She ordered me. What's up?"

"You and I have overseen her personal security since Geneva and yet, in a few hours, neither of us will be within five thousand miles of her. On her orders. Why?"

CHAPTER 45

I FLAGGED NADIA, STANDING AT the side of the room after her principal sidelined her for the party, and asked her to stand next to Betty. I needed air and room to think. The balcony called me like a siren. When I stepped out, there were only two clumps of people outside, one on each end. No Serbian soldiers and no Finns. I leaned on the railing and looked over the moonlit park two floors below.

The actress was right: I should've shot Griffith with the sniper rifle in Greenland. But no, I had to know what was going on, why everyone was lying to me, and what "Chaac" meant. Curiosity nearly killed my family. Tania's the best in the business and the Finns nearly got through her defenses. That was too close.

I looked over my shoulder to see Ms. Sabel mid-laugh with her hand on Griffith's chest giving it a playful push. That ruled out walking in there and killing the man right now. That and the fact I was still curious. And I didn't know why. Why did I care about Betty Bardon? Or Pia Sabel, for that matter? They were all lying to me. Was that my problem? Because I didn't want to die wearing a shroud of half-truths? Or was I like most humans: an unreasonable optimist believing I will fall in love again someday?

Jenny's ghost beckoned to me from the great beyond. Whatever the afterlife holds had to be better than this.

And you was this close to getting over it. Mercury stepped away from one of the groups of people nearby. *I am NOT in need of a dead evangelist, homie.*

Leave me alone, I said.

Mercury said, *Betty Bardon, your mom and dad, Pia-Caesar-Sabel—*

they all need a hero. And right now, you're just a washed-out has-been making a half-assed attempt at a desperate comeback. Saving Betty this afternoon? That was the old you. Whining about Jenny? That's just a sad imitation of Orpheus and you ain't even got a lyre.

I lost it and started yelling. *Screw you and your riddles! I don't get what Orpheus has to do with anything. The guy sang a song, a god liked it, he was supposed to get his wife back, but he made one little mistake—and Ariadne screwed him. The gods always screw us. What does that have to do with me?*

Mercury put out his hands, pushing me back. *Easy there, brutha. All the religions got a Orpheus-kinda story. Why did Lot's wife turn into a pillar of salt? Why did Eurydice disappear? What do these people have in common?*

I said, *Don't know. Don't care.*

Mercury said, *They all looked back. They longed for the way things were, not for the way things gonna be. You get stuck in the past you can't move forward. You can't be a hero. You can't trust yourself. In grief, Orpheus could only sing sad songs. He got back to the world after finally letting go of Eurydice, and everybody loved him again. He got on with his life.*

Nothing pisses me off more than learning how the ancients were dealing with the same problems thousands of years ago. And what makes it worse: my feelings are so common they had to come up with a myth about it. I prefer to be unique.

Mercury said, *Ain't no myth, homie. Orpheus really did that.*

I said, *Yeah, sure.*

Mercury said, *You don't sound convinced.*

I said, *Everyone lies to me. Why should I care about them or the future?*

You think they lie to you? Mercury stepped back. *What'd you think all them mortals are doing on their knees with their hands clasped in front of them? They be whispering lies like—*

I said, *Not my problem.*

Mercury said, *Look at all I done for you, homes. Look at the gifts the gods have given you and still you mope around. I brung you a woman looks just like Jenny only smarter. And she likes you. Holy Minerva! Y'know how hard it is to find a woman willing to put up with you? Listen up, bruh: you start believing in the one true messenger—how you and me make a great team—and good things will happen, answers to your questions will come.*

I said, *Is there a catch?*

He was gone. Sure there was a catch. There's always a catch and, like always, I'd find out the hard way.

Would it be better to join Jenny in the spirit world right now or join Betty in her quest to destroy Griffith? What did Mercury mean when he said the gods never told us what the next world was like because we'd all give up on this one and move on. Did that mean suicide, no matter how much or little *dignitas* it carried, would release us from the oppression of life on Earth? No more whimsical bosses dictating ever-changing rules. No more public humiliations from inexperienced masters born into their unearned positions. No more painful rejections after a lopsided love affair. Do we need the heartbreaking toil of forging ahead in this exhausting life?

The only reason we don't take the easy way out is fear. Fear of the unknown. Fear of the horrid imagery painted for us by everyone from the Ancient Greeks to Dante to the mad evangelist on the street corner crying, "Repent!" That's my fear: that when I get there, there will be no Jenny. Only a desolate landscape of nothingness. A void, a starless universe where I wander alone forever.

And if Mercury has any say in the matter, that's where I'd end up.

One thing was clear: I couldn't let anything bad happen to my family. A quick glance back to the cocktail party found all the players had moved one person over. Betty was giving Griffith a defiant smile, like the joke was on him. Did I owe her the trouble it would take to help her achieve her goal? Betty had saved my life. She'd torn the sleeve from her shirt for me. I owed her something for that. Ruining Griffith would be fine by me. And Jenny wouldn't mind me making her wait a little longer if it meant Griffith would pay for his sins. But what did that mean for me?

I watched Griffith walk away from Betty Bardon. She flipped him off to his back.

Yes. I could help a woman like that. I could take on one last battle—Finns and Knights and whoever else wants a piece—for the good of the world. Jenny would understand my tardiness.

Mercury said, *Aight, home-boy! Now I can look forward to getting my wife back.*

I said, *Just tell me what is going on. What in Bellona's name is Chaac?*

"It's a battery," Rafael Tum said.

He stood on the opposite side of me from Mercury, leaning his forearms on the railing, watching the evening breeze flutter the tree leaves in the park. He wore the dinner jacket Emma had tailored for him in Kyiv, with regular slacks.

"That's close to what Griffith told me," I said.

Rafael smiled mischievously. "I've decided to steal it. Would you like to help?"

CHAPTER 46

GRIFFITH'S RENTED VILLA IN BELGRADE was nothing to write home about. It was big. Three floors. And all red brick. It had a Cold War feel, all function and no form. My drone showed us views through the windows. Ground floor: a large sectional sofa surrounded a raised platform with a floor-to-ceiling stripper pole in the center. No occupants. The dining room showed three men scarfing fast food. Toward the back, two Finns argued about a soccer game on a large TV.

These were the reserves. That meant three times as many Knights of Mithras were out and about on the streets of Belgrade.

I texted Miguel and Isaiah my discovery. Miguel, having taken my place next to Betty, responded with, "Bring it."

Rafael brought the CIA agent I'd seen him with earlier. No introductions were exchanged, so in my head I named him Our Man in Belgrade, OMIB for short, sounded out like a word, oh-mib. But the man pulled his weight. He conjured up a visit from the Serbian authorities, claiming a neighbor's unspecified complaint, to draw out the Finns. That maneuver put them in motion so we could count them. Using heat lumps from through-the-wall thermal imaging, we counted eight in the villa. There could be more.

Griffith's boast about "a battalion" of Finns was plausible.

We left OMIB sitting outside in his Skoda Fabia with my drone to track the residents and a comm link keep us informed.

Rafael could climb brick as if stegophily was a way of life. It's not as hard as it looks if your fingers and toes are strong enough. We scaled the side of the house to the roof and entered one of the dormers in silence. We stood in an attic bedroom, listening for anyone or anything. The attic counted as a fourth floor, but with sloped walls and minimal living space, it hadn't been mentioned in the rental brochure we found online. Around us lay the signs of habitation: an open rucksack, a small knit laundry bag, a too-neatly-made bed. Across the tight hall, light snoring came from behind a closed door. I listened and determined from the rhythm it was a ninth man.

I snuck in, moving quickly to a shape under the sheets. The figure heard me and sat up. "Lukas?"

I said, "Shhhh…" And jabbed a dart into him. One down.

We came to a narrow stair leading down with a closed door at the bottom. We stepped on the sides of the treads to minimize creak-potential. Halfway down, OMIB let us know two Finns were coming up from second to third floors, putting them near the door in front of us.

A second later, we heard voices. Without any Finnish in my repertoire, it sounded like friendly chatter.

Rafael and I froze in place. He stood three steps in front of me, blocking my shot, should it come to that.

The men talking stopped in front of the door, finishing up with a laugh. We watched, holding our breath, waiting for the knob to turn. Their voices picked back up, as if saying, *oh, I forgot to tell you.* My heartbeat throbbed in my ears as I strained to listen. Rafael turned his gaze to mine with similar concerns. I felt adrenaline kick in.

Gently pulling my pistol, I prayed we wouldn't need it. We were outnumbered and wouldn't last long.

They stopped talking and their footsteps went in opposite directions. My guess was end-of-shift men turning in.

In the comm link, OMIB said, "Something's going on. They're mobilizing. Men in the living room putting on body armor. Did they make you?"

Rafael thumbed out a reply. "Uncertain."

We backed up the steps and headed for the window we came through. I checked the side yard below. Nothing. There were sounds of men scrambling around the back where I couldn't see. If we went down the outside, there was nowhere to go. On the floor below us, more men scrambled. If they rushed the attic, we were sitting ducks.

I never imagined checking out in a sleazy Serbian villa with a recovering revolutionary covering my six.

"Two men out front," OMIB reported. "Securing the driveway."

That could mean reinforcements were on their way. But the noise in the backyard told me different. I relaxed and waited. In the dark, Rafael turned to me, saw my calmness, and looked a question at me.

"They're leaving," I whispered.

"Emergency elsewhere in town," Rafael said, answering his own question. "They'll leave three behind."

"Counting sleeping beauty?" I pointed at my latest victim.

Rafael shrugged. "No."

A moment later, engines fired up. Our man out front reported, "Two SUVs, six onboard. Two standing guard out front."

"Run that drone by the windows," I said. "We took down one in the attic. Tell us how many are left."

We crept our way back to the stairs and trod lightly down to the door when OMIB got back to us. "One on the second floor, two out front. Inconclusive on the third floor. Too many bathrooms."

Rafael and I made quick work of the third floor. We found one guy with bedhead in the middle of suiting up. He looked surprised when I popped out of the quiet and jabbed him with a dart. That made eleven men at the villa. More than I bargained for.

Less worried about noise, we made our way down a level, then to the ground floor. When the two men out front determined the perimeter was secure, they came back inside. We put them down, then propped them up in the foyer for shock value should anyone walk in.

If Yeschenko was right and Griffith was executing his men, we'd just signed four more death warrants.

"All right, then." I turned to Rafael. "What are we looking for?"

"A server-quality hard drive with at least ten terabytes of data. Too much data for SSD or USB. It would be the old-fashioned kind, about the size of a small paperback."

We began ransacking the house in tandem, looking for the Chaac Project. He pulled cushions off the couch while I searched a bookcase filled with knickknacks.

"What's on this hard drive?" I asked as I moved to an empty credenza. "The plans for a battery?"

"I used the term 'battery' loosely." Rafael stepped on the cushions, feeling for lumps with his feet. "It's beyond that. But the word is good enough for now. It's a battery a thousand times more efficient than what we have today. Imagine a car that drives cross-country on a single charge. A phone that you plug in once a year. Whoever owns that patent will make the Saudis look like paupers." He faced me across the room. "The Keepers believe it should be public domain."

I wondered if his conversation with the Chinese general was about making the Chaac Project public domain. I decided to ask that question later when I had more background on them both.

"No capitalists in the Keepers, huh?" I checked the stripper pole and platform. Solid, no hidden chambers.

"All capitalists. But why be the richest of a species if your planet no longer supports your species?"

"Why do you want me in the Keepers?" I moved to the TV room and tossed the sofa.

"The Keepers intend to publish the findings online. Crowdsource the answers. Let the world seek a solution to fossil fuel pollution. Naturally, everyone at Griffith's party would be against that idea."

"Including Ms. Sabel," I said rhetorically, letting him dodge my question for now. "Why not tell me that at the beginning?"

Rafael came in and turned over a recliner, checking the underside. "What you did this afternoon, rushing to protect Betty Bardon, showed you care about something in today's world. You're acting like Jacob Stearne again. I thought it was time to tell you the whole story."

I knew damn well that wasn't the whole story. I also noted that everyone thought I'd been off my rocker lately. Including a Mayan college professor. I said, "You let me run around Monaco and Greenland, getting lots of people killed because you thought I wasn't ready? Are we playing Karate Kid here?"

"The Chaac Project doesn't work." Rafael pulled Playstation DVDs out of a bureau. "Not yet. There are a few critical pieces missing. In theory, the Chaac Equation has those missing pieces. But there is a third piece to the puzzle, and Griffith has it. It's a trove of data on failed tests that are invaluable in the search. It's called the Edison Data."

"What? Why care about failed tests?" I pulled the TV off the wall. No hiding places behind it.

Rafael jumped on the DVR, crushed the casing, and shook out the contents. Nothing. He tossed the pieces and said, "Edison famously said, 'I have not failed. I've just found 10,000 ways that won't work.' He won the race to create the first light bulb not because he figured out the right answer on day one, but because he tried thousands of different materials. Failures are the basis for success. What Griffith has is a large hard drive with ten terabytes of data on failures, which is why it's called the Edison Data."

I tried to wrap my head around why everyone was up for mass murder to get their hands on failure. We headed to the kitchen together. I stopped him in the doorway.

I asked, "Griffith's big investment pitch tonight is about his failures? These people came to hear about terabytes worth of 'ways that won't work?' Guess there is a sucker born every minute."

Rafael smiled and pushed ahead. He took the cabinets, pulling out pots and pans. From halfway in a low cabinet, he said, "Griffith doesn't know the first thing about Chaac. The Russians abandoned the project because leaders in the Kremlin became impatient. Careers crashed and burned trying to find the right combination of materials to make it work. They got rid of it. To this day, they don't know they were missing the Chaac Equation. Griffith knows. He thinks he's on the verge of success. He is not. To be successful, millions of combinations of element, temperature, pressure, and other variables must be tried. The Edison Data represents decades of work. Even if he procures the Equation, it will take another ten years without the Edison Data."

That made sense on some levels. They each had a piece of a whole and were trying to steal the rest from each other.

I thought about telling him how Griffith wanted me to betray him. But I canceled that idea. At some point, I'd have to betray one or the other. At that moment, I didn't know which.

I opened the fridge. The Finns had a lust for fast food. Two buckets of

KFC, three paper bags from McDonalds, and two boxes from some place called Burrito Madre. Poor bastards must've had nothing to eat back home but reindeer. I checked the freezer: four bottles of vodka. Then it came to me.

I closed the freezer and reopened the fridge. "Bingo."

Inside the most dog-eared KFC bucket: a shiny hard drive. I held it up and felt the weight. Seemed right.

"Well done," Rafael said.

"Hold on." I pulled my phone and opened the app to check for bugs. "Damn."

I tossed it back in the bucket, slammed the door, and grabbed Rafael. As I pushed him through the back door, I said, "It's a trap."

CHAPTER 47

THE OLD PROFESSOR COULD RUN like an Olympian when he had a horde of Finns on his tail. As we leapt hedgerows and fences, I pictured him as a young man, doing this same thing in the jungles of Guatemala before I was born. Three blocks later, OMIB screeched his little Skoda to a stop in front of us.

He didn't wait for the doors to close before accelerating at a light whine, its tiny engine straining with three adults. Headlights swept our back window before we got squared away. I glanced around inside the pocket-sized car for rifles. None.

"Can you pick up the speed?" I asked.

"The Belgrade office doesn't have a Sabel Security budget," he snarled as he gave me some side-eye.

What he lacked in horsepower, he made up for in driving skills. With a duck down an alley barely wide enough for our car, then two more clever turns, he lost the bigger SUVs. He got out of the suburbs and headed straight for the airport.

I texted Miguel, "Tell Ms. Sabel goodbye for me and keep close tabs on Betty. Oh, and don't forget to bring my sniper rifle with you."

It was killing me. Rafael was a nice guy who included me on the raid of Griffith's place. I craned around the headrest to face him. "Griffith threatened my family. He was going to kill them unless I earn your trust and betray you."

Rafael held my gaze with that blank look of his. After a while, he said, "We figured something along those lines."

"Why would you think that?"

"You left Greenland alive," he said.

"You still want me in the Keepers?"

"Yes."

"You never answered my question. Why?"

Before he could answer, a big SUV came up behind us too fast. Its headlights lit up the interior, the mirrors reflecting high beams in our driver's face.

The Finns had people all over town and good connections with the local police. They had figured out we were on the only road to the airport and tracked us down.

Without warning, OMIB yanked the wheel hard right, throwing the car up on two wheels and sliding down a cloverleaf. Our tires shrieked against the curb as he bravely clung to his high-speed exit.

The SUV behind us wasn't as nimble. They tried to make the turn but missed and flew down a grassy embankment, disappearing out of sight.

We merged into traffic on a major boulevard. Our driver slid between cars, leaving honking horns and obscenities in our wake. When he'd created enough havoc, he hung a U-turn and drove back the way we'd come at a calm speed. Rafael and I understood the maneuver and ducked. A minute later our driver reported a carload of Finns scrutinizing the passing cars as they went in the wrong direction—following the chaos he'd created.

As a precaution, he took us down street after alley, squeezing the Skoda through keyhole-sized passageways before driving out to the country. People following on lonely country lanes at night become easy to spot: headlights. When he was sure we were clean, he took us to the airport.

A white-haired Finn patrolled the main terminal at Nikola Tesla Airport. Snug in our footwells, he didn't see us but did recognize the Skoda as we drove by, heading for the executive terminal. He gave chase on foot.

Lurching through the gate and out onto the tarmac as fast as the little car could go, we slid to a stop in front of the airstair to Sabel One. Rafael and I bounded up the steps, where the pilot met us.

The pilot said, "The tower wants to know if we have Jacob Stearne onboard."

I handed him my passport. In bold letters, it read: James Lebon. The pilot stared at me. Then the passport. Then me. "Seriously? French, *le bon*, the bond? As in James the Bond?"

I shrugged. The 777X pilots were all business. Not fun like the Gulfstream guys. I said, "Permission to come aboard, sir?"

"Granted ... Mr. Lebon." He gave me a suspicious salute and disappeared into the cockpit.

I made my way through to the main seating area. Miguel, Isaiah, Rafael, and Betty raised their drinks to me.

"I told you to keep an eye on Betty," I said to Miguel.

He gestured with his hands as if she were an advertised product.

"Nice to see you too, Jacob." Betty, still dressed up, gave a quick smile and let it fade. Having dropped her cocktail-party act, her eyes jumped around the cabin. "I couldn't stay another minute in that room. The white-haired guy was there."

"The one from Greenland?" I asked. I took a seat near the window.

"Yes. Creep of the year. He got a call same time you texted Miguel. I thought it best to stick close to you." Betty brought back the sparkle in her eyes. "Since you were so kind to me earlier today."

Miguel's stoic face raised one eyebrow. Isaiah's expressive face formed a silent *wow*, ending with a guy's nod to me. I shook him off. I hadn't been *that* kind to her. She did look great, though. The bare shoulder and deep blue gown showed off her golden locks.

"Joona Forss," Rafael said.

I snapped to look at the old man. How did he know the Finn's name?

Before I could ask, the professor held up a hand and answered. "Our intelligence marks him as the head of the Knights' Finnish brigade. We know he's the most revered within their ranks, but he never took the field before you ran into him in Greenland. He's resourceful, clever, and relentless."

"And he's out for your blood," the pilot stood behind me. "He's talked the Serbs into holding us until the authorities can get here to search the jet. I've insisted they wait until the embassy can send someone. It's a stall tactic. Only thing I could think of. They'll cut through the red tape in less than half an hour and board."

I glanced out the window. Joona Forss, the tall, thin man with a shock of white hair stood on the tarmac, shouting at the ground crew.

"We have a labyrinth of holds below deck," the pilot said. "If you'd like to play it that way. My second officer can help you move from one to another. It might work. No guarantees."

I pulled my phone and got Neville on video chat instantly. The fact that he not only kept the phone I'd given him on the nightstand but also carried it in an easy-to-reach pocket told me he was serious about working with me. He looked different with his hair combed and wearing a suit and tie. I said, "Say, Neville, I need a favor."

"First, I must tell you how thrilled I am this request comes during daylight hours." he said deadpan.

"The Serbians are trying to frame me for some murders. I could—"

"Where are you?"

"Belgrade Airport." I turned to look out the window. White-haired Joona Forss had summoned a few heavily armed Serbian police officers. The ground crew had rolled the airstair back to the terminal and were trying not to let the cops have it. My time remaining as a free man was dwindling quickly. I said, "They're about to board the plane right now. Can you help me?"

"I'll make a call." He clicked off.

Betty moved to the seat next to me. "Where were you guys? Why did we have to run?"

"Those diamonds still belong to Ms. Sabel."

Betty's hand rose to her neck as if I were about to steal them. "You didn't answer my question."

"Broke into Griffith's villa. All we found were Finns."

After a quick glance at the professor, she asked, "You went looking for the Chaac Project?"

I didn't answer.

"Well, he would never bring it here." She looked disappointed.

"He has to show the investors something tangible," I said.

"Only a handful of people know what it looks like. He could show them anything." More disappointment saddened her gaze. "He might bring a fake, but not the real thing. That would never leave his precious

Nerve Center."

I watched Rafael as he engaged Isaiah in polite banter and realized Mercury had been right about Betty Bardon. She was smart. Very smart.

"Excuse me," I said and rose.

I went straight to the cockpit. The pilot held up a finger as he looked over his shoulder at me. Then he said, "Understood, tower. Runway 12N." He pulled his headphones off. "You have some serious friends. We're cleared for takeoff. Wheels up in three minutes."

I glanced out the window. The uniformed Serbs walked away while Joona Forss stood on the tarmac like a lonely loser.

"Change of flight plans," I said. "We're making a stop in Chicago."

CHAPTER 48

LEANING OUT OF THE DRIVER'S window in front of Griffith's mega-mansion on the shores of Lake Michigan in Winnetka, Illinois, I held my fake ID badge in front of the security camera. I raised my voice, "Like I toldya, your router's sending feedback down the line. We gotta trace it. And that means you gotta let us in to do our jobs, man. It's in your terms of service. Read the thing."

After a moment, the gate swung open. A man with a rifle pointed north to the service entrance. Isaiah rode shotgun.

The "home" of Joe Griffith could easily have been called Fort Griffith. It was built more like a castle with bulletproof glass, a tank-proof driveway, a battering ram-proof front door, and—since my last visit—a reinforced roof with secure access doors and an around-the-clock sentry. After dropping in from the roof a couple months earlier, I couldn't do the zero-dark-thirty skydive into this place again. So I got creative. We chose the second sleepiest time of day for our raid: the hour after lunch.

The guard pointed at what would be a significant home in any other neighborhood. On my last visit, I'd discovered Griffith bought his neighbor's house and used it for security personnel and an eight-car garage. A second guard waved us in like a ground crew signaling a jet. He pointed to a parking space at the side of the house.

When we climbed out, he wouldn't let us put our tool belts on until he'd gone through them. The tools were worn and slightly dirty. If we lived through this, I would send Emma a box of chocolates for getting the right props. I looked and felt like the internet service technician I was impersonating. Satisfied, he marched us into the house and led us into a small data center. Racks of lights and routers and servers and stuff I didn't know anything about faced me. The guard crossed his arms and watched me. Isaiah did the same.

That meant between the three of us, no one knew what we were doing.

Emma had a tech on the line. She said, "You're looking for a three-inch metal conduit coming out of the floor to about waist level. From it, there will be several cables. One of them is going to be a pair of thin, aqua colored, rubber-clad cables running to the ceiling, across a bundle carrier, and down to one of the racks."

Sure enough, against the far wall I found a pipe coming up from the floor with several cables coming out, one of which was a pair of aqua-colored fiber-optic cables. I followed it to a big black box taking up half one rack. I read her the model and serial numbers over the comm link under the guise I was reading them off to Isaiah. He pretended to enter them into a tablet.

Repeating what my tech told me over the comm link, I told the guard, "Let your people know, we're going to take you offline for about ten minutes."

"You can't do that," he said.

"Your system is sending feedback downstream. Technically, since it's coming from your side of the demarc, we should just shut you down until you guys get it fixed on your own. Fiber shutdown is half a day minimum. To minimize the impact, we're going to find the problem, isolate it, and let you fix it later."

"Wait here."

"Dude, I'm doing you a favor here. You guys are blowing up half the county. You got a dark fiber connection right here. You can fail over to AT&T. You'll be out ten minutes, tops."

"OK." He pulled a radio and warned his counterparts. He got an immediate response I couldn't make out. He said, "Hang on, our technician's coming."

I flipped the off switch and started following the orange fiber cables out of the room. Before I got to the door, a skinny guy with crooked glasses ran into me and bounced off.

"Easy there, tiger," I said. "You the guy who knows a transceiver from a multiplexer?"

"Yeah." He scrunched up his nose. "And I know we're not sending interference downstream."

I handed him one of the props Emma lined up for me. "Zat so? Suppose this fried 40gig-E transceiver I just pulled from your switch is in fine working order too, huh?"

He stared at the finger-sized piece of tin with astonishment. His gaze ran back to one of the big boxes whose lights were no longer blinking. "You can't be pulling our equipment apart like that."

"Have it your way." Turning to Isaiah, I said, "Tell them to cut it at the station."

"No!" Crooked glasses barked. "What do you need? Let's get this fixed."

"Show me where that one goes." I pointed to a cable tray overhead where a hundred cables of different types lay in what looked like a horizontal ladder. "The gig-E multimode."

He huffed and turned to the armed guard. "I got this, Gary. I'll get us back up in ten."

He waved me to follow him. He took us down to the basement and through a small maze to a junction box the size of a refrigerator in a dark corner of a storeroom. He pulled some keys and started to open it. Before he got anywhere, I stabbed him with a Sabel Dart and propped him in the corner with a comic book. I stole his magnetic access card.

"We're on the clock," I said to the team.

Pointing to the conduit running through the wall overhead, we located a door and followed it through two rooms. We came out to a loading dock of sorts. From here, an underground tunnel ran to the main house. All Griffith's food and supplies came through the tunnel after passing double security sweeps in the guardhouse. Griffith lived by Stearne's Law more than I did.

The techie's access card opened the locked door, as expected. Techies have better access than anyone so they can be summoned quickly when the boss accidentally deletes his life.

We jogged between the properties, coming out in an industrial pantry with five exits. A cook sorted through the food shipment for the day. She looked up, shrugged, and went back to work.

Working from memory, I found a dark hallway leading to an open area with one orange wall. This was what Griffith called the Nerve Center, a secure communications facility built inside a Faraday cage that blocked any unwanted signals from the FBI, NSA, or Sabel Security. Once we went inside, we'd be cut off from our specialists over the comm link. Time was critical.

Opening the door, I found a large oak table surrounded by twenty evenly spaced chairs, pushed in neatly. In the center, a multi-microphone with spider-like arms reached in eight directions. At the far end, a blank video screen filled the wall. Scattered across the table were fifteen three-inch thick binders, each one containing different information. At some point in the not-too-distant past, several people had huddled together, cramming for finals to make Griffith's presentation in Belgrade. They'd left in a hurry. Coffee cups, plates with bagel remnants, and crumpled napkins were scattered about. At least they'd pushed their chairs in.

"Notebooks?" Isaiah asked. "I expected computer files."

"Too easy to hack. And with this setup, we can't steal them. We'd never make it. Looks like ninety pounds of materials in big, awkward, slippery binders. Let me think."

Next to one binder lay a hard drive that looked just like the boobytrapped one in Griffith's villa. Was it the Edison Data? Isaiah started to reach for it. I held up my hand.

"Motion sensor on the last one I found," I said. I checked this one. A tripwire as thin as a human hair ran from it under the table to a black box. The box had an ethernet cable running to a hole in the floor.

Isaiah looked at me for direction.

I thought for a moment. "Pictures. Take pictures of every page on that side. I'll get these."

"Do we have time for that?"

"No. So let's get what we can."

Taking out our phones, we flipped each notebook to page one and started clicking away. Page after page. With fifteen of them, and four hundred pages each, we weren't going to get it all.

My skin crawled as if I sensed a nearby Finn.

As we clicked and flipped pages, I said, "Any of these look more important than others?"

"This one has a list of co-authors and contributors that runs five pages," he said. "I'm guessing it's the first binder." He clicked several more times then said, "And it has an executive summary."

To me, that meant he was getting the most important one. If we had to shoot our way out, at least we had a summary. I kept flipping pages and snapping pictures. With each passing second, my skin itched more and more. I checked the time. Fifteen minutes since we left the guardhouse. If there was a Finn in charge, he'd be looking by now.

I finished the third notebook and started on a fourth when we heard it. The rustle of pant legs rubbing against each other in stride. Isaiah had just finished a notebook and had both hands free. He drew his suppressed Glock and aimed at the door.

It flew open and two men came in, one squatting, aiming right. The other standing, sweeping an automatic rifle toward us. Both men saw us an instant before Isaiah dropped the standing guy. Dropping my phone and pulling my pistol took me an extra second. Allowing the squatter time to acquire me as a target. His shot skimmed my ear. Mine hit square. He slumped to the floor.

"Time's up," I said.

We dropped our tool belts and grabbed our phones. I stared at the hard drive. If our cover was blown, we could take it. But the wire might drop steel doors that would trap us inside or raise a larger alarm. The Finns had been a step ahead of me since I first heard of them. Tough call.

Isaiah ran to cover the door.

Life is risk. I waited until Isaiah wasn't looking, then grabbed the hard drive and ran to meet him.

Isaiah took one side while I covered the other. Working like a well-rehearsed team, we made it out of the room and halfway down the orange hall before taking fire. I was right about sensing a Finn. At the far end, a tall man marched toward us with a fearless stride.

Isaiah flattened against one wall while I used a doorjamb for minimal cover. We fired with a syncopated beat to confuse and disorient him. He didn't fall for it. He raised his rifle. We jumped to the middle of the hall and opened up with our pistols.

Our adversary was not invincible. He fell to the floor, facedown.

Behind us, rifles fired.

We fled down the hall and through the storeroom, where more guards were coming from the guardhouse.

"Plan B," I said.

"Yeah, I saw that coming." Isaiah was ahead of me, pushing through the servant's access.

In my ear, I heard Emma's voice. "Jacob, we just re-established comms. Are those gunshots?"

"Yep. Tell Miguel to bring it in."

I led the way to the stairs and went up a level. We made it outside before shouts erupted. Bullets ripped through the bushes next to us as we ran down the hill to the lake. We crossed the thin beach and hit the dock. I pulled ahead of Isaiah. No slouch in the competitive department, he tried hard to pass me on the right. I set the state track record back in Iowa. He didn't have a chance. But we were in open space, like target practice.

Coming at us, full tilt, was a big, roaring speedboat, aiming to ram the pier.

The wooden boards beneath our feet splintered and shredded from flying bullets. The air filled with the scent of sawdust.

The boat slewed sideways, its momentum carrying it straight at us while pushing a tsunami of lake water before it. Over the gunwales, Miguel emptied a thirty-round magazine from his MP7 over our heads at Griffith's property. We jumped the ten-foot gap from the dock to the boat, landing on top of each other in the stern. Miguel slammed the throttle and the boat shot forward, flying down the shore. Sprays of bullets trailed us, splashing water into the boat.

Within seconds, we were safely out of range.

Taking the long way back to avoid unnecessary lake patrols with difficult questions to answer, we headed out into the lake and the armadas of pre-summer boaters.

After exchanging post-combat survivor's hugs and hoots, I let my adrenaline cook off. At moments like this, when you steal the golden fleece from the dragon, life is worth living. Even if I couldn't share it with Jenny.

I reached in my pocket for the medallion. It wasn't there. It was still in Belgrade. How could I have left it behind? Intentional or subliminal? I felt a part of my life slide off the back of the boat and into the lake where it bobbed in the water as we sped away. A sad sigh left me.

Time to work. I took a chair, put my feet up, sipped the beer Isaiah handed me, and checked the pictures we'd taken.

None of it meant much to me. Math, diagrams, equations, explanations, footnotes. The notebooks were in Russian. I checked the photos for clarity and focus. Considering we were in a rush, we did a surprisingly good job. Then I came to the executive summary. Even though it was written in English, the summary meant nothing to me until I got to the last page. When I read the signature, I dropped my beer.

The author's name: Lloyd Aston. Pia Sabel's murdered biological father.

CHAPTER 49

BY THE TIME WE REACHED the Chicago Executive airport, I'd glanced through enough pages to give me a headache. Sabel One had returned to Belgrade so Emma had Sabel Three waiting for us. Miguel, Isaiah, and I trotted up the airstair.

Already onboard were two uninvited guests: Rafael Tum and Betty Bardon. I'd expressly shipped those two back to DC after Belgrade. I had a reason for that. The security of the intellectual property we copied was at stake. No one could know we had it, much less what it was. Not yet. Not until I figured out what it was and who owned it. I hadn't even uploaded the project pictures to the team yet. I didn't want Ms. Sabel finding her dad's signature without a preamble.

Rafael still wore the dinner jacket from when he'd fled Griffith's villa in Belgrade. Not a speck of dust. Betty, on the other hand, had changed out of the ball gown and diamonds. She had chosen the same kind of athleisure fashions Ms. Sabel wears—but in a whole different way. Ms. Sabel wears the tight, stretchy fabrics for the range of motion it yields her athletic lifestyle and does it in a form-follows-function, almost chaste way. If skin-tight can be chaste on a tall, athletic woman. Betty chose similar fabrics with a bare midriff, swooping neckline, and strategically placed vents along the legs and ribs. She knew how to catch a man's gaze.

No doubt that was how she'd conned the pilots into letting her aboard.

"What the hell are you doing here?" I asked.

"We flew here this morning," Rafael said.

"Commercial," Betty said as if I'd forced them to eat spoiled meat.

Miguel and Isaiah marched through and went to the back. They knew

I wanted to question our stowaways discreetly. I took a chair facing the gatecrashers.

Mercury leaned over my shoulder and said, *Question Rafael first, homeboy. He's the one you're after.*

I said, *Because Griffith claims the Keepers have the answer to solving the Chaac Project and Rafael hasn't admitted it?*

Mercury sat on the arm of my chair, *No, because when you talk to a pretty woman, you get all blubbery and can't think straight. Get what you need out of the old man, then you can blubber all you want.*

I said, *I don't blubber. I talk to beautiful women all the time. Watch.*

I stared at Betty for too long with my mouth trying to open and getting nowhere.

Mercury laughed and shoved my shoulder, *See what I mean, dawg?*

I said, *It's the audience. I don't like working under pressure.*

Mercury said, *Oh, yeah. Sure thing, brutha.*

I turned to Rafael. "Miguel wants to talk to you about indigenous cultures."

After a long stare deep into my eyes, my favorite Mayan went to talk to my favorite Diné.

I sensed fear lurking beneath Betty's uber-confident façade. A healthy dose of it. I could envision working with her. She had a lot to offer: inside information on Griffith; a master's degree; and she took the shot in Belgrade when she was supposed to and not when she wasn't. On the downside, she was distractingly beautiful and knew how to weaponize it. And I was just dumb enough to fall for it.

I said, "Thank you for letting me know the Chaac Project was at Griffith's Chicago place. I'd like to think I would've figured that out eventually, but you saved me a lot of cycles."

"You're welcome." Her dimples kicked in and her eyes sparkled. "Did you find it?"

"Why did you go to Belgrade with us?"

"Pia didn't leave me much choice."

"All right," I said. "I'll ask it another way. Why did she make you go to Belgrade?"

Betty chewed the inside of her cheek for a moment before answering.

"That's a question you should be asking her."

"And if I did?"

Betty's dimples and sparkles faded. She squirmed.

"You said we could be allies," I said. "What kind of partner won't answer a simple question?"

Her hard gaze never left mine. She breathed several times before answering. "She wanted me to evaluate Griffith's proposal. I told her my skills are rusty. Acting is a demanding business; I haven't had time to keep up on physics. But she insisted."

She rubbed the palm of her hand on her yoga pants as if wiping away nervous sweat.

I let her sweat.

People don't like silence. Especially actors. And especially extrovert actors. She wiped her palms again, her eyes wandered, her knees clamped together. Then she chose sides. Mine. "She thought I knew something about Joe Griffith. Wanted to use me the same way you did, to throw him off. She set up a meeting. Just the two of us and him. He was supposed to have proof that his project has legs. I was supposed to look at it. Evaluate it. Instead, I got kidnapped in the elevator."

I rolled back time in my head. Miguel showed her the video camera. She blew up. Then stormed out. At the time, I didn't question it because it felt like an appropriate reaction. But now I realized that going outside the suite was the opposite reaction to what she should've done: stay inside and demand my protection. She was going to meet Ms. Sabel.

Another bit of that afternoon played out in my head. After the kidnapping, Ms. Sabel went to help Betty get ready for dinner. A typical girl-thing. But that wasn't what she wanted. She wanted to talk about Griffith's proposal. Why didn't she tell me anything about meeting Griffith? I would've had Betty at that meeting with double security.

After regrouping my thoughts, I asked, "What did she say when you left Belgrade?"

"Nothing. She watched me walk out as if I were leaving her in the lurch. Well, I guess that's what I did. She must hate me now."

"You keep telling me you want to kill Griffith, yet you're here in Chicago instead of Belgrade. Every time I turn around, you're appear to be chasing the Chaac Project, not him."

She tightened her mouth and narrowed her eyes. "After Greenland, I realized you were right. Killing him was hyperbole on my part. I said those things—and thought them too—but I don't really have the stomach for it. I want to destroy him though. And his little circle of royalty and ultra-rich, his business, everything. Burn it to the ground. I'm going to steal Chaac from him and turn it over to the public. And when he's stripped naked and paraded in front of the world—then he's all yours. I won't care if he lives or dies."

I leaned back in my seat and thought.

Mercury leaned to my ear. *You called it with this girl, homie. Just like you thought after that not-so-romantic dinner on the way to Belgrade. She wants to destroy Griffith. She'd make a damn fine emperor's wife. And you'd make a damn fine—*

I said, *I'm not going to be an emperor.*

Mercury peeled back, *Not with that attitude, you ain't.*

"Betty," I said and leaned forward, "I get that part. He abused you and destroyed your family, so revenge makes sense. What I can't figure out is why you went back to him and made those movies. You landed a scholarship to a prestigious quantum program at Santa Barbara. You got a masters at Caltech and were working on your PhD. Then you drop all that and run back to the man who abused you. You made a few movies. And now, out of nowhere, you show up anywhere the Chaac Project is mentioned. You want to be allies. Fill me in. What am I missing here?"

Her gaze darted around my head. A faint sweat broke out on her brow. She worried her fingers, then put her palms together, resting her elbows on her knees. "OK, I get it. You don't trust me. I earned that, so I'll own it." She took a breath. "You're right, there's more to it. Griffith and his buddies, the Duke of Kingston, the Earl of Wesley, and the Sultan of Sulu used me like a whore until I was sixteen. When they dumped me, I poured myself into my studies to avoid my classmates. A lot of therapy helped me finish high school. I found quantum physics fascinating and I was good at it. I won the attention of a Russian physicist in need of new talent. He had a project his country was under-funding, the Chaac Project. They hired me. I worked on it for a year and figured out how world-changing this thing could be—if we could figure out the last few steps. Then the Russian Federation closed up shop. They said they were going to sell what they had to the highest bidder. They sent me home. I knew how close they were. I wanted to bid on it—but I don't have that kind of money. The only rich people I know who—"

"Griffith and his friends," I said for her.

She shuddered, then continued, "The only thing holding back renewables is when the sun goes down, or the breeze stops blowing. A storage system like the Chaac Project could change that overnight. For the good of the planet, I sucked it up and went to him. He toyed with me, made me take roles in those movies while he drummed up investors. Or so he claimed. Next thing I know, he bought the project, cut me out of the deal, and claimed my movies were bad investments."

For once, I felt like I had a reliable story. She was a good actress, and she could be playing me, but this felt real. Then Stearne's Law flared up my concerns about her ability to distract me. I said, "Are you working with Rafael?"

Betty's face scrunched up, offended by the question. "We came here separately. Seems like we have the same idea. But I don't know him at all. Only thing I know about him is he's one of your sidekicks." She softened to a husky bedroom voice. "Why work with one of your lieutenants when I can work with you?"

"Trade places with him." I pointed to the aft section.

She looked down the aisle, then back at me as if I'd insulted her. With a clenched jaw and a miffed sniff, she went back.

A text dinged my phone with an odd sound. Not one of my regular people dings. I checked it. A picture of my family, Mom, Dad, Joyce, and Louis were standing in line on Navy Pier just below the Centennial Wheel.

Griffith. Or his Finns.

I forwarded the picture to Tania with a note, "Got this from Griffith. They're near you."

She texted back immediately. "Yeah, we saw him. Tossed him off the pier. Turns out, he knew how to swim. Disappointing. But whatcha gonna do? Relax, Jacob. We got this."

I texted Griffith back. "Nice. I tried reaching out to your mom to tell her what kind of useless man-child you are, but the motel manager said she was busy giving a massage to three sailors."

I slipped the phone back in my pocket as Rafael took the hot seat.

"You're not going to tell me what you found," he said before I could say anything. "You don't trust me. You shouldn't. Not yet. As an overture, I'll explain why you found Lloyd Aston's signature on the executive summary."

I couldn't mask my shock. How did he know I'd found anything, much less the summary?

"You should take a few acting lessons from Ms. Bardon." A wry smile crossed his face for a split second. "You came back with the air of victorious warriors. Yes, you tried to hide it and you did well. Betty, the pilots, the ground crew have no idea." He watched my eyes. "The difference between triumph and defeat can be observed in the shoulders."

"We didn't get it. We saw it but couldn't carry it out."

"You got close. A moral victory, as they say in sports."

"What's the answer?"

"A young grad student was working on a world-changing storage cell, a metacapacitor, as his doctoral thesis. Unbeknownst to young Aston, his professor's department was largely funded by fossil fuel companies. When the Chaac Project showed promise, they sent a representative from one of the largest fossil fuel reserves in the world: Russia. They killed Aston and his girlfriend, stole his research, and left his daughter Pia to be adopted by Alan Sabel."

"I figured that out when Ms. Sabel showed a picture of Lloyd Aston to Betty." Which wasn't quite true. I hadn't figured it out until I said those words, but the facts lined up in my mind as I spoke. And that meant Ms. Sabel knew all about Chaac. There was no need to shield her from seeing her dad's signature on the summary page; she knew it was his work. She'd told me she wasn't sharing with me because she wanted my objective opinion. Objective opinion about what, exactly?

Rafael looked surprised for the first time since I'd met him. He craned over his shoulder for a look at the actress. Slowly turning back to me, I could see the gears working in his head. He was trying to figure out the enigma we call Betty. Then his face resumed its normal deadpan. Which told me they weren't working together. Yet they claimed to have the same goal: to take Chaac public.

Four people had put me in the center of their separate efforts to secure the Chaac Project and Equation: Griffith, Rafael, Betty, and Ms. Sabel. In theory, Ms. Sabel should be the rightful owner. Griffith's motivation was pure greed combined with might makes right. I had Betty's motivation figured out to a certain extent.

That left Rafael as the only pure question mark. Despite the many answers he'd provided, a larger mountain of questions remained. It was time to find out what was going on between the Keepers and the Knights of Mithras. I had only one card left to play with Rafael.

"Griffith told me you have the Chaac Equation. So. Where is it?"

"To answer that," Rafael said, "we need to go to Calgary."

CHAPTER 50

I PARKED THE SQUAD AT the Banff Springs Hotel, a stone fortress built in the late nineteenth century deep in the Canadian Rockies west of Calgary. The next day, Rafael and I drove to Lake Louise, outfitted horses, and rode up public trails into the Valley of the Ten Peaks. Ominous black cliffs stood out in high contrast under snow-covered peaks. Eighty million years ago, one slab of North America dove under a younger plate of rock and shoved it ten thousand feet into the sky. The resulting mountains of knife-sharp shale and sandstone gave us breathtaking views.

On the far side of Moraine Lake, we left the day hikers and rode above the tree line. The marked trail disappeared. Rafael rode like an old cowboy with no concerns about the darkening skies, the increasing cold, or the ever-deeper snow. We crested a ridge between two of the ten peaks, the horses kicking through powder on a trail only the professor could see. On the downhill side, we rode into a primeval forest with a stronger scent of pine than I'd ever experienced before. Squirrels watched us from halfway up tree trunks. It was late spring elsewhere in the world but this far north, it felt more like the first thaw.

After a full day of riding, we came to a deserted compound of five log cabins, a barn, and a corral. The barn was stocked with fresh hay even though ours were the only horses and the only tracks in the snow. Fresh straw lined the open stall area. The strong smell of horses and leather gave me the sense there were others here.

We went to one of the cabins, where I stopped to look around before mounting the half-log steps to the small porch. Aging mortar barely held the pitch-coated logs together. Across the way was a cabin that looked exactly like the one in Neville's fishing trip picture. I imagined Neville, Rafael, Ms. Sabel, Alan Sabel, and Griffith standing in front of it.

We went inside. It held three rooms: a great room with a fireplace, a kitchen, and a bedroom. The outhouse was a short walk. The place smelled of old wood and campfire. Fresh trout lay in the kitchen sink, cleaned and ready for grilling. Rafael tended the fire while I cleaned up some veggies.

A long day on the trail makes anything you cook taste ten times better. It was the finest trout ever. We enjoyed our meal at a rough-hewn table. When we finished, I started to clean the kitchen. Rafael stopped me.

"There is something you need to see." He beckoned me to follow him.

We went to the bedroom where he opened an armoire and stepped through. I followed, half expecting Narnia. Instead, I found a long stone corridor dug into the mountainside. After a quarter mile, we came to a steel door. It unlocked with an automatic clunk.

"OK," I said. "So, this is the Bat Cave?"

Rafael didn't even glance over his shoulder.

We kept going down a dimly lit passage chiseled out of solid rock. Marks from picks and wedges were evident on every surface. Eventually, we came to a cavernous room, fifteen feet high, sixty in diameter. Hundreds of niches lined the perimeter wall. Each one held an object lit from above and protected by a thick slab of glass.

"The Keepers is an ancient order of academics, statesmen, revolutionaries, visionaries, and philosophers." He welcomed me with arms spread wide. "Our mission has been to safeguard dangerous knowledge that might destabilize civilization. And to introduce the same when it will benefit all of humanity."

"Yeah. Sure." I moved to one of the display cases. I'm no paleographer, but it looked like a stack of Mayan codices. Of tens of thousands of pre-Columbian books handmade by ancient Mayans, only four were known to have survived the flames of the Spanish Inquisition. In this niche were at least twenty.

"You can tell what I mean more through our failings than our successes," he said. "We failed to stop the Manhattan Project. Hundreds of thousands died, and many millions still live in fear of annihilation. Then there was the rape of the Americas. While we convinced King Alfonso V of Portugal, and later King John II, not to finance a trade route to Asia by sailing west, we failed to stop Christopher Columbus from convincing the Spanish crown to pay for it."

"I get the atomic bomb," I said. "Why were you trying to stop Columbus?"

. "Look what came of it." He raised his hands, palms out as if crucified. "Cultures destroyed, millions enslaved, genocide, destruction. At that time, the Europeans were not ready for the responsibility of conquest."

"Yeah, that's one way to look at it." I stared at another niche. Stacks of parchment scrolls lay under one that was partially unrolled. I tried to make out the lettering. It looked vaguely Greek.

Mercury leaned over my shoulder. *The history of Alexander the Great, written by Ptolemy Soter, homes. One of the greatest works of all time.* He choked up. *A loss to all y'all mortals.*

I thought it burned in the Library of Alexandria, I said.

Mercury said, *That was the official story. Maybe the Keepers wanted to release it at some later date when it suited them.*

"Why did you 'keep' Ptolemy's history of Alexander?" I asked.

Rafael's stone face showed a flicker of surprise that I knew what it was. "Alexander's legend was greater than the actual man. What you believe today is much different from the murderous, genocidal maniac whose own soldiers murdered him and covered it up so they could go home to their families."

He was right. That was not what I'd been taught. I looked at the scrolls and wondered, why not tell the truth about him? But Rafael was moving on.

He pointed at another display holding a sheet-metal box with a strange lens on the front. "This is one of our successes. In the '50s, a group of scientists working for the military came to us with a dilemma they compared to the atomic bomb. They'd invented this device: a focused microwave that could kill a man at up to three miles. Point the beam at a victim's head and it cooked his brain in a second or less. No smoke, no trace, no evidence left behind."

"A death ray?" I asked.

"Exactly. Consider the implications for assassination. Dictators would be unstoppable. The scientists gave us the research for safekeeping and reported the experiment a failure."

Footsteps on stone approached us. I reached for my pistol, but Rafael waved me off.

A woman entered the chamber holding a three-inch thick notebook, like the ones we found at Griffith's. She strode straight to Rafael and handed it to him.

She turned to me and extended a hand. With a thick accent, she said, "Pleased to meet you. I am Amit Sofer. I provided your vegetables. My husband Eli provided the trout."

I shook her hand. "Thank you. Both were delicious."

She bowed her head and tracked around me and left down the hall.

"Housekeepers?" I asked.

"We rotate working vacations here. This location provides a cathartic sabbatical from the stresses of life."

I could see that. There are times when killing people becomes tedious. I could do with some downtime in a quiet place like this. Maybe joining up with the Keepers wouldn't be such a bad thing.

He opened the notebook to the middle and held it in his arms for my inspection. "A friend of Lloyd Aston's, a fellow grad student, approached us. He feared something terrible might happen to Mr. Aston's research. We met with Aston and tried to convince him to let us handle the Chaac Project. Like many brilliant young men, he was reluctant to turn over his life's work to strangers with strange tales. However, we did convince him to keep a key part of the project in a different place from the main body of work."

I turned the pages. Lots of Greek letters in complex formulas. I can handle math with epsilons, even the occasional delta, but when they start throwing omegas and thetas in the mix, I get a headache. I squinted at the footnotes.

Mercury stood behind Rafael, tilting his head in curious thought. *So now whatcha gonna do, homie? You could beat him over the head, steal the notebook, give it to Griffith and free your family. Or give it to Pia-Caesar-Sabel and maybe she gives you a bonus. Or, hey, here's an idea: keep it for yourself and get in on the action. You could be a billionaire! Then you could build me a great big temple in Central Park.*

I said, *I don't even know if it's real. He could be showing me a dishwasher repair manual.*

Mercury stroked his chin. *Now where could you find an expert to verify this thing?*

To Rafael, I said, "You wanted to jump me into the Keepers. I take it this is why. So what do you want from me?"

"Griffith said this belongs to him. Pia could make the same claim." He left it there, his gaze like steel.

I considered the implications and tried to figure his next move. "You said you wanted to make it all public. Why not publish this on the internet?"

"It would be the equivalent of giving it to him," Rafael said. "We asked you to find out how far along he was. You did that, albeit unwittingly. When you raided his house to get the project, you confirmed what we suspected: he was quite close. If he had been far from the end, we would've found the notebooks in Belgrade."

"Why? That's not a secure location."

"Human nature is easy to read. It's all about confidence. He's confident because he's close to solving the problem. If not, he would have no confidence and would've shown off more."

That sounded like Griffith, all right.

"You want me to negotiate something with him." I thought through where the old man was going with his fantasy that I could solve all his problems. "A negotiation that results in you—I mean, us—the Keepers, having everything."

Rafael stayed still.

I kept thinking. "You want me to lure him into a negotiation with this piece, then screw him out of his part so you can publish the whole thing?"

The slightest twitch of an eyebrow confirmed my theory.

"And the reason you're so keen on signing me up is that you think of me as expendable. If the whole thing goes south and I wind up dead, you still have this piece of the puzzle. You can try again with some other guy."

"Yes, we see you as an option." Rafael closed the notebook. "There are tremendous risks to you. There is no need to pretend otherwise. But we want you, not because we consider you expendable, Jacob. Quite the contrary. We consider you the best hope the world has to bring the Chaac Project—including this critical piece, the Chaac Equation—into the light where it can benefit all of humanity."

Mercury leaned an elbow on the old man's shoulder. *Ain't that sweet, my brutha? He butters you up before he asks you to die for his cause. You wanted a chance to die with a truck load o' dignitas—well here's your opportunity, wrapped with a bow.*

I said, *Why do I feel like that's pure sarcasm?*

I never faked a sarcasm in my life, Mercury said. *C'mon now, I'm trying to get my wife back. I only win if you win. Last time I checked, dying ain't winning.*

"Did you really want the Edison Data?" I asked the professor.

"There are three equally important components to this: the Project itself, the Equation, and the Edison Data. The solution is theoretical, never proven. To test the theory 22.8 billion combinations must be tried. The Russian's failure data constitutes nearly half that. If three factions had the Project and Equation parts, and a fourth faction had all three components, that last faction would win the race by virtue of having half the work done for them."

It felt like the first straightforward answer he'd given me. I asked, "Have you asked Ms. Sabel about this?"

"Alas, she declined to work with us."

I found his answer puzzling. Teasing the ideas in my head, I tried to figure it out. She allowed the Keepers to conscript me while she foots the bill. Yet she won't share her communications. She had a legitimate claim to ownership, more than any other player. Why not tell me?

Mercury said, *Cuz you wasn't being you. She knew you'd get back to being my true believer one day. Until then, she couldn't have you spillin' the beans to the Keepers.*

I said, *Why not work with the Keepers then? What's she up to?*

Mercury tossed his hands in the air and paced impatiently. *She's up to the same thing Caesars always be up to: playing the odds, making and breaking alliances, testing the loyalty of her partners. She's gonna reclaim the Chaac Project.*

I said, *Their idea of putting it in the public domain is the kind of thing she loves. She could change the name to the Aston Project and everyone would know it was her dad.*

Mercury wiped his face and shook his head. *Dude. Dude! DUDE! Rich people do not get rich by giving shit away. Don't you get that yet? Ah, you're useless. See, that's why you're a worker bee and she be the queen.*

I understood what he was telling me, whether he believed it or not. I applied that same theory to Rafael Tum and figured he was doing the same. Everyone was out to screw everyone else. The only person I understood was Griffith. Criminals can always be trusted to choose the criminal option, while nice people only chose the criminal option when it's more convenient.

But I had a trick or two up my sleeve as well.

"If this checks out to be what you claim, I'm your man." I extended a hand to shake.

Before Rafael took it, he asked, "How do you intend to check it out?"

"Just let me look at a couple of the key pages. I'm not bad at math."

He opened the book. I leaned in to get a close look. I stared for as long as I dared. I love math, but the equations on those pages were so far over my limited education, it could've been anything.

None of that mattered. I didn't care what the book said or if the Equation even existed. What I cared about was taking down Joe Griffith, for Jenny and Betty, and women everywhere. And the old man was giving me a way to make that happen. With this notebook, I could lead Griffith to slaughter and, maybe, just maybe, get Ms. Sabel's inheritance back.

"I'll double-check later," I said, "but for now, I'm in."

CHAPTER 51

JOE GRIFFITH PICKED UP THE next proposal in the stack. The parties were over, the attendees were gone, the show had gone well, and now it all boiled down to a room full of accountants. Who had turned in the best offer? He opened the binder and smiled when he saw the logo: Sabel Industries. He flipped through the pages to the financial commitment. Pia Sabel was serious. The highest commitment for research and development funding by far. She was now the front runner in his mind. He turned the page to most important consideration: the ownership request.

Shit.

He tossed Sabel's proposal on the table.

Rising to his feet, he looked at the assembled accountants typing away like hamsters on wheels. "Damn it! I told you, any bid requiring operational control gets trashed. That's a non-starter. Who let this one through?"

Pointing at Sabel's proposal as if it were an armed grenade, he glared at each one of them.

"I did, sir." A large guy leaning back raised a weak hand. "The board representative said he wanted to see them all."

"Is the 'board representative' here?" Griffith mocked the phrase.

"No sir, but he inventoried them before he left."

"Who the hell let him do that?"

The accountants all looked at each other as if pointing fingers. He'd expected them to watch his back, take care of things, but no, they had no loyalty at all. Not a pair of balls in the lot of them. He should've had Joona watch these fools instead of letting the man run off to Canada. His gaze fell back to Sabel's proposal.

He picked it up and started scanning for reasons to shoot it down. There had to be something. The board would get all starry-eyed and drool over the R & D budget instead of seeing it for what it was: a takeover. He knew Pia Sabel would work this like an ancient Egyptian stonemason. To build the pyramids, they cut small holes with a hammer and chisel, drive a wooden wedge into the holes, then soak them with water. The water would swell the wood and split the stone. Let her in and the Knights of Mithras would be splintered into warring factions within a month.

His phone rang with the Duke's special ring. He answered.

"How are the bids looking, old boy?" the Duke of Kingston asked.

"Analyzing is tedious business, but I'm plowing through it."

"My money's on the Red Army," the Duke said. "Have the Chinese come through for me?"

"They didn't leave a proposal."

"And why would that be?" the Duke snarled.

Griffith thought about telling him the truth. They had seen the Russians crash and burn. How many generals and bureaucrats had lost their careers digging in that salt mine? Instead, he said, "They spun their wheels trying to work out a partnership with Sabel."

"Poor fools. Like working with a rock. Did she put in anything worthwhile?"

"I just read the summary," Griffith said. "She believes she owns the intellectual property."

"Possession is nine tenths of the law. Let her cry about it in court."

"My thoughts exactly. But we won't need any of them if we can get inside the Keepers."

"Stop wasting your time." The Duke laughed. "Never underestimate the stubbornness in a coven of self-righteous old bastards. They've believed in their cause for so long, they've lost the plot. You'll never turn one of them."

"You're quite right. That's why I've sent in an infiltrator."

"You never. Who?"

Telling the chairman of the board a lie could end his career. And

Joona Forss, for all his loyalty to Griffith, would never lie to the board for him. The Knights of Mithras meant more to the Finn than any individual. Griffith bit his lip and told the truth. "Jacob Stearne."

"The man who destroyed your predecessor in Germany?" The Duke's voice grew louder with each syllable. "The man responsible for the fiasco in Monaco? The man who outwitted you in Belgrade?"

"Uh. Well. We had him in Greenland, and he committed to bringing me the Chaac Equation. His family hangs in the balance. We need only a bit more patience—"

"You're not even certain they have the Equation! We can't wait for your risky plans. The Koreans and the French are a year ahead of us. We need a partner, the right partner—one with deep pockets. Get those proposals analyzed and bring them to me. Stop wasting time on those doddering old fools, the Keepers. They mean nothing."

"Just a few more days is all—"

"The board is not happy with your performance now, Mr. Griffith. Deng Zhipeng and Mikhail Yeschenko chose not to bid. Why do you suppose that is? I'll tell you why. They think they can steal it from you. We need partners with money, and we need them fast. Get moving, Griffith. There are others ready, willing, and able to stand in for you if you can't get the project underway soon."

The call ended.

Griffith looked at his reflection in the window. He could see Sabel's damned inscrutable poker face sitting across from him at Klub 20/44. At the time, he thought he had the upper hand. She probably knew then she'd have the winning bid. She probably chased off the Chinese herself. And if that proved to be the case, he'd have to work with her.

That was an image he couldn't stomach.

He called Joona. "You're losing to a farm boy from Iowa! He put your men to sleep. To sleep, Joona!" Spittle flew from his lips as he shouted. "He didn't even respect them enough to kill them. He doesn't fear you. Make him regret that. Kill one of his family so he takes this seriously. Leave nothing undone. I want Stearne in my grasp in twenty-four hours!"

He clicked off without letting Joona say a word.

Griffith grabbed the Sabel proposal and tossed his jacket over his shoulder.

The accountants stared with open mouths like a school of fish at feeding time. He'd forgotten they had ears. "Whatever you think you heard, you're wrong. Anyone who thinks otherwise will face serious consequences."

He stared them down until they went back to work.

CHAPTER 52

STRIDING INTO THE SUITE IN midafternoon the next day, I made straight for the bathroom to get a quick shower and change of clothes. I like riding horses as much as anyone, but two days on the trail is a lot of pine, leather, dirt, and horse.

While I undressed, Ms. Sabel sent me a text. "Did you find anything?"

She loves wide open questions that make it hard to lie to her. I responded, "I'm not sure." Rafael could've shown me gibberish for all I knew. "I need to check a few things before I get your hopes up."

That seemed to pacify her. For now. It wasn't a lie, and it wasn't obfuscation. The Equation felt real, it looked real, and I had a feeling it was real. But before I became someone's accomplice, I wanted to know their intentions. Why was Ms. Sabel being so uncharacteristically mysterious about her actions? Who were Neville and Rafael? Were they the trustworthy noblemen they portrayed?

Whatever the answers to those questions, I knew the time for sneaking around was over. I would make Rafael's crazy plan work. Not because it would get the result he desired—it wouldn't—but to bring Griffith to his knees. I considered a major bonus to the idea: I could also flush out the one yet-unseen faction who had remained in the background since they tried to dig a tunnel into the Sabel Operations Center. Griffith claimed it wasn't him and I believed him. It was time to force their hand and bring them into the light.

When I stepped out of the shower, Betty handed me a towel. Her eyes sparkled and her dimples grew with her snow-white smile. Yet the faint sheen of fear still trembled beneath her skin. The attack in Belgrade had shaken her to her core.

Betty stared and let out an, "Oh my."

Mercury leaned against the sinks. *Forgot you had a two-bedroom suite, huh, dawg?*

Taking the towel and winding it around me, I said, *Yeah, bad planning on my part. What is she doing in here?*

Mercury looked heavenward. *Hey Cupid, are you there? Our intellectually challenged mortal here needs another one of your lessons cuz he's a slow learner. Apparently.*

I said, *I mean, why is she here in Canada? Why did I let her come along? It's dangerous.*

Mercury said, *Are you asking me, 'what was I thinking?' or are you asking me, 'was I thinking?' cuz it looks pretty simple to me what you was thinking. You was thinking she looks a lot like Jenny only with dimples and a master's degree. Did you know she loves jazz? Jenny weren't too keen on it, if you recall.*

I said, *She was learning about it.*

To Betty, I said, "Thanks for the towel, but I could've found—"

The instant I had myself covered, she threw her arms around me and squeezed the air out of me. It felt good. Undeniably good. In the instant, I felt both the erotic and the compassionate benefit of a good hug. For once in my life, the compassionate benefit outweighed the other. The sensation that someone else on Earth cares about you is a powerful feeling. My arms encircled her for a moment. She felt good. Very good. Then I felt myself pushing her away from me, despite wanting to continue the embrace.

"What?" She searched my eyes. "You can hug me after I kill someone, but I can't hug you when I've been worried about you for two days?"

"Worried?" I moved to the sink and grabbed my toothbrush. "You have nothing to worry about."

"Your life has been in danger from the moment I met you." She waited until my mouth filled with toothpaste lather, then she said, "I care about you, Jacob. Don't pretend you haven't noticed. You care about me too. You wouldn't have saved me in Brest or Belgrade if you didn't care.

And don't pretend you're still mourning your girlfriend. She's gone and she's not coming back. On an intellectual level, you know that's true. You're pushing the world away, trying to dive into a chasm of sorrow. It's a waste. It's time to start looking forward."

I gave Mercury a dirty look in the mirror. He tossed up his hands and mouthed the word, *Truth.*

What the hell. They were both right. Ms. Sabel had said as much, too. And Betty was smart. My grandfather once told me, "You can marry for money, beauty, or brains. Only one of those will last a lifetime." He never mentioned a woman who had all three.

Whatever the case, Betty Bardon suddenly looked like a movie star.

My arms encircled her again. "Didn't want our first kiss to be marred by bad breath."

My phone rang with Tania's tone. I held up a finger. "Hold up, I've got to take this."

Betty stepped back, crossed her arms, and frowned.

Due to my wet fingers, I answered it on speaker. Just as Tania began a fast rant, Miguel appeared in the doorway. Tania said, "We got problems, Jacob. I ain't gonna lie. We kept them at bay but as of a few hours ago, they've taken the gloves off. I got Finns coming out of my grill. I'm thinking of telling your folks what's going down and taking them out to the new Sabel Ranch in Montana. It's isolated, with a long, winding road leading in. No one can get there without us seeing them miles in advance. But your folks are itching to get back to the farm now. They're not going to the ranch without an explanation."

Tania never gave up. She never admitted she was in trouble. That meant she was losing control of the situation and didn't want anything to happen to my family. Which meant she cared. Lots of people cared.

Except Miguel. He had his nose in his phone. A rarity for him.

"Jacob?" The strain in Tania's voice came across loud and clear. "You there?"

I started to respond. Miguel grabbed my shoulder to stop me. After thumbing something one-handed on his phone, he looked up. He answered for me.

"Better plan," Miguel said. "Trombone Shorty's playing in

Backatown tonight and Tremé tomorrow. I'll meet you there. Who you got with you?"

I started to say something. He squeezed my shoulder again. Even if you're good friends with a man as big as a bear, when he squeezes your shoulder, you keep your mouth shut.

"I got Cody, Dhanpal, and two from the Chicago office," Tania answered.

"I'll leave Isaiah here to cover Jacob," Miguel said. "You can ditch the Chicago people. They're good, but I know a few agents out of New Orleans that're top shelf."

"What's wrong with my ranch plan?"

"Two things," Miguel said. "These Finns are resourceful. If they aren't trained paratroopers, they'll read the manual on the way down. The other is: we don't want to tell his folks. They'd get mad and save the Finns the trouble of killing Jacob. Especially that sister of his."

"Hold on there," I said. "I get to have a say in—"

"No you don't," both Tania and Miguel said in unison. He let Tania continue. "I know you want to come along, but you're like a lightning rod. It'll make things worse. Besides, right now, I'd rather have Miguel's brains than your brawn."

Miguel stabbed the disconnect button and looked up at me. "You've got something big going down with the professor." He glanced over my shoulder at Betty. "And other opportunities demanding your attention. I've got this."

The fact that Tania was losing ground to the Finns worried me. I've trusted her with my life plenty of times and never regretted it. Double for Miguel. But trusting them with Mom?

Mercury said, *Dude, you've had some rough patches in New Orleans. I can't protect you down there in Voodoo country. They've got gods lurking in the swamp ain't nobody ever seen before. Didn't go to god college or nothing. They're like feral gods and they—*

I said, *Feral gods? No. Don't explain that one. Just stop talking or I'll have to go back on my meds.*

Mercury said, *Short version, homie: You trust Tania because she's almost as good as you. You trust Miguel because he's better'n you.*

Together, they're invincible.

I said, *Yeah, you've got a point.*

Mercury said, *Besides, you've got business in Banff. If you know what I mean.*

I said to Miguel, "You're right. Thank you."

He turned and left.

Maybe Tania and Miguel were right, but it would've been nice if they let me argue about it for appearances sake.

"What was that about?" Betty asked. "Where is Backatown?"

"Trombone Shorty is the top horn player in the world right now. Backatown and Tremé are the neighborhoods where the best jazz is played. They're behind the tourists-only French Quarter. My parents are big jazz fans. They won't think twice about a trip to NOLA."

"Part of me wants to go with them," she said. She stepped in close, her breath brushing my lips. "I love Trombone Shorty."

I leaned in for a kiss.

Just as my lips came within range, she turned to the side. "Hey, where's that professor of yours? Is he going to come wandering in like everyone else?"

Stearne's Law crept into my head. She asked for details about where Tania was taking my family. Now she wanted to know about Rafael? While my paranoia rose, I answered. "He had to go to the big city. He'll be back in the morning."

"You're going to meet him." She pressed her cheek to my chest. "I'd like to be there."

"And I'd like to be the king of France." I pushed her back. "Dress for dinner. I made a reservation for the two of us."

CHAPTER 53

THE MAÎTRE D' CALLED THREE times asking if I wanted to cancel. Three times I told him we would be just a few *more* minutes late. They were holding the most exclusive dining experience in western Canada for me, and they weren't going to let me forget it. Finally, Betty was ready. She made the wait worthwhile. Recycling the diamonds and blue gown from Belgrade, she did a twirl for me in the living room. She'd hadn't lost a single sparkle on the whole trip.

What is it about shoulderless dresses that makes them so eye-catching? Is it the subliminal message that it might fall to the floor at any moment? Or is it the expanse of skin so often hidden from view? In this case, I decided, it was simply Betty. Her charm, warmth, and ability to calculate the strength of a Lamborghini's hood while on the run—not to mention fashioning a bandage from her shirtsleeve—towered over any other attributes.

The bright red lipstick didn't hurt either.

"Do you still like it?" she asked.

"You still look like a Hollywood bombshell from the golden age. But I told you to send the diamonds back."

Her hand covered the jewels as if I were trying to snatch them from her.

I waved at the door. "Tomorrow."

We made our way to the 360 Dome on the Garden Terrace, where the glass enclosure had been cleared of everything but one table for two. Waiting for us were candles and crystal and silver and linens and gracious staff. Betty looked them over with a skittish glance. After the maître d' acquainted us with the surrounding peaks, still visible in the late dusk, he poured our wine and left us.

"Our second romantic dinner," she whispered across the table.

"Let's hope it ends better than the first."

She looked surprised for a moment, then apologetic as she recalled her outburst. "Your attitude has greatly improved since then."

"Is that your way of saying, 'Thanks for saving my life?'"

"About that," she said. The sparkle in her eyes came back and her dimples accented her smile. "I have a present for you."

Reaching into her clutch, she produced a small, square jewel box and presented it with that beautiful smile. I took it with an appreciative bow and opened it. A shiny Canadian silver dollar stared back at me. On one side was written, "Lake Louise Mount Assiniboine," and had a relief of the famous peak just a few miles away.

A token given to me in the same spirit as Jenny's. I winced at the thought I'd lost Jenny's medallion. Betty had never seen Jenny's; hers was an original thought. A keepsake to preserve our moment. Part of me wanted to cry. Part of me wanted to kiss her. The result was a dumb and unappreciative expression. Realizing my rudeness, I said, "Thank you. It's very nice."

It was too late.

Her dimples disappeared and she avoided me with a glance around the spacious room. "Where is Isaiah? Shouldn't he be protecting us?"

"The poor guy hasn't slept in three days." I swirled my wine in its glass, checking the clarity and legs. "I told him to take a nap."

"How convenient." She held up her glass. "Here's to the only hero I need."

I clinked and decided to ignore etiquette, which said never to drink a toast to yourself. I sipped a surprisingly superb cabernet. This deep in the wilds, gourmet becomes a relative term, yet the wine was as good as any I'd tasted. Our waiter arrived with our amuse-bouche, a potato-and-chive croquette with crème fraiche and caviar.

I held up the coin and twirled it in my fingers before slipping it in my pocket. "I'll carry it with me wherever I go."

She smiled politely and sipped more wine.

"Do you ever feel like you're abusing Pia's generosity?" Betty asked.

I raised a brow for her to explain.

"Buying out this dome for dinner?" she asked. "Grabbing the highest-priced suites in hotels? Flying around on her jets like borrowing a friend's car?"

"She's never complained. Her accountants used to raise a stink, but they got tired of her brushing them off."

"That's an interesting relationship you have." She tried a croquette.

On that point, she was right. We had a unique relationship. We'd saved each other's lives on multiple occasions. But the concerns about my spending didn't go away until after she got mad and shot me. Long story. Do I abuse her guilt? Since my annual tab amounts to pocket change for her, I never felt bad about it. But Betty had a hint of jealousy in her voice. I decided to exploit it by leaving out the explanation.

"Do you ever wish you were independent?" she prodded.

My attempt to go solo lasted two weeks. Another long story I decided to skip. I sipped my wine and tried the fish eggs. Above our heads, the sky turned a darker blue. Hints of stars began to twinkle, uninhibited by city lights.

Once she realized there would be no answer, she plastered a croquette with caviar. She looked around again.

"You're nervous about something," I said. "Want to talk about it?"

Betty bit her knuckle until it turned white. Her eyes darted around us. She dropped her elbows on the table and leaned in.

"How do you live this lifestyle?" She lowered her voice to a whisper. "How can you put on a dinner jacket and casually eat caviar days after watching a man die? I'm barely holding it together. I need therapy. Every time I close my eyes, I see that man's head explode. You've done that hundreds of times. How do you live with it?"

I picked up the remaining croquette, since a woman would never take the last piece. Knifing the last bit of caviar on top, I chewed slowly, never breaking her gaze. She waited.

"Everyone makes choices in life," I said. "He chose to play a dangerous game and lost. He was ready to end my life right there. But you got him first. That's why I thanked you afterwards. But now, it's done."

She peered at me in disbelief. "Is it that easy? At the cocktail party, I was acting. Doing my best. But it took every ounce of concentration not to vomit. I've been acting ever since you pushed me out of the casino window. I understand the thrill in the moment, the adrenaline high, the hypervigilance, the feeling of being alive—totally alive! But moments later, I'm a total wreck. How do you sleep?"

"I've never killed a man whose death didn't make the world a better place."

"You convince yourself of this stuff, don't you?" She crossed her arms, pouted, and leaned back. "Like that trite line you dropped about how you can read a man when you hold a gun to his head. This is all one big joke to you, isn't it?"

Mercury leaned over her shoulder. *Here's your chance, homeboy. Tell her how you really handle the fear and the gore and the high of being a quasi-legal serial killer. Tell her about me. Tell her who makes you tick.*

I said, *Tell her I'm as mad as a hatter?*

Mercury looked insulted. *Dude, tell her you're a hero because you were chosen by god. And that I'm the one who handles your nightmares for you. Say, you know what? I could handle her nightmares too. I would not mind having Babelicious Betty Bardon as one of my flock. I'll fit her in my calendar somewhere. Why not introduce us?*

Recalling that most Greek and Roman gods did things that would get a mortal arrested for assault—or worse—I said, *Maybe later.*

"I take life very seriously," I said to Betty. "The people who die are on the wrong side of the cause."

"How do you know you're on the right side?"

Stars came out in full bloom. We looked up through the glass dome protecting us from the frigid air to see the Milky Way in all its natural glory.

The waiter cleared our dishes and left roasted beet tarts with whipped ricotta. I waited for her to take the first bite. She tried one and mimicked an orgasm for a second.

"You told me," I said, "that you intend to wreck Griffith. Did you think that was going to happen by accident?"

"Well, no." She recoiled. "I no longer want anyone to get killed."

"You plan to tackle a man like Griffith—child molester, money launderer, serial rapist, executioner—without anyone getting hurt? He shot you at point blank range and had no idea you were wearing body armor. Does he deserve to live? Do his henchmen?"

She blushed and ate her tart. I finished mine. A waiter appeared, refilled our wine glasses, cleared our plates, and brought the third course: Wagyu beef carpaccio with crispy capers. The paper-thin slices of beef tasted like culinary poetry.

When she could meet my gaze again, I said, "Are you out to save the world? Or play nice?"

She set her jaw. "I want him destroyed. Forever."

"By releasing the Chaac Project to the public?"

"That's one part." She took a big gulp of wine. "The Chaac Project is missing critical information. The Russians thought they could figure it out by testing all 118 elements on the periodic table. But there are too many variables of pressure—"

"And temperature combinations," I finished for her. "So I've heard. What's the other part?"

"I get him to admit his abuse of minors in a recording. Something I can use to destroy him and his friends. For people like him, humiliation is better than a death sentence."

I admired her determination. Now that I understood her better, I liked her. She had an agenda that might clash with mine, or it might align. I could work with that.

We inhaled the raw meat in seconds without noticing how fast it went down. The waiter brought the next course. I would've called it bacon-wrapped scallops, but the delicately interwoven flavors of Granny Smith apples, basil, and maple put it on a whole different level.

Mercury leaned over my shoulder in the discreet way a waiter whispers that your credit card was declined. *Homie, this is the moment you've been avoiding. Show it to her.*

I said, *The Chaac Equation? No way.*

Yes, way. Mercury stood up and looked at me like I was stupid. *You need to know if he showed you the real thing. She can answer that. She worked on the freaking Project.*

I said, *Trust her with this? I don't even know her.*

I trust her, Mercury said.

I said, *One call to this Joona-from-Finland character and I could be dead.*

C'mon, brutha, Mercury said. *Did she shoot a man to save your life? Is she dealing with all that PTSD-stuff now—just for you? And you still ain't even kissed her. Speaking of which, what is with you two anyway? What kinda man passes up a shot at a woman like that?*

I said, *She said her skills are rusty.*

Mercury said, *She be talking about her physics skills not her ... other skills.*

We finished our scallops in silence. The waiter appeared, swept the table, and left behind passion fruit sorbet as our palate cleanser. A strange look came over her.

"You're in a good mood for once," she said. Her dazzling smile returned with her adorable dimples. The sparkle in her eye matched the diamonds. "Wait a minute. I get it! You found something. You really found something. Talk to me, Jacob."

The waiter cleared our sorbet dishes.

Her sudden expectation that I would confide everything in her struck the wrong note in me. I've been betrayed too many times. I believed her but I still wasn't sure I could or should trust her. I grabbed her wrist. "You're too glib for my taste. Do you know what happens to people who violate my trust?"

When she looked into my eyes—the eyes that had been to wars too numerous to count—she inhaled panic and stopped breathing. I let go of her wrist.

The waiter froze mid-stride four steps from our table, uncertain about our exchange. I twitched a smile his way. He brought bison short ribs resting on polenta and mushrooms with a side of cornbread. After rushing through "Bon appétit," he scurried away.

"I'm sorry, Jacob." She exhaled her stress. "I feel like we're getting close to destroying that bastard and I'm getting excited. But I take your point. This is serious business. Too many people have died to take this lightly. Please, I'll do anything to bring him down. Tell me what I need to do."

We finished the bison, an excellent dish. The waiter cleared, poured wine, and brought us our last course: apple beignets with vanilla ice cream slathered in a luscious bourbon caramel.

I asked, "You wanted to be allies. Is that still the case?"

She reached across the table and scooped up my hand. Her eyes glistened with sincerity. "I want that more than anything. More than allies."

Could I trust her? Those eyes said yes, but she was an actress. An actress with firsthand experience working on Chaac. Mercury was right, though. Whatever she knew about the project, she was the only person for five hundred miles who could even read the equations.

I pulled my phone and pulled up the picture of a single page from Rafael's notebook taken with my button-camera. When I had pretended to memorize the page, I was leaning in to let the camera take a high-resolution photo without Rafael knowing. I didn't even feel bad about it.

Betty leaned in with a curious expression. She studied the picture, then grabbed my phone, pulled it in closer, zoomed in, panned around, and squinted. She let go and looked up at me. "Holy shit, Jacob. Where did you get this?"

"What do you think it is?"

"What the Russians tried to find for twenty years. What Griffith is killing for right now." Her face lit up like she'd just won the lottery. "Jacob—that's a page from the Chaac Equation!"

CHAPTER 54

WHEN THE WINE BOTTLE WAS empty and the beignets reduced to crumbs, we stared at each other for a long time. There was nothing more to say about the Chaac Project or the Chaac Equation. She understood when I said nothing about where it was, or how I came to have a picture of it. Instead, we talked about our favorite books. Then movies and plays. My words were spilling out, but I wasn't putting much thought into them. There was something about her eyes that kept me distracted.

Suddenly, she sat up and said, "Hear that?"

"Hear what?" The 360 Dome didn't have piped-in music. It was a quiet place.

"Glenn Miller playing *In the Mood*." She rose and tugged my hand until I faced her. Despite being a little drunk, or perhaps because, we started dancing.

The wait staff watched us swinging in silence hearing music only we could hear. When the song concluded, she said with an impish smile, "Do you know *Northwest Passage* by Woody Herman?"

"One of the early bebop tunes by the master?" I grinned. "Of course."

We picked up the pace. I felt a warmth growing inside me. My paranoia began to recede. It would take a great actress to conjure up Glenn Miller. But only a true jazz fan would know Woody Herman. No one could fake that much arcane knowledge. Dancing picked up our spirits and our energy.

When we finished the song, a bottle of El Dorado aged rum waited for us. Instead of sitting, we swayed in a warm embrace and reached for our glasses. We toasted our new partnership silently and sipped.

For the first time since Jenny left me, I felt good.

She tipped her face to mine. "I'll have that first kiss now."

We brushed rum-wetted lips lightly before diving in with pent-up passion. She seemed to melt in my arms, leaning into me like a blanket of affection. For the first time in a long time, everything felt right. Then she broke it off.

"I simply must visit the powder room," she said and tugged at my tie.

I smiled and watched her walk away. Before she made five steps, she turned and blew me a kiss.

I stared up at the stars. After a few minutes, the waiter came over and said, "The lady had to meet a friend, she asked that you meet her in the suite."

A smile crept across my face. We had separate beds in that suite, yet I had a feeling one of them would remain empty tonight. I complimented the staff and sent my appreciation to the chef.

Then I went outside where the evening had dropped below freezing. Warmed by alcohol and Betty, I wandered across the hotel's garden terrace, looking at the inky silhouettes of the Rockies. Propping my forearms on a railing overlooking the river, a sense of dread began to fill me. I couldn't place where it was coming from. Was it too soon to move on from Jenny? Was I plagued by guilt?

Mercury descended from the heavens next to me. He said, *Dude, what is it that makes you so stupid?*

I said, *I'm having a great evening, here. The first in a long time. Can't you say something nice for once?*

Mercury said, *OK, how 'bout this: Ain't it nice that you be the only friend Babelicious Betty has in Canada? And ain't it nice she's about as hot for you as a woman can get with her clothes on?* His voice shifted to a harsh tone. *And ain't it nice that she's making you wait while she talks to a friend? Who showed up in middle of nowhere? Now why would she make you wait?*

I said, *Because she didn't send that message, Griffith did ...*

That's when I saw them. Thirty feet below the terrace, two men struggled to subdue a woman in a blue dress. Her borrowed diamonds gave away her identity over the dark distance. The tall, thin man with white hair supervised. They put her in the bed of a pickup.

I leapt the railing and climbed down the retaining wall until I was within jumping distance. The pavement stung my feet on landing. The bullet that broke my ribs in Brest reminded me I hadn't fully healed. I took off after the truck. It pulled away even as it entered a sharp hairpin turn. I cut through the trees downhill to meet them as the driver shoved the pedal to the floor. Grabbing a branch, I swung out over the road and dropped. The truck sped past underneath me.

I missed.

Landing on the pavement, I rolled to reduce any additional sting. My roll slammed me into a tree trunk. Only one more hairpin remained that would bring them close. Last chance. With aching ribs, I rose and ran down the remaining slope toward the river.

Before the truck came toward me out of the last turn, it swerved off the pavement into an off-season cut-your-own Christmas tree lot. A sign read, "You cut it, we ship it." The truck pulled into an empty Quonset hut with truck-sized doors open on both ends. A second before it disappeared into the dark chasm, I counted four silhouettes including the white-haired leader, Joona. They appeared to be holding Betty down.

I ran at top speed for the building. Angling for the shortest distance forced me to give up a line of sight to the inside. Rounding on my approach, I saw the truck pull to the far end. If they left the building, I'd be miles behind them in minutes. With my pistol out, I swung around the opening.

At the far end, the brake lights went out and the truck began to leave. I lined up my shot.

A giant barrel, wider and taller than me, dropped from above. I found myself strangely encased in plastic netting inside the barrel. My struggles to break it were interrupted by the whole barrel being tipped over and landing on the ground. I landed on my broken ribs; my pistol unable to move. The barrel suddenly tilted up near my feet, spilling me onto the ground. But it wasn't ground. It was something like a table with rollers. Rough hands spun me around and sent me back into the barrel. More netting enveloped me. The barrel tilted up again. They spun me around a third time, more netting. Followed by fourth and fifth trips through the barrel.

Then I landed on my feet. My hands held hard to my side by Christmas tree netting. My Glock was pinned to my thigh, useless. I could see through a few triangles where the netting's mesh lined up.

Joe Griffith clapped his hands as he strolled toward me. "Well done, Joona. A round of drinks for the boys."

He put his face close to the holes I could see through. "Are you in there, Jacob?"

I felt a knife slicing through the netting near my pocket. A hand reached in and fished around. A moment later, Griffith held a Sabel Dart where I could see it. He said, "I think turnabout is fair play, don't you?"

The world went dark.

CHAPTER 55

I WAS NEITHER AWAKE NOR asleep. A groggy world that smelled of pine needles and sap and plastic and cologne. The space around me was silent but there were voices in the distance. How distant was a question I couldn't determine in my woozy state. It was dark. Blinking repeatedly didn't help much; the netting still blocked most of my view.

Christmas tree netting. That was clever. When improvising a mission, you have to make use of any tools available. The Finns demonstrated extraordinary resourcefulness. I had to give them that.

After my moment of appreciation, my heart raced as I realized I was at their mercy.

Mercury leaned over the table and looked into the small spaces where I could see.

I said, *Why didn't you warn me about this?*

There you go again, homes, Mercury said. *Starting things off on the negative. Did I tell you about my wife? How I gotta win this thing to get her back? You think they gonna let me tell you everything? That's not how gamblers operate. How about once, just once, you take personal responsibility for your actions?*

I said, *Thanks. First it's 'listen to god' but then it's 'you're on your own.' Can you at least tell me who betrayed me?*

Mercury said, *What makes you think anybody betrayed you? These Finns are smart, yo. They can call every fancy hotel in western Canada to ask if some fool's gone and rented the most expensive suite on Pia-Caesar-Sabel's credit card so they can deliver the flowers for his engagement party.*

The sad part was that calling hotels sounded like something I would do. Not that it would do me any good against Joona's people. I imagined the Finns bivouacked in attics unbeknownst to the homeowner. Calling hotels wouldn't work to find them.

Mercury said, *What you shoulda done is apply Stearne's Law and realize you ain't safe at the freaking South Pole. Why'd you let your guard down?*

I couldn't answer that. Why had I suddenly felt safe when I had no reason to think the Finns suddenly went on vacation?

All cuz of a woman. Mercury shook his head. *You was just born to be a sucker for a pretty face. Don't feel bad—same thing happened to ol' Julius. And Mark Antony too. They both fell for Cleopatra when I was jumping up and down screaming, 'Don't do it!' But ... mortals be what mortals is: fools.*

Without mortals, you don't exist, I said.

"Is that supposed to be a compliment?" Griffith asked.

When I blinked, his fingers stretched one of the openings in the netting. He said, "You didn't sleep long. Does that mean Sabel employees are given vaccinations against Sabel Darts to prevent accidents?"

"Something like that."

"We'll do this right here then." He gauged my eyes to see if I was alert enough for whatever he had in mind as his next step. A moment later, I felt his next step as something sharp touching my side.

I could hear his voice but not see him when he said, "I can never understand why people resort to torture in the movies. Getting information is a simple process. If you simply kill someone slowly enough, they give it up long before they die. Mother Nature makes pragmatists of us all in the end."

The sharp thing in my side punctured my skin in the same place the bullet in Brest had cracked a couple ribs.

"What you're feeling now," he said, "is the tip of a large hunting knife slipping between your ribs just above the diaphragm at the bottom of your right lung. I'm going to twist it now for proof."

I shouted when the pain hit me like a two-by-four.

"And it's only a quarter-inch in," Griffith said. "I plan to drive it all the way."

Holding a deep breath behind clenched teeth, I waited for the pain to subside. Then I blew it out.

"We had a deal, Jacob." He sighed with disappointment. "Are you ready to hold up your end of the bargain?"

"I never made a deal."

"Oh, but you did." The knife slid in farther, widening the slice in my rib muscles. Pain shot through me from head to toe. "In Greenland, remember? I promised not to kill your parents if you brought me what belongs to me."

"Too bad. Haven't seen anything of yours."

"Don't lie, Jacob." The knife dug in deeper.

Electric shocks shot through my spine. Orange lightning bolts of pain crossed my vision. I breathed heavy and hard, trying to dissipate the agony. I wondered how far in it could go before I died.

This was not the death with *dignitas* I'd hoped for. I'd done nothing to save anyone yet. If Griffith killed me here and now, mine would be a pointless sacrifice.

"You didn't come to Calgary for the weather," Griffith said. "Rafael showed you one of his fishing cabins, I'm sure. We know these things. And that means your family's last hour of life hangs in the balance."

"You have my family? Prove it."

Griffith fell for it. He held up a picture in front of me. Dusk in front of Navy Pier, Mom and Joyce talking to Louis while my father looked skyward at the Centennial Wheel. I counted the hours in my head. Driving and flying, Miguel would've arrived in New Orleans about eight hours after he left my suite. Tania would meet him there with my family in tow. That meant when Betty and I were having dinner, he and Tania would've connected. Had anything gone wrong with that plan, they would've called me. They didn't. So Griffith didn't yet know his people were in the wrong state. My people were safe.

"Damn," I said and closed my eyes. "Did you kill them?"

"Not yet. Tell me what I need to know."

He twisted the knife in both directions, forcing the already-broken ribs apart. Hot jags of pain shot through my body. I involuntarily cried out. Black and silver dots appeared on the periphery of my vision.

What the hell had he been talking about? This was torture of the worst kind. The anticipation alone made me want to make up stuff to tell him. But giving in to a man like Griffith only hastens the end.

When he stopped twisting the blade, I coughed out, "You'll kill them anyway."

"I'm a man of my word, Jacob."

"Worthless." I couldn't get another syllable out. It took every ounce of strength to keep breathing away the fires shooting through my bones. My mind was ready to shut down, bring this nightmare to an end.

"Where is the Chaac Equation?" Griffith asked.

"Don't ... know."

The knife twisted again, shredding the muscle, tissue, and edges of both ribs.

Griffith whispered in my ear. "If you tell me, I might spare Betty this same terrible procedure."

Hands grabbed my body, turned me on my side, driving the knife in deeper, and giving me a glimpse of another table a few feet away. Betty was strapped at the ankles, knees, hips, waist, shoulder, and forehead. Blood streaked down the side of her face and stained the diamonds. The white-haired man, Joona, loosened the strap on her head and turned her to face me. A ball gag prevented her from saying anything. But her eyes spoke volumes. She felt my suffering as if it were her own.

They rocked me on my side, driving the knife halfway through the bone of one rib. Trying not to, I screamed again.

I couldn't conceive of her going through this ordeal.

They rolled me on my back.

"How ..." I breathed hard to stay conscious. The black and silver stars in my vision crowded into the middle. "How can you prove ... unharmed."

"Are you asking how I can guarantee you Betty will be unharmed if you tell me what I want to know?" He laughed. "You just gave away that you have some intelligence to bargain. Therefore, you have no position, Mr. Stearne. I need not make any assurances."

The knife, already embedded in the bone, twisted yet again. This time, it was one twist too many.

The black and silver stars closed in, blanking out the world.

CHAPTER 56

SUDDENLY, I FELT TERRIFIC AND sick and confused and pained—all at once. An opening had been cut in the netting around my mouth. I could feel cactus-like needles of the plastic netting around my lips. The knife was still stuck in my ribs. And yet Jimi Hendrix was playing in my head. I felt like I could kiss the sky.

"Yes." Griffith's voice somewhere near and yet so far away. "It's an unfortunate side-effect when slipping a knife between a subject's ribs: they often pass out."

My stomach tried to hurl everything on Griffith. I stopped it.

Griffith said, "It's too hard to find medical-grade morphine or even simple opioids for work like this. There are so many forms to fill out and all that red tape. It's easier to buy heroin." He leaned in. "For your sake, I hope the dealer wasn't spiking it with something awful like fentanyl. That would be regrettable."

"I … I ain't telling you shit." Not my most eloquent speech, but it was all I could manage.

"Oh, but you are." Griffith ripped the netting away from my eyes and face. "Have you forgotten about Betty?"

He pushed my head sideways.

She lay in the same place as before. Not much time had elapsed, judging by the blood rolling down her cheek like slow raindrops on a window.

Griffith snapped my head back where all I could see was the ceiling and him leaning over me. He said, "You didn't seem to care much about your family, but your eyes gave away your feelings for Betty. You poor sucker. Oh well—not the first man to fall for dimples. You know, we always look for the greatest point of vulnerability. Saves time. Now. Where were we? Oh yes, you were going to tell me how to retrieve my Chaac Equation before Betty goes under the knife. So, Jacob, I'm asking nicely: Where is it?"

"He showed it to me," I said. "Then he left with it."

Griffith's face shot up with disbelief. "He left with it? Do you expect me to believe that? He took it out of a secure location? Jacob, come now, tell me the truth or we go back to twisting that little butter knife back and forth. You don't want that, do you?"

"Shipping it to me … giving me time … set up exchange."

"A what?"

"Exchange." I tried taking deep breaths. I couldn't tell if I was getting air or not. I felt as if someone were giving me a huge, hard hug. "I want the Chaac … Project. I'll bring you …"

I couldn't finish. I wanted to sleep.

Griffith shook me. "You plan to make an exchange?"

"Yes … Project for Equation."

Griffith, stroking his chin, disappeared from view. From a short distance, he asked, "Rafael agreed to this exchange?"

"Not exactly."

Griffith came back into view, examining my eyes with an intense stare. "He wants you to take it for safekeeping. You're going to double-cross him. I'm supposed to believe that?"

"Take it … or …"

"Makes no sense, Jacob. What do you plan to do with the Project portion?"

"Ms. Sabel." I breathed five times. "Owns it. It's hers. Deserves it. Investor."

"Yes, yes," he said and waved away his impatience. "She thinks it's hers. Why would I give it to her?"

"Pursue you … and Finns to the ends … the Earth."

"She'll do that anyway."

"She's business … bottom line. Invested in Project. Gets what she paid for. No idea the Equation exists. Done."

Placing his hands on either side of me, he put his face close to mine to watch my eyes. "Why would you do this? Double-cross your friend, shortchange your boss?"

I chinned toward Betty.

"Well, well, well." He stood up and looked over at her. "Isn't that romantic? Jacob. I'm touched. But I don't believe you. I think you're going to make a copy of the Equation and give it to her."

"Then may ... the best person win." I breathed heavily. "You have ... advantage. You have Edison Data."

"How do you know about that?" He came into visual range, stroking his chin. "Rafael, no doubt. Naturally, you'll need to provide assurances that she won't send you after me." When I nodded, he continued, "Where do you envision this exchange going—"

The phtt-phtt-phtt of a silenced Glock cracked the quiet. I heard the dying exhale of a man near me a split second before his body hit the floor.

The Finns returned fire. No silencers.

Griffith flinched at every round and crouched beside my table, his knuckles gripping the wood so hard they turned white.

It had to be Isaiah. And that meant my opportunity for making a deal was drawing to a close. I couldn't let Isaiah know my next move. Getting rescued was nice. But I needed to set up the exchange or a lot of people could die. I didn't want Betty to be one of them.

I said, "Joe ... Joe."

He crawled closer to me. Sweat broke out on his pale brow. His voice cracked. "Call them off or you're a dead man."

"I can't ... raise. Voice."

I felt a sting in my arm. Seconds later, my head began to clear. My nausea improved. He must've given me Narcan, the anti-opioid drug. Not enough to sober me up, just enough to keep me lucid.

"Call them off," he snarled in a whisper.

"You're the only one in this whole thing—" I stopped talking to breathe. I was feeling better but not all the way back. "—who told me the truth. Let me return the favor. No criminal dies in their bed. The fact that you're alive says you're a survivor. So far, your success has been making sure what happens in your Nerve Center stays in your Nerve Center.

Make sure you keep it that way. *And* do the exchange."

His face filled with confusion. Another exchange of gunfire sent him back to cowering. Then he raised his head above the table and looked at me with understanding. My message got through to him. He disappeared from my view. I twisted the other direction and found him huddling near Betty.

What was he doing? She was his ticket to freedom from this place but releasing her would put her in danger. A stray bullet could kill her. He knew that would be the end of his hostage shield. Too much risk. He wouldn't do that. So what was he up to?

Suddenly, Griffith shouted to Joona. Then he turned and ran out of the building. Joona's white hair ran past me a second later. The shooting stopped. A truck started in the distance.

Footsteps approached at a run.

"Narcan," I said.

Isaiah came into my limited view. He holstered his weapon and began cutting the netting away from me.

"NARCAN!" I repeated as loud as I could.

His scissors slid up the side of me, freeing me. I felt the rush of freedom.

Isaiah's eyes blew open wide. He stared at the knife in my side. He looked out at the exit, no doubt calculating the odds of catching Griffith.

"No!" Grabbing his arm, I shouted, "Narcan! Now. Find some. The hotel infirmary. Get help! He gave Betty an overdose of heroin."

CHAPTER 57

ISAIAH WAS A FINE SOLDIER. He accepted my order without hesitation and ran out of the structure.

Griffith knew how to survive. He had huddled by her side to give her a fatal dose of the drug, knowing full well that I'd save her life before pursuing him. Evil and clever.

I swung off the table and kicked away my netting. Then I took a few seconds to steady my dizziness. The knife handle sticking out of my ribs begged to be yanked out. Since that could deflate a lung or open the bleeding or both, I opted for the macabre solution: leave it in.

Grabbing the scissors, I sliced the netting away from Betty. She looked like an angel with her hands folded across her stomach, eyes closed, and lipstick still bright red.

"Can you hear me, Betty?" I asked.

She mumbled something. Her eyes fluttered and closed again.

"You need to stay with me," I said. "Stay awake."

The thought of losing her filled me with fear and dread. There was no way I could let her slip into oblivion. I couldn't lose someone I cared about. Not a second time. She had to live.

I pulled her limp body to the edge while my ribs shrieked in pain at every exertion. I swung her feet over and pulled her torso upright. I almost pulled her arm over my shoulder on the right before realizing the jostling would hurt like hell. I switched sides and pulled her weight onto my left shoulder.

She could barely stand up. I wasn't doing a whole lot better. What addicts like about the drug is beyond me. On a few rare occasions, I'd seen it in the trenches. More often, I saw men using back home when they couldn't get the war out of their heads. This was my one and only heroin experience and it was making me ill. Worse, Narcan doesn't work for long. If Isaiah didn't come back with some quickly enough, Betty and I were in trouble.

Pulling the Canadian silver dollar out of my pocket, I held it where she could see it. "Thank you for this. It kept me going."

She mumbled something.

I got her walking. It wasn't quick, but we made it across the building. Her bare shoulders were cold. I wrapped her in my blood-soaked jacket. I told her we had to walk the length of the building, a hundred feet. She mumbled a response. We got to the entrance, where I'd been caught. Hanging from the rafters was a block-and-tackle setup. The owners dropped the barrel on larger trees. Not something that comes up in battle very often. I decided not to blame myself for getting caught in a trap that rare.

On the ground were two piles of spent casings. One on each side of the entryway. I stared at that until my muddled brain made sense of it. We turned around and headed for the far end.

I said, "Betty, are you with me?"

She mumbled something.

I wondered if she had alerted the Finns to our Canadian destination. Yes, Mercury was right, they could've called all the hotels. But the last time they saw us, we were in Chicago with a flight plan filed for DC. How would they even know to call hotels in Canada, much less Alberta? Then again, would she have made the call after the assault in Belgrade? Maybe she accidentally alerted someone else who might have tipped them off. Did she post something on social media? There were too many possibilities to consider. And my brain wasn't fully functional.

We were halfway to the opposite end when the whir of a golf cart approached.

"You're ... the only one," Betty slurred. She wiped drool from her chin with the back of her hand. "Only one who cared enough ... only guy man enough to care ... about me. To ... save. Me."

I squeezed her. "Keep walking. We're not out of the woods yet."

"Don't you know ... I'm saying?"

"Anyone would do as much."

"No." She pulled away from me with woozy anger in her eyes.

It only lasted a second. Then she started to topple. I pushed my shoulder under hers and righted her. We walked.

The golf cart whirred through the entrance at the far end and zoomed to us. Three people: Isaiah, the hotel manager, and a woman who had "doctor" written all over her: a focused, assessing gaze, purpose in every movement, and determined to save a life.

Betty tugged at me. "Aren't you going to say you love me too?"

She tried to look up at me. Her eyes wandered and her head lolled.

I had no answer. Was that the drug talking? Was she that serious about me?

Was I serious about her?

Mercury looked at me like a car accident. *You with me, homie? You look worser'n Nick Nolte's mug shot.*

I said, *What do you want?*

Mercury said, *I wanna know what you been thinking. What's with this harebrained plan to give Griffith everything? That's not how Ima win this bet, boy.*

I said, *No way any of them give up Chaac. First, I need to expose whoever dug the tunnel to the Ops Center, then I'm going to take everything from all of them. I have a plan for the long game.*

And you ain't gonna share it with me? Mercury asked. He thought about it and came to a conclusion. *That means you ain't got no plan. Say, you ever notice Neville and Rafael don't seem to be singing out of the same hymnal?*

I said, *Exactly.*

Mercury said, *And Pia-Caesar-Sabel be working on something behind your back. Don't you dare be upsetting her. I'm just using you to get to her, y'know.*

I said, *I'm not worried about her. She's after the same thing everyone else is and I have a plan for that, too. Besides, she would never do anything that would hurt me. Again. I think.*

Mercury said, *You ever notice Yeschenko and the Russians, Deng and the Chinese, and Remmo Nidal and OPEC all just up and disappeared on you? Those people don't just disappear.*

I said, *That's a problem for another day. First, I have to take out Griffith. I owe Betty that much.*

The doctor jabbed a needle in Betty's arm. Betty looked offended.

The doctor gasped. Her gaze came up from the knife sticking out of my side.

They gingerly placed us in the golf cart and ran us back up the hill. Betty in front, quickly mending, me in the back with a second dose of Narcan. The downside being that it let the knife-pain back in. Every pebble the cart popped over, every expansion joint in the pavement, every speed bump in the parking lot sent lightning bolts ricocheting through my brain.

Isaiah helped me off the cart and through the lobby. The manager guided Betty. The doctor ran ahead.

The lobby clock read 0320. Beneath it sat a short, wiry man with a cap of black hair and dark eyes, reading a newspaper. No one reads newspapers anymore. Especially at that hour.

In my suite, the doctor laid me out on a pile of towels. People ran between my suite and the infirmary fetching things for the doctor.

I grabbed Isaiah. "Bug sweep … Betty, you, me. Griffith got a tracker on one of us. That's how he found us."

Then the doctor pulled the knife out. I slipped into another world. A dark, hazy world of pain and agony where my brain sorted through colors and shapes and thoughts. I thought about Rafael Tum and why he wanted me to exchange the Chaac Equation. I thought about Betty and why I suspected her of anything bad when everything she'd done since Kyiv lined up with her goal of destroying Griffith. Images of Ms. Sabel drifted in and out of focus. Why did she send her most trusted friends to the opposite ends of the Earth? Why had she asked an actress to help her in a meeting she didn't even tell me about? But my thoughts constantly returned to Betty Bardon.

Was I serious about her? Was that wise?

CHAPTER 58

WHEN I WOKE, MS. SABEL was rubbing my hand between hers as if kneading dough. Her gaze crossed the room to the window. Her eyes glistened. She wore a business suit that looked like she'd just walked out of a board meeting. Daylight knifed between clouds and through the glass, reaching the floor at a steep angle. Late afternoon. Sharp, jagged peaks of huge mountains lay just outside. I was still in Canada. Had to be. They don't grow them like that anywhere else. I mumbled something that snapped her attention to me.

"You're awake?" she asked. "How are you feeling?"

"Thirsty," I said. Twisting slightly to look at her, my ribs shrieked in pain. A groan escaped. "How long have I been out?"

She looked around for water as she spoke. "Most of the day."

"Aren't you supposed to be in Belgrade?"

Her gaze came back to me, concerned. "That ended two days ago."

"Guess things were moving pretty fast on the ground here. Lost track." I closed my eyes and mouth, hoping to rehydrate my sticky tongue.

Lost track, dawg? Mercury grinned over her shoulder. *Didn't lose track of Betty Bardon.*

I'm not interested in Betty, I said. *Am I?*

You sure was last night, homie. She told you to meet her in the suite. You know what that means.

What it means to women and what it means to men are two different things. Where is she?

"Who?" Ms. Sabel asked.

"Betty."

"I sent her out on a trail ride." She tried to smile and squeezed my hand sympathetically. "She recovered physically but has been in shock ever since. Apparently, she heard Griffith torturing you and is sick about it. She needed fresh air and time to calm down. Don't worry, I sent along two bodyguards and a shrink. She'll be back for dinner."

That made sense. Even I would've found it hard hearing someone take a slow knife to the ribs. "Thanks."

"She's fallen for you. When she speaks of you, she has dreamy eyes."

Curious if she were teasing me or telling the truth, I started to lean forward only to have my ribs send jagged zaps of pain through me. I fell back.

She let go of my hand as she resumed her scan for a water bottle. "What did Griffith want?"

"The Chaac Equation."

"Did you give it to him?" she asked. Her grey-green eyes snapped back and searched mine.

"That implies I had it."

"And?"

"I didn't," I said. I checked the nearby tables for water. I couldn't see much without twisting my ribs.

"Do you know who does?"

"Rafael."

She whistled in shock. Her gaze shot to the window. She was thinking hard. And not sharing her thoughts. When she looked at me again, she had that extra-focused, everyone-better-get-out-of-my-way look in her eyes that carried her through championships and World Cups. "Where is he now?"

"Last I heard," I said and smacked my lips, "he was going to Vancouver, where he planned to put the Chaac Equation in a box and ship it to a shipping company with instructions to put it in another box and ship it somewhere else. Seven stops so that anyone looking for it won't find it until it arrives at a final destination. Keeps it out of anyone's hands until he's ready."

"Ready for what?"

"He has a crazy plan to screw Griffith."

"Will his plan work?" she asked.

"Will yours?"

She frowned at me. "What's that supposed to mean?"

I pushed up on my elbows to look around for water, but my ribs freaked out, so I relaxed back into the pillows, still thirsty. I said, "You scheduled Betty to meet with Griffith. You didn't want Tania or me there. It's your company, your money—but don't I deserve to know why?"

"Backup plan," she said. She worried her fingers as her face flushed with anger. "Sorry, but I'm anxious about the Chaac Project. It belongs to me. The Russians killed my father for it—with help from our government, I might add. When they realized they couldn't make it work, they invited criminal organizations to bid on it. Can you believe that? It's mine. MINE!"

I'd never seen her get that angry—or possessive—before.

"So, you bid on it," I said. "If your bid wins, you'll be partners with a man I'm planning to kill."

She shrugged. "Don't let anything stand between you and your goals."

Mercury said, *Dang. That was cold. Is that the same Pia-Caesar-Sabel talking? The one who saved children from the CIA and killed terrorists in Dubai? The same lady who stopped an insurrection? The one who—*

Yes, I said. *Doesn't sound like her.*

People get funny about inheritance. You shoulda heard Mark Antony talking about Julius AFTER he died. 'I come to bury Caesar, not to praise him.' A whole different song from what he was singing the day before. Maybe you should try to help her.

I said, *I would if she'd talk to me.*

"Sorry," she said after taking a few breaths. "I let it get to me."

"But Griffith came here to work me over—after you submitted a bid. Why?"

"He didn't show any tangible proof that he had the Chaac Project. It was all smoke and mirrors. I'm the only one who believes him at all. And my bid requires a controlling interest. Yeschenko didn't bid because he's planning on stealing it instead of buying it. Deng probably has the same idea. Those who did submit bids put in minimal numbers."

"Why does he need investors?" I asked.

"Criminal organizations can't raise capital by issuing stocks or bonds. The fact that he came here means none of the bids gave him what he wanted."

"Rafael was there, but he left with me, so the Keepers didn't put in a bid." I kept my mouth closed, hoping to collect enough moisture in it for my next sentence.

"If they were to bid, they would do it under a shadow company," she said. "I doubt they have that kind of capital anyway. What's this plan of Rafael's?"

"He thinks I'm going to talk Griffith into the exchange for him."

"Are you going to do it?"

I looked at her and asked, "If Rafael's strategy was solid, wouldn't he do it himself?"

"He must have an angle."

"Yeah. I just don't know what it is." My lips stuck together.

Ms. Sabel leaned close to my face, peering into my eyes. "You have a plan. I know you do. Otherwise, you'd have gone back to DC last night. What is it?"

"Do you still have that ranch in Wyoming?" I asked.

She shook her head. "I donated it to the university for wildlife research. But Sabel Property bought another one in Montana just outside Glacier National Park a couple weeks ago. Need it for something?"

My throat was so dry, I wasn't sure I could answer. But I had a few more sentences to croak out before I died of dehydration.

"Yes," I said. "Text me the address. I've got to make a call."

She took the chair and looked up *spare ranches* on her phone while I dialed.

I didn't want her to hear my call. I did my best to put moisture on my lips with my bone-dry tongue. "Could I have that water now?"

"Oh!" She jumped up. "Sorry. I got engrossed in … I'll find the nurse. I can't believe they don't have any. Be right back."

A moment later, Joe Griffith answered.

I put him on speaker and said, "Joe, in two days, I'm going to text you an address. You're going to go there immediately. I'll forget your little knife trick if you're on time and have no more than two bodyguards. You're going to bring your part, like we discussed just before you tried to kill Betty. I'm going to do my part. I'm going to deliver the Chaac Equation."

I clicked off before he could argue.

Standing in the doorway with two water bottles, Ms. Sabel stared at me with wide eyes and her mouth hanging open. "You're going to do what?"

CHAPTER 59

MS. SABEL TOSSED ME THE water and stormed out with a good deal of anger bubbling up inside her. Maybe I should've told her my plan. After all, it is her money I'm spending and it's her inheritance—but she'd say no. She'll get over being mad at me.

Isaiah passed her in the doorway and pointed at her exit with a curious expression. I waved him off before he could ask why she was pissed off.

He strolled in and asked, "How's my favorite junkie?"

I chugged half a bottle of water. "Not funny."

"Yeah, actually it is." He smirked.

I drank the rest of it. The satisfying flush of rehydration filled my body and improved my mood. "Thanks for saving my life."

"You're welcome."

"You're right," I said, grabbing the second bottle. "That was kinda funny."

He laughed. "Hey, we found the trackers. About the time we left for Greenland, every corporate pilot received a new Sabel luggage tag. Even the chef on the big new jet got one."

"Diabolical."

"They didn't know exactly where we were, but they knew what city we landed in. A new bug sweep procedure came out of it, crews are now included."

"Well done, Isaiah."

"Hey, I was on my way in because I found something you need to see." He pulled up his phone and spun through pictures until he found one. "OK, so this is one of the shots we took of the Chaac Project in

Griffith's lair back in Chicago. I haven't figured out much from looking at them—this stuff is way over my head—but I found this and thought you should have a look at it."

He held the phone where I could see it. Written in Cyrillic, the Russian alphabet, I made an educated guess it was a list of contributors in volume nine of the fifteen notebooks because of the page numbers. It contained a paragraph of what appeared to be names with degrees after them. I looked at him. "Am I looking for something specific?"

"Yulia Nyakhaychyk," he said. "I saw that name in your field report from Brest. That was Betty Bardon's birth name, right?"

"What does that mean?" I looked at the page again. I blinked. It was still written in Cyrillic.

"She worked on the Chaac Project," he said triumphantly. "She didn't tell you that. I don't know what it means exactly, but in my opinion, she should've told you."

My decision not to share everything with Isaiah Reddick had proven wise.

I looked at him, then looked at the document in question. Nowhere on the screen did I see Nyakhaychyk. All I saw were Cyrillic characters. I met his gaze again. He beamed, expecting heaps of praise for his discovery. Instead, I decided it was time to have a serious heart-to-heart with him.

I pointed at the chair Ms. Sabel had been sitting in. "I have questions for you. Pull up a chair."

He hesitated before taking it. "Yes, sir."

"You're smart, Isaiah," I said quietly.

"Thank you." He smiled nervously while waiting for the other shoe to drop.

"Very smart. A lot smarter than me. I checked your history. You got into Dartmouth not because you were the head of your class in high school, but because you were the top Merit Scholar in your state. That's smart. But you're not this smart." I tapped the phone. "No one is smart enough to go through all the pages we scanned, all written in a foreign language, looking for the birth name of Betty Bardon—in Cyrillic."

"Uh." Tiny beads of sweat broke out on his forehead. "What are you saying, Jacob?"

"I'm saying, you had help. Help that you think I'm not aware of—but I am. When we first met at the Sabel Operations Center, you jogged down a tunnel dug by criminals without any idea if they were lying in wait for us—because you knew they weren't. That's when I knew it was you who alerted the diggers to the alarms."

"Hold on," he said, holding up his hands.

"I'll give you a chance to explain things in a minute. See, I thought it was the Knights of Mithras who dug it. But they don't leave tunnels abandoned. They'd hold their ground. When we didn't get killed coming to the other end, I knew you would eventually tell me who dug it. Add to that, the fact that you haven't slept since Belgrade. Being a double agent requires long nights sneaking out to contact your handler. By the way, don't ever think you can lose Miguel when you're creeping around after hours—the man has eyes in the back of *your* head. You were supposed to be catching up on sleep when Griffith was torturing me. Instead, you were meeting with OMIB."

Isaiah frowned. "OMIB?"

"Our Man in Belgrade. OMIB. The guy I thought was CIA. The one working with Rafael. The guy who helped you take down the Finns in the Christmas tree shop. Don't shake your head, I know he was there. There were two piles of spent shell casings, one on either side of the entrance. I'm talking about the guy who was later reading a newspaper in the lobby—at 0320. I take it you don't know his real name."

"Oh shit." Isaiah rubbed his face in his hands. He blew out a long, mournful breath as he got up and paced a circle next to my bed. "OMIB's as good a name as any. You sure he's working with Rafael? When he dropped you guys on the tarmac at the Belgrade airport, I was shocked to find out he was even in Serbia."

"That's because Rafael is at the top of OMIB's chain of command and you're not." I waited for him to recognize where he stood in OMIB's pecking order. "Ready to tell me about it?"

Isaiah dropped into the chair, put his elbows on his knees, and his face in his hands. When he was ready, he met my gaze and said, "Got out of the Marines and started a security company. I'd saved up to cover the early dry months. But I only landed a couple rich people digging for divorce-dirt. Nothing lucrative like the corporate contracts Sabel Security gets. This guy OMIB comes to me, says the government needs someone inside Sabel. Says it pays well and it's a matter of national security. He had identification. He had references inside the State Department. I double-checked the references. They vouched for him and sent emails confirming his project status: Diplomatic Security Special Agent on Special Assignment. Everything checked out, Jacob. I swear. Well, everything except his name. I expect that was an officially sanctioned legend because the name he gave me was Sid Reilly."

"Cute," I said. Sidney Reilly was an international spy working for nineteenth century England, and the real-life archetype for James Bond. "And he asked you to do what?"

Isaiah took a minute to consider what he was doing. The government would have made him sign a secrecy document that would land him in jail for the rest of his life if he talked to anyone for any reason. I was asking him to commit a felony. He weighed his loyalty to them versus me. When he met my gaze with unwavering determination, I knew he'd made the right choice.

"First, I was to work my way onto Pia Sabel's personal security team," he said. "That turned out to be a hard assignment to get. He kept pressuring me, but there weren't any openings. After riding around on her jets and spending her money like it was water, I can see why no one ever transfers out.

"When I was assigned the Ops Center, OMIB saw an opportunity and changed things up. He kept asking me to search for anything in the inventory that said *Chaac* on it. Nothing, of course. That's when they did the tunneling thing. He was convinced pieces of the Chaac Project were stored there. When that fell apart, he disappeared. I didn't hear from him again until Kyiv. He popped out of a hotel service elevator in a waiter's outfit and told me to report our movements."

I waited a few beats to see if he was done. "And did you?"

"If you knew about me," he said with heat, "why did you take me everywhere with you? Why didn't you fire me then instead of waiting until now?"

"You're not getting fired," I said. "If we fired every smart guy who made a dumb mistake, I wouldn't have made it out of new hire orientation."

He watched me with a puzzled look that slowly faded.

I said, "Your mistake was trusting a government agent to tell you the truth. After a stint in the Marines, I'd have thought you were smarter than that, but no big deal. Dartmouth might ask for the diploma back, though."

He squinted at me, shaking his head in disbelief.

"And did you keep OMIB updated?" I asked again with a hint of impatience.

"Not really. I didn't know what the hell we were doing in Brazil, and that's what I told him. After that, I was having so much fun with you guys, I just told him nothing you did made any sense. Which was true. In Greenland, I was ready to tell you about him, but things turned ugly before I worked up the nerve. He cornered me when we got back to the States, tried to put the fear of violating national security into me. Then somehow he knew we were in Chicago."

"Rafael," I said, thinking out loud. "You sent OMIB the scans we took. He has a team of people researching it and that's how you found Betty's original name. He told you."

Isaiah nodded and looked down like a chastened boy. He pulled himself together. "If I'd done that in the Marines, I'd face the firing squad."

"Yeah, normally I'd shoot you myself and spare the squad the trouble of dressing up for the occasion."

"Normally?" he asked.

I held up a finger letting him know to wait. He folded his hands in his lap and sat still.

I looked to the ceiling where Mercury reclined as if he were right side up.

Mercury said, *Getting soft as the Pillsbury doughboy in your old age, huh homie. Just a couple weeks ago, you'd have shot him right there and called housekeeping to haul his ass away.*

I said, *I never shoot an intelligent man, and he's smarter than me.*

Besides, he's an operational asset on Miguel's level. We need him.

Mercury said, *You breezed over his connection with Rafael pretty quick. They both be talking to OMIB. Why not dig deeper?*

I said, *He's at the bottom of OMIB's food chain. If I want to know more about OMIB, I'll ask him directly. Which isn't a bad idea. Think I'll do that.*

Mercury said, *Are you gonna trust Brother Isaiah or not? Cuz you ain't killed nobody in a long time and that's pretty rare for you. Also, kinda boring.*

I said, *You're the one who told me to take him on.*

Mercury said, *So's you'd have someone to kill. Thought it would cheer you up. You was in a mood.*

Killing people doesn't cheer me up, I said. *Well, maybe some people. But he's a good man, made a mistake, he's fessed up now. Everybody makes mistakes. I made a mistake once and Ms. Sabel got mad and shot me.*

Isaiah's eyes looked like a pair of full moons. "She what?"

"Long story. No firing squad for you. Not today. Go get OMIB and bring him back here. I want to thank him for saving my life."

He rose to leave, took a few steps, then faced me. He asked, "Did you really know about me from the beginning?"

"One day you're a shift supe at the Ops Center who should be under investigation. The next, you're flying to London with the legendary bear of Sabel Security, Miguel Rodriguez. Did you think that was all about your charm and good looks?"

"Well, yeah," he smiled. "But I expected to be sent home to wait for the investigators."

I thumbed through the emails in my sent file until I found the one from the internal investigations department. Their email to me was an order to make Isaiah Reddick available for questioning. My reply was one word: No.

I showed it to him. He pursed his lips and tilted his head with a question. He was about to ask why I did that.

To avoid having to tell him *god made me do it*, I said, "Ground penetrating radar to find the tunnel was smart. There was a sensor that told you exactly where to look. But you spent time digging out the equipment and getting it running. You bought OMIB enough time to pack up and get out of town." I waited for him to look away. "Then there's Chicago. Three operators on a mission to break into Griffith's Nerve Center. Which job should've fallen to the new guy?"

He closed his eyes as the realization hit him. "Driving the getaway boat." He shook his head and reopened his eyes. "You brought me to the Nerve Center on purpose. You wanted me to tell OMIB what we found in there. I don't get it. Why would you do that?"

"Go get OMIB."

CHAPTER 60

HIS FACE GLOWING RED WITH rage, Joe Griffith hurled a paperweight at Joona Forss. "One extra man you didn't know about? How is that possible?"

Joona caught the paperweight one-handed and set it on the side table. He resumed his at-ease stance.

"I had him right where I wanted him!" Griffith shouted. "He was seconds away from telling me where to find the Chaac Equation and his man shows up with an accomplice? This is total FAILURE!"

Joona's stone face gave him nothing.

Griffith's phone rang. Jacob Stearne delivered his demands: Griffith and two bodyguards were to show up at an address to be texted in two days. Griffith was to bring "his part, like we discussed" and Stearne would deliver the Equation. Then, before he could say a word, Stearne ended the call.

"What the hell does he mean, 'like we discussed?' What did we discuss?" Griffith stroked his chin and paced quickly while he thought. "Damn it, this puts him in control of everything. He sets the location. He sets the terms. There's no way I can go through with that. He knows damn well I won't agree to those conditions. Why bother making the call?"

Griffith marched to the far end of his office and stared at his bookcase as if the answer could be found there.

"Stearne thinks I'd put myself at his mercy? He's mad. Stearne thinks I'd bring the Chaac Project to his location for the promise of the Equation in return? Please. Only a fool would do that."

Joona coughed.

"Go ahead," Griffith said, rolling his hand impatiently. "What is it?"

"You told him to bring it to you."

"Exactly!" Griffith shouted. "I told him to bring it to me. I didn't tell him to demand I come to him. Obviously, he knows his family gave your Knights the slip. But he's a smart operator and knows their safety is still at risk. Sooner or later, they'll have to go home and then we have them. Not only that—Betty is his Achilles heel. So why would he make unreasonable demands?"

"He doesn't have it," Joona said. "He can't bring it to you. He's meeting in the middle."

Something about that made sense. Griffith strode back the length of his office and stared at Joona. His right-hand Finn stared at a distant horizon only he could see. Griffith turned to the window.

"I remember now," Griffith said, "just after the shooting started, Stearne told me, '... what happens in your Nerve Center stays in your Nerve Center. Make sure you keep it that way.' What the hell does that mean?"

Joona raised his chin.

"You have a thought on that subject too?" Griffith asked.

"Don't bring the originals," Joona said.

Griffith gave his man a curious once-over. "You mean make copies?"

"Fakes."

"Risky." Griffith clasped his hands behind his back. "I'm inches from getting the Equation. Fakes could jeopardize the whole thing. Let me think this through from the beginning."

He stroked his chin and resumed pacing the room. He said, "Stearne set the terms, the location, he dictated everything. That means he'll have an expert to verify the Project. I don't get what's in it for him, though. He said if two sides have the same information, it's a race. And I'll have the advantage because of the Edison Data. He thinks Pia Sabel will leave us alone if she has the Project and the Equation. But he told me, in so many words, to bring fakes. If I give her fakes, she's going to know it at some point. But by then, if I act fast, I'll have all three pieces and can complete it, get the copyrights and patents, and win. Does that make sense?"

He glanced at Joona. The Finn stared into the distance. No comment, apparently.

"If I screw him, it's reasonable to assume he's screwing me. What's to stop him? He said he's doing it for Betty. I don't believe he'd screw his boss and benefactor to save his girlfriend. Then why would he do it?" Griffith turned to the window. "Whole thing is a setup. It couldn't be though, could it? Why set it up if it's just an exchange of fakes? Maybe he really means it. Maybe some people really do fall in love and sacrifice everything. Suckers."

"He's a romantic," Joona said.

"What do you mean? Oh, yes, he was pining over the last girl and now he's pining over this one. He probably is dumb enough to do it for love. That means he'll have to produce the original in case I discover him. Hmm. And he'll have to verify fifteen notebooks where I'll only verify one. I can give him the first five, enough to pass the verification process. Then the rest are fakes, copies of the first five. If he tries verifying more than that, I'll get impatient and make him stop. He'll get away with only a few of the older materials. OK. My plan is coming together now. But I need insurance. If he controls the location, there is a potential for him to just take it all."

"All my Knights were *Utti Jaegers*," Joona said. "Special forces paratroopers."

"I know what we'll do!" Griffith cried. "I'll wear a locator beacon. You keep a platoon in the air, circling my general location. I'll press a signal button, and your people can parachute in and kill Stearne and his 'expert'. Whoever else he might have lying around. Yes, my plan is brilliant!"

CHAPTER 61

THE INSTANT ISAIAH LEFT, MERCURY materialized. *You got yourself into one whale of a mess now, homie.*

I said, *You're going to help me figure it out, right?*

Mercury said, *I can't be giving you any help. Mars is all over me about cheating. He be whining to Juno already. But whatcha expect from a mama's boy? Amiright? Heh. Get it? See, Juno's the bookie for our bet. She's also his mom.*

I know. I got it, I said.

Mercury said, *Whatcha gotta do is think about the people involved. It's always the people. The Chaac Project ain't nothing but a theory in someone's head. All them people want to be the hero who saves the world. Which one is worthy?*

I said, *Ms. Sabel is the rightful owner. Her dad came up with it. And she expects me to bring it back for her. But she's been in a mood about this ever since it surfaced. The global-impact question is: Does the world need another ultra-billionaire? Jeff Bezos has more money than 2.7 million median American households combined. If this works, she'd be worth ten times more than Bezos—she'd be worth more than the rest of the USA. Does the world need that?*

Mercury said, *If you could talk her into building my Temple of Mercury, I'd be fine with her being richest-ever. It was nice back when Augustus was worth four trillion of your dollars. He built me temples all over the Empire. Ah yes, now he was a good man.*

I said, *She's not building you a temple.*

Mercury said, *Screw her then. What about Betty? She'd build me a temple, wouldn't she? Let's set her up with it.*

I thought about Betty. The infectious charm that flowed from her smile. Calculating the Lamborghini's hood strength on the fly was impressive. She saved my life. And those dimples. The sparkle in her eyes.

I said, *Has she told me everything? I keep getting the feeling she's up to something.*

Mercury said, *She's up to that sparkle. You know what that means.*

I said, *Not everything means what you think it means.*

Mercury said, *So what? Consummate the 'sparkle' you two got going and you guys come out bizzillionaires and—for Jupiter's sake, brutha—build me my damn temple.*

I said, *Betty wants to make it public so all humanity will benefit.*

Holy Diana! Mercury shook his head. *Are all your friends bleeding-heart socialists? I mean, where is the sense in giving it all away? May as well be a Christian, do like Jesus said, 'Give all your money to the poor.' Except none of them ever do. Oh, dude, you should see Jesus jumping up and down outside that preacher's mansion in Houston. He be shouting, 'How does this make sense?' Yeah. That preacher should be one of my flock. Oh. Where was we? Yeah, Betty. So scratch her off the list.*

I said, *Then what's next?*

Mercury said, *Focus on Rafael, lil' dude. Did he go to Vancouver to mail that package to you? Will it arrive where and when he said it would? And why did he do that? Why not hand it over when he showed it to you?*

I said, *Because he knew a horde of greedy killers like Griffith and OMIB would descend on me and take it. This way, he bought time to figure something out. He's an old Mayan revolutionary, working out his tenure at the university and keeping the Keepers going. He's too old and tired to do it himself, so he recruited me for the dangerous part. It all makes sense.*

Mercury said, *OK, well then, whatcha gonna do about Griffith?*

I said, *He's a criminal. I can trust him to screw me—and everyone else—out of the deal. That's why I told him to bring fakes. He wouldn't come if I told him to bring the real thing.*

Mercury said, *Yeah. About that, homie. How is that supposed to work? You ask a guy to bring nothing so you can give him the real thing and somehow you're going to end up with everything?*

I said, *Yes.*

Mercury said, *Are you gonna share this plan? I mean, normally I can read your mind but right now, it's looking kinda blank. Come to think of it, that's how it usually looks.*

I said, *I've got two days to figure that out.*

Mercury said, *That's where we started! How come you're grinning like Willie Nelson? Whoa, look at the time. I'm officiating at the Miss Goddess pageant in a few minutes. Ceres thinks she's gonna win this time. We'll see about that.*

Isaiah politely knocked on the open door. I waved him in. An angry wiry guy with a cap of black hair followed him. OMIB. His dark eyes tried to burn through me.

I rolled mine. "Thanks, Isaiah. I'll take it from here. Call Miguel. He'll have a new assignment for you when he gets back from New Orleans."

To his credit, Isaiah didn't look at OMIB, he saluted and left for Miguel's room down the hall. OMIB watched him with a good deal of concern crossing his face.

As soon as I heard the suite's door close behind him, I said, "Have a seat."

He took the chair.

"Thank you for saving my life," I said as we sized each other up. "Don't take this the wrong way. I appreciate your help, but there are questions that need answers. Don't worry, I'm not going to ask you anything. You won't have to divulge state secrets."

I pulled up my phone and video-called Secretary of State Neville Townsend.

Neville didn't answer until the sixth ring. When he did, his face filled the frame from holding it too close. "I'm at a formal reception for the Japanese Ambassador. I'll call you back after."

"Won't work," I said. "I need you to tell me who this guy is."

I flipped the phone camera from selfie to the other side. OMIB came into view. He grimaced before trying to kill me by burning through me with his glare. Again.

Neville said, "I've no idea. Now, if you'll excuse me—"

"Then I don't need to hand over the Chaac Equation to him?" I flipped the phone back to selfie mode.

"You have it?" Neville's face widened to accommodate his shock. His camera angle widened as well, showing a conservative bow tie and tuxedo jacket. He stood in what looked like a powder room, judging by the wallpaper.

I said, "I just asked you a question and you lied to me. Let's try it again. Who is this guy?"

"He's a special agent." Neville wiped his face with a handkerchief. "He's my backup plan in case you fail. Reports directly to me."

"Does the president know about him trying to break into the Sabel Operations Center?"

Neville did a double take before resigning himself to telling the truth with a labored exhale. "Not specifically, no. President Williams authorized necessary measures. I would never tell him operational details. Plausible deniability, you know. Put my man back on."

I turned the phone to face OMIB so he could see who I was talking to.

Neville said to him, "Leave the room. I need to have a chat with Jacob."

OMIB got up and headed out. At the door, he stopped and tried to burn a hole through my head one last time. I flipped him off. He left.

I turned the screen back to me and gave Neville a nod that we were alone. I said, "Have you heard from Rafael in the last forty-eight hours?"

"No. Do you have the Chaac Equation or not?"

"Not with me," I said. "Since you asked, you've confirmed my theory: Rafael is working without the full authority of your organization. Tell me this: are Amit and Eli Sofer part of the Keepers?"

"How do you know those names?"

"Here's how this goes down, Neville: I ask a question, you answer it. Then, you can ask—"

"Yes, yes, all right. They're both Keepers. They're Israelis on a mission for us in Korea. Where did you hear about them?"

"They were at your little hidey hole in the Canadian Rockies—with the Chaac Equation."

"You saw it?"

"Yes. And I had it verified by an expert who worked on the project."

"Damn it." Neville pursed his lips and stared off camera while he thought. "Jacob, can you recover the Equation?"

"Maybe. Rafael had a crazy plan in which the Equation winds up in my hands. I have to warn you: at first, I thought he was nuts, but now it feels like it's coming together. So, I might have it in a few days."

"Listen carefully, Jacob. President Williams has issued an Executive Order making the Chaac Project, Equation, and the Edison Data matters of national security. I am hereby ordering you to retrieve any and all copies and turn them over to my representative. Is that understood?"

He and I both knew executive orders can't seize intellectual property; that takes an act of Congress. We also knew he couldn't order me directly, but he could go to the Pentagon and have me recalled to active duty, then have a general issue the orders. Something I'd rather not do, since they'd take away my Sabel Security Centurion card and make me fly on troop transports, not Gulfstreams and Boeings. That and the fact that the US Government was a good deal bigger and better armed than Sabel Security meant there was no point in fighting him. I said, "Understood, sir."

"And no more of these churlish calls." He clicked off.

Perfect. Everything was falling into place as planned.

CHAPTER 62

THE DOCTOR GAVE ME A local anesthetic to keep the pain at bay so I could sleep. My right side felt numb from hipbone to armpit. She changed the bandage, gave me antibiotics, and told me to ice it. Housekeeping brought me a mini-freezer and ten ice packs. The doctor ordered sleep, which felt just about right. Then she left.

Mercury showed up with a golden goblet in one hand.

I said, *No way. I'm not drinking that.*

Mercury said, *Vejovis hisself sent it. He's the god of medicine. This here's the elixir of the gods! You be fixed up by morning and ready to rumble. How do you think Tom Cruise comes back to win the day after he was shot twenty times and dumped in the Thames? Or was it the Seine?*

I said, *That was a movie called* Mission Impossible, *not real life.*

Mercury said, *Shut up and drink the elixir.*

I said, *That's no elixir, it's Bellona's menstrual flow—I'd rather die.*

Mercury jumped on the bed and straddled me. He grabbed a fistful of my hair and forced my head back, mouth up. *Damn it, dawg, you gonna drink this shit. I got a lot riding on this bet and I ain't letting it all go down the tubes on account of you being squeamish about a little nectar.*

He held my nose until I opened my mouth to breathe. He poured the whole goblet down my throat and slammed my chin closed. He said, *For Junos' sake, just take your medicine like a good little mortal and quit your whining. The crap I gotta do to save some random-assed white boy is beyond my divine duties.*

He disappeared. And worse—I felt better. I also felt like throwing up.

I got up to relieve my bladder and changed into my sleepwear. Which is easy because I sleep in the buff. When I stepped out of the bathroom, Betty stepped into the bedroom.

"Oh," she said, staring without blushing.

A thousand questions had been piling up in my head waiting for a chance to ask her. I wanted to know how she felt after another brush with death. I wanted to ask if she was up for the next phase. I wanted to ask a lot of things. They all slid to the back of my mind. Because: I was buck naked.

I stood still.

She wore riding clothes from the boutique downstairs. Khaki pants with black cowboy boots and a plaid shirt that a more modest woman might have buttoned up one notch higher. Her eyes grew larger. So did her pupils.

She rushed to me with her arms outstretched. Six inches before slamming into me, she pulled up. "I'm sorry, I shouldn't … um, can I hug you?"

"Mind if I put some clothes on first?"

"Yes." She said before gingerly sliding her hands around me. "I do."

She squeezed my upper body gently, her hands exploring the muscles of my back. I leaned into her embrace, equally gingerly, and put my cheek on top of her golden locks. She felt good in my hands. And my wound remained numb.

Feelings began to stir that hadn't stirred since … too long.

We pulled back to look at each other. Tears filled her eyes. One rolled down her cheek.

"What's wrong?" I asked.

"You." She sniffled. "You're the only one who's man enough to care. Well. Since my dad." She pressed her face to my chest again. I could feel her tears hot on my skin. "I feel bad that you're hurt because of me."

I started but stopped myself from saying I'd do the same for anyone. That wasn't what she wanted to hear. After a bit of thought, I said, "For you, anything."

"That's nice to hear. I would like to say the same thing, but I'm worried about making your injuries worse."

"I'm fully stitched," I said, leaving out Mercury's elixir. "And the doc numbed my side."

The sparkle in her eye caught the light and some more things stirred inside me. She kissed a line across my chest. That made a lot more things stir.

"You smell of horses," I said, trying to think of calming subjects while fully exposed.

She inhaled deeply. "And you smell of antiseptic."

She pushed me back an arm's length. I felt the bed at the back of my knees. I cupped her face in my hands and kissed her. She tasted like cherries, sweet and tart. We kissed for a long time before coming up for air.

"How was your ride?" I asked.

"Second best way to relax there is." She looked up at me with deep dimples. "I just love riding."

I tried to think of calming subjects again. Things like grooming horses after a ride, but all I could visualize was massaging warm, smooth flesh.

"Do you like riding?" she asked.

With outstretched fingers, she pushed me another inch. The bed held my lower legs in place. My butt dropped to the sheets. My ribs screamed through the local and the elixir, but I didn't let it show. She squeezed my knees together and put her knees on either side them.

"Love riding," I said. "But I'm not big on bridles or saddles."

"Not a leather man? Noted. Bareback is my favorite, too." She unbuttoned the third button down from the neck of her shirt. Then she stopped. "Wait, can you survive a ride with your injuries?"

I inhaled long and slow. She smiled and loosened the next button. She moved in so close I could see nothing but a little red bow between two lace cups. And skin. I exhaled long and slow.

I said, "I can survive anything."

The remaining buttons took her less time. She pulled the tail out of her riding slacks and pressed my face to her stomach. I kissed a circle around her belly button. Grabbing my hair, she pulled my head back and gave me her best ingénue pout.

"Can you help me?" She asked. "I memorized the Schrödinger equation when I was seventeen, but I still can't figure out belt buckles."

CHAPTER 63

TWO DAYS LATER, THE RANCH manager picked up Betty and me at the airport. With his weathered face, worn flannel shirt, and broad-brimmed hat, he could've stepped out of a Frederic Remington painting. He reported that Ms. Sabel had arrived hours earlier and he was impressed by her. Which meant he was smart enough to brown-nose whenever possible. He gave us the ranch history and told us we were nestled between Glacier National Park and Idaho, just south of Canada.

The location I'd requested after looking at the map—two cabins a couple miles apart with an open meadow in between—was seldom used and had been cleared of grazing cattle. Nonetheless, he advised watching where we stepped. Ten Sabel Agents from the Seattle office had arrived and were in place. Ranch hands had been given notice the area was off limits for the duration. We had a small corner of the ranch—about 5,000 acres—to ourselves.

Ms. Sabel met us at the cabin. She brought saddled horses "just in case." The elixir of the gods had patched up about 60 percent of my injuries. Mercury claimed I needed another dose. I'd been ducking him. Nonetheless, the mere thought of jostling on horseback made my ribs shriek in agony.

The cabin was no prop on a movie set. It was the real thing. Ancient logs with chinks of mortar missing and gaps wide enough to put your hand through. No glass windows, just ancient shutters hanging onto their hinges for dear life. The four-plank door had to be lifted an inch to scrape it over the buckled floor. Not that we cared. We only needed the porch. From it we could see across the mile-wide meadow to the road.

Armies of big, white puffy clouds marched across a bright blue sky heading for a roundup in the east. The nearest range of peaks scratched at the bottoms. The scent of pine with a hint of cow manure wafted on the breeze. Birds sang in the trees. A turkey vulture made a reconnaissance tour of the valley, waiting for the spoils of war.

The ladies sat cross-legged on the splintered gray boards, complimenting each other on their western outfits as if it were opening day at summer camp. They'd gone all-out for the gear. They had the finest cowboy hats, boots, jeans, and leather belts money could buy. The hats were felt. The shirts had snaps instead of buttons. Ms. Sabel had her hair back in her trademark ponytail. Betty had her golden locks harnessed by a western leather-and-stick barrette. They both looked great. They were ready for their close-ups.

I had a different fashion concept. My black t-shirt had white lettering that read, "Bullet Catcher." My jeans had holes because they'd worn through. My combat boots had better traction than the high-heels people think of as cowboy boots. My jacket had gone through four of my eight combat tours. All three bullet holes were the autographs of our nation's enemies.

I showed Betty the tablet I'd brought. "I'll send you a livestream video from my button-camera as I look through the books."

As I spoke, I realized Betty's snaps were also button-cameras. She didn't get them from me, which left only Ms. Sabel as the source.

Betty started to ask, "Are you sure you want me to verify—"

"Using these buttons here," I said. I had cut her off with a glance at Ms. Sabel. Betty checked me and understood that I'd not told the boss we were going to verify everything as authentic—whether it was or not. "Red for wrong, and green for good."

"Easy enough," she said. Her eyes sparkled as she flashed a smile. "I'm ready."

Ms. Sabel held up her phone. "Emma wanted me to tell you: they tracked forty Finns, all former *Utti Jaegers*, who went through customs in Chicago yesterday. That's a lot more than we brought in from Seattle."

I nodded. "Risks. Always risks."

"Where are Miguel and Isaiah?" she asked.

"On a special assignment," I said.

She didn't look satisfied with my answer. They were my go-to guys, and the fact they were nowhere to be seen rattled her. She said, "This is my inheritance, Jacob. The only thing I have to remember Lloyd Aston. Alan Sabel tried to retrieve it and died in the effort. You helped me try to get it back, but we came up empty. I can't lose this time. Not to these people." Her voice rose in volume and her brows closed over her eyes. "I don't want bastards like Joe Griffith getting their grubby little hands all over my father's work!"

I nodded and put a calming hand on her shoulder. She shrugged it off.

Her gray-green eyes seared into me. "This is going to work, right? I end up with my legacy. Not those filthy cretins who have it now. Right? Jacob?"

"That's the plan."

"You don't sound terribly confident."

"My experience: things never turn out as bad as you feared nor as good as you hoped. I'm not setting expectations either way. Too many variables. My aim is to walk away with as much as we can."

She said, "We should call this off."

"We'll never get this close again." I watched the dust cloud thrown up by an approaching truck.

She shook her head, unsatisfied.

Pulling my binoculars out of my pack, I glassed across the meadow to the tree line on the far side. A properly maintained cabin, complete with glass windows and a painted front door, waited for our guests. The map listed both cabins as "unused line cabins" without distinguishing which one had been spruced up in the last century.

The truck turned onto our lane and came toward us at a good clip.

"Is that Griffith?" Ms. Sabel asked. "He's early and he's heading for the wrong cabin."

"FedEx," I said.

The delivery man stopped fifty yards from the cabin due to rough ground. I met him halfway and signed for the ten-pound package. I walked back to the porch, where Ms. Sabel waited with a curious scowl. I pulled the Chaac Equation notebook out of the package and handed it to Betty.

"Is this the real thing?" I asked.

Betty took the book and started thumbing through the pages.

"How did you get that?" Ms. Sabel asked with strain in her voice. "Rafael sent it here?"

"He sent it to the hotel in Canada and I had it forwarded."

She did the math in her head. It was obvious I could've told her more than I had about my plan. Her expression indicated she wasn't happy. Couldn't be helped with the mood she's in. Not that I blamed her. If she knew what I was about to do, she'd shut it down. And that would ruin everything. While Betty turned pages, her finger tracing diagrams and equations, Ms. Sabel's steam rose.

When it bubbled to the surface, Ms. Sabel said, "Tell me again how this plan works."

"You won't like it, so I'm not going to tell you."

Betty's head came up from her homework. She checked Ms. Sabel's burning face, then glanced at me and followed my gaze across the meadow. She dropped her face back into the book, wanting to stay out of the brewing fight.

Ms. Sabel bit the inside of her cheek and willed herself to trust me. She took a few long, deep breaths, then got up and paced with her arms folded tight across her chest.

After a few minutes, Betty looked up and said, "As far as I can tell, this is the real thing. There's no way to be 100 percent sure without completing the experiments, and no one's done that, so, this is as close as we get."

Ms. Sabel's locked jaw, tapping foot, and hard glare told me my employment—if not my life—could end shortly if things did not go well.

I pointed at a dust trail rising at the end of the valley. "They're here."

CHAPTER 64

JOE GRIFFITH STEPPED OUT OF the rented Suburban and took in the cabin. It had a newish front door, a picture window, and an occasionally maintained drive with minor ruts. A dense forest surrounded the cabin on three sides. It was so thick it was hard to see more than three trees deep. He creaked up the steps to the recently refinished porch, where a tripod held a massive pair of binoculars. He opened the door and peeked inside. Two rooms: a kitchenette and great room with fireplace took up half the cabin; a double bed and chair took the other half. No sign of an indoor bathroom. No need to ask if anyone was home. The whole thing could fit in his closet back in Chicago. He closed the door.

He took the sturdy pine chair next to the bench. After securing the area, Joona and his lieutenant brought the notebooks from the truck and stacked them in three piles of five on the edge of the porch. The lieutenant kept watch, tracking around the empty site. No sign of anyone.

A phone rang. Griffith looked at Joona. Neither had found mobile service since they left the Kalispell airport over two hours earlier. Joona found the phone, a Sabel Satellite unit, under the bench. The caller ID read "Jacob Stearne." Griffith took it from his hand.

"What's your game, Stearne?" he asked.

"Look through the binoculars. They're aimed at a spot in the meadow."

Griffith peered through the glass. "OK, I see you."

"As you can see, I'm alone and I'm holding the Chaac Equation."

Through the binoculars, Griffith could see a man. As he claimed, he was alone and held a four-inch notebook over his head. After adjusting the focus, he could see it was Stearne and the notebook had the same

359

appearance as his Project notebooks.

His heart raced with excitement. If this deal was on the level, he was inches from having it all.

He turned to Joona, looking for a high five. But the cold Finn had his own field glasses out, scanning the valley.

"OK, Stearne," he said. "I have the Project books as promised. What's next?"

"You and Joona will pack them on the horses and ride out here. You'll leave the other guy at the cabin."

"What horses?" he asked.

A split second later, a rider came out of the forest leading three horses. Two with saddles and one with panniers. The rider had an H&K MP7 slung across his chest, and a calm demeanor. His black cowboy hat hid his gaze, but Griffith felt the man take his full measure. His anger rose. Stearne never said anything about horses, wranglers, or pack animals. He looked at Joona.

The Finn held a stoic pose and quietly said, "Salvation rains from the skies."

Griffith heard the buzz of a distant airplane. A skydiving rig circled a few miles away, waiting for their signal. He calmed himself and focused his thoughts on the expression Stearne would have when he saw all those Finns descending from on high. A wry smile stretched his face.

The rider stopped at the porch and tipped his hat.

"I suppose you expect me to ride down there?" Griffith asked.

"You promised to leave Betty and my family alone if I brought you this. I held up my end. If you want it, this is what you're going to do. So. What's it going to be, Griffith?"

"Fine. See you in fifteen." He clicked off.

The cowboy—who looked more like a mercenary with a hat instead of a helmet—pointed at Griffith. He said, "All your electronics on the porch."

"I don't have any," Griffith said.

Three men stepped out of the trees wearing full military gear, body armor, helmets, camo—and MP7s leveled at Griffith and his men. Another pair stepped out of the cabin and started patting them down.

They took everything out of the men's pockets and holsters: three pistols from the Finns, a Sig P320 from Griffith, and two knives. Along with their phones, wallets, and keys, everything was placed in a cardboard box. The box was placed on the driver's seat of the rental and the keys given to the wrangler. The soldiers melted back into the forest.

Joona shrugged at Griffith. Then he and his lieutenant packed the notebooks into the paniers.

Griffith mounted his horse. Joona mounted his. Their guide moseyed them down the slope into the meadow.

Griffith turned to Joona. The Finn nosed in the air. The airplane banked in the distance, heading their way.

CHAPTER 65

I WATCHED MY MAN LEAD Griffith and Joona across the meadow toward me.

Mercury spoke into my ear. *Hey, homie, you see horses walking, but you hear a horse galloping. Whazzat all about?*

After jumping and slashing the air as if attacked by bees—because I hate it when he comes out of nowhere—I turned to see Betty riding at full throttle from my side of the meadow.

I said, *Holy Minerva. What the hell is she doing?*

Mercury said, *Maybe she gots an urgent message from Caesar.*

I said, *The days of couriers on horseback are long gone, my friend. She'd have called.*

Mercury said, *This be your end game, boy. Will it be your swan song or your curtain call? You're gonna win my wife back for me, right? I said, RIGHT?*

Absently, I replied, *I hope so.*

As I waited for her to ride in, I took a side glance at him. *How did the Miss Goddess thing go?*

Tough times, my man. He shook his head. *See, androgynous gods are a dime a dozen in most religions. I mean, even the apostle John keeps getting mistaken for Mary Magdalene in Da Vinci's* Last Supper. *A bunch of the old-fashioned judges wants everything defined in a certain way, right? So, they put me in charge of making sure all the goddesses was actually goddesses. Well, I ain't looking up nobody's toga. They want to play goddess, why spoil the party? Turns out, in some circles, it's all right and in others it's not. They's all back there arguing still. I'm done with the lot of them. Don't have to mess with them 'til the next gods convention.*

I blinked at him and wondered if I should tell Doctor Harrison that story. How would he counsel me? Would he say I'm falling apart under the stress of imminent combat? Would he say I'm having a psychotic break to avoid dealing with my responsibilities? Or would he say I need mass quantities of lithium?

Betty pulled up her galloping horse, sliding his front hooves into the dirt with a flourish John Wayne would've envied. I said, "You know how to ride a horse?"

"I played a barrel racer in the contemporary update of *The Searchers.*" She dismounted like an expert.

"I didn't know there was a remake of *The Searchers,*" I said, referring to the classic John Ford movie of 1956.

"Neither did anyone else," she said with a sad smile. "The story of my career."

"What are you doing here?"

She walked up to me, real close, and looked up at me. "I came to stand by my man."

I waited for a punchline that didn't come. She was serious. I glanced over at the approaching riders. Three minutes out, tops.

After a few beats, I said, "Betty, go back to the cabin. Use the tablet. Things are going to get dangerous down here. There are forty Knights, trained special forces guys, who will be arriving soon. You're not safe here."

"I'll be just as safe as you," she said. "You won't let anything bad happen to either of us."

"You're the math wiz," I said. "Forty men are coming, and I have a pistol with seventeen rounds. What are my chances?"

She wrapped me up in a tight squeeze. "I can't imagine a world without you."

Griffith and Joona were a minute away. It was too late to send her back. I could protect her better here. Even if it meant using my body as a shield. At least it would be death with *dignitas.*

She released her grip as the riders approached.

My wrangler pulled up ten yards shy of where I stood. He jumped down, drove a heavy stake in the ground, and tied the lead horse to it.

Griffith climbed down from the saddle. He shook himself and inhaled a dose of arrogant attitude. He tucked his thumbs in his belt and strode toward me.

Joona brought a stack of notebooks out of the paniers. He piled them in three stacks of five at my feet.

When they were all done, the wrangler untied his horse from the other three and jumped back in the saddle. He shook the rental keys until Griffith looked his way. Then he threw them twenty yards into the knee-high grass, turned, and rode away at a lope.

Griffith sneered as he said, "Time to show your cards, Jacob."

Betty stepped forward, facing him. "Surprised to see me here, you sick bastard?"

"Not at all." He smiled his reptilian grin. "You've done well reporting Jacob's movements."

"You can stop trying to make me distrust her," I said. "We found the luggage tags. We know how you tracked us."

"What happened to His Grace, James, Duke of Kingston?" Betty snarled. "Was he too chicken to make the trip?"

"He dumped you fifteen years ago," Griffith said. "Past your prime even then."

"Why do you do it, Joe?" she sneered. "Why pimp high school freshmen for your friends?"

"The world revolves around supply and demand, Betty." He raised up on his toes and settled back down as if he were explaining something to a child for the tenth time. "There are certain people in powerful positions who demand high-quality virgins. Men have been doing it for all recorded history. The Duke is a connoisseur of fine young ladies, that's all. You should be honored to have held his attention for a time. You were quite willing, as I recall. Eager—if not talented."

Her fists balled up, Betty stormed toward him.

CHAPTER 66

I GRABBED HER ARM BEFORE she could get far. I said, "Before you two resolve your differences, we have a deal to complete."

Bellowing, Griffith pointed at the notebooks and said, "Well, if she's your expert, have her look at a few books then. Let's get moving. I haven't got all day."

Betty took a tentative step toward the stack. I backed up to give her the go-ahead and some space. Kneeling, she opened the first notebook and fanned through the pages. Checking the table of contents for specific entries, she then double-checked those pages to make sure they matched. She did the same for a few random index entries. Other parts she simply read. When she was satisfied, she set the first volume down forming a new stack and took the second book.

"Is this really necessary?" Griffith asked. "I'm not standing around while she reads six thousand pages."

"No shortcuts," I said. "You get to look at the Equation after she authenticates your end."

Griffith stared at me in disbelief. He scoffed and turned away. "You know, I could have my man jump you and walk away with everything."

"You could try."

"Say, where is that Indian always watching over you?" he asked.

"On a special assignment. He's Native, Diné to be specific. Calling him an Indian shows your geographic ignorance by 8,000 miles."

He hmphed.

Betty finished the second volume and added it to the first. She went back to the third stack and jumped to volume eleven. She got comfortable cross-legged on the ground with the book in her lap.

"Hey, what's she doing?" Griffith pointed angrily. "Go in order."

"She does what she wants."

"Well, if she doesn't have a method, she'd going to get everything mixed up and screw the results. I'm not letting this whole thing blow up because you—"

"Just because you don't know what it is, doesn't mean she doesn't have a method."

"Give me the damned Equation, then!" he shouted. "Least you can do is let me confirm the wait is worthwhile."

It was a reasonable demand. I didn't see a downside, so I handed it to him.

Griffith paged through the book. I watched him. Joona watched him. We both wondered when he would admit he had no idea what it said after the table of contents. He was fifty pages in when he said, "Your people took my phone. I had some reference points to look for on there. Have your man bring it to me."

"That book hasn't seen daylight since a long-dead genius handed it over to the Keepers twenty years ago. You don't have any reference points. But you do have someone who worked on the project with the Russians. She could tell you what you want to know."

"Have it your way," he said. With derision dripping through his words, he continued, "Betty, would you please authenticate this for me?"

"I looked at it when it arrived an hour ago," she said. "As far as I can tell, it's the real thing. There's no way to be 100 percent sure, so this is as close as you're going to get."

Joona tensed up like a snake ready to strike. We were coming close to them executing their endgame. I looked to the clouds.

Griffith waved at the stacks of unchecked books. "You can verify the rest of this on your own time. Trust me, it's all there. At least, whatever the Russians gave me." He turned a disdainful glare at Betty. "None of my experts actually worked on the Chaac Project."

Betty pulled her hair back and re-worked her barrette. Our pre-arranged signal that the Chaac Project was not what he claimed. As expected. She raised a brow, asking permission to call him out. I shook her off with the subtlety of a pitcher on the mound.

"That's fine," I said. "You're free to go."

He started to look for his car keys.

"Hey, before you leave, you should check out why they call it Big Sky Country." I pointed into the air over a mile and a half across the valley. "Plenty of room for all those paratroopers to practice. Don't they look tiny from here?"

His Finns had jumped from fifteen thousand feet, a mile behind the forest at the back of Griffith's cabin so they could swoop in without being seen. It was where Griffith's locator beam had called them— unbeknownst to Griffith.

Griffith looked in the air, then at Joona. The Finn looked confused, staring in disbelief as his men headed in the wrong direction.

"Parachutes are magnificent, aren't they?" I asked. "Dang near silent right up 'til the final flare for landing. Of course, that's when they're most vulnerable, too. For my guys, it'll be like ducks in a barrel. They'll just run up and stab each guy with a Sabel Dart when he tries to land."

It would be a lot more difficult than I made it sound. If the Finns spotted our ambush, the guys higher up would shoot my agents. But just as we figured, they came in over the treetops going for the element of surprise. Their cover would also block their view of the ground until it was too late.

"You ... you can't do that." Griffith said. "Who called them in?"

"You did," I said. "We figured you'd have a panic button for reinforcements. When my guys patted you down, they pressed every part of you to trigger it. Looks like it worked. We weren't sure, and that had me worried this whole time."

Pulling a locator device hidden in his belt, Griffith turned to Joona. "But why are they landing over there?"

Still mystified, the Finn shook his head and watched his men coming in over a mile off target.

"Don't blame him, Joe," I said. "We figured you'd keep the locator on your person. That's why we put multi-spectrum radio jammers in the bottoms of the paniers."

Both men's eyes darted to the pack horse.

"Right now," I said with a grin, "they're heading to your last known location."

"Why, you son of a bitch!" Griffith shouted with clenched fists.

Joona wasn't big on words. Instead, he pulled a tactical knife out of his belt buckle and ran straight at Betty. It was a smart move on his part. He expected me to be armed. I was. The only way he could fight was to charge Betty, forcing me to step in front of him without time to pull my weapon. If I went for my 9 mil, the time it took would allow him to get around me, putting Betty in mortal danger. I couldn't shoot him without a high risk of injuring or killing her. That evened the odds in Joona's favor.

The fact he was using a belt-buckle knife pissed me off. That was my trick. I rarely ran into anyone else using it. And I wouldn't have time to pull mine, for the same reason as the pistol.

I charged Joona like a linebacker sacking a quarterback. Seeing me, he staggered a step and tried to send me over his back. I adjusted but caught only one of his shoulders. I yanked it as hard as I could and landed face-down on the ground. He spun across my back. My ribs sent agonizing electric shocks through my nervous system.

Joona gained his feet before I did. He tried a massive kick to my ribs, knowing right where to find my wound. I rolled away and jumped to my feet. I was too slow to catch his foot and push him backwards. But I tried. I caught his leg for a second, sending him staggering back a step. The maneuver made my whole ribcage lock up in distress.

As he regained his balance, I landed a solid blow to his face that sent blood spewing from his nose. It wasn't enough to faze him. Instead, he leaned forward, pounding his elbow into my jaw and slashing at me with his knife on the backswing.

I stumbled back. Realizing I was on the defensive, I took two more steps back, trying to draw him in. He didn't fall for it. He lunged at Betty. Again, I had only time to react and not enough to find a weapon. I tried to tackle him with the wrap-method, both arms outstretched, hoping to grab any part of him.

Betty spidered backward.

He expected my move and somersaulted. My arms wrapped his calves as he went over the top. He kicked wildly, hitting me in the cheek. My wounded side began to spurt blood. I could feel it, along with jagged spasms of pain. I could barely breathe. By the time I picked myself off the ground, the Finn was lunging directly at me. I rolled, my injured face joining my knife wound in complaint.

Joona's knife skimmed over me and stuck in the dirt. The Finn pushed to his knees.

During my roll, I freed my pistol. I did the fair and honorable thing: I waited until he gained his feet. "I don't have a beef with you, Joona. Drop the knife. Walk away."

Eyes blazing hatred, he charged me.

I fired. He was still crouching, which gave me the perfect angle for a decisive kill-shot. My bullet pierced his forehead just above where his eyebrows met and roared through the front of his skull. From there, it drove through the bottom of his frontal lobe on its way to shatter the amygdala and sever the brainstem. It exited through the cerebellum, crashing out of the back of his skull trailed by a mixture of brains and blood.

Griffith shrieked in horror. His Knight without shining armor was gone.

Betty grabbed my arm and pointed at Griffith. She said, "Give me that. I'm going to kill him."

I shook her off, but she didn't let go. I had to grab her hand with my left and peel her fingers off my pistol. "Remember the last guy? You don't want to live with that. You're after humiliation."

"Not anymore." She glared at me as if I were no better than Griffith.

I said, "Look away."

She didn't.

"No, Jacob." Griffith dropped to his knees, a coward in the end. "We had a deal."

"You had a deal." I stepped closer while maintaining a sporting distance, about the length of a ranch house. "You put a plan in motion in Germany that cost Jenny Jenkins her life."

"I had nothing to do with that." He clasped his hands in submission and shook them. "It was all that crazy—"

"You had plenty to do with destroying Betty Bardon's childhood, didn't you? Killed her father and co-opted her mother. Are you proud of yourself?"

"I had no choice." His tear-filled eyes turned to Betty. When he saw no mercy, his cowardice turned to anger. "She went willingly to the Duke, if you must know. Couldn't wait to offer herself to a real man—"

I shot him in the left shin. He screamed. I shot him in the right shin.

"No! Please!" Griffith cried. "You're doing that thing."

Betty squeezed up behind me, holding my bicep and leaning around my shoulder to watch with horrified satisfaction.

I shot him in the right thigh. He called for divine intervention, like so many of his victims. I shot him in the left thigh. I said, "What thing is that?"

I put a bullet through his right arm.

"You're ..." He gasped for breath in a last-ditch attempt to keep the pain from overwhelming him. "You're torturing me. Seamus said ... professionals ... shoot without killing."

I put a bullet through his left hand. "Don't know where he got that idea. You're going to die—eventually."

The next bullet went through his spleen. I think. When it comes to the little organs, I forget where they are exactly. So I put the next one through his lower left lung. I knew where that was.

"I beg..." he gasped with a sickening wheeze. "Don't ... stop."

"Don't stop? OK."

I was tired of listening to his shrieks anyway. I pumped the rest of my magazine into various parts of him, saving the last one for his forehead.

CHAPTER 67

I GRABBED AT BETTY'S HAND as she walked past me to Griffith's body. She pulled out of my grip. She said, "I want to know he's dead."

"You'll never un-see that," I said. "Come back."

She didn't. I let her walk the fifty feet on her own.

From up the hill behind us, I heard a horse at a gallop. I didn't need to check to know it was Ms. Sabel. She pulled up next to me in a cloud of dust and jumped down. Striding up next to me, she watched Betty.

"You pulled the trigger, right?" she asked.

"Yep."

"That'll spare her a few more nightmares." She blew out a breath. "Reports are in from the other cabin. All but four of the Finns are sound asleep. Two are caught in the trees and two are making a break for it. So that part went well." She waited a beat. "Now, I have to thank you for bringing me the Chaac Project and Equation."

"Don't thank me yet." I pointed at a tiny triangle in the sky directly overhead. "Triton."

She didn't need an explanation. Sabel Weapons Systems was bidding to replace the Triton spy drones used by US Naval Intelligence. They were good machines that could stay at 50,000 feet for more than a day. And they were built to stalk something as small as a squirrel for more than twenty-four hours at a stretch.

"What's does the Navy want?" she asked.

Betty started walking back.

"It's not them," I said. "They're just handy. They operate those out of Whidbey in Puget Sound. They're the eyes and ears for those guys."

I pointed due south, where three Chinooks labored their way toward us.

"What the hell are those?"

"Dual-rotor helicopters operated by SOAR. The 160th Special Operations Aviation Regiment, call themselves the Night Stalkers. Based at McChord outside of Tacoma. They can carry a platoon each. I can guess who's commanding this operation, but you've never met him, so I'll let him introduce himself."

Ms. Sabel's gray-green eyes drilled a hole through the side of my head as the thrumming noise of the choppers grew louder.

One of the Chinooks came straight to us. The other two headed for Griffith's cabin.

Ignoring the noise, Betty walked up, put her arms around me, and buried her face in my chest. "You were right. I shouldn't have gone. Let's get out of here."

"Good idea," Ms. Sabel said.

"Nowhere we can go they won't find us."

Across the valley, near the cabin, soldiers fast-roped down from the Chinooks. We'd already subdued the Finns for them, so it was more theater than necessity. But that wouldn't matter to them. To the US military, there's no success like excess.

Ms. Sabel watched the lead chopper drop low and swing around. Gatling guns in portals on the side trained on us. Still several feet above the surface in what special ops pilots call the pinnacle maneuver, they dropped the loading ramp in the back. The whole platoon spilled out as if they were taking ground in a war zone. The first men out dropped to the ground, securing the area. The rest flooded out in a precision maneuver.

Seconds later, we were surrounded by well-trained, heavily armed, but silent soldiers. We stood still.

"What do they want?" Betty asked, squeezing my arm and moving behind my shoulder.

"Same thing everyone wants: Chaac."

Both women turned their fury-filled faces to me.

"You knew?" Ms. Sabel asked.

"Expected, would be more accurate."

"Then why not call it off?"

"This was our only chance." I watched OMIB step out of the helicopter and march toward us. "We ran out of time."

On one side of me, Betty grew increasingly afraid. On the other, Ms. Sabel grew increasingly angry.

When he was still a few feet away, I said, "A bit of overkill, don't you think?"

"Did you expect us to trust you for delivery?" His glare hadn't softened any since the last time I saw him.

"Army operations aren't allowed inside the country."

"Training mission, Stearne." He assessed my companions. "Just a game of capture the flag."

He turned to the piles of notebooks. He snapped his fingers. Soldiers slung their rifles and picked up two each.

"Who the hell do you think you are?" Ms. Sabel screeched loud enough to scare the elk for miles.

He lifted his chin and supervised the soldiers.

I turned and grabbed her shoulders and turned her to face me. "He's a covert special agent for Secretary of State Neville Townsend. Your friend President Williams declared these materials a matter of national security. He's securing them on behalf of the government."

"Like hell!" She yanked free of my grip. "These belong to me! They're mine, damn it. I never heard of the State Department having covert operators."

"That's the idea behind covert," I said quietly.

She reached for the pistol concealed in the small of her back. I grabbed her hand with a calm, steady grip. She relaxed a little but her eyes flashed death rays at the soldiers.

OMIB gave me a look that told me to get her under control.

"It takes an act of Congress to nationalize something," she kept going at full volume. "The president can't unilaterally nationalize my inheritance—MY BIRTHRIGHT! You can't do this!"

I put an arm around her and whispered, "He has the twenty-four rifles that say he can. For now. We have legal remedies. Just try to calm down before these guys get jumpy."

Looking up at OMIB, I said, "Rich people think everything belongs to them."

He nodded knowingly.

One of the soldiers picked up the Chaac Equation and walked away.

Betty pounded on my shoulder, "You can't let them take that! NO! We worked too hard for that. You can't let them have it. It's not fair."

She broke down in sobs.

OMIB shot me a disdainful look and followed the last man carrying notebooks.

"Hey!" I pointed at the two dead bodies. "You take anything, you take everything."

He stopped and looked at Griffith's carcass. He looked back at me with a harder scowl. Then he snapped his fingers and pointed. Soldiers grabbed Joona and Griffith and carried them back to the Chinook.

OMIB walked into the cargo bay and disappeared. The last soldiers backed in, their weapons covering any potential threat. Then the loading ramp folded up and the chopper rose into the sky.

Ms. Sabel watched it go and turned to me. "Tell me you have a plan. You damn well better have a plan."

"Lawyers," I said. I looked skyward at the tiny triangle of Triton spy plane. "It's a legal matter from here on out."

Ms. Sabel followed my gaze and began to understand my reticence to talk. Betty continued crying.

Leaning close, in a confidential tone, Ms. Sabel said, "Our people will delete the video from Betty's button-camera from the Finn on. Nothing about shooting Griffith will get out. But the Navy drone is a different problem."

"They can't release anything from the drone without exposing this operation. My secret's safe."

I thumbed out a message on my phone's screen and showed it to them both. It read, "Not another word about Chaac until we're on the jet and airborne."

CHAPTER 68

AT GRIFFITH'S COMPOUND IN WINNETKA, Illinois, Miguel Rodriguez walked back into the guardhouse where Isaiah double-checked all the camera displays.

Isaiah pointed at the monitor banks as he craned over his shoulder. "You were right. They took everyone to Montana and left only a skeleton crew. Looks like we got them all. I'm not seeing a single guard still awake."

"Who are those two?" Miguel pointed at a monitor where two people worked on something on a broad counter.

"Cook and her assistant. They're in the kitchen on the way to Griffith's Nerve Center. We'll knock them out as we go by."

"No," Miguel said. "We take them with us. They're non-combatants."

"If you say so." Isaiah groaned. "I'm not fond of prisoners. But, since we have a couple hours before these guys wake up—"

"We have fifteen minutes." Miguel waited until Isaiah rose and tilted his head for an explanation. "The feds aren't stupid. We don't know how many people they have working on this but at some point, they'll do the same critical thinking we did and come to the same conclusion: Griffith would never hand over the real thing to Jacob."

They headed down to the basement, Isaiah leading the way to the underground tunnel between the guardhouse and Griffith's mansion.

"Is that why you have the guy from the Chicago office working the drone?" Isaiah asked. "You're expecting company?"

"Stearne's Law at work. I even sent another guy out to monitor the FBI office where they keep the SWAT team. And another at the Bureau of Diplomatic Security's SWAT team."

"Diplomatic Security? The State Department has a SWAT team in Chicago?"

"Amtrak has a SWAT team. They're all the rage at federal agencies these days."

Emma texted them: "FBI is mobilizing SWAT. Estimated 14 minutes out."

"You called it," Isaiah said. "I'll start a timer."

They marched through the dark tunnel side-by-side. After a few moments of silence, Isaiah said, "I have to ask you: am I forgiven for my sins?"

Miguel gave him some side-eye. "Jacob left your execution to my discretion."

After a few more silent strides, Miguel elbowed the shorter man.

Isaiah laughed weakly. "It's not all that funny, you know."

"Suppose not. Jacob and I talked about it. He asked you a question and you came clean. Good enough for us. If you'd lied, the Canadians would never find your body. But you didn't. You risked a lot defying the papers OMIB made you sign. We understand how hard that made your decision. You're one of us now. Inner circle and all that."

Isaiah beamed with pride. Then doubts withered his expression. He asked, "Shouldn't there be some form of punishment?"

"You've been hanging around white people too much. America is hell-bent on vindictive retribution. They throw people in 'corrections' institutions every chance they get. Instead of being corrected, the offenders go from bad to worse. Where does that get anyone? No good.

"When I joined Sabel, I proposed we use traditional Diné methods of dealing with people. The Navajo have a saying, 'He acts as if he has no relatives.' When someone acts badly, selfishly, untrustworthy, the relatives are asked if they will take responsibility for that person. If they do, they keep a close watch on him. If they won't, the offender has nowhere to go. No one will let him in."

"Sounds like intra-platoon discipline." Isaiah stopped and checked Miguel. "Who vouched for me? Who are my relatives?"

"The team discussed it. Pia, Tania, Jacob, me, a few others. Jacob and I are your relatives. We've seen you in action, we know how smart you are. How valuable you are to the team. We have full faith in you." Miguel squeezed his shoulder. "Of course, if you'd prefer, we could always beat you with a stick."

"No, this is good. Thank you."

They walked into the kitchen and explained to the cook, a gray-haired older woman, and her helper, a young man, that they were needed as tour guides. The shocked pair placed their phones on the counter as instructed and came with them. Despite repeated assurances they would be unharmed, they appeared frightened. Which Miguel chalked up to his size rather than his charm. Of course, it may have been the automatic rifles they carried.

Emma sent an update. The FBI SWAT team was eight minutes out.

The cook led the way to the orange wall and into the Nerve Center. Isaiah stepped inside and announced, "Exactly the way I saw it with Jacob a week ago."

Miguel wasn't pleased. "Don't move for a second."

Isaiah stood still. The cook and helper parked themselves against the built-in cabinets on the side.

Something was off. Miguel circled the large table while staring at the open notebooks. The conference table was made of oak and had twenty evenly spaced chairs pushed in neatly. A multi-microphone with spider-like arms waited for a conference call. On the far wall, a video screen sat blank and black. Fifteen three-inch binders lay open. It appeared someone left in a hurry. Coffee cups, plates with bagel remnants, and crumpled napkins remained between the notebooks.

"Exactly as you saw it last?" Miguel asked.

Isaiah nodded and tilted his head with curiosity. "There's one thing missing. There was a hard drive over there. Jacob said it was boobytrapped. It's gone now."

"They had time to push the chairs in but not to throw away their bagel plates? That's interesting." Miguel flipped pages in a notebook. "Jacob told him to make a fake set and bring them. How would you make a set of fakes?"

Isaiah scratched his chin. "He's not a physicist, or engineer, and a lot of it's in Russian, so he wouldn't know how to read this stuff. If I were him, I'd make copies of the first and last twenty pages, then stuff the middles with random pages from just one book. It would pass a field inspection. What else could he do?"

"If these are the real thing, how could he make a fake without taking these off the table?" Miguel nodded as he completed a full circle. "If he made fakes, he had to use a different set. He had to make it look half right. He couldn't bring fifteen dictionaries stuffed into three-ring binders. And he sure as hell wouldn't bring the real thing to Montana."

"I see what you're saying," Isaiah said. "The Chaac Project is here, but this isn't it."

"This might be it, might not. He wouldn't make copies for fakes, then lay them back down exactly as you saw them a week ago. There's one other thing."

Isaiah waited as Miguel stroked his chin.

"Griffith told Jacob he made sure the Russians had given him everything," Miguel said. "They left nothing behind. So there's one big problem with this scene." He pointed to the open notebooks. "Lloyd Aston didn't speak Russian."

Emma sent another message. The FBI were four minutes away.

Miguel tracked around to the cook and stood in her space, his big frame towering over her. "I hope you can help me, ma'am. I need to find the other set of notebooks that looks exactly like those. You bring him bagels, coffee, lunch. Would you please tell me where he works on them?"

The cook stammered with her eyes glued to the floor. After a moment, she looked up with glistening eyes. Her lips trembled, her skin shook. But she couldn't get any words out.

The assistant took off his apron and handed it to the cook. "Worst job I ever had. They're all scared to death all the time. I quit. I'll show you."

Miguel turned to the cook and said, "You're going to be better off sleeping through the rest of this."

She never saw the Sabel Dart, she only felt it strike her thigh. Miguel laid her out gently on the floor. Then she slept.

The young man led them upstairs to a study off the master bedroom. In a wall cabinet were fifteen notebooks—the first eight in English.

That's where the Russians took over adding the next seven notebooks.

Stuffing them into large duffels, Miguel and Isaiah ran back to the guardhouse. They climbed into the cable service van and offered the cook's assistant a ride home. He climbed in with them.

Four blocks away, on a quiet residential street, they pulled to the curb to let five FBI personnel carriers scream past them, lights flashing blue and white.

CHAPTER 69

IT TOOK A FEW MINUTES for Betty to tire of pounding her fists on my chest. Ms. Sabel thought about it but let me off with a glare of pure hatred. They were livid about the Feds making off with the notebooks and I was nearest lightning rod for their fury.

Neither woman's temper had settled by the time the ranch manager collected us and headed for the airport. Ms. Sabel got in the back and Betty took the seat next to her. Both slammed their doors behind them, leaving me to ride shotgun up front. Betty's last scowl told me whatever we had was on the rocks.

I wasn't sure what we had, much less how to salvage it.

After ten minutes of silence on the two-lane blacktop threading through the valley, the ranch manager said, "You folks all right?" He tossed me a side glance. "Aside from that gash in your cheek, I mean. There was a whole lotta noise and several big helicopters—"

"Not to be rude," I said. "There are matters of national security at stake. Today didn't happen. You didn't meet me, or Ms. Sabel, or Betty. No one came to visit, no military training exercise happened, nothing at all."

He did a double take and craned around to Ms. Sabel. She must've nodded her agreement because he turned back around and faced front. "OK then. Just trying to be neighborly."

"What you need to know," I said, "is that you're evacuating your employer from Dunkirk. It was a tough loss, but the war is far from over."

"Gotcha."

"Beautiful country," I said. "If I ever quit this business, I could live out here. That is, if the West still needs gunslingers."

"Come visit in January before you pack your bags," he said with a laugh. "Snow gets deep."

That was the last of the conversation for the next hour and a half. He tuned the radio into a country station. The music seemed to soothe Ms. Sabel and Betty.

When he dropped us in front of the Glacier Jet Center, Sabel Two, a better fit for the smaller airport, waited on the tarmac with the airstair down and the pilot waiting for us. He saw we were in a mood and backed away to give us some privacy. We stood on the apron facing each other. Both women stared at their boots.

"Look, Betty," I said, "today didn't go the way I wanted, but there was nothing—"

"You let them have it!" She stepped back, fire in her eyes. "You just stood there and did nothing. Where was the hero who can get out of anything? Where was the guy who defused a bomb in the middle of seventeen children? Where was the guy—"

"That's not fair," Ms. Sabel said.

"And what happened to you?" Betty screeched. "Don't you have twenty thousand more where he came from? Wasn't this important to you? You brought him and me, a few guys hiding in the trees on the other side of the valley—that's it?"

Ms. Sabel put her hands out as if she were pushing down a helium balloon.

"I'm not going to calm down," Betty kept going. "I worked damn hard to get near that thing and now it's gone. Gone!"

"We'll get another chance," I said. "It's not over."

"How? How are we going to get near it? The government has it. It may as well be at the bottom of the ocean. It's over, Jacob. It's gone."

"The real one is still out there."

Ms. Sabel's gray-green eyes snapped to mine, half-filled with fury and half with shock.

"That was the real one," Betty said, almost slipping into tears again. "I authenticated it."

"It couldn't have been, and you know it." I crossed my arms and waited for Betty's glare to meet mine. It didn't come.

"You wouldn't have arranged this whole thing for nothing." Betty tightened her arms across her chest, refusing to look at me. "As far as I know, that was the real thing. What do you know about it?"

"What are you so high and mighty about?" Ms. Sabel pushed Betty's shoulder to make her look up. "It's mine! Not yours. My dad developed it. My dad died for it. It belongs to me."

"Like hell! It belongs to the people. The whole thing should be made public." She frowned at Ms. Sabel. "That's what we were working for. That's what we were trying to do. Tell her, Jacob."

Betty looked at me.

So did Ms. Sabel. "You WHAT?"

"Is that all I mean to you?" I asked Betty. "Just a means to retrieve the Chaac Equation?"

She looked up at me with tear-filled eyes and pressed against me. The warmth of her body against mine reminded me of our two nights in heaven. My arms slipped around her waist.

"What the hell, Jacob?" Ms. Sabel shoved my shoulder. "What is she talking about? You know who you work for, right?"

I held up a hand, asking for a moment. "I'll explain. Just …"

Betty tore away from my arms and backed up. "Tell her! Tell her, Jacob! Chaac belongs to all humankind. The world doesn't need another fucking billionaire milking the rest of us. Jacob. Tell her!"

I stared at Betty. Her nostrils flared, her mouth clamped tight, her fists clenched. "Where is the real Chaac Equation, Betty?"

She turned on her heel and stormed toward the building. "Fuck you! I'll find my own way home."

We watched her rip open the executive center's door, storm across the lobby, and out the other side, heading for the commercial terminal. Long after she disappeared from view, we hadn't moved.

"Is this where you turn in your resignation and chase after her?" Ms. Sabel asked.

"I don't know."

"Word from Banff was you two connected and brightened up the place. Did you fall in love?"

"I don't know."

She studied me. I couldn't bring myself to look at her. My gaze was locked on the last place I saw Betty in full sunlight. Walking into the executive center.

"What was that crap about making it public? Was she serious?"

"I don't know."

"Jacob, were you going to take the only thing my father left me in this world and make it public?"

"I don't know."

She grabbed me, this time, both shoulders. She pulled me to her, face-to-face. "Jacob. Tell me the truth."

A lot of pent-up questions exploded like a fireball in my mind. Heat flowed up from my chest through my neck and flooded my head. I did my best to get it under control. But I had to know.

"You want the truth?" I shouted at her. "How about you start? You submitted a proposal to invest in Griffith. How could you do something like that? You knew he was a child molester. You knew he ran the Knights of Mithras. You—"

"I told you, it was a backup plan." She put her hands on her hips and leaned even closer. "Better to be in the deal than locked out of it. If this deal went south—and it did—then working with him would have become a necessary evil."

"Why not sue for it?" I felt blood dripping from my wound, soaking my shirt. Exhaustion from the fight weakened my resolve.

"With what evidence?" Ms. Sabel asked. "You know Viktor Popov sent assassins over twenty years ago and took it back to Russia. His assassins didn't give me a receipt. It took years for you and me to track down Popov. And then, which court am I going to sue Griffith in? He had the meeting in Belgrade for a reason." She caught her breath. "Hey, when were you going to tell me Betty worked on the Project? What was that all about? And what was that thing where you said she knew it wasn't the real thing?"

"In Banff, Rafael showed me a book written in English. Betty authenticated it after looking at one page. The one that showed up today was written in Russian."

"My dad didn't speak Russian." The realization hit her. "They worked on the Chaac Project and some of those notebooks should be Russian, but they never had the Equation. Rafael sent you a fake and she knew."

Pain weakened my ability to remain standing. I nosed at the jet. "Let's go."

She started toward the airstair with her long strides, then stopped. Turning back to me, she said, "If I were her, I'd be expecting you to come running through the terminal shouting my name right about now. Last chance. Are you going to chase after Betty?"

"I don't know."

CHAPTER 70

I DIDN'T CHASE AFTER BETTY. I boarded Sabel Two. Reluctantly. And with a heart full of questions.

Ms. Sabel noticed the blood dripping down my jeans. Instead of talking, she helped me out of the chest brace and went into Nurse Sabel mode. She cleaned my wound, took out broken stitches and put in new ones. Then dressed it with new gauze. She joked about being in so many dangerous situations that she'd learned how to stitch lacerations but never learned to cook. Then I lay down. Exhausted. She left me to rest.

There was a lump under my hip. I reached in my pocket and found the Canadian silver dollar. And that raised the question: Where had Betty gone?

Then I passed out. I had a nightmare about Mercury showing up with a golden goblet filled with the elixir of the gods—or so he claimed. I fought him hand-to-hand, but he pinned me to dungeon walls with manacles and chains. He forced me to drink the horrible-tasting fluid from his chalice. Thank the gods it was just a dream.

When I woke up, we were just south of Pittsburgh, descending into Dulles. I felt better. I was still stiff but most of the aches and pains were gone. The bruises felt healed.

"Are you awake?" Ms. Sabel asked.

"Sure," I said. "Where'd we leave off?"

"I sent the video of Griffith to the British Ambassador," she said. "They arrested the Duke for child molesting an hour ago. They had been working a case against him but didn't have hard evidence. Betty achieved her goal of destroying those men."

"Glad to hear something good came of this."

"Before you woke up, Miguel texted us both that he'd meet us back at Sabel Gardens with a 'qualified success.' What is that about?"

"It means you might have two of the three Chaac pieces. But we don't know for sure because I was relying on Betty to authenticate the information Miguel's bringing. But now she seems … unreliable."

"Want to explain that one?" she asked.

"While I kept Griffith occupied in Montana, Miguel and Isaiah went to Chicago to retrieve what we hope is the real Chaac Project. We can't be sure because of our lack of expertise. Last time I was in Griffith's house, I stole a hard drive that might contain the Edison Data. I suspect it's encrypted to self-destruct if not plugged into the right machine. I haven't had a chance to give it to Bianca and her tech wizards yet. That's what I mean when I say you 'might' have two-thirds of Chaac. All we need is the Equation."

"That's what everybody needs." She nodded. Her face twisted in thought.

We landed and crossed the apron to a nearby executive helicopter. We climbed in and put on headsets.

"Why did you set up the exchange with Griffith?" she asked. "Especially if you knew there was a chance the government would take it."

Her voice had that chopper-radio quality, the incongruously crisp voice that should be drowned out by the engines directly over our heads but wasn't due to the extraordinarily effective earcups protecting our ears.

"To flush out who's who. Belgrade was nothing more than Griffith's last parade. He didn't know it, but by letting everyone know he had the Chaac Project, he aligned some powerful people against him. At first, I thought Rafael planned to do something that would secure the whole thing for the common good. Now I'm not so sure."

"You think Rafael is working for someone other than the Keepers?"

"Hard to say, but he did some strange things. He made me an honorary Keeper without Neville Townsend's blessing. He wanted me to set up the exchange of the Equation for the Project knowing Griffith was a criminal and would do what criminals always do: lie, steal, and cheat."

I leaned over and looked out the window. We were coming up on the Potomac River.

She asked, "Didn't he make you a Keeper because he wanted you to keep the Chaac Equation out of the hands of criminals?"

"That's what he said, but that's not what he did. He took me to a remote location with better natural security than anything I could provide. He was going to ship it around in a circle and have it land in my hands a few days later. Why bother? It was safer where it was. The smart play would've been to leave it there and ask me to mount an attack on Griffith's stronghold. The idea that he would ship the most valuable notebook of the twenty-first century to me at a Canadian hotel was laughable. Plus, he had two Keepers with him who were supposed to be in Korea. That's when I knew he was planning to steal it for himself."

"Damn," she said. "Rafael went rogue?"

"I set up the whole thing in Montana to flush that out. I thought we'd have a good chance at getting Griffith, and that worked out. But I didn't know if Rafael and Neville were on the same page. Neville asked me to recover it but didn't mention taking it from Rafael. When I saw the Navy drone overhead, I knew those two had different agendas. Neville sent in overwhelming military force to take it all back—and that means he thought the Equation would be there. Whatever Rafael is planning, he didn't tell Neville."

She thought about that while we landed at Sabel Gardens. Ducking under the rotor wash, we walked to the car barn. She chose a convertible McLaren in volcano yellow and helped me into the passenger seat. Then she took the wheel.

Isaiah appeared, her bodyguard for the day. He chose a matching McLaren in red for a chase vehicle. I called out to him, "Still like working with us?"

"It doesn't suck, sir. I mean, Jacob." He slid into the car with a big grin.

Ms. Sabel drove me home, testing Isaiah's ability to keep up while she drove like Mad Max. I made a mental note: if we were keeping him on the team, he would need to attend tactical driving school. Without training, no one could keep up with Ms. Sabel.

Once underway, she asked, "Why did you call Betty unreliable?"

I exhaled my emotional pain. "Right up until the point where she walked out on us, I thought she was serious about me. Against all odds, I thought she meant it. Hell, I still want to believe she's serious. Maybe there's an explanation for her behavior. If she cared about me, she would've had faith I'd get it fixed. But no. All she cared about was getting her hands on the Chaac Equation."

"What about Betty and Rafael. Do you think they're working together?"

"When Rafael showed me the notebook in his fortress, I managed to get clear pictures of four pages with a button camera. Later, I showed them to Betty. She looked at the one page, zoomed in on it, then declared it legit."

"Oh," Ms. Sabel said. "That's too quick."

"All acting aside, I don't think they knew each other," I said as she pulled into my driveway and stopped. "But. They both tracked the Project and Equation for years and they both had plans for it, so it makes sense they appeared to be working together."

"They spent a good deal of time together in Kyiv, Belgrade, and Chicago. They could've hatched a plan."

"She had to know the original was written in English," I said. I opened the door but didn't get out. "But she authenticated one in Russian. She knew Rafael was trying to pull a fast one. Now she's chasing the Equation."

"Can you get it back? Can you find the Chaac Equation? I have to get it back, Jacob. It's mine. MINE."

"You worry me." I held her gaze for a moment. "I've never seen you get so upset about material things. I've never seen you care about money—"

"It's not about that!" Fire flared in her eyes. "Think about who wants it. Think about the people who didn't bother submitting a bid to Griffith. What if Rafael reached out to them and told them he would have it in a few days?"

The people who bid on it were straight shooters, like Ms. Sabel. The governments of Germany, France, and South Korea. Corporations like

Microsoft, Volkswagen, and Exxon. Who didn't bid? I began to see her concern. Mikhail Yeschenko, the unofficial head of the criminal syndicate known as Russia; Deng Zhipeng, the internet mogul who was either trying to flee China or had been ingested by it; and Remmo Nidal, shadowy consulting company for OPEC, known for their expedient methods of obtaining signatures on contracts. Not good.

I climbed out.

She grabbed my hand and said, "We can't let Rafael sell it to one of them."

CHAPTER 71

THE NEXT MORNING, I ARRIVED as dawn cast a pale blue hue over the treetops at Sabel Gardens. Making my way through the mansion, I tromped through the great hall past the drawing room and the library, heading to Ms. Sabel's home office. An old guy burst out of it, barreling across the marble, brushing past me with a scowl.

"If you're the ghostwriter," the man called over his shoulder, "forget it. She's not in the mood."

I walked in, pointing a thumb over my shoulder at the stranger. Ms. Sabel thumbed out a message on her phone while leaning against her desk.

"Seeley James," she said without looking up.

"The writer?"

"Yes." She finished her text and looked at me.

"What did he want?"

"To write my *authorized biography*." She rolled her eyes while enclosing the last two words with air quotes. "Like I'd let that hack anywhere near my life story."

She dropped her phone into her open purse on the corner of her desk and tracked around to her chair. She sat and motioned for me to take one of the chairs in front of her.

"Why did you keep so much from me?" I asked as I dropped to the seat. "With all that was going on, all that was at stake, don't you think I deserved to know more about Chaac?"

She watched my eyes carefully before answering. "The thing is like Tolkien's One Ring. Everyone who gets near it is consumed by its promise. You're not immune."

I couldn't argue with that. She was showing signs of channeling Gollum herself.

"Right." She read my mind. "Same goes for me. But it's my father's dream. The fossil fuel lobby killed him for it before I knew him. If someone else puts Chaac together and then claims it doesn't work, I'll never believe them. I'll think it was a conspiracy to bury the project. If I control the R & D, whether it succeeds or fails, I'll know the truth."

"Then let's plan on getting it," I said. "What intelligence do we have?"

"Rafael went through customs in Shanghai an hour ago. Betty booked a flight to Riga with a connection in Paris."

"Is that a coincidence?" I asked. "Viktor Popov, the man who set this in motion by ordering the hit on your father, had a dacha in Riga."

"Do you think I forgot the shoot-out we had there?" She peered at me with concern. "Have you been in so many firefights you forget who was with you?"

Too true to admit. I tried to laugh it off. "Ah, good times, right?"

"But we searched Popov's place back then. No secret chambers, no hidden laboratories. Why would she go there?"

"It was in a Russian ex-pat compound near the beach. Maybe she's looking up someone else?"

"Bratva?" she asked, referring to the Russian mob. "Officials? Is she enlisting help?"

"Let's find out and get this resolved."

"One step at a time. You have a question to answer first, Jacob. What do you want to see resolved: Chaac—or Betty?"

I choked. She may as well have hit me with a two-by-four. I tried to make light of it by saying, "Both."

"Hard to do since she's in the Baltic and he's in Shanghai."

"It's a problem," I shrugged, "like any other. I'll figure out how to solve it on the fly."

"A woman is not a problem you can *solve*."

She made me stop and think. What did I want from Betty Bardon? To get even, beg forgiveness, yell at her, get yelled at by her, catch her and drag her home? I had no idea. I felt something between us, brief as our time was. What did she think? How much was acting and how much came from her heart? Why should I care? She was the one who walked away. Right when I was ready to get involved again.

I said, "I'll go to Shanghai and track down Rafael."

"While your head is in Riga?"

"OK, I'll go to Riga." I tossed up my hands. "I don't care. You pick. Do you want to go after Rafael or Betty?"

"Neither. I'm meeting Deng Zhipeng in Monaco tomorrow. After that, I'll look up Yeschenko and Remmo Nidal."

"That's a nasty crowd. You'll need me with you."

"Tania's packed and waiting." Ms. Sabel rolled a pen around on her desk. "You need to find Betty first."

When it was my idea, I had all the confidence in the world. I knew exactly where I would go and what I would do. Now that she exposed the gravitas of it, I felt anxiety shredding at my insides like a wolverine clawing its way out. At that moment, I'd rather go to war and face impossible odds against an overwhelming force than face Betty Bardon. Why?

Ms. Sabel was right. Betty was a ghost I had to exorcise. I said, "OK. I have a list of questions for her anyway."

"You might not like her answers."

I took a deep breath and let it out slowly and painfully.

Ms. Sabel rose and gestured toward the door. The meeting was over. She was going to Monaco, and I was going to Riga.

"Do you care about her?" she asked as she walked me out.

A question I'd been asking myself since Betty tore her sleeve off to make my bandage. When did I first feel my heart skip in her presence? Swimming for the storm drain in Brest? Her grand entrance at the restaurant in Kyiv? Buying me a drink at the bar in Monaco? When she sat in my lap and figured out the tensile strength of a Lamborghini's hood? Thinking about her caused me more pain than Griffith's knife.

Why? Was I afraid to find out that she really cared about me? That would make me vulnerable again. I never wanted to see someone I care about running down a cave carrying a bomb. I said, "I can't see a future with Betty Bardon. Not yet. But I can see a tomorrow."

Ms. Sabel's phone buzzed with a text message. She read it and looked up. "Neville Townsend insists we meet President Williams and him at the Truman Building immediately."

CHAPTER 72

A SECURITY OFFICER LED US to the Adams Drawing Room in the Truman Building, headquarters of the State Department. Neville greeted us at the door. On a couch in the center of the room, two anonymous suits crowded President Williams. Williams was an average-sized man with piercing eyes, the fitness of a man twenty years younger, and a commanding presence. He waved away his companions. They rose like guard dogs given a command they didn': like. They obeyed without enthusiasm, their suspicious eyes fixed on Ms. Sabel and me as they exited the other end of the room.

CIA. Had to be.

Neville gestured broadly at two facing sofas. He looked better in daylight, wearing a suit, with his unruly hair plastered down than he did during my frequent pre-dawn calls and midnight visits. We dutifully sat. Before us was a plate of homemade gingersnaps. No milk. They had to be from his bodyguard Dan. They had that same golden hue, crisp edges, and begged to be eaten.

Neville took a seat next to President Williams, so it was us versus them.

Neville cleared his throat. "You are here because the President didn't want to have you arrested."

He let that hang in the air. Neither of us even batted an eyelash. Ms. Sabel kept her gaze fixed on President Williams. And he returned the favor.

After rolling mine, I landed them on Neville. "Yeah, yeah, yeah, get in line. So, what's up?"

Neville continued like a hanging judge delivering his favorite sentence. "I ordered you to secure the Chaac materials and bring them back. I told you it was a matter of utmost urgency and that national security was at stake. Nonetheless, you offered them to the leader of a criminal organization. Further—"

President Williams raised his hand, palm down. "Let's not stress over specifics. Ms. Sabel has been a generous supporter of the party and always has her nation's interests at heart. Perhaps we could hear her point of view."

I wanted to reach for a cookie, but Neville was in the middle of turning red and shaking with anger. His voice barreled out of him. "These two set up a fake exchange! They purposely led my people to the wrong location while their agents raided Griffith's house—moments before the FBI could get there. They did not have their nation's interest at heart."

Mercury popped up from behind the couch and put an arm around both men. *Looks like you woke up Grandpa Townsend one too many times, huh homie?*

I said, *How bad is this?*

Mercury said, *You heard the boss man say who's boss of this here meeting. The one with the deepest pockets. Why do you think I call her Caesar?*

I said, *Then I've got nothing to worry about?*

Mercury said, *Hold up there, son. I didn't say nothing like that. There's more to this Chaac business but I'm the messenger of good news, so ... Catchya later.*

Mercury began to rise toward the ceiling.

Wait, I said. *Did you get your wife back?*

Mercury stopped in mid-air. *Yeah. In theory. See, I won when you killed Griffith and foiled his Finns. But when I got back to Mars' crib to claim my winnings, there was a party going down. Bacchus is everywhere these days. Anyway, Larunda likes to party like it's 1999. So, I gotta get back before she forgets who brung her to the dance. Feel what I'm saying?*

I said, *In this case, didn't Mars bring her to the dance?*

Mercury said, *Hey! Whose side are you on, bruh?*

Everyone was staring at me as if I'd said something strange. I rolled back the video in my head and realized the President of the United States had asked me a question. I keep forgetting to pay attention to reality when god's talking. Gotta learn to multitask.

"I couldn't tell Neville everything," I said, "because the Keepers have a leak. They're an unreliable partner."

Neither man batted an eye when I mentioned the organization, so I gathered Williams had been briefed.

The President turned to Neville and waited for an explanation.

I was perfectly willing to wait for Neville's version. I reached for a cookie.

Before my hand got into the cookie plate's airspace, Neville leapt to his feet. "You cannot be serious! We kept that and thousands of other things safe for years!"

"Then where is it now?"

Neville fumed and stomped and wandered away, Williams watching him the whole time.

That's when I realized how bad things with the Keepers really were. My mind thought it and my mouth said it at the same time: "Rafael scammed you, didn't he?"

"I don't know that." Neville stormed his way back. "I know you did."

Williams held up his hand again. Neville ran his hands over his thin wisps of hair and turned away.

"We need your help." Williams was looking directly at Ms. Sabel. "By we, I mean the people of the United States. I know you have a vested interest in Chaac. There's too—"

"It's not a vested interest, it's mine. MINE."

"—much at stake to trust the NSA or the CIA. Everyone who knows it exists wants to profit from it, regardless of their dedication to country or cause. It's like the *Lord of the Rings* meets *Lord of the Flies*. When they understand what they're chasing, they turn into bloodthirsty pirates out for themselves. You command loyalty unlike anyone in government." He chuckled. "That might be because you pay them a lot more. But that aside—"

"I get it," she said. "You want Jacob." She leaned toward the president, and he leaned toward her, the intensity in their eyes reaching a scary level. "And I want Chaac."

And Jacob wanted a gingersnap. But it didn't seem like a good time to take one. Instead, I said, "What does Jacob want?"

Everyone turned to me as if it just occurred to them the hired man was a human being.

I looked at Neville. "How are the Keepers organized at the top?"

He glanced at Williams, then at Pia. "Nothing I say goes anywhere beyond this room. Understood?"

"Your ancient organization has seen its day," Williams said. When Neville turned an angry glare his way, he shrugged. "The same goes for those other guys, the Knights of whatever."

Neville sat back down, his hands waving aimlessly as if he didn't know what to do with them. He said, "Rafael and I are, or were, the Keepers' executives. Think of me as the chairman and Rafael is the president. We have three others who form the board. We make critical decisions together."

"Until now," I said.

Neville folded his hands between his knees. "Until now."

"Did anyone know Rafael had taken the Chaac Equation?"

He shook his head. "We're a compartmentalized organization. Need-to-know basis. But this ... this was something we needed to know. There was too much at stake not to keep us informed. There's no excuse for his actions. None I can see at least."

President Williams said, "Neville, what did you know of Ms. Bardon's involvement?"

Neville shook his head. "Only what we've discovered since she came into the picture. She's an orphan. Her father died twelve years ago. Her mother died two years ago."

Ms. Sabel whispered to me, "They sent her a picture of someone else's finger?"

I shrugged. She shivered.

"I won't have you running this operation anymore," Williams told Neville. "You've lost control of your organization. As I said, the days of the Keepers are over. You'll continue as Secretary of State—but forget everything you know about Chaac."

Neville nodded, a defeated man. I felt sorry for him. I almost offered him a cookie. But then, if he turned it down, I'd end up taking one and it would look like a self-serving gesture. Which might be worth the awkward moment. They were really good cookies.

My phone buzzed with a text from Betty. I checked it as surreptitiously as possible. It read, "Walking away from you was the biggest mistake of my life. Forgive me?"

I leaned the screen to Ms. Sabel. She glanced at it, then at me with an expression that said, *Good luck figuring that one out.*

"What's your take on Rafael?" the president asked me. "Is he selling the Equation to the Chinese?"

I said, "He had a long conversation with a Red Army general in Belgrade. It's possible."

Ms. Sabel leaned forward. "Deng Zhipeng led the Chinese delegation in Belgrade. Their top scientists were with him. Right now, he's in Monaco with the same delegation, including the Red Army general."

Curious how she knew his whereabouts, it occurred to me she most likely endured an endless string of his salacious invitations. Deng was spying on himself and didn't know it.

"My best guess," Ms. Sabel said, "Rafael's arranging an R & D auction like Griffith's. In Belgrade, I alerted the governments and corporations of my claim to ownership. Most of them won't touch it for fear of losing in court. That leaves the criminal element as Rafael's auction bidders. Remmo Nidal will represent OPEC; Mikhail Yeschenko will represent the European criminal element; and Deng Zhipeng will act on behalf of himself or China, I'm not sure which."

"What happens if they form alliances?" Neville asked.

I said, "We're screwed."

Williams rubbed his palms together. "We've been working on cold fusion for a hundred years. We started hoping for manned flight around the time of Golden Age in Athens, but it took over two millennia before the Wrights made that happen. Chaac might be a pipedream."

His eyes were clear and sharp and drilled down into my brain, then Ms. Sabel's. "But I'm an optimist, and I don't believe that. We need

Chaac for the sake of humanity—we can't afford to let it end up in the hands of mobsters or dictators. Look at how OPEC has held the world hostage for the last fifty years. We can't let that happen again."

"I agree, Mr. President," Ms. Sabel said.

"Good. When Chaac happens, we need to make sure it happens here, in the USA. I know, we're not perfect, but we're a far sight better than the likes of Yeschenko and Zhipeng." He softened his voice. "Pia, I'm going to risk sounding melodramatic. I need you and Jacob to save the world. You need to save it from climate change, and you need to save it from economic domination by grossly unworthy men. I have every faith that you can do this. Will you?"

Ms. Sabel looked as serious as I've ever seen her. She chewed the inside of her lower lip for a moment, then said, "I want to see that happen as much as you do, Mr. President. Leave it to us."

Williams shifted his gaze to me.

You don't say "no" when a good man asks you to save the planet. "Or die trying, sir."

"There's no time to lose." Williams faced Ms. Sabel again. "You will report directly to me."

"I own Chaac," she said. "I want to be clear about that."

"I believe it should belong to the country first, and the world second. But we can hash that out later. Right now, we have nothing."

There was a long silence while the two of them—one with power and the other with money—stared each other down. He blinked first, but Ms. Sabel spoke first.

She said, "We'll bring it home."

We rose and shook hands, exchanging goodbye-for-nows. As we turned away, Neville held out the plate of cookies and said, "I nearly forgot. Dan wanted me to give these to you. His way of saying thanks for not making a career-ending deal out of the other night."

It was all I could do not to scarf down the plate right then and there. I took the cookies and thanked him. We headed for the door.

Mercury put an arm around me. *Now ain't you glad I didn't let you die under that dump truck, homie?*

THANK YOU!

Thank you for choosing my book. I hope you enjoyed reading it as much as I enjoyed writing it. As an independent writer, I am dependent on word-of-mouth referrals and book reviews. If you liked this book, please tell everyone, and leave reviews all over the place. I will be eternally grateful.

When you do write a review, send me a link to it and I'll put you in the next drawing for an autographed book. I run at least three or four drawings a year.

If you can't get enough of Pia, Tania, Miguel and Jacob*, checkout the series at SeeleyJames.com/books. While you're there, join my newsletter to get discounts, drawings, fun, news, outtakes, and more about the Sabel Agents club on Facebook! Every week (or so, sometimes I'm lazy), I'll let you know about the book in progress, personal triumphs & tragedies, what I'm reading and other fun stuff. I even had one person write to me to say, "I don't like your books, but I love your newsletters." To which I replied, "Thanks, Mom." Yeah … whatcha gonna do?

I'd love to hear from you. Please write, message me on Facebook, let me know what you think.

*I like you already.

**NOW THAT YOU'VE READ THIS BOOK, WHICH ONE SHOULD YOU READ NEXT?
HTTPS://SEELEYJAMES.COM/BOOKS**

TRUTH IN FICTION

As an avid reader of fiction, I'm often curious about the facts, physics, and philosophies of the books I read. I once read a book in which the hero traveled 2,000 miles in two hours—in a helicopter. It was otherwise a good book, so I didn't worry about it. But I do strive for a certain adherence to reality, the laws of nature, and so on. From time to time, I get emails inquiring about the validity of certain premises in my books. I have one fan who finds mistakes. (IE: as it turns out 300 kph is 186 mph not 174, which was due to me doing the math at 280 kph then rounding up during the editing process without recalculating. Oh well.)

I feel that, because you are a nice person and read all the way to the end (right? You're not a skipper, are you?), you deserve a peek at the research and notes I've taken during the writing of this book. To address and preempt commonly asked questions:

1) **Do the locations really look like that?** Yes! Probably. Like most modern authors, I rely heavily on Google Maps. I also research travelogues and other sources for impressions and information. Before beginning a book, I look up a lot of interesting places—some of which I've visited and others I'd like to—and drop those in my OneNote folder under Places+Things. Some places never make it into the story, others have entire neighborhoods moved or rivers rerouted to bring you a better story.

2) **Are there really electric airplanes?** Yes! They are different from the one described in this book. Mainly, they tend to be single seaters. They aren't ready to replace your beloved automobile, but they have promise. To make a two-seater, I mathematically calculated weight and distance for the Sabel E-Airplane. But I'm not an engineer, so if someone offers you a ride in one, be suspicious.

3) **Christmas Tree Netting? C'mon.** Yes! These machines exist. Writers are constantly searching for new and interesting ways to

confound the hero. James Bond once chased the bad guys in an airplane that lost its wings in the first few seconds. He slid to a miraculous, and hilarious, stop and rescued the damsel. Since that one had been done, I came up with the netting machine after stumbling on an amusing video on YouTube about a garden shop in the UK that will wrap you in tree netting for a donation to charity. My scene required a larger machine (for larger trees, naturally) and the result was, in my opinion, terrific—and possible.

4) **Is the Roman history and philosophy accurate**? Absolutely! Except where it isn't. Ancient Rome spanned a thousand years and never had a single religious or philosophical "bible." Many leaders rewrote history to make themselves look better and their predecessors look terrible in contrast, so what we know is often debatable. I'm not a Romanophile, but I've found any psychological or philosophical point to be made can be found in Roman mythology or history. With a quick internet search for "time to move on," I discovered the story of Orpheus and Eurydice. Searches like that uncover many other gems as well. I tuck them in my notebook. Some get used, some get misused, others will be misused in the future.

5) **Is the Chaac Project possible?** I hope so! I find quantum mechanics fascinating, but with my limited brainpower, it just gives me a headache. However, there are a few riddles in that field which point to terrific possibilities. Everyone with an R&D budget today is trying to build a better battery. Whether it will be discovered before or after civilization collapses is the question of the day. I live with the fervent belief that humankind always finds a way to survive.

Still don't believe me? You're not alone. So, here is a link to my OneNote file for this book.

Thanks for reading, you're now my favorite reader!

ACKNOWLEDGMENTS

My heartfelt thanks to the people who, without hesitation or concern for bodily injury, gave their time and attention to make *DEATH AND REDEMPTION* the greatest book ever written by a human. (In my opinion, anyway.) Without the insightful contributions of these few selfless, hardworking readers, editors, and writers, the story would teeter on the verge of putting you to sleep better than a Sabel Dart. I am forever in debt to these brave souls:

- **Extraordinary Editor and Idea man:** Lance Charnes, author of the highly acclaimed *Doha 12, SOUTH,* not to mention the DeWitt Agency series: *THE COLLLECTION, STEALING GHOSTS, CHASING CLAY* and, if you like ass-kicking heroines: *ZRADA and ENGAÑO.* I highly recommend his exciting novels, visit http://wombatgroup.com. With his contribution on nearly every scene, this book is a more powerful story.
- **Medical Advisor and Character Diviner:** Dr. Louis Kirby, famed neurologist and author of *SHADOW OF EDEN.* http://louiskirby.com Before his analysis recommended ratcheting up the tension, the final showdown failed to cleanse the reader's soul. Now, it rocks.
- **Amazing Editor and Character Arc Speicalist:** Mary Maddox, horror and dark fantasy novelist, and author of the *DAEMON WORLD* series and the fantastic thrillers: *DARK ROOM* and *HOMETOWN BOYS.* http://marymaddox.com. Her analysis took Betty's character from a confused starlet to a dynamic force of nature.

And my additional thanks to the beta readers who aided and abetted my endeavors. No amount of proofreading, professional or amateur, can match their diligence in finding the niggling little malapropisms, mondegreens, spoonerisms, homophones, and other typos: Rick Tara, Michael Davis, Fritzi Redgrave, and Serena Montague. But don't blame them for my bad grammar. It's intentionally bad. (That's the story I'm telling this year.)

A special thanks to my wife whose support, despite being a tad reluctant, has gone above and beyond the call of duty. Last but not least, my children, Nicole, Amelia, and Christopher, ranging from age twenty-one to forty-eight, who have kept my imagination fresh and full of ideas.

SEE THE SEELEY JAMES COLLECTION

SEELEYJAMES.COM/BOOKS

ABOUT THE AUTHOR

His near-death experiences range from talking a jealous husband into putting the gun down to spinning out on an icy freeway in heavy traffic without touching anything. His resume ranges from washing dishes to global technology management. His personal life stretches from homeless at 17, adopting a 3-year-old at 19, getting married at 37, fathering his last child at 43, hiking the Grand Canyon Rim-to-Rim several times a year, and taking the occasional nap.

His writing career ranges from humble beginnings with short stories in The Battered Suitcase, to being awarded a Medallion from the Book Readers Appreciation Group. Seeley is best known for his Sabel Security series of thrillers featuring athlete and heiress Pia Sabel and her bodyguard, unhinged veteran Jacob Stearne. One of them kicks ass and the other talks to the wrong god.

His love of creativity began at an early age, growing up at Frank Lloyd Wright's School of Architecture in Arizona and Wisconsin. He carried his imagination first into a successful career in sales and marketing, and then to his real love: fiction.

For more books featuring Pia Sabel and Jacob Stearne, visit: SeeleyJames.com/books. Also, check the sales and discounts page for special offers: SeeleyJames.com/sale.

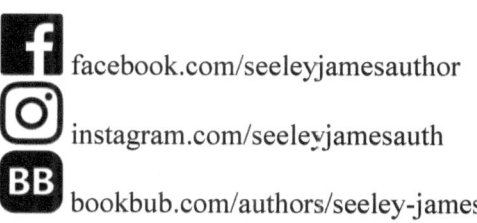

facebook.com/seeleyjamesauthor

instagram.com/seeleyjamesauth

bookbub.com/authors/seeley-james

www.ingramcontent.com/pod-product-compliance
Lightning Source LLC
Chambersburg PA
CBHW020235110726
47898CB00004B/1271